BURNING FOR THE BARON

BOOK THREE IN THE LORDS OF DISCIPLINE
SERIES

ALYSON CHASE

Cover image by Dar Albert.

Visit the author website: http://www.alysonchase.com

ISBN-13: 978-1-944802-03-5
ISBN-10: 1-944802-03-7

A Note from Alyson

WARNING: This book contains scenes of fire play, a highly dangerous activity. My characters are trained professionals. Also, they're fictional, so they can't actually get hurt. So, what I'm trying to say is, DO NOT TRY THIS AT HOME!!!

Seriously, all I did was a little internet research on the subject of fire play. This is definitely not a how-to guide on how to heat up your love life. (Hee hee. I love my puns. *clears throat* But enough of that; back to the serious warning.) I did try to play my own game of snapdragon, to see if I could actually stick my hand in a bowl of flaming liquor without getting burned. And I have to say, it hurt. I don't know how those Regency ladies were able to grab that raisin. So, if I can't even play a parlor game safely, I'm not someone to listen to when it comes to instructions on lighting a loved one on fire. If fire play interests you, go to classes. Do you own research. Do not read this book and decide to experiment. And, if you learn any neat tricks during your research, feel free to email me with any tips. :)

On to more general warnings, the characters in this book are all fictional. Except for Liverpool. He was a real dude, but I fictionalized the heck out of him. Any resemblances to people living or dead are purely coincidental. Yada yada yada.

Chapter One

London, 1815

Colleen averted her gaze, but the sounds still created a vivid picture in her mind. The slap of skin on skin. The grunting. The moaning.

The barking?

She slid a glance out of the corner of her eye. Yes, the woman was most definitely barking like a dog. The collar around her neck, the man plowing into her from behind holding the attached leash, gave definite confirmation.

One of her girls was pretending to be a dog.

Colleen tilted her head heavenward and sighed. For the thousandth time she asked herself what in the blazes she had gotten herself into. Colleen Bonner was a respectable woman of business. A God-fearing woman. How she had managed to let that silver-tongued devil talk her into managing a bawdy house, she'd never know. And not just any bawdy house. The Black Rose. A Venus club for those with unusual tastes – and the blunt to pay the high membership fee.

Colleen sidled around the edge of the Gold Room. It was one of the smaller back chambers in the club. The walls were painted a rich amber hue, and the thick pile carpet underfoot was a light olive-brown that was the color of an antique locket. Plush pillows in varying shades of yellow were piled in the center of the floor, a soft, makeshift bed for the tomfoolery that went on under her roof.

Pulling her watch from the pocket of her waistcoat, she tried to gain the attention of her girl, Lucy. Who was currently howling like her fur, er, hair, was being plucked from her skin.

The small cluster of spectators made the task more difficult. Men and women lounged about on the semi-circle of settees surrounding the pile of pillows. Colleen slunk around the edges of the room, keeping her eyes firmly planted on Lucy's face. Too many hands were creeping where they shouldn't on the settees. Too many body parts exposed that only a doctor should see.

Lucy looked up, her glance sharp, but her howling and barking never ceasing. Colleen tapped her timepiece, and Lucy nodded, the motion small and quick. The girl dug her fingers into the carpet, and pushed back into the man's thrusts, yipping and moaning like mad. Quite the performer her little Lucy. A performance she'd promised to another member in fifteen minutes.

Message delivered, Colleen escaped from the room. She leaned back against the closed door and stared at her feet, willing her stomach to settle. Working under this roof was a trial, but it was a trial she deserved. And her penance would soon end. Still, the urge to leave, to tell *him* just where he could shove his job, was as tempting as sticking her toes in a cool stream on a hot summer day.

Having a roof over her head and food in her belly was a greater temptress. Much as she hated her new role, she couldn't deny the relief at having a room to herself and a full meal to look forward to each day.

Her cousin had been all kindness and condescension, allowing her to share a room with his daughters when her own home had burned.

And he'd spent every day reminding her just how kind he was.

Insufferable man, her cousin. Almost as bad as *he* was.

Colleen smoothed her hand down her cotton skirts and strode down the hall to the main room of the club. The crystal chandelier hanging from the high ceiling scattered soft light throughout the room. The gold painted paper covering the walls shimmered under the one hundred and eighteen candles in the chandelier. The one hundred and eighteen candles that still weren't sufficient to brighten the room to its current warm glow if not for the gas lamps burning discreetly on each wall.

Those one hundred and eighteen candles cost a fine penny to replace each day, and Colleen made a note to herself to ask *him* if they ought not rely solely on the gas lamps from now on. Not that *he* ever appreciated her thrift.

A three-piece band played a waltz from their nook on the small landing that separated the main room from the upper floor. Couples danced under that glittering chandelier, holding each other indecently close. The women wore diaphanous gowns of silks and satins, necessary uniforms for most of her girls if they wanted to project the right image to the club's patrons.

Colleen looked down at her own apparel. When she'd first married, she and her husband hadn't had the luxury of a maid, and Colleen had taken to wearing her husband's loose shirts with skirts she'd fashioned to conveniently wrap about her waist. Easy to slip on and remove. After a while she'd paired it with an old waistcoat her husband had no longer worn and the look had become her daily uniform. Simple. Efficient. No-nonsense. The outfit she sported now was the one she'd had on the night of the fire. None of her other clothes had survived.

As the manager of The Black Rose, not one of the doxies, she thought her clothes appropriate to her position. She'd packed up the frivolous gowns the owner of the club had left behind in her chamber upstairs and donated them to the girls. If *he* had wanted a different sort of woman managing the club, *he* should have found a different woman.

Molly, one of the club's higher-earning lady-birds, sidled up to her, a glass of champagne in her hand. Colleen resisted the urge to pull the shoulder of the woman's gown up.

"We have a good crowd tonight." Molly took a sip from the flute. A large blood-red stone on her ring glinted in the light. "It's a shame Madame Sable isn't here to see it. After all, you had said she might be back by now."

Colleen gritted her teeth. "I said I didn't know when she'd return from her tour of the continent. She could return tomorrow or a year from now." That was the story she was to tell, anyhow. That her dear friend had needed a respite and had asked Colleen to act as manager of the club until her return. Colleen knew the true reason for the woman's departure as much as she knew the woman. That was to say, not at all. But the need for secrecy had been impressed upon her.

"Yes, where did you say she was?" Molly asked. "The south of France?"

A serving girl passed by, and Molly grabbed another glass of champagne. Colleen narrowed her eyes. That champagne ran two hundred quid a cask. "I didn't say. Madame Sable's letters are too infrequent for me to keep track of her whereabouts." Reaching into a deep pocket sewn into her skirts, she pulled out a small notebook and a bit of black lead. She scratched herself a note. "How many glasses of that wine have you had tonight?"

Molly snorted. "Are you going to dock my pay? Madame Sable was never so stingy."

"It isn't only the expense." Although keeping an equal or greater level of profit as Madame Sable was important to Colleen. "But you girls need to keep a sober mind, what with all you get up to. An impairment of any kind could be dangerous."

"What would you know about it?" Molly edged into Colleen's space, her slight form vibrating with animosity. "Your knees are bound together so tight, I don't see how you even manage to walk."

Colleen kept her expression placid, but a pulse

throbbed in her temple. Her new workers liked to push her, test her boundaries, and no one more so than Molly. "And yet I walk quite well. I can even climb stairs. If I wanted, I could climb to my office and write a note of dismissal if the urge took me." She was gratified when the girl stiffened beside her. She needed the workers to respect her. A touch of fear, even, wouldn't go amiss. It was difficult to wield authority when Colleen didn't know her own limits. Could she fire someone? She didn't want to write to *him* to ask.

One of the members, Lord Halliwell, swaggered up and clicked his heels together as he bowed. A broad smile was plastered across his face. "Mrs. Bonner. A treat, a real treat to see you down here. You so often hide your lovely self away from us."

Colleen stifled a groan. With a smirk, Molly raised her glass in farewell and sauntered away. Colleen looked around for the serving girl. She could use a glass of that obscenely-priced champagne.

"Good evening, Lord Halliwell," she said. Her shoulders sagged. The alcohol was on the other side of the room. "I hope you fare well."

He shrugged and dipped his chin. "I did something quite naughty today. I was hoping to confess my sins."

Colleen huffed out a sigh. "Lord Halliwell, I will tell you again that I only manage the premises. I am not available for ..." Her mind whirled, searching for a polite form of speech that wouldn't insult the paying member before her. "I'm not available for entertainment purposes."

The earl slid his gaze up and down her body. Colleen didn't quite understand what he was looking at. Unlike the scantily-clad doxies, Colleen's high-necked shirt and mannish waistcoat hid her attributes. Of all the peacocks flitting about, she was the boring brown hen.

The earl leaned close. "Can I tell you a secret, Mrs. Bonner?" He didn't wait for her response. "Something about you reminds me of my old nurse. She raised me to be the man I am today. If I ever misbehaved, she was there to correct my course."

Colleen stepped back. "Flattering as that may be, I'm not available. I believe Molly is free, and I know how much she enjoys your company." Colleen felt a slight qualm at the lie. But not enough to take it back. "Now if you will excuse me, I have to go, uh, check a room."

The earl stood in front of her, so she turned around and disappeared down the hall with the play rooms. The thick carpet muffled her footfalls. She glanced over her shoulder, but the earl had disappeared. Probably to find a woman to correct his misbehavior.

A group of young bucks crowded the entrance of the hall, laughing and jostling each other, obviously deep in their cups. She could only hope they didn't have similar nurse fancies.

She opened the door next to her and peered in. Only to pull it tight. A shudder ran through her body. No hiding in that room. One of the young men at the end of the hall playfully shoved a friend, and the group surged towards Colleen. She hustled to the next door and peeked within the chamber. Dark and empty. She darted inside and leaned her back against the wall. But the sight of what went on in the room next door lingered.

What was wrong with people? She'd been married for over eight years, and she'd seen more of the male anatomy in a night under this roof than in her entire marriage. Why they felt the need for the toys, the odd positions, the games, she didn't know. Relations were meant to be under the cover of night, the man doing his business to procreate, and getting out. She didn't think Mr. Bonner had ever seen her entire body all in one go. A leg here when he raised her gown. A shoulder there if it slipped down her arm. Their intercourse had been efficient, with a sole purpose in mind. As God intended.

Making her way to the nook where an oil lamp held the faintest of glows, she found the screw on the side of the lantern and lengthened the wick. The room brightened, and Colleen fisted her hands on her hips. Her workers hadn't straightened the chamber after its last use. A web of ropes hung from the sturdy rafters instead of laying coiled neatly in their spot on the wall.

She trailed her fingers along the tails of hemp that hung like vines to the floor. Pieces of rope were knotted horizontally between the vertical lengths. The arrangement could almost be used as a net. She fingered the rope that hung at hip height. Or a swing.

Colleen glanced at the door. No one had reserved this room for the rest of the night, but that didn't stop members from popping in. Gripping one of the ropes, she tugged. It seemed sturdy enough. She leaned her weight on it and held on with both hands. The hemp shifted against the rafter but didn't slip.

With a sidelong look at the door, Colleen slid her torso through a rectangle created by the ropes. Raising up onto her toes, she pulled a length of hemp beneath her bottom. Her boots slid against the smooth wood floor, and she wrapped her arms around the ropes above her. Tentatively, she raised one foot from the ground. Then the other. Her body swung easily, and for a moment, she felt like a child again. One without a care in the world.

Bending her knees, she kicked her legs out and leaned into the swaying motion. The hemp creaked against the beam. Colleen floated, enjoying her moment of solitude. The club boasted plenty of rooms, and she could always find somewhere to be alone. That was the one thing about this place that she was going to miss.

She pointed her toes towards the ceiling and swung higher. Cool air slid beneath her skirt and petticoat as she flew through the air, causing a delicious shiver to dance up her spine. Her mind emptied. She forgot the sad state that her life had become, enjoying this moment of escape.

It didn't last. The web shifted, and Colleen clutched the rope at her chest. The left side of the net dropped another inch, and Colleen yelped. She tried to wriggle from her seat, and one of her feet tangled in the hemp. Her grip on the ropes slipped, and she fell backwards, rope snapping tight against her thighs.

Colleen blinked. The floor was inches away from her face, and she swung in a lazy spiral above it. Wiggling her legs, she tried to slide free of her bonds. She grabbed a rope by her hip and heaved. She struggled until she was out of breath. It was no good. She was stuck.

The ropes gently swayed, creaking softly against the beams, and Colleen's breaths slowed. Not her most graceful moment, but at least the ropes had saved her from knocking herself senseless on the hard wood floor. She tugged again at her trapped leg, but three ropes had seemed to loop themselves around it. She shimmied her hips. The rope at her bum slipped, and she dropped an inch. Her skirts crept up her legs. She wiggled some more but achieved nothing but louder creaking from the beam above.

The scrape of hemp against wood couldn't hide another sound. One far worse. That of the door opening.

Pushing at the hair that had fallen around her face, Colleen tried to see who the intruder was. She rather hoped it was a member. There was no way she would improve her position of authority over her workers if one of them caught her like this.

"Hallo? Who's there?" With one hand pressed to the floor, she pushed her skirts back over her knees.

A pair of black top boots edged into view, a smudge of soil dirtying one of the toes. Colleen levered her head. Wool trousers disappeared into the wheat-colored leather bands that ringed the top of the boots. Her gaze rose over broad thighs to the bottom of the trousers' falls. And the bulge behind. Try as she might, she couldn't crane her head to look higher than that bulge.

The man dropped into a squat, a bushy black beard replacing her view.

Colleen closed her eyes and dropped her head to the

floor. She wished it had been a worker.

"This is a splendid way to greet a man," said Maximillian Atwood, Baron of Sutton. He rubbed his jaw, his fingers disappearing into the beard that looked as soft as a beaver's pelt. "Like a fly trapped in a spider's web. I wonder who the lucky man was who was supposed to eat you."

Chapter Two

Max bit back a laugh. He couldn't help but draw one of the ropes forward and release it, making his lovely manager swing softly to and fro. Her skirts slipped past her knee, exposing the edge of her stockings and a thin slice of creamy skin. His mirth turned to something else.

Mrs. Bonner batted at his hand. "Will you desist. Matters are bad enough already without you adding making merry to the mix."

He sighed. One thing he'd learned from these months of association with the woman was that she smiled little. Not that he could blame her. She had little to smile about.

He swallowed past the thickness in his throat. "Let me assist you." Reaching for the rope around her ankle, he tried to slide it past her boot. The rope caught at a small hole in the heel.

She slapped him away. "I can untangle myself."

Max rocked back on his haunches and gave her a couple of moments of flailing about. He wasn't sure, but it looked like she managed to wrap another rope about her elbow. Her chances of success were low, but she looked delightful twisting this way and that. Strands of dark red hair had escaped the tight knot at her nape but they couldn't hide the angry flush reddening her face, or the heaving of her breasts.

"Do you concede defeat?" Really, he had all evening to enjoy the spectacle. Her skirts crept past her knees, and he would love to see just how far gravity would take them. But he began to suspect the blood in her face had more to do with hanging upside down than pique. And the way she was managing, she could end up wrapping one of those ropes around her neck.

"No. Just ..." She heaved a sigh, and a lock of hair blew away from her face and drifted back to her lips. "Fine." She reached out a hand. "Please help me up."

He pulled her upright and set her on the one foot that was free. Max eyed the harness, trying to determine which rope to attack first. "Do you mind my asking what, pray tell, you were doing?"

"I was putting the ropes away." She tilted her chin up and sniffed. Her left leg was still caught in the ropes, torqued at an indecent angle away from her body, ruining the sanctimonious effect. She swayed, hopped on one foot, and clutched the ropes.

"An inventive method, to be sure."

Mrs. Bonner narrowed her eyes, and he bit back a grin. The woman was all starch and misguided propriety, and Max enjoyed ruffling her tail feathers.

Ignoring her yelp, he hefted her to his shoulder and dragged the now slack ropes from her body. His fingers scraped across her hips and thighs and he forced himself to make the contact as fleeting as possible. His face was at her waist and he couldn't help but breathe her in. Her clothing smelled of lavender with an undertone of lye, a combination that shouldn't be appealing. His cock didn't agree and gave an interested twitch. It was such a mismatch of odors, a contradiction much like the woman. He wondered how long it would take a man to know Mrs. Bonner completely.

He set her on her feet and gripped her shoulders when she wobbled.

She shrugged him off. "I'm fine. I thank you." Shaking her skirts, she heaved a sigh. "This place is awash in filth and oddities, and I cannot understand how it continues to turn a profit."

Max unknotted the ropes and began to loop them

around his hand and elbow. "What exactly is so filthy about people seeking pleasure?" He slid the coil on his shoulder and started on another rope.

"What happens under this roof is a sin, as you well know." Mrs. Bonner took one of the coils and strode to the far wall. She hung the rope from a large nail. "I am quite happy that my employment here is almost at an end."

Max plodded to the wall, avoiding her gaze. When her employment ended, so would their association. He would miss her wide-eyed shock at the scenes played out in The Black Rose. The way she would press her lips together in disapproval, but sneak glances of the so-called sin when she thought no one was looking.

Perhaps convincing her that The Black Rose wasn't a den of iniquity would help change her mind. She needed employment. His paid well. It was only sensible. "How can it be a sin to enjoy what God has so freely given us? Minds and interests, and bodies to revel in it all. Isn't it more sinful to waste our lives by denying our blessings?"

She shook her head as she pulled a coil of rope from his shoulder. "By that way of thinking, we'd have license to do anything we wanted. Steal, cheat, murder ..." She paled and turned for the wall.

He hung the last length of rope. "Has your time here been so unbearable?" he asked hesitantly. "I had thought when I offered you this job that it would help your situation."

Clasping her hands together in front of her, she stared up at him. In the dim light, her deep blue eyes looked as dark as the night sky. "No. I was fortunate to get the work and I don't mean to sound ungrateful. But you *were* high-handed about it. Ignoring my objections to the manner of work, insisting I take the apartments here above the club." She shook her head. "I almost thought you were going to drag me to your carriage unless I agreed."

Max remained silent. He wasn't quite certain he wouldn't have. The woman had been damn stubborn. And he was responsible for her well-being. Knowing she was safe and provided for had eased his mind.

"But, much as I dislike this establishment and your general bossiness"—she arched an eyebrow and his damn cock twitched again—"you have done more for me since my husband died than anyone. I need to remember that."

"I would have done more, if you'd let me." That still burned. The fact that she wouldn't let him set her up in her own apartments after the fire. That she'd lived in a cramped home with her cousin, his wife, and his five children. But she hadn't wanted charity from a stranger. When The Black Rose's former owner and manager, Madame Sable, had been arrested, asking Mrs. Bonner to replace her had seemed the perfect solution. Honest work for honest pay. Even though it was work she loathed.

Maybe he should have told her he was responsible for her condition. Maybe then she would have accepted his help freely.

"You did plenty." She strode for the door. "No other landlord would have done so much for a tenant. Especially as you'd only just purchased the building the week before it burned to the ground."

He'd bought it a week after, making sure the previous owner wouldn't sustain a loss. But if she knew that, she'd ask questions. And if she asked questions, he'd have to tell her more lies. And lying to such an honest woman made his stomach tighten and his throat go dry.

She'd refused the damn fire insurance he'd offered. Saying she knew she and her husband hadn't purchased it and she didn't want anyone to be cheated. How many people did that? She was broke, a widow, her home and clock shop burned to the ground, and she refused easy blunt.

He followed her down the hall and into the main room. A raucous game of Beast of Burden had broken out. Max couldn't see which club member was down on all fours bearing the woman about on his back. The beast crawled around the room, carrying the chit to every gentleman. The places on her body where she received her kisses were most ... inventive. The music from the small band on the landing competed for dominance over the howls of laughter.

"Why don't we go to your rooms?" he asked. "I need to discuss something with you."

"Of course." She circled the edges of the room, on the opposite side of Lord Halliwell, Max noticed. That man needed a talking to.

She led him up the staircase to her private rooms. Her threadbare skirts hinted at shapely legs and displayed to admirable advantage the swaying of her wide hips. Max greedily ran his eyes up and down her form. Unlike the other women of Max's acquaintance, Mrs. Bonner had neither the gracefully sloping shoulders of the lady-birds of the club nor the affectations of languor practiced by the coquettes of the ton. From the determined set to her broad shoulders to her firm steps upon the stairs, Mrs. Bonner looked capable instead. Sturdy even. Like a woman with the strength to face the world.

She was completely unfashionable, and Max found her unutterably appealing.

She took him to her office instead of the sitting room and settled herself behind the elegant Queen Anne table that served as a desk. She indicated the chair across from her. "Have a seat."

Max turned to the fireplace instead. Picking up the tongs, he laid more coal on her fire and stoked the flames higher. "As you know, when you first agreed to manage this club, it was on the condition that it would be for three months."

"Or until the owner found a permanent manager. Whichever came first."

"Yes. About that." Max lit a taper in the fire then went about the room lighting the rest of the candles. He considered how to broach the subject.

"That one candle there is quite enough light." Mrs.

Bonner pointed to the taper on the corner of her desk.

"You'll ruin your eyesight with how stingy you are with the wax."

"It's not stingy to avoid extravagance. Which reminds me, I wanted to talk to you about the candles in the chandelier downstairs. There are one hundred and—"

"The candles stay. They add ambience." He set the taper in a candlestick on the mantle then strode to the chair in front of her desk, taking a seat.

He eyed the woman across from him. She'd been so reluctant to work in a Venus club. But she had a roof over her head now and three square meals a day. Surely, she'd come to appreciate the employment. "I now own this club. Madame Sable ran into some difficulties, and she had to sell in order to pay her legal fees. I purchased it."

Mrs. Bonner gaped at him, her full, open lips giving him all sorts of indecent ideas.

He gritted his teeth. Why was he always attracted to the strait-laced women? The ones who were shocked by his predilections? Who thought him immoral?

"But why would you want to own a bawdy house?" she asked. "I knew you were interested in its management and in ensuring the club's survival, but to actually enter into such a trade ... You're a member of the peerage!"

"And the peerage are above such filth?" Max raised an eyebrow. She truly was too naïve for words. "All the members are of the Beau Monde. With the fees we charge, they need to be. Why is it so surprising one of us would own it?"

Mrs. Bonner rested her elbows on the desk. "But you don't ... that is, I've never seen you ...." A delightful blush crept up her cheeks, a lighter shade of red than her dark auburn hair.

"You've never seen me use one of the rooms?" He hadn't, not since Mrs. Bonner had become manager. But she'd have to find out sooner or later. Especially if she acceded to his wishes. "I've been busy lately."

She pushed a piece of paper back and forth with the tip of her index finger. "Everything here is so strange. What is it, exactly, that you do here?"

"Next time I play, you'll have to come and watch." Blood rushed to his groin at the thought, and he draped one leg over the other. It hid his burgeoning erection, but the pressure on his length only made him harder. "Or, if you're interested, I'll even let you play with me."

Her eyes flared before her spine snapped straight. "No, thank you," she said, her voice clipped. "Now, would you like to look over the books? My three months here are almost at an end, and I believe you'll see that my management has maintained sufficient profit for you to pay me the premium you promised."

She jumped to her feet and reached for a ledger resting on the shelf behind her. She laid it on the desk, spun it around, knocking a piece of parchment to the ground. She ran her finger down a neat column of numbers. "As you can see, net earnings have grown by two percent. Not a huge increase I'll grant you, but as I'm not certain of my authority to change vendors, it was the best I could do."

Max picked up the fallen piece of paper. "Would you like to have that authority?"

"What do you mean?" A tiny dent appeared in her forehead. "After you pay me my premium, I won't be working here anymore."

He tapped the paper against his thigh. "I wanted to discuss your leaving. What would you say to staying on? Now that I'm the owner, I'll need a full-time manager. And as you said, you're doing a fine job."

"Absolutely not."

Max pursed his lips. "You don't need time to think about it?"

Mrs. Bonner tugged at the hem of her absurd waistcoat. Even amongst the lower classes, a woman wearing something so masculine was unusual. But Max had to admit the fitted garment did cup her breasts and torso nicely.

Much better than those formless gowns women typically liked to wear.

"No. I already have plans for my premium." She fingered the chain than ran from a buttonhole in the waistcoat and disappeared into a pocket. "And frankly, I've spent all the time I should at this establishment. It isn't proper."

Well, that was disappointing but not unexpected. Not with how difficult it had been to get Mrs. Bonner to agree in the first place. But he did need a good manager. He glanced down and frowned. "What if I offered you a pay increase? I could ..." His eyes flew to the paper again. "What is this?" He pushed from his seat and slapped the letter down on the desk.

Mrs. Bonner flicked her gaze down and up. "That is one of many correspondences directed to this business and a good example of why my time here must come to an end. To engage in such lewd behavior is bad enough, but to discuss it so openly is beyond reproach. Why that Mr. Zed thinks I'll tell him stories about what goes on within these walls, I don't know."

Grinding his back teeth together, Max tried to swallow his frustration. She couldn't possibly be so simple. "The author of this letter isn't asking you to write a lewd novel. He wants information on the members."

"Yes, that was clear." Mrs. Bonner leaned back in her chair. "I believe his exact words were, 'I will make it more than worth your while if we came to a mutually-beneficial arrangement. I'm more than willing to pay, and pay well, for information regarding your members' less savory inclinations.'" She sniffed. "I don't know how he wants me to determine which behaviors are more or less savory when every act in The Black Rose is shocking. It would be like choosing between the Tyburn Tree or the guillotine."

It didn't surprise Max that she would remember the letter word for word. From running numbers to solving problems, Mrs. Bonner had proven herself a most intelligent woman.

She was also the stupidest smart person he'd ever met.

"Do you not understand why Zed wants this information?" The alias burned in the back of his throat. It was one he recognized. "The man isn't planning on reading your little stories in bed as he pleasures himself." Mrs. Bonner's mouth dropped open, but he ignored her dismay. "He wants information about the members in order to blackmail them."

"He doesn't say that."

"Not in so many words, no, but the intent is clear." Max blew out a breath and reread the letter. Zed had been the head of a crime ring that he and his friends had been instrumental in taking down several months ago. The Crown had arrested many perpetrators, including The Black Rose's proprietress Madame Sable, but others had fled England, evading capture. The identity of Zed had never been determined. The man had been as elusive as smoke, and Max had thought he had drifted out of their reach.

Tension coiled in his gut. He'd thought that part of his life was over. He'd wanted a fresh start, and purchasing The Black Rose was the first step. An investment that would keep him as occupied as he'd like, one that did nothing more than make money and people happy. No more sneaking and spying for the Crown. He was done soiling his soul for the greater good. Finally, he could live a life of peace and pleasure.

But Zed was back. And sniffing around his club. That idyllic future would have to wait. Tucking the letter into the inside breast pocket of his coat, Max stood. "I have to go."

"What about the books? You wanted to see them." Mrs. Bonner tucked a lock of hair behind her ear. "And we have yet to discuss the exact date of my departure."

"Later." He strode for the door.

"But, my premium—"

"Later." Max turned at the door and bowed. "I'll return

tomorrow and we can discuss your employment." He fled, not wanting to see the confusion crossing her honest face.

The letter changed everything. His options for his new club were now forced. And Max had a creeping suspicion that Mrs. Bonner wouldn't like the new terms of her employment.

* * *

"So, he's back." John Chaucer, Earl of Summerset tossed the letter onto the low table in front of his chair and kicked his feet up onto it. He pulled out a lilac pocket square and wiped his fingers, as though the blackmail letter held a taint.

Marcus Hawkridge, Duke of Montague, and Sinclair Archer, Marquess of Dunkeld, laid down their cue sticks and strode over to join them. The men were in a private billiard's room at Simon's, a gentleman's club they all belonged to, and a favored location for confidential conversations. Dunkeld knocked Summerset's boots off the table and picked up the letter.

The marquess ran a hand through his copper hair. "What is this 'Zed' business, anyhow? I detest affectation."

Montague snatched the letter from his friend's hand. "Says the man whose castle in Scotland boasts a dungeon holding fifty suits of armor chained to the walls."

"Sixty-five. One for each Englishman who dared fight my clan at Prestonpans."

Summerset crossed one silk pantalooned leg over the other, swinging his foot back and forth. "And which clan member was it who sold out to us English in order to receive a marquisate?"

A deep growl rumbled from the Scotsman's burly chest.

"Gentlemen." Montague raised a hand. "Can we please get on to the matter at hand? I was on my bridal tour when you took down this crime ring. I don't know who this Zed fellow is." Marcus and his new duchess, Elizabeth, had faced trials of their own when they'd first met. But fortunately for them, the pair had missed Zed's arrival to

England.

Max picked up a cue stick and rolled it between his hands. "That's the problem. Neither do we. All we know is a man—"

"Or woman," Summerset interrupted. "We never had any confirmation of the miscreant's sex."

"Someone, calling himself *or herself* Zed"—Max glared at Summerset, daring him to interrupt again—"was the head of the ring. They gathered intelligence on men in the highest levels of government and business and blackmailed them in order to influence the regime. Of the many co-conspirators that we've picked up, not one of them had ever met Zed. Or were too terrified to admit to it."

The door was flung open, and two young club members, barely out of their leading-strings, stumbled in. The ripe odor of whiskey and ale followed closely behind. Max flipped his cue stick so he held the narrower end in his hand and placed the wide end against one of the lad's chests. He prodded the duo back out into the hallway, ignoring their drunken protests before closing and locking the door.

Stalking back to the table, Max bent over it and took a shot. The ball bounced around the corner pocket but didn't drop in. "We'll need to contact Rothchild. He was running point on this investigation." The fifth member of their group, Julius Blackwell, Earl of Rothchild, was recently married, as well. His bride, Amanda, was the Duchess of Montague's sister. Rothchild was enjoying his newly-found nuptial bliss at his country estate in Dorset.

It would have to be interrupted, poor sot. But Rothchild would want to know that Zed was back. He'd almost lost his wife to the bastard.

Montague refolded the blackmail letter. "That last paragraph. It could be construed as a threat against your manager. If she doesn't play nicely, take his money in return for information, he implies he'll resort to less savory means of convincing her."

Max's arm jerked, and a red target ball bounced over the edge of the table onto the carpet. He forced his hands to ease their grip on the cue stick. He'd picked up on the threat, too, even though Mrs. Bonner had remained oblivious. She was an unsophisticated woman, too straightforward to understand how she could become a pawn in a deadly crime ring. It would be all too easy for someone to take advantage of that. All too easy to hurt her.

Dunkeld bent down and picked up the billiard ball. With one bushy eyebrow raised, he placed it on the table and rolled it towards Max.

Tossing the stick on the green baize, Max turned and leaned against the wall next to a heavy silver candelabra. He crossed his arms over his chest and stared into the flames. "Mrs. Bonner is anxious to end her employment. With this threat against her, I figured now would be a good time to send her on her way." He ran his fingers through the flames, watching them flicker and bend around his skin. If his friends agreed with him, all would be well. He'd miss the little puritan, but it would be for the best. With her premium, he would have made amends for the wrong he did her, and they could part on good terms. His friends would agree. They—

"Of course, she can't leave," Montague said. "She will have to remain as manager. It would look too suspicious to Zed if another proprietress of The Black Rose left so quickly."

"Suspicious or not, this Zed must know that we have Madame Sable under house arrest." Summerset examined his nails. "And should know that Max is now the owner of the club. Why come after the manager that is under his control?"

Max held back his snort of derision. There was very little he controlled about Mrs. Bonner. Yes, he'd been able to remove her from her cramped living conditions, and the salary had improved her resources, but she'd only agreed from desperation. And with the premium he'd promised her for three months of service, she would no longer be desperate.

"Yes." Dunkeld threw himself down on a padded leather armchair, and the rest of them held their breaths, waiting to see if the chair would survive. Max was a large man, but the Marquess of Dunkeld had him beat in size. The Scotsman was a veritable giant.

The chair remained in one piece. "Zed must have suspected Max would read that note," Dunkeld continued. "So, what's his game?"

"We don't know that for sure," Max said. He held his hand over the fire until the heat grew too intense. He turned to his friends, shoulders slumping. "But if it is a game, I guess we'll have to play along to find out."

Summerset pushed to his feet and clapped Max on the shoulder. "Why so glum, chum? This is our best chance to finally catch the bastard." He rubbed his hands together, anticipation making his eyes gleam as bright as the jewels on his fingers.

Summerset loved their work with the Crown. Relished the chase. The danger. He'd never understand.

The muscles in Max's shoulders drew tight. "I had a meeting with Liverpool yesterday." One that the prime minister had been less than happy with. "I resigned from the special service that we provide to him. I'm tired of the clandestine assignments."

Varying degrees of shock crossed his friends' faces.

Summerset was the worst offender. His jaw hung wide enough to swallow a cod whole. "You can't leave the service. It's who we are. What we do."

"Not for all of us." Montague gave Max a small smile, understanding in his eyes. "Some of us do grow tired of the intrigue. Grow tired of the games."

Max nodded, and the tension eased the slightest bit from his shoulders. He could only imagine how Montague and Rothchild felt now that they had wives to attend. A family to build. The thrill of near-death experiences must lose its luster knowing all that you would be leaving behind.

"Games are what make life worth living." Summerset fisted his hands on his hips. "I swear, the lot of you are turning into a bunch of tight-kneed biddies."

Max leaned against the pool table, weariness attacking his limbs. He rubbed his eyes. "Game or not, with Zed raising his head, my retirement has come to a quick end. What should we do?"

"I'll write to Rothchild, tell him to get his arse back to London." Dunkeld shoved his hands in his coat pockets. "Summerset, you go talk to Liverpool. Tell him what's happened."

"Why do I have to talk to him?" Summerset pursed his lips. "Tedious man. Why don't you offer him a year's free membership to The Black Rose?" he asked Max. "That should take the starch out of his falls."

"It turns out proximity to bed sport and games doesn't necessarily lead to wanton behavior." Although Mrs. Bonner had shown a flicker of interest when it came to discovering Max's predilections. But mere curiosity could account for that. "Should I have Mrs. Bonner respond to the letter? Send the man some false information?"

Montague nodded. "Even if he knows the letter is coming from you, we still need to engage. Play his game."

Shrugging into his lime-green coat, Summerset added, "And even if he knows the information is false, he might not know that we know he knows." The earl tipped his head to the side. "You know?"

Dunkeld grumbled, the sound reverberating from deep in his chest. "I can't believe I followed that load of toss."

"My manager won't be happy that she has to stay on," Max said. "She has dreams beyond the club."

"But you'll find a way to keep her." Montague's words weren't a question.

Max slumped his shoulders. Yes, he knew a way. But he was under no illusions about what lay ahead in the next couple of months. His manager would be as angry as a cat in a burlap sack. When he finally released her, there would be hell to pay.

He put his cue stick away and trailed his friends to the door.

Summerset placed a hand on his arm, stopping him at the threshold. "Are you serious about leaving the Crown's service?"

Max nodded. "I'm tired of the company we keep. The things we have to do to protect our country. The filth we must roll in. There must be a better life out there, and I want to start living it."

Summerset narrowed his eyes. "Do you remember what you told me when our government first asked for our help? Years ago, when we'd just returned from the East?"

Max pursed his lips, wracking his brain. He was sure he'd said many things.

"You told me the indolent lives peers lead disgusted you. How barren and useless they seemed." Summerset crossed his arms. "You said you couldn't wait to work with the government, that you could start fresh and finally start living. Sound familiar?"

"What's your point?" So being a spy hadn't turned out the way he'd thought it would. Dealing with the dregs of society had a tendency to make a person reevaluate his life.

"My point," Summerset said, stepping close, "is that you're never quite happy with where you are. You always think there's some utopia lurking just out of reach. Something better. Cleaner. And you're always disappointed."

"You don't know what in the hell you're talking about."

Summerset shrugged, the gesture careless but his eyes serious. "If you say so. But for a man who is always so perceptive when it comes to reading others, you can be quite the lackwit when it comes to understanding yourself."

Chapter Three

"Poor Mary still hasn't been able to shake her cough, and we were hoping to send for a leech. And the smithy said he'd take Jonny on as an apprentice, but that will cost ten bob a month." Robby Polcock, Colleen's cousin on her mother's side, rubbed his rotund stomach and belched. He wiped his mouth with the back of his hand and continued naming his expenses to provide for his family. The list was interminable. And manipulative.

Colleen closed her eyes. He had been kind enough to take her in when her husband and home had been taken in the fire. It was only fair for him to expect some recompense for feeding and clothing her.

But did he have to be so sly about it? Each week she had taken her earnings to Robby, trying to repay all that he'd spent on her. There was still twenty quid of rent—and she nearly snorted at the idea of charging rent for sharing a bed with two little girls—that remained of her debt. Once she had her three-month premium, she would be able to pay it off. With plenty left to spare.

"And did I tell you that Julia—"

"Yes. You did tell me about your wife." Colleen had to interrupt. She couldn't take the litany of woe any longer. "I'm sorry to hear your situation hasn't improved." She pulled a small bundle of coin from her reticule and pressed it into her cousin's hand. "I hope this will help. Soon I'll be able to pay you everything that I owe."

"Well," he said, hefting the bag and giving her a hard smile, "that's what family is for, isn't it? To help each other when times are tough. Just think, if I hadn't been there to give you a roof over your head, buy you a whole new wardrobe, put food in your belly, just think where you'd be." He narrowed his eyes. "Just think of it."

Colleen swallowed. She didn't want to think of it. London was a city of extremes. The nobs lived in their mansions with their ladies' maids and gold-encrusted carriages while the poorest of the poor rested their heads in the mud, hoping to beg or steal enough to put a little food in their bellies. She had been fortunate enough to land somewhere in the middle. The day after the fire, she'd stood looking at the burned-out shell of her old home, and tentacles of panic had wrapped around her throat. She'd known how close she was to becoming one of the unfortunates. Living, and most likely dying, on the streets, with no one to even mourn her passing.

She would have deserved nothing less.

"You know I can never thank you enough, Cousin." She took a deep breath. "And as I said, I hope to repay all your kindnesses very soon."

He shrugged. "The money means little to me, as you know. I'm only glad you've landed on your feet. Where did you say this club was that you worked?"

Colleen hadn't said, and never would. If Robby ever snuck his head through the door, Colleen would have to pick his jaw off the floor. His shock and disgust would be unbearable. Another possibility reared its ugly head, and a legion of ants skittered down her spine. She could imagine another reaction laying below his outrage and Colleen had no desire to see her cousin in one of the rooms of The Black Rose.

Her stomach settled. He'd never be able to afford it.

"Speaking of the club, I must be getting back to work." She jumped to her feet. "It was lovely seeing you again, and I'll be back next week with the rest of your money."

Robby stood. "I look forward to it."

Colleen shouted a goodbye to the rest of the family and

scuttled from the house. The cold air slapped her face, and she inhaled deeply. Although a fire had been burning in the hearth, her cousin's house held no warmth. Her tidy room at The Black Rose, although in a house of sin, was a safe haven she relished. But it wasn't her own. It was controlled by someone else, someone who could kick her out on a whim.

She fingered the chain to her pocket watch and sighed. No, that was inaccurate. The Baron of Sutton wasn't the sort of man who would leave a widow without a home. He would always find work for her, try to ensure she was provided for. Even though he could be demanding and insupportable, he was also an unusually kind man with enough blunt to be generous.

Still, she longed for independence. Why rely on another's generosity when she could provide for herself? She had a mind for numbers and solid business sense; at least, Lord Sutton told her that often. She had to admit it was partially his belief in her, his flattery, that had induced her to accept the position at the bawdy house.

And in a week, she'd be leaving it. Would she ever see the baron again? She pushed that thought away and focused on her anticipated independence.

She turned and headed for the street a couple miles away where she hoped to attain that independence. The bottom of her feet ached from walking in her thinly-soled boots, but she hurried on. She strode into a small side street, the crowded buildings blocking the afternoon sun. Wrapping her coat more tightly about her, she followed her nose to the flower shop near the corner.

An old man looked up from the high table he sat behind, tying bunches of flowers together with string. He smiled pleasantly. "Yes. What can I do you for?"

"Good afternoon, Mr. Ridley. It's me."

His watery eyes crinkled around the edges but never focused. "Mrs. Bonner! I was wondering when you'd come back to brighten an old man's day. Ever since you moved out of the neighborhood, it's been as dull as tea with a vicar."

"Stuff and nonsense." Colleen turned to a large bouquet in the window and buried her smile in the petals. The light, innocent scent of the primrose reminded her of springtime. "I was here just two weeks ago. And from what I hear around the neighborhood, you're not lacking for female companionship."

His cheeks turned ruddy. "I don't know what you're talking about."

"Uh huh." Striding to the table, Colleen tugged off her gloves. "So, Mrs. Hutchins doesn't bring you dinner every other day of the week?"

Mr. Ridley lifted his chin. "The widow is being neighborly. Unlike some, who forget their friends and move halfway across the city."

Colleen rested her elbows on the table, her sleeve brushing a cut stalk of lavender. "I'm close to coming back. If you still want to sell, in a week I'll have enough saved to make the down payment on this building and your business."

With his failing eyesight, Mr. Ridley had talked of selling the place for years. He lived in the upper apartment and had run the florist shop downstairs for as long as Colleen could remember. But the income from the sale of the building and the business would be enough to see him comfortably through his remaining years. His daughter had offered him a room in her cottage in Surrey, and Mr. Ridley was of a mind to take it.

Colleen wanted the flower shop with a longing so strong it stole her breath. While married, she'd been surrounded by hundreds of timepieces. The endless tick-tocks, the sterile whistle from the rare cuckoo clock imported from Germany, all had created a cacophony loud enough to drive a person mad. Her refuge had been this shop. It was vibrant, abounding with life and vitality. The scents and colors were a feast for her senses.

Her husband could never understand her wasting her money on a bouquet that would wither within a week. But, then, Mr. Bonner had been as mechanical as the clocks he'd repaired and sold.

The old man patted the table, searching, and Colleen slid the knife under his hand. He cut the end of the string and knotted it around the spray of lavender. "I wish I could give the place to you. No one else seems to feel the same way about it. But I'll miss it."

He slid the knife into an apron pocket and walked into the back. Colleen followed. Four tables were piled high with mounds of loose flowers. Mr. Ridley felt along the tables, picking up stems and smelling the blooms, forming a bouquet. "My wife and I had a lot of good years here. Well, you know what it's like working with someone you love."

Her heart pinched. She wasn't quite certain she did know. She'd started out her marriage with high hopes. Each year that passed, Colleen had begun to suspect that whatever it was she felt for her husband wasn't love. And then—

She slammed the door on those thoughts. "I know you've been patient with me. You must have turned down other offers waiting for me to come up with the money. I can't tell you how much I appreciate it." She looked through the watery glass of the back window into the small yard behind the building. Rows of flowers punched out of the soil, the newer buds starting to defy the strict order in which Mr. Ridley had sown them. Weeds escaped notice because of his failing sight. Colleen knew he purchased most of his flowers wholesale each morning. But the idea of growing and harvesting her own seeds sent a lick of anticipation shooting through her.

He snorted. "I haven't had that many offers, though I am glad you're almost ready. My daughter asks nearly every day when I'm going to move." Wrapping the bouquet in yesterday's paper, he dampened the end. "Let me know when you can close the deal. Mrs. Hutchins's nephew is an attorney, and he said he'd draw up the paperwork. I already told him the terms we agreed to."

"Sounds perfect." Colleen clasped her hands together and blew out a long breath. Her heart thudded in her chest. In just over a week, this would all be hers. Hers, and something no one could take. Not a husband, not a landlord, not a bank. She bounced on her toes. And because she couldn't help herself, she skipped over to Mr. Ridley and kissed his bristly cheek.

His ears turned bright red. "Aw, go on with you. You'll be making Mrs. Hutchins jealous, you will."

"So, you admit there's something there to be jealous of."

He shooed her from the back room. "Scoot. Or I'll sell to that Friday-face next door."

"I can't have that." Although having such a sullen man as *her* new neighbor didn't exactly fill her with glee, either. But she could handle living next to a cranky man. "I'll see you next week." She gripped the door's handle.

"Wait." Mr. Ridley shuffled towards her. He held out a woody stem with a delicate starburst of white petals.

"It's beautiful." Colleen took the flower and rubbed one of the leathery leaves between her thumb and forefinger. She slid the stem into the buttonhole of her old coat.

"Smells even better," he said gruffly. "It's bridal wreath. Supposed to bring you luck."

From the depths her life had sunk to six months ago to being a week away from purchasing her dream, she didn't know how much more luck she needed. But she supposed every bit helped.

"Thank you." She squeezed the man's arm and slipped out the door. Her good mood lasted three blocks. Colleen stopped in front of the remnants of her old home. The burned-out shell of the structure remained, a discarded carcass. The bottom floor of the building next to hers had also burned, but the owner had rebuilt. A new tenant was slapping paint on a sign above the front door announcing a bakehouse.

Colleen stared at the charred pile of rubble that represented eight years of her life. She'd lived there since the day of her marriage at age nineteen. Eight years of her life, and it didn't feel real. Her memories of that time were already fading, becoming obscured, as though she was looking through a window covered with a heavy sheen of oil, distorting all the images. Nothing in that time felt as real as her life now at The Black Rose.

As a woman, her husband had owned everything. She'd worked in the clock shop, increased its profits, and it all belonged to Mr. Bonner. Nothing was hers. Even if she'd worked outside the shop, her wages would have belonged to her husband, as well. As a widow, her rights had changed.

Her throat thickened. Of course, she'd give all those rights up if she could go back in time and change what had happened six months ago. But she couldn't deny the heady rush when she received her pay each week and knew it was hers, and hers alone. The Black Rose had provided her with the means to determine her future. For that, she owed Lord Sutton a large debt of gratitude.

Yes, the club was immoral. Colleen chewed on her lower lip. But a proper establishment would most likely never be managed by a woman. Strange to think a den of iniquity was more forward-thinking than the rest of London society. Perhaps ... perhaps the club wasn't *all* bad. And like the baron had said, no one was hurt by it, except perchance the salvation of some everlasting souls. But that was a decision best left up to God and not hers to pass judgment upon.

Eyes dry, she turned and walked away from her past life. Night was falling by the time she reached the club, and she suspected a large blister had formed on her right heel. The footman opened the door for her and gave her a polite nod. "Molly's been looking for you, ma'am."

"Thank you." Looking longingly at the door to her apartments, Colleen turned into the main room of the club instead and searched for the girl. Molly wasn't dancing with the members. Or drinking champagne. Or sitting down to a game of cards. Nowhere semi-respectable. Colleen turned for the unrespectable parts of the club.

She found her in the Cellar Room. Not an actual cellar, but the walls and floors were a dark grey stone and a damp chill hovered in the air. It was the name Colleen had given the room. She preferred it over what the girls called it – the Dungeon.

It took a moment for her eyes to adjust to the dim torch light. About fifteen members gathered on hard benches to watch the scene playing out before them. None of the spectators made a sound, either too awed or too afraid of the consequences. And Colleen could see why. Molly stood in the center of the room wearing a gown of crimson organza. The skintight pantaloons that were visible beneath the dress made her look dangerous. Fierce. The outline of her bare breasts beneath the sheer fabric did little to soften the image. Molly looked like a female pirate.

The whip in her hand didn't hurt that image, either.

A naked man knelt before her. Even in the low light, Colleen could see the long, red welts marking his back. Four leather cuffs wrapped around each of his knees and wrists and were attached together with thongs.

Molly placed her booted foot to his side and tipped him over. He landed on the stone with a groan.

"Get up!" Molly cracked the whip. It didn't seem to strike the man, but the noise was enough of a motivation for him to try to right himself. The ankle and wrist harness hampered his efforts, an effective hobble. After two more cracks of the whip, he managed to heave to his hands and knees. He crawled towards Molly and kissed her boot.

Colleen slid into a spot on the wall next to Lucy. "How much longer?" she whispered.

Lucy shrugged. "Almost done, I think," she murmured. "The scene started with him forced into his restraints by four of our men. He was cursing Molly's name. Now he is all slavish devotion."

Colleen could see that. The man practically purred when Molly smoothed his hair, a glazed look softening his face. Molly bent over and whispered something in his ear. She stroked the handle of the whip down his spine and between the cheeks of his bum.

The man mewled and arched his back.

"She is skilled," Colleen admitted. Had someone put a whip in Colleen's hand, she'd as like end up choking herself with it than control anyone else.

"She should be." Lucy shifted, leaning closer to Colleen. "I heard she's been on the streets since she was twelve. You can learn a lot in that time. And that's why I watch as many of her dominance scenes as I can. To learn from her."

Colleen rubbed at the ache in her chest. She didn't care overmuch for Molly, but her heart broke for the little girl she'd been. And that any man would touch one so young .... Colleen clenched her fists, and her glare landed on the unfortunate male who sidled through the door.

Lord Sutton closed the door behind him, caught her look, and raised an eyebrow. He leaned back against the wall, crossing his arms over his chest, looking content to wait.

Colleen turned from his scrutiny, her scalp prickling. Insufferable man. It was easy to forget his kindnesses when, with just one look, he could make her as uncomfortable as a cat in a room full of dogs.

Molly lashed her customer twice more before grabbing his member and tugging none too gently. With the handle of the whip, she pointed at one of the house servants lounging in the shadows. The man wore breeches but no shirt, and claw marks streaked across his stomach. He stepped forwards and unbuttoned his falls.

Molly cracked the whip, and the tail bit into the customer's buttock. "You injured that young man when he was kind enough to restrain you. I believe he deserves some recompense." She kicked him before striding to the servant and stroking his freed prick. He hardened quickly.

"Yes, Mistress." The bound man shuffled forwards on his hands and knees. With his wrists bound to his knees, he had a hard time raising his head high enough to put his mouth on the servant's length but he finally managed.

Wet, slurping noises filled the chamber. Colleen averted her eyes, looking everywhere but at the tableau. More than one of the male spectators had unbuttoned his own falls and was bringing himself pleasure. The wife of one of the members knelt before her husband and took him in her mouth.

Colleen stared at the floor. There was nowhere safe to look. Sutton shifted, drawing her attention. He had one leg crossed over the other, the toe of one top boot planted firmly next to his other foot. She looked up the dark leather shafts, up to the trousers tucked into the tan-colored band circling the tops of the boots. His thighs bulged behind the wool of his black trousers, and .... Her cheeks heated. Was he hard behind his falls? Was he watching this licentiousness and becoming aroused?

She darted a glance at his face and lost her breath. One of his shoulders was propped against the wall, and he was facing her, ignoring the scene in the center of the room. He stared at her, unblinking, his countenance indecipherable. The man was an enigma. He rarely showed his thoughts or emotions, yet he seemed to always know hers, a condition that was becoming increasingly annoying.

Soft moans filled the chamber, and she didn't know if it was the house servant's pleasure or that of the other members' that she heard. The gentle sucking noises developed a rhythm, each tug sending a low thrum to her center. The tips of her breasts tingled, and she stared into Sutton's eyes, finding it impossible to look away. The air in the chamber warmed, grew heavy from the heat of all those bodies and the scents of their desire.

She shifted her thighs together, trying to will away the ache. The moans grew louder. The delicate sucking sounds picked up tempo. Sutton's eyes were black in the dim light, dark, burning embers. She needed to look away but was ensnared. Sweat dampened her back, rolled down her skin, joined with the moisture pooling between her thighs.

And still he stared at her.

Her breath clogged her throat. Her chest heaved. Slowly, he pushed off the wall. Took a step towards her.

Molly planted herself in front of Colleen, severing the connection.

All the air left Colleen in a hiss, and she slumped back against the cold stone. She needed to gain control of herself. She was a widow and a woman of business, with no time for such nonsense as ... well, as whatever that was.

She cleared her throat. "You wanted to speak with me?" she asked Molly. "I can wait until after your scene." Glancing over the girl's shoulder, she took note of the house servant gripping the customer's hair, yanking the man's mouth over his length in deep, rough strokes. "It is almost over?"

Molly tapped the handle of the whip into one hand. "Bernard can wait. I can have him service every male in the room as his punishment if need be. But I did want to speak with you."

"About?"

"Mr. Harper. He's one of Suzy's regulars. I want him."

Colleen waited for more, but the girl remained silent. "That's it? You want something so you think you should have it?" Molly hadn't had parents for most of her life, Colleen had to remind herself. No one to teach her the sins of selfishness.

"Yes." Molly dropped the tail of the whip and drew circles on the floor with it. "I'm a better courtesan than Suzy. Why shouldn't I have him?"

"And how does Mr. Harper feel about this?"

Molly looked at her scornfully. "He's a man. He'll feel what I tell him to."

"I hope you don't hold all members of my sex in the same low regard." Sutton stepped behind the girl's shoulder. "We don't all care to be led around by our ... noses."

"My lord!" Something dark flashed across Molly's face before she spread her lips in a pleasing smile. Turning, she dropped a saucy curtsy. Resting her hand on his forearm, she leaned close. "There are exceptions to the general rule, of course. But I would love a chance to prove you wrong. Show you just how sweet life can be when guided by the firm hand of an experienced mistress." She tapped his shoulder with the whip's handle. "It can be a battle of wills. Trap us in a room for a couple of hours and see who's the first to crack."

Sutton leaned away from her and side-stepped towards Colleen. "As delightful as that sounds, forgive me if I pass. I have no desire to break or be broken myself."

Molly inhaled deeply, and her breasts pressed against the organza, her hard nipples poking against the fabric. "Pity."

Colleen stepped between them, blocking the baron's line of sight to that exhibition. "My answer is no, Molly. Mr. Harper can request any girl he wants when he visits the club, and if he wants Suzy, he'll get her. I won't assign him elsewhere."

"But—"

"That's final."

"Of course, mum." Molly wrapped the tail of the whip around her palm. "I'd best get back to my slave." She tossed her head, her sheaf of silky, nutmeg hair swinging, and marched across the room.

Sutton followed Colleen from the chamber. "You're tough."

"I have to be to keep people like her in line. I had thought of asking you if I could fire her, but as Molly said, she is one of the better courtesans. The club's profits would take a hit if she weren't here." Colleen turned left, away from the main room, and made her way through the back halls to the second staircase leading to her private rooms.

The baron was only a step behind, so she kept her back rigid, her steps firm, even though she longed for a bucket of ice water for her feet and a hot bath for the rest of her body. "Did you want something, my lord?"

"I wanted to know where you'd been all day."

She slipped past her half-open door to her office, but he pushed it wide, filling the frame.

She tossed her reticule on her desk. "Out."

"Out? Is that all the answer I am to receive?"

"It's all that you're owed." She tugged off her gloves. "You're my employer, not my father."

He narrowed his eyes. "And as your employer, I expect a certain level of responsibility from those under me. You're supposed to manage this place, not go traipsing around London. Unattended, no less." He stalked towards her, and she backed around her desk. He followed. With his bushy beard and wild black hair, he was the very image of a rampaging Visigoth, or what she imagined one to look like.

Barbarians didn't scare her. She planted her feet and tipped up her chin. "If you are displeased with my managerial style, I'm happy to conclude my employment now rather than next week. I'll just take my premium and get out of your way."

Rubbing the back of his neck, he sighed. "I apologize. When I couldn't find you, and after that letter .... I apologize. Of course, I don't want you to leave." He pulled out her chair from behind the desk. "Please, sit."

Ignoring the pain flaring in her heel, she stepped to the chair. She tugged off her coat and lay it across her desk before dropping into her seat.

He lowered his gaze, his dark green eyes growing hooded. "You're in pain. Where?"

Colleen gaped. "There's no way you can know that."

"And yet, I do." Pulling around another chair, he sank down in front of her. His gaze tracked up and down her body, assessing. "Are you ill?"

"No. I'm quite well."

"Are you suffering a megrim?"

She gritted her teeth. "I said—"

"And I can play this guessing game all night until I hit upon what ails you." He fingered the flower in her coat. "Why don't you save us both the time and trouble?"

"It is of little account. I walked too far and my foot is sore." Gripping the edge of her desk, she scooted her chair under the tabletop.

Sutton dragged her back around. "Let me see." Picking up her left foot, he studied her face, and replaced it with her right.

Colleen tried to keep her expression even. It was blasted annoying how the man could see past her façade, always knowing what she felt and thought. He hadn't believed her when she'd told him she was content living with her cousin and had installed her at this club. And she suspected he didn't believe her when she feigned indifference to the activities that took place within these walls.

He unlaced her boot, and she didn't argue. It was highly improper, of course, but her standards of propriety had become distorted these past couple months. A gentleman's hand on her stockinged ankle was hardly enough to blink an eye over. When the worn leather of her boot slid over her blister, she winced, and then sighed in relief when cool air caressed the wound.

Trailing the tips of his fingers along her heel, the baron said, "That's a beautiful example of Stephanotis floribunda."

Colleen bent her knee and looked at her heel. "There's a name for my blister?"

He laughed, the deep rumble crashing over her like waves on the shore. Fine lines softened the hard set of his eyes, and the wild beast suddenly looked human.

Her heart twisted like the mainspring in a clock, setting things in motion in her body that she didn't want to acknowledge.

He nodded at her coat. "I was speaking of the flower."

"You know the Latin names of flowers?" The baron didn't even look like the type of man to know the common names.

"Botany is a hobby of mine." He rested her ankle on his thigh, close to his hip. "One I hope to pursue more fully in the future."

A slight tingle spread across the arch of her foot and down through her heel. His muscles made a hard bed beneath her ankle and one of the buttons on his falls just scraped her big toe. She was inches away from something most inappropriate.

She shifted her hips on the seat. "I can't see a man like you studying plants. Ripping them out to plant a crop, perhaps."

With one hand, he cupped the top of her foot. He stroked his fingers up to her toes and back down, pressing his thumb into a fleshy pad on her sole. His movements were slow, the pressure delicious. She could hardly sit still.

"I'm happy to surprise you." He raised her foot, and Colleen pushed the fabric of her skirt tight between her legs. From his angle, he might look right up her petticoat. Lowering his head, he blew cool air across the blister. "That flower is fairly unusual here in England. Where did you get it?" He lowered her foot back to his thigh and picked up her other. Her blisters no longer hurt, but she missed the soft caress of his breath. Liked the way his lips pursed inside the circle of his beard. He untied the laces of her other boot.

"A florist in Wapping." Would he furnish the same treatment on her left foot? It felt like thick syrup coursed her veins, making her limbs heavy, her body languid. She needed to keep talking, anything to prolong his ministrations. "I'm buying the flower shop with my premium. It's a lovely store, and the owner is the sweetest old man. I've wanted to buy it for years."

He paused before sliding off her boot. "Have you signed

a contract?"

"Not yet, but an attorney is writing one up." His hands engulfed her foot. They were large. Strong. She had no doubts they were capable of wringing a man's neck, yet he cradled her foot as gently as though he were holding a babe. Something deep inside of her tugged. "Why?"

His chest heaved, and he blew out a long breath, not meeting her gaze. He rubbed circles into her ankles, each thick digit a patch of warmth that soothed her tired bones. She relaxed back into her chair.

"You can't buy the shop. Not yet." The baron raised his head, his piercing green eyes pinning her in place. "I'm not going to give you your premium. I need you to remain manager."

Jerking her feet from his hands, she shot up. "You can't! You promised me that money for three months' service. It's been three months."

"I'm sorry, but circumstances have changed."

Fire burned in her chest. How dare he? Wasn't that just like a swell? Ignoring his commitments when it suited him. "You promised," she said through gritted teeth. "I held up my end. I've managed this club competently and efficiently. I've earned that premium."

"I agree." Sutton lounged in his chair, stretching out his long legs. He might act high in the instep, but Colleen could see the tense set of his shoulders. The press of his full lips. "But the letter you received has changed our circumstances."

"What letter?"

He slid a folded piece of parchment from his pocket and tossed it on the desk. "The one you showed me yesterday. The one that threatened you with harm if you didn't provide Zed with information."

Colleen frowned. "No one threatened me." Unfolding the letter, she reread the contents. The end bit didn't sound quite friendly but it hardly qualified as a threat.

Sutton sighed. "It's right there in black and white." He

pointed at a couple lines.

"There is nothing there." This couldn't be happening. Not another dream taken away. Her throat squeezed, and she forced the tears back where they came from. "You're seeing something that doesn't exist. And even if it is a threat, that is only an added reason for me to leave The Black Rose."

Sutton stood, crossing his arms over his wide chest. "You read things too literally, but communication is in the nuance. The threat is there. And it is a threat from a very dangerous man."

"How do you know that? Who is Zed? And who are you?" Normal toffs didn't run around with dangerous criminals. But, then, she'd always known the baron was different. That there was more to Madame Sable's disappearance and her *legal* troubles. She narrowed her eyes. "Who do you work for?" There was only one option that made sense.

He ignored her questions. "I need to catch him, and in order for that to happen, I need you. Here."

"No." She matched his stance. She didn't care if he did work for the government. "I refuse to stay here any longer. I'll take my money now, thank you."

"It pains me to say it, but you have little choice." Bending, he swiped her boots off the ground and held them in one hand. "Not if you want your premium. But once Zed is in prison, I promise to make good on our arrangement. In fact, I'll even double it."

"You bleed freely," she bit out. She turned to face the wall and wiped her fingers across her cheek. "And pardon me if I don't believe your promises. They no longer hold any weight." The air shuddered in her chest and her lungs refused to completely fill. She'd been so close. The loss of her flower shop hurt more than it should.

More than when she'd stood before the charred remains of her life.

She hung her head. She was lower than scum.

She heard a clatter before he cupped her shoulders. The weight was reassuring and warm, but she refused to find comfort. Not from the man who'd just ripped her future from her. She jerked forwards, but he drew her back.

"I know I've let you down, and it pains me to do so." His voice was soft as velvet. She didn't want to find it attractive. There could be nothing about the brute that she liked, not after his betrayal. She'd thought him better than the rest of the Quality. He'd seemed to care about her and her dead husband, genuinely wanting to help her. And he looked nothing like the coifed and pampered swells that she'd seen rolling about in their fancy carriages.

She'd thought he was different, but he was like all the rest. Only in it for himself. No faith behind his words, only carelessness.

She swallowed past the thickness in her throat. "How long?" she asked, pleased with how even her voice sounded. He wouldn't know how deep his lies had cut.

"It could be a week. Or several months." He rubbed her upper arms, the thin fabric of her shirt scraping against her skin. "Investigations like this take time."

She turned and cocked her head. "And why are you investigating? Isn't this a matter for Bow Street? It's not like a toff to get his hands dirty."

She thought his smile looked tight, but it was difficult to tell with the beard covering his cheeks.

"Not all toffs behave the same. This man is threatening my club. Threatening my manager." His nostrils flared. "That isn't a situation I'll tolerate."

Colleen's mouth became moist, and she swallowed. He didn't raise his voice or punch a wall, but his anger was intense, nonetheless. It wrapped around her, promising protection in its power. Her anger leeched away, replaced by a sharp longing. The baron wore a look she'd hoped to see on her husband, back when she'd been young and romantic.

She stepped from his grip. Picking her boots up from

the desk, she strode from the room. The baron was silent, but she could feel him following. She pushed into her chambers and placed the boots at the foot of her wardrobe. Hands on her hips, she examined her options. Without the premium, they were few. And putting her feet up and snoozing by the fire wasn't one of them. It was time to get back to work.

Her options for footwear were just as limited. Either the stiff boots that had caused the blisters, or ... With a sigh, she slid out the discolored and frayed slippers from under the wardrobe and went to sit on the bench at the foot of her bed. She covered the guinea-sized hole the fire had burned through the toe of one of the slippers with her hand and slid it onto her foot.

Sutton stood in the doorway, her coat tossed over one arm, his eyes tracking her every movement. "Why haven't you purchased anything with your clothing allowance?"

She stood and shook her skirts out. Unlike the floor-length gowns the upper class and her lady-birds wore, her skirts ended at the ankle. Doing little to hide her pitiable footwear. "I have no need to dress like a fancy lightskirt. That isn't my position here."

"Forget 'fancy'. It would be nice if my manager didn't walk around in shoes that didn't allow her feet to touch the floor. And didn't wear coats"—he held out her borrowed wool one—"that would serve better as a rag."

She moved to him and snatched the coat from his grip. Removing the flower from the buttonhole, she hung the coat in her wardrobe. "Most of my things were destroyed in the fire. My cousin gave me this. It serves its purpose."

"Your cousin." Sutton curled his upper lip. "From the little I know of the man, I suspect his act wasn't done out of charity. Giving his old coat to you likely saved him the bother of burning it."

Colleen refused to feel ashamed of her appearance. All she had was honestly earned, and that meant more to her than fancy gowns or delicate kid slippers. A man like the baron wouldn't understand that.

She tipped her chin up. "Now that you've *convinced* me to remain on as manager, what is it exactly you wish me to do? Write back to your Zed with shocking stories? I don't know where to address the letter."

Sutton rested his forearm against the doorjamb above his head. "No, the man will have to find a way to contact you again. Another letter, a courier. If Zed wants a response, he's going to have to reveal himself. And I'll be waiting."

"So, I continue running The Black Rose and when I hear from the blackmailer again, I contact you?" It didn't seem like much of a plan. Not the zealous and speedy prosecution Colleen would have preferred.

He smiled, one side of his mouth curving higher than the other. His beard framed his sinful lips, and she wondered what it would be like to kiss such a man. He had the sort of smile she imagined a highwayman would have. It did funny things to her knees and made her breasts heavy and achy.

She swallowed and fought back the illogical blush that threatened to sweep her cheeks. Just because she was standing in her bedchambers with a man was no cause to think such improper thoughts. Besides, the baron could have no way of knowing what was running through her mind. Nothing to feel awkward about.

His smile deepened, and his gaze flitted to the bed and back to her face.

She refused to believe it. There was no way he was that discerning of her unspoken thoughts. "My lord?" She clasped her hands together, forgetting about the flower and crushing the bloom. "Am I to contact you when I receive another letter?"

"There'll be no need." He leaned forwards, that slight tilt of his shoulders feeling like he'd invaded her space. "Until this matter is resolved, I'm going to stay so close to your side it will feel like our bodies are joined as one."

Nothing could stop her blush that time.

Chapter Four

For one so small, Mrs. Bonner burst with energy. Max had been following her around for days, watching as she settled this dispute before moving on to fix that problem. She was like the commander of a ship, always walking the decks, sleeping with one eye open. He hated to admit it, but the woman wore him out. The soles of his feet yearned for a reprieve from constantly being upon them; he could only imagine how hers, in her flimsy footwear, fared.

That, at least, was something *he* could fix. "Mrs. Bonner, a moment."

She turned from a discussion with one of the maids. "Yes, my lord?"

"Will you follow me? I have something to show you." Without waiting for a response, he strode across the main room and held the door to the private upper rooms open for her. His palm was slick on the latch, and he wiped his hands on his coat. It shouldn't be so nerve-wracking presenting small tokens to a woman. Especially as these were necessary for her to do her job properly. But gift giving of any sort was a practice to which Max was unaccustomed. And to a woman such as Mrs. Bonner ...

She was so unlike the women of the ton that he knew. With her, there was no pretense. A man got exactly what he saw. A straightforward, hardworking woman who deserved more than the lot she'd received in life. Her honesty gave him hope for society, and he couldn't help thinking that in a perfect world, all women would be like Mrs. Bonner.

She glanced at him curiously but went through the door and led him up the stairs. Her round bottom swayed three steps in front of him, and Max shoved his hands in his pockets. Her unconventional outfits showcased the hips that most women hid behind shapeless gowns. Those hips gave him ideas. Max adjusted his cock. The urge to touch his manager was great, and it didn't help that he saw desire trapped behind her eyes when she looked at him. If he seduced her, pressed slow, soft kisses to her neck as he lifted her skirts, would she give in to her cravings? Or slap his face and call him a fool?

It would be better if she rebuffed him. He didn't deserve Mrs. Bonner. Not after what he'd done. Although, if he brought her pleasure as well as himself, would it truly be so wrong?

She hesitated at the top, and Max directed her into the sitting room. "Through here, please."

She strode through the doorway and stopped short. Max bumped into her back and grabbed her shoulders, making sure she didn't topple over.

"What on earth is all this?" She inched to the settee and fingered one of the many dresses thrown over the back. The room was littered with clothes, the garments draped over every chair and sofa. Neat rows of slippers, and with a nod to Mrs. Bonner's practicality, several pairs of sturdy boots lined the floor.

"Two men's shirts, a waistcoat, two sets of skirts, two pairs of shoes, and one ratty coat seem to be the entirety of your wardrobe." Max scraped his palms down his trouser legs. Women liked this sort of thing, right? Presents and frippery and such. Even practical Mrs. Bonner couldn't differ that much from the rest of her sex. "I know the fire destroyed most of your belongings. You've done such good work here, you've earned a few things."

"A few things?" Mrs. Bonner dropped her chin and stared at him. "Perhaps to Marie Antoinette, God rest her soul, this would be a few things. But there's no way I could wear all this in a lifetime." She narrowed her blue eyes. "Are these guilt offerings? A new wardrobe in no way makes up for you reneging on our agreement."

"I know that." This was the one thing he'd done for her that hadn't been because of guilt. The urge to put his mark on her, even if it was only by clothing her with garments he'd paid for, was strong. He spread the fingers of his left hand and gestured at the room. "You need a new wardrobe, and as I've said, you've more than earned it."

She ran the tip of her finger along the lace neckline of a pale purple silk gown and bit her lip. "Highly impractical. I could never wear such things."

Gathering up the dress she admired, he held it to her body. "Practicality isn't everything." He wondered at the type of things her husband must have bought her. A clock repair man couldn't have had much blunt, but with a woman like Mrs. Bonner waiting at home, he must have given her some small trifles. The more serious the woman was, the more Max wanted to lavish her with unserious things. She'd been dry-eyed and stoic at her husband's funeral, showing a strength Max could respect. But it had been six months since she'd been widowed. Max wanted to see her smile.

Mrs. Bonner had been without the resources to garb herself in widow's weeds after the fire. She'd refused Max's offer of financial help, and her dreadful cousin hadn't dug within his purse to clothe her appropriately. And for that, Max was grateful. Such a serious woman would be swallowed in all black. He cocked his head. Although, perhaps the paler colors didn't suit her personality, either.

Tossing it aside, he plucked up another gown, a deep maroon that reminded him of her hair. "I'll call up a maid. Why don't you go try this one on?"

She fingered the soft fabric. "Who do these belong to? The former proprietress?"

"They're yours. I had a modiste make them up."

"But ..." A tiny furrow appeared between her

eyebrows. "How did she create them without knowing my size?"

Max didn't need to look. He'd memorized her dimensions by their third meeting. But his eyes were greedy, and he dropped his gaze and ran it up and down her body. "I described you to the modiste." Every last curve and inch. "She'll come here to alter anything that needs it."

Alterations shouldn't be necessary, not if the modiste had done her job right. His description of Mrs. Bonner had been thorough. The silly waistcoat nipped in at her middle, and her hips and breasts flared around it. It covered everything yet hid nothing. She was a luscious hourglass that he'd imagined spread out beneath him more nights than not. The hem of her skirt exposed a good two inches of ankle, and that tiny expanse of skin beckoned to him like an invitation. How easy it would be to slide his hands up under her skirts, under the petticoat she wore, stroking along that smooth skin until he found her hot and wet and ready for him.

He shook his head. His fantasies could wait until he was alone. But the real Mrs. Bonner was just as alluring. She stood toe to toe with him, looking up with eyes that were wide and curious and without a hint of affectation. A lock of her dark auburn hair had come loose and coiled around her neck.

He couldn't help himself. Reaching up, he brushed the strand back, his fingertips trailing over her silky skin. The contact was fleeting. As light as a summer breeze.

It made every hair on his body stand at attention.

Her eyes darkened to a night sky. She parted her lips then stopped moving. He didn't even know if she breathed. They stood there, motionless, as though caught in a moment between time. The air thickened around them, grew heavy with want, and Max swore he could smell her desire.

He blinked, and time sprang forwards. The stillness

broke. Colleen swallowed thickly, her neck undulating with the motion, and he bit back an oath.

She stepped back and looked at the floor. "I don't have time for such nonsense. Return all this. Besides, all these clothes would never fit in my wardrobe."

"I've had two more wardrobes installed in your chambers."

Her eyes flared wide. "Two more? Is there even room to sleep in the room anymore?"

"Of course." Plenty of room to do a lot of things on that bed. "Why don't—"

"You know I can't accept this." She laced her fingers together in front of her, her hands resting at the cradle of her hips. Always so proper. "You pay me a salary, and that is enough."

"None of this is returnable." Max had no idea whether he could return the gowns and shoes he'd ordered. And he didn't want to find out. He shrugged, trying to look casual. "If you don't want the items, fine. But they will only go into the dustbin."

"You wouldn't." Her eyes flashed, shining outrage at the thought of such waste.

Max kept his smile to himself. One of the many delights of such a forthright woman was that she was quite easy to manipulate. And like any man, Max liked to get his own way. And right now, he wanted to see Mrs. Bonner out of her rags and into his clothes.

"I'll have the footman hang the gowns in your wardrobes, and if you come across something you don't want to wear, throw it out." The new shifts and stays were already in their place. He hadn't bothered buying her new petticoats. They were out of fashion, and for the life of him he couldn't see why she wore the thing. There couldn't be a more useless garment for such an efficient woman.

Taking her elbow, he guided her out of the room and to the top of the stairs. "Now, I believe you said there was a problem in one of the rooms that you wanted my opinion on?"

She looked like she wanted to argue further, so Max trotted down the steps. A temporary retreat was in order.

She followed more slowly. "It wasn't your opinion I needed, but your authorization. I have enough opinions of my own."

"Indeed." Max smiled. She wasn't lying. "Why don't we go to the site of the problem and you can tell me all about it."

Squaring her shoulders, Mrs. Bonner marched across the main room, taking a sharp detour when Lord Halliwell spied her. The earl lowered his champagne glass and gazed after the manager, his eyes as sad as a hound dog's. Max couldn't fault the man's taste. But his infatuation was highly irritating.

They turned down the back hallway. At the door to the Plain Room, she hesitated before easing it open and peeking inside. Max followed her in. "Don't you know which rooms are being used?" All the private rooms in the club were styled differently, with singular needs in mind. This room was bare except for a narrow bed with a thin mattress. Fist-sized iron hooks were spaced evenly along the wall at eye-level. It could have been a monk's chamber.

"Yes, but you never know if one of the members is going to slip in without requesting a room." Mrs. Bonner gave him a sidelong glance. "We at The Black Rose are here to cater to the customer's every need. And spontaneity is always welcome." She gave him a wide smile, all teeth and no sincerity.

"Christ, is that the pitch you give to potential new customers?" He shook his head. "No wonder we haven't increased membership these past months. Profits have only increased because you've reduced costs."

"Yes, it's past time you found a manager with a brighter disposition. I will happily relinquish my position as my promised term has ended." She paused, looking at him expectantly.

He gave her a small smile but said nothing. She was like a terrier with a bone on that issue.

With a huff, she strode to the corner of the room and the bucket of water on the ground. She hefted it up and staggered.

In two steps Max was at her side, taking the bucket. "Where?"

She pointed to the middle of the room, and he set it down as directed. Colleen dropped to her knees on the wood plank floor. "I've noticed that more of our members have small injuries after leaving this room than any other. Mainly cut knees. I'd like your permission to install a carpet."

"That wouldn't be wise."

She plunged her hand into the bucket and pulled out a rag. Frowning, she scrubbed at a mark on the oak floor. "Why ever not? By what we'd save in bandages alone in a year, it will be worth it. And several of the other rooms have carpets."

A pyramid of tapers lay piled on a shelf built into the wall, and Max picked one up. He lit it from the oil lamp by the door. "Did it never occur to you that the hard floor is one of the attractions of this room?"

She looked up from her scrubbing and drew her eyebrows together. "No. Why would it be?"

He dropped to a squat and lowered the candle, trying to discern what the stain was. "It's not nearly as much fun making someone crawl on a plush carpet as it is upon a hardwood floor. Or stone. If there wasn't a little suffering, what would be the point?" He dragged his eyes from the lovely flush traveling from her face down her neck and disappearing behind her high collar. "What is this? And why isn't the maid cleaning it up?"

"Do you truly need me to explain the different excretions that produced this?" she asked tartly.

Max wrinkled his nose. "Leave it for the maid. This isn't the manager's job."

"Mrs. Hudson's back is ailing. I told her I'd finish the cleaning." Mrs. Bonner scrubbed until a foot-wide circle of oak was stained dark from the soapy water. She tossed the rag back in the bucket. "Can we at least sand the floor down? I'm tired of wiping up blood."

Grasping her hand, he pulled her to her feet. "Yes. But I guarantee we'll get complaints."

"I don't understand you people." She tightened her mouth, as though tasting spoilt milk. "Why do you do this?"

He stroked her skin with his thumb. Turning her hand over, he ran his fingers up and down her palm. Her hands weren't the pampered ones of a lady. Small calluses marred the surface, badges of hard work. He traced a line up her palm to the vein in her wrist. Her pulse raced beneath his fingertips.

"Do you sincerely want to know?" Max asked. "Or are you merely expressing your disdain for what you don't understand?"

"I ..." She sucked her bottom lip into her mouth and let it go with a pop. "I'm curious," she whispered.

Max's body tightened. It wasn't smart engaging in bed sport with a business associate, but Max didn't pretend to great intelligence. Cradling her hand, he lifted her wrist to his mouth and pressed a soft kiss to the inside. He slid the tip of his tongue between his lips and tasted the salt of her skin. She hissed in a breath. Taking his lips away, he blew gently over the moistened flesh.

"You asked earlier what my personal predilection is." He stared into her eyes. "May I show you?"

"Show me?" she asked, voice wobbling.

Blood raced to his groin. He'd known she was attracted to him. Seen it in the unconscious way she slightly parted her legs when he sat next to her at her desk. In the delightful flush that would cover the freckles on her face when they stood too close. But every time that attraction was confirmed, he went hard. Every damn time. "All your clothes will remain on," he assured her. "Just a small taste to show you what I like."

Hesitantly, she nodded. Her gaze followed his hand as he raised the candle above her wrist. She bit her lower lip, the plump flesh going pink around her white teeth, and Max's budding erection went full-blown. Fuck, he loved the slight apprehension of a woman when she didn't know what was coming. Her restless anticipation. He craved the way a woman tensed as she waited for the heat, and her shudder as the nip of pain slid into pleasure.

But apprehension could turn into fear given too much time. And that was an emotion he never wanted Mrs. Bonner to feel. With an efficiency he thought she'd appreciate, Max tipped the candle and dropped a neat splash of white wax on the spot he'd kissed.

Her hand jerked in his hold, and she hissed in a breath. Keeping their gazes locked, Max blew over the area again, soothing away any sting.

"You drip wax on women?"

"Yes." He traced a line across her wrist. His fingertip slipped across the slick wax to her soft skin. "Wax, and I also play with fire."

"How do you play with fire?" She tugged her hand free with a wary look at the candle flame.

He licked his thumb and forefinger and snuffed out the flame, enjoying the small hiss. "Don't worry. The wax demonstration is as far as we go for now." Wax was a good introduction into fire play. Gave a hint of the heat, the pleasure, that fire could produce. And Mrs. Bonner's fair skin would look beautiful dripping with wax. He wondered if freckles covered more than just her face. If he could connect the dots of her body with strings of wax. His hips shifted closer to her of their own accord, his aching cock seeking her heat.

He tucked a lock of her hair behind her ear and let his hand rest at the nape of her neck. "But when we do play in earnest, I want you to know that the flame won't hurt you.

Not if I'm the one holding the torch. But it will make you feel more alive than you ever have in your life."

Her breasts stilled and her eyes went dark. Max thought it was from desire, until he remembered her dead husband. And how he'd been killed. He cursed. "Forgive me, Mrs. Bonner. I'd forgotten."

She blinked, and her forehead cleared. "Mr. Bonner. Yes, I dare say the fire didn't make him feel so alive." Bending, she grabbed the bucket's handle. "A good reminder of my place. I'm a widow, and it's best if we pretend such foolishness never happened."

Max took the bucket, disappointment that their intimate moment had ended weighing against his chest. He stopped the door before she could open it fully. "You might be a widow, but you're still a woman. With needs and desires." He stepped close, and a hint of lavender teased his nose. "I want to be the man to satisfy your every need." He ached to be that man.

A flicker of self-reproach tried to ignite in his heart but he stamped it out. His past misdeeds were of no consequence to a potential liaison with Mrs. Bonner.

She turned, her breasts brushing his chest, her abdomen achingly close to his need. They were like puzzle pieces, joining together. "Thinking about what can never happen only leads to disappointment," she said.

"So, you were considering it?" The woman wasn't as proper as she liked to think she was. What would it be like to peel off her high-necked shirt, strip her of her petticoats, uncover the real woman beneath all her protective layers? Max had a feeling she burned hotter that any fire he'd ever struck.

"We'll never know." Mrs. Bonner strode down the hall to the edge of the main room. She bent her head to speak to Lucy, a woman he'd painted with wax many times before. He should turn to her. She was a professional who enjoyed her work and had no inhibitions. His prick was throbbing behind his smallclothes, needing relief. Lucy was the easy choice. Anything between him and his manager would be too complicated. Yes, he would go to Lucy and see if she was available. The chit nodded at something Mrs. Bonner said and wandered off.

Resolved, he squared his shoulders and turned in the lady-bird's direction. His feet had other ideas and padded after Mrs. Bonner, like a dog looking for a scrap from his master. Easy was overrated. And so were brains, apparently.

Mrs. Bonner drew up short and held up her hand. "You can't take a bucket of dirty water into a room with our guests." She pointed towards the end of the hallway, back the way he'd come. "Leave it around the bend. Lucy has gone for a footman to come collect it."

He complied and returned to her side. This business with Zed needed to come to a quick conclusion. If he was to be near Mrs. Bonner so often and not be able to touch her, he—

"Are you listening?" She placed her hands on her hips. "Do you agree to give me that authority?"

"Uh ..." He scratched his beard. His finger got tangled in a knot, and he tried to comb it out. Blasted beard was becoming more trouble than it was worth.

She sighed. "May I have the authority to rid The Black Rose of some people in our employ? If I'm to remain here as manager, it will be necessary."

"Necessary?" He raised an eyebrow.

"Well, helpful."

Max glanced through the throng of people in the main room. The men were in full-dress, the women somewhere between full-dress and scandalous. He couldn't pick out the woman she'd just spoken to among the swirl of colorful gowns. "What's the matter with Lucy? She always seems most pleasant to me."

Mrs. Bonner snorted, the unladylike gesture somehow made charming. "I'm sure you find all the women here 'most pleasant.' They are paid to ensure that members feel that way." Turning on her heel, she strode across the main room. "But Lucy is fine. Some other workers like to push their boundaries with me. Show me disrespect. It's almost too bad Molly brings in so much blunt. If I got rid of her, the others would fall in line. But I may have to remove some who aren't as valuable." As they walked, she surveyed the room with a critical eye. Max could see her counting the wineglasses, how many girls were on the floor, looking for any signs of trouble. Her face was as open and easy to read as a book.

If only the rest of the world were so apparent. There would be no need for spies.

"What's wrong with Molly?" And which one was Molly? He couldn't remember. He didn't think she was one of the girls he played with.

"It's not surprising you can't tell them apart. Why all the girls here decided on names that end with 'Y', I don't understand. Lucy, Molly, Felicity, Suzy, Daisy ..." Mrs. Bonner sniffed. "Is that common of prostitutes? Do they think they'll earn more money with such a name?"

Max shrugged. He couldn't imagine any man giving a shit about the name of a doxy.

"Anyhow, Molly's the one fondling that poor man's nether region." Mrs. Bonner shook her head, her shoulders drooping. "It's sad what no longer shocks me. My husband would have been most ashamed."

"You do what you have to survive," Max said gruffly. "You have nothing to be ashamed over."

"No, men like you feel no shame. If someone found out you were here, nothing would happen to your status in society." She fingered the delicate chain that disappeared into her waistcoat pocket. "But every one of these girls would be publicly shunned if their occupation came to light. And if my acquaintances learned what sort of establishment I managed, I would be disgraced. It's fortunate for me none of my sort ever come down this street, much less have the means to enter the club." She turned reproachful eyes on him. "But don't try to teach me about shame."

Lord Halliwell slunk over. "My dear Mrs. Bonner." The earl swept a dramatic leg, and Max rolled his eyes. "Can I say how ravishing you look tonight. Truly incandescent."

Mrs. Bonner inclined her head. No feminine curtsies for her. "Thank you, my Lord. Now, if you will excuse me." Without waiting for an answer, she turned for the door that led to her private chambers.

Lord Halliwell shot his hand out, grabbing her arm.

Little spots danced in Max's vision, and he blinked.

"Not so hasty, my dear." With two fingers, the earl beckoned a serving girl. "How about a glass of wine?"

"I don't drink spirits with customers."

"Nonsense. It's only wine." Halliwell pressed a glass into her hand. He slid his own hand up her arm, over her shoulder, and down her back.

Max dug his fingers into his palm until he couldn't feel his knuckles. Is this what the women here had to deal with? He'd thought the members had more self-control, that they only pursued amenable women. The women and men who worked for the club made their money entertaining the customers, but it was well established that no one had to participate in an activity he or she didn't wish to. Ever.

And Lord Halliwell should damn well know that.

Max stepped forward, his gaze locked on the man's roving hand.

He didn't see Mrs. Bonner's hand moving until it was too late.

"Oh, I'm so sorry!" She swiped at the hem of the earl's coat. "So clumsy of me. And I do believe I got some of the wine on my skirts, as well. I must go and change." She sidestepped out of his range. "If you gentlemen will excuse me." With shoulders thrown back, she strode away.

Max smiled grimly. The woman could take care of herself, no doubt. He turned to the earl. But that didn't mean he wouldn't teach the sot a lesson. "Let's go get you cleaned up. I know just where a bucket of some water is." Clapping his hand on Halliwell's back, he shoved the man towards the back hall.

He almost wished Mrs. Bonner hadn't left. She would enjoy the sight of the earl cleaning himself with the filthy water.

Max looked over his shoulder, seeking out her sturdy figure. The door to her staircase was easing closed. His view of the person behind the door narrowed until it disappeared completely.

Max froze, Lord Halliwell purged from his mind.

The person closing the door to Mrs. Bonner's private rooms hadn't been Mrs. Bonner. Nor anyone who worked at the club.

A man Max didn't recognize had followed his manager into her inner sanctum. And Max saw red.

Chapter Five

Colleen strode past her sitting room and stopped dead. Leaning backwards, she peered inside. The jungle of gowns and mountains of slippers had disappeared, leaving the room as tidy as her office desk. She ran to her bedchambers and pulled open the door of the first wardrobe she came to. Neat rows of gowns, organized by color, hung inside, matching footwear lined up beneath. She opened all the wardrobes, all crammed full of impractical nonsense.

She pressed her lips together. The baron was absurd, thinking she would ever wear one of these concoctions let alone thirty of them. And if he thought a roomful of clothes made up for his oath-breaking, the man was sorely mistaken.

She traced a finger down the bodice of a silk evening gown, the fabric as soft as a rose's petal and about the same color. What would such a gown feel like against her skin? Would she look pretty in it, or like a fool playing dress-up? She glanced one last time at the dress and closed the wardrobe door. The wife of a clock repair- and salesman didn't wear silk. She couldn't think of anything more absurd.

Trudging to her office, she flopped onto her chair and kicked off her threadbare slippers. She couldn't let the daft man throw away all those clothes. The wastefulness of that would be a sin. She sniffed. There must be some way for her to fashion something practical from that abundance of fabric. And all those lovely shoes ...

She shook herself. Attractive footwear was no substitute for hard work. If she wanted to ensure a way to support herself for the rest of her life, she needed to convince Mr. Ridley to wait to sell his business until she had the blunt to buy it. Pulling out a crisp sheet of paper from a drawer, she started a new budget.

A scuffing sound made her look up. A man with a cap of dark curls stood at her door. His mouth was pressed into a hard line, and his right hand disappeared into his coat pocket.

A trickle of unease rolled down her spine. "Yes? Can I help you?"

"You're Mrs. Bonner? The proprietress of The Black Rose?"

The man's accent was twangy, crashing over her like a brass instrument. She couldn't place it.

"Yes. And you are?" Pushing to her feet, Colleen rested her palms on the desk. "Are you here as a guest of one of our members?"

The man snorted. "Not hardly. Even if I had the coin, I'm not one of your loose screws." He looked down his nose at her, like the peculiarities of people's desires were her fault.

She rolled up onto her toes, wishing she wore her boots. "If you aren't interested in joining, then why are you here? In my private rooms?"

"We have a business matter to discuss." Striding to her guest chair, he pulled out a pocket square and swiped at the seat.

Colleen narrowed her eyes. "This is my office, not a den of iniquity. Nothing inappropriate happens here." And really, what call did some foreigner have to come into her establishment and insult the clientele? And they weren't all loose screws. Most just wanted to have a bit of amusement in this harsh world. There was nothing wrong with that.

She poked her tongue into her cheek. She was starting to sound like the baron, defending this lot and their predilections. What was happening to her?

The man seated himself, and Colleen followed suit. Resting her elbows on the desk, she asked, "So, what can I do for you?"

"I'm here to arrange a mutually-beneficial agreement between two parties." He flicked a piece of lint from his trousers. "I believe you have received some correspondence indicating a desire to enter into a business arrangement?"

Colleen sat back. "You're Zed." Finally, the snake had revealed himself and she could get this business over with. She glanced at the open doorway. But where was that blasted baron? For the past week he'd been underfoot so much she'd tripped over him. Now, when she needed the man, Sutton was nowhere to be found.

"Who I am isn't important," the man said. "It's what I can do for you that is." Pulling a cheroot from an inside pocket, he looked to her fireplace and started to his feet.

"I don't allow smoking in my office." That rule was as recent as her last breath, but it seemed like a fine one. And it was always an advantage to put an opponent in his place in a business negotiation. And that's what this was to her. A business matter to be resolved. The sooner she could obtain the evidence implicating this Zed and deliver it to Lord Sutton, the sooner she would receive her premium, and her flower shop.

With his bum hovering over the chair's seat, the man looked at his cheroot like it was a dying friend. He dropped back down. "Fine. This isn't a social call in any event." He tucked the cheroot back in his pocket. "Zed is interested in coming to terms with you. You have access to information he'd find interesting. He has access to money you'd find useful. It seems like a fair trade. He's willing to pay you from ten to one hundred pounds per communication, depending on how valuable your information is."

"How generous." Extraordinarily so. Enough to pay off all her debts and more. Colleen laced her fingers together.

"And what will he pay me to betray my customers and my morals? Surely there must be an extra reward for that."

He blinked. "That cost is embedded in the price."

"And how much are you paid to deliver this message." Pulling a piece of parchment towards her, she picked up a quill and dipped it in her inkwell. "If I'm to go into business with someone, I must know all the numbers. Only by having a full picture can I make a decision about whether to partner with that business."

He narrowed his eyes. "You wouldn't be a partner. Are you cracked? You'd be a very small cog on the wheel."

"How many cogs are on this wheel?" Picking up a pen knife, Colleen shaved the end of her quill. This investigation business wasn't so hard. A few more questions and she'd have the information Sutton needed. And then her premium would be as good as in the bank.

"Look, lady, I don't think you're understanding how things work." Pulling out his cheroot, he rolled it between his fingers. "You see a tasty tidbit you think might be worth money, you tell me. I give you coin. But you don't ask questions. And you don't tell anyone else about this deal. Got it?"

"What happens if I tell someone else about the deal?" Sutton already knew about it. And she supposed he'd told others. Really, this Zed should know better than to buy a pig in a poke.

"You don't want to know what happens."

"But if I did," she persisted. "Full disclosure is only sensible." As was not looking like easy prey. She tapped the flat of her small blade on the desk, holding his gaze.

He shook his head. "Lady, if you talk ..." He brought the end of his cheroot to one side of his neck and started to draw his hand across to the other side. The cheroot snapped in two, dropping clumps of tobacco onto his coat and pants. He cursed.

Colleen drew a pocket square from her skirt's pocket and handed it across the desk to the man. She frowned. "I don't see how covering me in ash will do me much harm. You're going to have to be more explicit."

He brushed the tobacco from his shirt onto her floor. "Not ash, lady. This!" He brought his hand up to his throat, scowled at the handkerchief dangling from it, and snatched the linen away with his other hand. Pinning her with a glare, he slowly drew his finger across his throat.

Colleen's shoulders snapped back. Of all the ... "Sir, I can only assume you are ignorant of the horrors of the French Revolution as there is no way you would invoke it otherwise." As a child, one of her uncles had told the family the story of what he'd seen during his time in Paris. He made the very same motion to describe a poor man losing his head to the guillotine. She'd had nightmares for a week.

She eyed the sot across from her. It was a nasty threat, to be sure, but hardly practical. One which no sane person would fear. Did Zed have his own personal guillotine in his rooms? Colleen snorted at the thought. Really, if this Zed was going to send someone to intimidate her, he could at least have found a suitably villainous-looking scalawag, and one whose threats held some real teeth. "Guillotined? Truly?" She shook her head sadly.

The man swore under his breath. "It figures. I'd have to be given the dizzy ones to manage. Not dirtied up. Not guillotined." He jabbed one broken half of the cheroot at her. "You really need me to spell this out for you?"

Colleen nodded. "I'm afraid you'll have to as your pantomimes are incomprehensible. And it's best to have all terms clearly defined in a contract to prevent any confusion later on."

"And you don't understand this?" He sawed the cheroot back and forth in front of his neck, making odd squeaking noises with each jerky movement.

She wrinkled her nose. He sounded like a rusted water pump.

"I believe what our blackmailer is trying to say, however inarticulately, is that he'll cut your throat if you talk." Sutton leaned against the doorjamb, his arms crossed over his chest. A slight smile floated on his lips and he looked the very figure of ease. But the muscles beneath his trousers were taut, his legs ready to spring into action.

Of course, *now* he would show up, interrupting before she could get her visitor to reveal the identity of Zed. Just like a man. Never around when she needed him and underfoot when she didn't. Her irritation almost made her miss his words.

"Wait ..." She glared at the stranger in outrage. "You're saying you'd cut open my neck?" If properly delivered, that would have been a threat she would have taken notice of.

Jumping to his feet, he stumbled back, away from the monolith at the door. "I wouldn't want to! It would just be business."

Sutton shrugged his coat off and tossed it on the back of a chair. He wore no waistcoat beneath, only a snowy white shirt. Every drape in the linen emphasized the strength in his arms, the hard planes of his chest and shoulders. "'You wouldn't want to.'" Sutton shook his head. "I guess that makes it all right, then."

Colleen stood and fisted her hands on her hips. "It does no such thing. How he feels isn't relevant. I'd still be dead."

Both men stared at her.

"Dizzy bitch." The visitor shook his head, pity in his eyes.

"She's too straightforward to understand sarcasm," Sutton said. "It's one of her many charms." He cracked his neck from side-to-side and prowled towards the man. "So, for her sake, and yours, I'm going to speak quite literally. Unless you tell me who you are and whom you work for, I'm going to rip your arms from their sockets and beat you to death with them."

* * *

Christ, Max threatens a fellow just once with dismemberment, and the bloody fool turns into a fucking wet-nurse. Zed's accomplice had turned into such a puddle of snot and blubber, Max had felt it necessary to send Colleen from the room. No need to humiliate the man further.

"This is my office," she argued. "And I'm the one he threatened with ..." She drew her finger across her neck and tried to mimic the man's earlier noises. She sounded like a cat in heat.

He winced. "Yes, but I think he might speak more freely if it's just the two of us."

"Oh God," the man wailed. "I can't tell you anything. I'll be killed if I do." He eyed Max. "And killed if I don't." He pounded both fists into his head, cursing.

Max worried about permanent damage. He'd seen battle-shocked men act such, and their instability could be dangerous. "New plan. Go downstairs," he told Mrs. Bonner, "and announce that the club is closing early tonight. Once it's empty, we'll be down to join you." He strode to the desk and dashed off a quick note. He folded and addressed the missive. "And give this to a footman to deliver. Tell him to make sure the earl gets it immediately, even if the lazy bastard has to be kicked out of bed."

"All right," she grumbled. She took the letter, her fingers grazing his. "But I expect to be fully informed of any developments."

"Of course." Within reason. He waited to hear her step on the stairs and handed his handkerchief to their visitor. "Clean yourself up, man." Two other pocket squares littered the floor. Max picked up the one with the letters C and B embroidered on it, folded the cloth, and tucked it into his pocket.

The man dropped into a chair, burying his face in his hands. They waited, unspeaking, for several minutes, the occasional sniffle and curse from the bugger the only sounds in the room. Giving Colleen plenty of time to clear the club, Max jerked his head at the door. "All right, let's go." When the man didn't move, Max grabbed his wrist and twisted his arm behind his back, careful not to inflict too much pain. Not yet. He marched him out the door and down the back set of stairs reserved for the servants. It led to a narrow corridor. The kitchen was to the left. Max steered them to the right where the hallway connected with the club's back rooms.

He headed for the room he and Mrs. Bonner had been in earlier. It should be perfect to scare the shit out of someone.

Max pushed the man inside. "Go. Sit on the bed." Locking the door, he slid the key into the top of his boot. He strode to a tall, rough-hewn bureau and pulled it open. Thick coils of chain lay coiled in the bottom, a row of attachable manacles lined up on the shelf above. Lengths of rope were tied in neat bundles and hung from nails hammered into the back of the bureau.

Picking up two manacles and a small two-foot chain, he walked to the side wall and slid the metal through a hook screwed in the wall. "Come here."

"Like hell." The man jumped to his feet and backed away. "What the fucking hell is this room? You Brits are goddamn—" His tirade broke off in a gurgle.

Max dragged him by his throat to the wall and slammed him against it until the fight drained away. Picking up a limp hand, he attached the manacles to the dazed man and let him sag against his bonds.

Max wiped his palms on his pants. "Now, let's say we have a chat. After your many threats upon Mrs. Bonner's person, I'm not predisposed to like you." He bared his teeth. "And I assure you, you want me to like you."

The man struggled to stand. His eyes rolled back in his head, and he slumped forwards.

With a sigh, Max slapped his cheek. "Focus. Let's start with something easy. What's your name?"

The man mumbled.

Max cocked his head close. "Pinkie?" That couldn't be right.

"Pinkerton." The man blinked several times then

opened his lids wide. "William Pinkerton. And that's all I'm telling you. It's more than just my life I have to protect."

"You have a family?" Max nudged the man when he remained silent. "Come now. You've already given me your name. Telling me about your family won't give me anything more than I could discover in a couple hours' time."

"A wife. A son." Pinkerton glared at him. "Who are now almost destitute thanks to you and your friends."

Max stepped back. "What did we do?"

Heavy pounding rattled the door. Pulling the key from his boot, Max unlocked it and cracked it open.

Julius Blackwell, Earl of Rothchild gave him a gimlet eye. "I spent all day on the back of a horse responding to Summerset's letter and was in need of a solid night's rest. One of your persistent footman didn't allow that. Care to explain what was so bloody urgent?"

Max opened the door wide. "Glad you could make it." He eyed his friend. Aside from a slight puffiness under his eyes, Rothchild looked good. Content. His marriage agreed with him. "I haven't seen you since your wedding breakfast, such as it was." A quiet meal of not more than ten people. And the couple seemed to be settling into an even quieter life at Rothchild's country estate. Max was sorry he had to interrupt it.

"Come in. Meet our guest." Max swept his hand out in front of him.

Rothchild strode through the door. Before Max could shut it, Mrs. Bonner scuttled in behind him.

Max took her elbow and tried to guide her back out. "This isn't the place for you."

She jerked her arm free.

"I'm the manager of this club until the time you see fit to hold up your end of our bargain." She crossed her arms over her waistcoat. "I should be aware of everything that goes on under its roof."

She caught sight of Pinkerton chained to the wall and her eyes flew wide.

Rothchild lounged on the narrow bed. He covered his mouth with his hand as he yawned. "I'd like to get some sleep tonight. Can we move this along?"

Mrs. Bonner kicked the door shut. "You'll have to pick me up and throw me out if you want me gone." She turned the key in the lock and dropped it into her waistcoat pocket, shooting Max a challenging look.

It was tempting. He had no doubt she'd fight like a hellcat, and that was always entertaining. But this man had threatened her. Perhaps she deserved to hear what he had to say.

"Fine. You can stay." He rested his hands on his hips. "But don't interfere."

"Now that's settled," Rothchild drawled, "care to tell me why I'm here." He jerked his head at Pinkerton. "Not that the wall hangings aren't intriguing. Do you have a new decorator?"

"Please." Pinkerton tugged at his restraints. "That man is goddamned soft in the head. He chained me up for no reason." He stared imploringly at Rothchild. "Let me go and I won't tell anyone about this."

"An American?" Rothchild asked.

Max nodded. He'd recognized the accent, too. How a continent had managed to butcher their shared language so quickly was a mystery. He stepped forward and slapped Pinkerton in the face. Not too hard, but enough to get his attention. "First, watch your tongue in front of a woman." Although, Mrs. Bonner had insisted upon staying. She was going to hear a lot worse than rough language. "Second, you're appealing to the wrong man. I brought my friend here because he's so much better at convincing people to talk than I am. I can bloody and bruise you"—and break bones, but he thought that was better left unsaid—"but my friend here will make you beg for death. And he does it all without leaving a mark."

Rothchild slid his coat off, folded it. "Is that why I'm here? You should have given me some notice. I would have brought my ropes."

Mrs. Bonner furrowed her brow. "We have plenty of rope in the club. But why? He's already restrained."

Rothchild sent her a wolf's grin. "Rope can do so much more than restrain." He turned back to Pinkerton but spoke to Max. "This man works for Zed?"

"So we think. Unless he is the man himself." Max cocked his head and looked at the sot drooping from his chains. "But that would be a disappointment. I have his name and the fact that he has a wife and son. The rest is up to you."

Locking his fingers together, Rothchild straightened his arms, palms out. His knuckles cracked, a startling sound in the still room.

Mrs. Bonner inched closer to Max, and he kept one eye on the widow and one eye on his friend. Zed's organization had nearly killed Rothchild's wife. It was before the couple had married, but still, not something a man forgot. Or forgave. Max needed to make sure his friend wasn't overzealous with his interrogation.

And Colleen ... well, she was an unknown. How she'd react in this situation was anyone's guess.

Rothchild stepped close to the American, dragged his nose along the curve of the man's neck and up to his ear. Rothchild's lips moved, but Max couldn't hear what he said.

The American shook his head, setting his jaw.

Max huffed. Why did people insist on making life hard for themselves? With the application of enough pain, everyone talked. He focused on Mrs. Bonner. Saw her eyes widen with shock, her fists clench tight when the first scream tore from the American's throat. She stepped forward, and Max grabbed her about the waist, pulling her back to his front.

"If you're here, you have to let us work," he whispered in her ear.

"But ..." Twisting her neck, she stared up at him. "All your friend did was touch him. I don't understand."

Rothchild loosened Pinkerton's cravat, slid it from his neck, revealing the man's throat. "The human body is made of a series of meridian lines. Certain points on those lines are especially sensitive. If I apply the right amount of pressure"—he notched his thumb at a spot in the side of Pinkerton's neck and pressed, earning a strangled gurgle— "the individual will experience an alarming amount of pain."

"It's effective, with no lasting damage." Max ran his thumb along her arm. "Also, less clean up than doing it my way."

She planted an elbow into his midsection. "This isn't a time for jokes."

"No, ma'am."

Pinkerton screamed again. Rothchild dug a knuckle into the man's shoulder, holding him steady with his other hand so the American couldn't writhe away from the pain. It seemed to go on forever but was probably no more than twenty seconds. Twenty seconds of bone-chilling screams that reverberated through Max's head and turned his stomach.

Colleen clapped her hands over her ears and squeezed her eyes tight. Her body jerked, as though the screams were a tangible force striking her frame.

Max gripped her shoulders and turned her away from the wall. She held herself tight, even after the screams had ended. She had gone a bit green, and Max could feel the pounding of her heart against his torso. Turning her body, he gathered her close and rubbed soothing circles into her back. "Mrs. Bonner? Colleen. It's over now. You can open your eyes."

She cracked first one eyelid, saw his face, and opened her other. The gesture would have been endearing if the circumstances weren't so terrible. "He's really loud," she whispered.

"Yes." He drew his hand up to the back of her neck, frustrated by her high collar. Her skin had been so soft on the inside of her wrist. Kneading the base of her skull, he waited until the tension left her face. "This is necessary if we're to discover the man responsible for many deaths. The man who's threatening you. Perhaps it's time you waited outside."

She shook her head, an auburn lock escaping from her tight knot. "I'm partly responsible for the man being here. I can't turn my back now and pretend I have clean hands. It seems the least I should do is watch what I'm accountable for."

Warmth spread through Max's body. She truly was a commendable woman. Stalwart and courageous. Her husband had been a fortunate man.

Max's throat went thick. And he'd taken her husband from her. It now fell upon his shoulders to be her protector. Even if she didn't want one.

"That's an admirable sentiment but unwarranted." He needed an argument for her to leave the room that she'd accept.

His friend saved him the necessity of coming up with one. "There'll be no more screaming, so you and Mrs. Bonner don't have to worry. I believe he's ready to talk. Isn't that right, Mr. Pinkerton?" Rothchild gripped the man's shoulder.

Pinkerton heaved and vomited on the wood floor, the splash catching Rothchild's boots.

Max shook his head. "I didn't want there to be any clean-up."

"What the hell are you complaining about?" Rothchild shook his foot. "I'm the one who got it on me."

"Men." Colleen pressed her lips into a flat line. "You're all such babies when it comes to life's dirty bits. I'll clean it up, and I'll even clean your boots, too, Lord Rothchild. Just, find out what we need to know."

"Yes, ma'am." Rothchild gave Max a look, raising his eyebrow.

Max tugged Colleen closer. The move was instinctive,

and Max chided himself on his own folly. His friend was a happily-married man. But he was finding any man's interest in his manager, casual or not, to be most aggravating.

Rothchild gave Pinkerton a sound shaking. "Now, you were about to tell us how you came to be involved with the individual known as Zed."

"I was on the board of directors of the Chesseworth Corporation." The American drooped, his fetters clanking. "I'd made my fortune in America and came over here on a world tour. I met my Isobel. She's the second daughter of a Scottish baronet, and he wanted her to marry a peer. My money persuaded him to accept me for his daughter, instead."

Colleen snorted. "Isn't that just like a man? And your wife? Did she want to marry you, or was she only bought and paid for?"

"Of course, she wanted to marry me! We're in love." Pinkerton looked at her with big doe eyes. "Isobel is the kindest, most beautiful woman I've ever known."

Colleen lowered her shoulders, the tight set to her back relaxing. "How sweet."

Max met Rothchild's gaze, and they both rolled their eyes. Women were so easy.

"We don't want your life history," Max told Pinkerton. "Jump ahead to when you got involved with a crime ring."

Colleen elbowed him in the side and took a step back. "He's getting there. There's no call to be rude."

"As I said, I was on the board of Chesseworth." Pinkerton straightened and jutted out his chin. "It was doing well. I invested most of my money in its stock."

A stab of pity struck Max but he repressed the emotion. He could see where this story was heading, but it still didn't excuse the American's actions. Max and his friends had discovered that Zed and his crime ring had infiltrated the boards of numerous corporations. When the Crown had gone after the criminals, many of those businesses had gone under. Chesseworth had been one of those that had gone bankrupt. The stocks had become worthless.

"How much is most of your money?" he asked the American.

"Nearly all." The man glared at Max. "Because of you and your friends, my wife is forced to wear rags. Clothes hardly better than Mrs. Bonner's." The man jerked his head at Colleen, who looked down at her outfit, a wrinkle of confusion puckering her forehead. "My son won't be able to go to Harrow. This is your fault."

While Max felt some sympathy, that was a step too far. "Who's the idiot that put all his eggs in one basket? Besides, those businesses had become part of a criminal enterprise. The government had no choice but to shut them down."

"And I had no choice in my actions," Pinkerton said. "I have to provide for my family."

"By threatening to cut a woman's throat?" Max's skin prickled with heat. "How low were you willing to sink to keep your wife in the latest fashions?"

"I wouldn't have done it." Pinkerton's voice was hoarse, his chin trembled. The man probably didn't know whether he believed that himself.

"How did Zed contact you?" Rothchild brought them back on course. "Did you meet?"

"No." Pinkerton rattled the chain at his wrist. "Can we take these off?"

"When you've told us everything," Colleen said.

Max glanced at her in surprise. She rested her hands on her hips and tapped her toe. Max waited for it, waited, and when she arched one burnished eyebrow, heat flooded his body and his bollocks drew tight. A tiny taskmaster shouldn't stir him so. Disciplinarians were never his predilection. But the more Max was around his manager, the more he ached for her.

"I've never met the blasted man," Pinkerton said. "I received a note. And included in that note was the payment for the back rent on our townhouse. Zed said more of the same was available if I worked for him. It was my salvation."

Rothchild leaned against the wall next to the American and crossed one leg over the other. "And what will happen to your family when you're in prison?"

"Prison?" Pinkerton jerked his wrists, the chains clanging.

"That is the normal course of affairs for someone caught assisting in blackmail and threatening murder." Rothchild buffed his nails on his waistcoat. "Or perhaps the courts will ship you off to Australia. That does seem to be the latest furor."

"Please." Pinkerton closed his eyes, his chest heaving. "Please. I need to take care of my wife and son. If I'm sent away, they'll starve. Her father won't take her back; not if her husband has disgraced the family."

"You should have thought of that before you disgraced your family," Colleen said tartly. She turned to Max. "He doesn't know anything that will help us. Will you call for a magistrate?"

Pinkerton blanched.

"He might be helpful yet." Curious, Max examined her face. "Have you no problem sending this man to prison?" Australia was a better alternative. The prisons in London were filthy, miserable places filled with desperate men. Even if a person wasn't sentenced to hang for his crime, death resulted from the imprisonment more often than not.

"We all have to pay for our crimes." She blinked rapidly. "We don't ever escape what's coming to us, not really. Justice will be served, either in this life or the next." Fingering the brass chain of her pocket watch, she chewed on her lower lip. She took a deep breath and turned to the American. "But I have no objection if you wish to release him. So long as he promises not to cut my throat."

"A full release is out of the question," Rothchild said. "But"—he clapped a hand on Pinkerton's shoulder, and the man winced—"if our prisoner is a very good boy, he just might get to see his urchin matriculate."

Pinkerton licked his lips. "What do you mean?"

Max smiled, feeling that for once, they just might have an advantage over their enemy. Their very own double-agent. A low-level one, to be sure. But it was more than they'd had yesterday.

He pulled the key for the manacles from his pocket. "That means, my dear fellow, that you now work for us."

Chapter Six

Colleen sucked in a deep breath, her stomach a bucket of writhing eels, and pushed open the door. Mr. Ridley's cheerful face and clouded eyes greeted her, along with a thick cloud of perfumed air.

"Good morning, Mr. Ridley. It's Colleen Bonner."

"Good morning, my dear!" Keeping a guiding hand on the large table in front of him, he circled it to stand before her. "I wasn't expecting you for another couple of days. You're that anxious to send an old man into the country, are ye?"

She pressed a hand to her abdomen. The telling wouldn't get any easier by delaying it. "About that, I have some bad news. I ..." She swallowed, but the pressure in her chest didn't ease. "I have to stay at my current employment for a little while longer. I won't have the earnest money this week as I'd promised."

"Well." Mr. Ridley pursed his lips. "Well, well."

Colleen felt lower than pond scum. "It shouldn't be too much longer. The owner of the club promised he'd give me my premium as soon as a certain job is completed. And it might be finished soon. Days even." She cleared her throat. "But it could take up to several months, too."

Picking up a wrapped bundle of irises, Mr. Ridley shuffled to the front window and arranged the flowers in an old milk jug. "You see, it's not just for me. My girl is going through some tough times. The money for my shop would help us both."

"I know." Colleen traced a pattern on the dusty floor

with the toe of her boot. A thorough cleaning of the shop from top to bottom had been the first item on her to-do list when she became owner. If she became owner. "And I know I promised you I'd be ready. I can't tell you how sorry I am that I can't keep that promise. But if you could only wait for a little bit longer. Maybe ... maybe I can increase my monthly payments to you, if you'd only wait for me to sell."

He separated the stems, the blue veins in his wrinkled hands looking like they might burst from his skin. "I'd like to. I truly would. I just don't know how long I can wait. Not when my neighbor is making me a good offer, too."

Colleen's chest grew tight, her breaths short. She tried to swallow down her rising panic. All her dreams were slipping away. She'd been able to console herself after her husband's death, after she'd become the temporary manager of The Black Rose, that from all her horror and shame, at least something good would take root.

Perhaps this was her punishment. She'd said that everyone must pay for their sins. She deserved much worse than losing the shop.

"I understand." She inhaled a shaky breath. "I'll check in every week. And I'll hope that by the time I'm able to make the earnest payment, you won't have sold the shop yet. But I'll understand if you have."

Mr. Ridley nodded, his posture stooped, his upper back beginning to curve with age. "Good luck, dear. Here." He felt among the bouquets and found a spray of daffodils. He pressed the small clutch of blooms into her hand. "I always think daffodils are the brightest flower. Sure to cheer you up."

Colleen looked around the small room, chock-full with color and growth, and thought nothing could ever cheer her. Not if she couldn't have this. She wanted to be surrounded by the shop's vibrancy, not locked away in a sterile office.

But an office was where she was needed. Pulling her

pocket watch from her waistcoat, she popped the lid open and checked the time. She'd invited the staff of The Black Rose to a luncheon and she needed to head back to make sure the kitchen workers had everything they needed.

"Goodbye, Mr. Ridley." She tucked her watch away and pressed her free hand to the old man's gnarled one. "I'll be in touch."

And without a backwards glance at her lost dreams, she swept from the shop and marched down the street. She convinced herself that the burning in her eyes could be wholly attributed to the yellow fog that choked the neighborhood.

A hand snaked out of the alley she passed and grabbed her elbow. She yelped as the man hauled her close.

"Would you care to tell me what, exactly, you are doing out of The Black Rose without an escort?" Sutton glowered down at her. His hunter-green eyes darkened to smoldering coals.

"My lord." Colleen sketched a short curtsy, hoping to placate him. She'd known he wanted her under watch until Zed was caught. But she'd thought she'd make it back to the club before he detected her absence.

"Don't 'my lord' me. Pretending deference to my title, when we both know you have none, won't work with me." He pinched her chin between his thumb and forefinger. "You, little goose, forget that your life is under threat."

She jerked her chin from his grasp and stomped from the alley. "And you forget that I'm not a child," she threw over her shoulder. "And I'm not anyone's wife. Not beholden to any man and not under anyone's control. I will move as I please." Besides, now that Mr. Pinkerton had agreed to work for Max and his friends, how much danger could she be in?

He matched her strides. "Mrs. Bonner, I know you are a most capable woman. But the escort is for your own safety. Please take pity on my nerves and abide by my request."

His words wrapped around her like a fur cloak. She

couldn't lie. The concern in his voice did queer things to her heart. Made it twist and twirl. It had been awhile since she'd felt cared for. Mr. Bonner, God rest his soul, had looked at their marriage in a practical light. She was a companion, a help in the shop, a body to create children with.

Sutton cupped her elbow and drew her around to face him. The heel on her new boot slid on a cobblestone, and she tumbled against his chest. He didn't step back. Neither did she.

The baron inhaled deeply, the buttons of his coat pressing against her breasts, making her tingle all over. The black centers of his eyes grew large, became so wide and liquid she thought she would drown in them. He was an enchanter, ensorcelling her, and she was unable to look away.

Cupping her neck with his warm palm, he brushed a wisp of hair from her cheek with his thumb. "I'm trying to prevent any harm from coming to you, Colleen."

The hair on her nape raised. Hearing her Christian name on his lips ... When he'd used her given name the night before in front of Pinkerton and the earl, she'd thought it a mere slip of the tongue. And she'd berated herself over the thrill it had given her. Such a small thing, hearing her name from a man's mouth. Small, but precious. Her husband had rarely called her Colleen, preferring to address her as Mrs. Bonner. The baron's deep rumble calling her name felt like a feather tickling her eardrum, and she wanted more.

Their chests rose and fell as one. Sutton lowered his head an inch, and her gaze dropped to his lips. What would his mouth on hers feel like? He was a hard man, forceful. Would his kiss be the same?

She'd never know. Stepping back, she ignored the chill that swept her body. Burying her head in the blooms, she inhaled, trying to replace Sutton's raw, masculine scent. "A laudatory goal, to be sure." She took another step back.

"But as Mr. Pinkerton now works for you, I hardly see how I am in any danger."

Sutton's hand slipped from her arm, and their connection broke. A numbness spread through her chest.

"We can't trust Pinkerton, not fully." Sutton rubbed the back of his neck. His black hat sat crookedly over his large crop of dark curls. "And we don't know how many others might be under Zed's control. You can't let your guard down."

"Well, isn't this a treat?" a lilting voice cooed from behind Sutton.

Colleen stepped to his side. Molly and Lucy stood there, each with a hat box wrapped in string dangling from their fingers. They both wore wispy gowns and tight pelisses that were just a smidge on the right side of decency, looking smarter and more daring than this neighborhood usually saw.

Sutton nodded at the women. "Ladies. How are you today?"

"Not as well as some." Molly gave Colleen a significant look, one Colleen didn't even try to interpret. "Lucy and I were shopping at one of my favorite milliners."

"In this neighborhood?" Colleen arched an eyebrow. The women at The Black Rose were paid well for their talents. Colleen could hardly fathom they'd purchase any of their clothes in this working-class district.

Lucy glanced over both shoulders. "It wasn't my first choice. But Molly insisted. And the shop did have good prices."

"And what are the two of you doing here together?" Molly stepped forwards and laid her gloved hand on Sutton's sleeve. She arched her back and lifted her chest. "If you were looking for female companionship, all you had to do was ask for me."

Colleen tightened her fists, crushing the stalks of the daffodils. The strumpet was practically shoving her breasts in the baron's face. The pair of them looked quite absurd together. Molly, dainty and delicate, and the baron a wild-bearded mass of masculinity. He needed someone much more sensible than an insubstantial lady-bird. Someone he wouldn't be afraid to dishevel.

For the right price, however, Molly could be whatever he needed. She was by far the most skilled lightskirt at The Black Rose. Molding her personality to suit whomever she entertained. The members clamored for her time, and Colleen had spent many an hour trying to calendar the girl in so she could meet the most requests. The members loved how perfectly attuned Molly was to each of their needs; and each of their needs were quite varied. She was a chameleon in a silk gown.

The men found her mysterious and alluring. Colleen was not so easily misled. Molly liked money. She liked shiny things. And she liked telling men what to do. Colleen had witnessed the girl at the handle-end of a whip too many times to mistake the glee in the girl's face when she made a man beg. Molly could play the servant when called upon, but her true nature reveled in being in control.

Sutton shifted closer to Colleen, and her heart warmed. "A kind offer," he told Molly, "but I assure you I am not without companionship."

"As I see." She looked Colleen up and down. "But unless our new manager has an untamed side she keeps hidden under that waistcoat, I'm sure you're not getting everything that you need. If you ever want to play, come find me. I can take the heat." And with a wink at Sutton, she threaded her arm through Lucy's, and the two of them strolled to a waiting hackney.

Sutton pressed his lips into a white slash. "I believe she thinks that you and I have begun a liaison."

"Yes." The harlot believed that Colleen was *untamed* enough to set aside her morals and engage in an affair with the baron, but too domesticated to meet the baron's more exotic needs. Her shoulders sagged, her body feeling heavy. Not for the first time, Colleen wished she were that woman.

The type to loosen the strings on her stays and kick off her petticoats. But that wasn't how she was raised. She wouldn't know how to be that woman. And even though such behavior might be pleasurable, it still wouldn't be right.

"I'll catch her up and set her straight." Sutton tugged his hat down and took a step towards the hackney.

"Don't bother." She grabbed his sleeve. "It hardly matters." And a tiny part of her didn't want the boring truth to be known. She wanted someone out there to believe her just a little bit dissolute.

"Now"—Colleen pulled her pocket watch from her waistcoat and checked the time—"I need to be getting back to the club. That luncheon isn't going to serve itself."

Setting her shoulders, she started off down the street.

"Where are you going?" he asked.

"I told you." She looked over her shoulder and lowered her brow. "Back to the club."

"You're walking?"

"That is how I typically make it from one point to another." She paused when a group of dogs ran in front of her, the lead mutt carrying a meaty bone in its mouth. This morning's walk had been almost enjoyable wearing the boots she'd pulled from the bottom of her wardrobe. The thick soles had cushioned her feet and lengthened her stride.

Sutton turned her around. "I have a carriage. I'll give you a ride back to the club." A footman hopped down from the back and opened the door when he saw them coming. Sutton handed her in. "Why didn't you hire a hackney, woman? It must be seven miles to The Black Rose."

"Hackneys cost money." Colleen tucked her feet under the bench seat, trying to hide her new boots under the hem of her short skirt. "I've been saving up every penny I can." Sutton settled next to her, and she scooted to the wall, placing the daffodils on the seat between them. Best to head temptation off where she could. "I guess that doesn't matter anymore."

Sutton pounded on the roof. He took off his hat and tossed it on the seat across from them. "Why does it no longer matter?"

Turning on her hip, she glared at the man. "Is that a serious question?" She didn't wait for a response. She poked his biceps. "It no longer matters because of you. You broke your word to me, and now Mr. Ridley will most likely sell his flower shop before you give me my premium."

For emphasis, and because she liked the contact, she poked him again.

Quick as a snake, he locked her finger with his own. "Won't Mr. Ridley wait a bit longer?"

"Says the man with pockets as deep as a grave." She pulled on her finger, but he refused to let it go. "To men like you, waiting a couple of months for five hundred quid isn't of great concern. But for people like Mr. Ridley and me, it matters."

Bringing her finger to his mouth, he pressed a glancing kiss to the back of her knuckle. His beard tickled her skin, and she repressed a shiver. His lips were as soft as she'd imagined.

"Forgive me, Mrs. Bonner. I don't mean to make light of your situation."

"Colleen," she told him, her gaze trapped on his mouth. A small dent creased the center of his bottom lip, and she licked her own. "And if you feel badly, you can pay me what you owe and we'll call it even."

He was silent a moment. "You wish me to call you by your Christian name?"

She faced forwards, a move made awkward by her trapped hand. Their carriage rolled past Parliament, and her stomach rolled with it. She shouldn't have opened her mouth. He was her employer, not an intimate.

But once she'd heard her given name on his lips, returning to Mrs. Bonner seemed a shame.

She jerked her head up and down.

He lowered their hands to his lap. "Well then Colleen,

tell me, if I were to give you your premium now, would you stay at the club until this matter is resolved?"

"Or course not."

The skin around his eyes crinkled. "Most people would lie, tell me what I want to hear and then take the money and run. But not you." He rubbed his thumb on the back of her hand. "I'd be honored to call you Colleen."

Colleen had never been so happy that she hadn't put on her gloves that morning. His hand was bare, as well, and he circled the tip of his thumb on her skin until she felt the pattern imprinted down to the bone.

The caress was so small, so innocent. But as the seconds dragged on, a low hum started deep in her body, a heat that pulsed with every swirl of his finger. Her mind blanked of rational thought, and all she could contemplate was the softness of his lips. The scratch of his beard. Of how her whole life she'd behaved as she ought, as society dictated.

Molly had thought her adventurous enough to take a lover, and Colleen wanted to live that, if only for a day.

She took a deep breath. Two. Her desires were sinful, but she couldn't find it within herself to care at the moment. Gathering her nerve, she crawled onto the seat on her knees and dug her free hand into Sutton's beard. His mouth rounded in surprise, and she took full advantage. Closing her eyes, she crushed her lips to his.

Warm. Sweet. And a little scratchy on her cheeks. Altogether quite nice. A marked improvement on Mr. Bonner's kisses, God rest his soul.

But not the fireworks she'd been expecting.

Sutton drew back. "Are you certain you want this?"

Was she? Not entirely. But she was sure she didn't want to go through the rest of her life abiding by all the rules. She wanted to be able to look back and say that she'd stepped off the expected path once or twice.

Holding her breath, she nodded.

He circled her ribs with his large hands and lifted her into a straddle across his thighs. With one palm at the base of her spine, he wrapped the other around the nape of her neck and pulled her close.

The carriage rocked beneath them, and her sex rubbed against something hard and long. "Oh my," she whispered, their mouths inches apart.

His breath feathered across her lips an instant before he closed the distance.

This kiss was nothing like their first. Angling her head, he took her mouth, sucking at her bottom lip, sending sparks racing to her center with each pull. He bit down, tugging at her lip, creating an opening. When he swept his tongue inside, Colleen jolted in surprise.

He explored every inch of her mouth, taking his time, making her feel like she was someone worth getting to know. Her scalp prickled, her core ached. The sensations coursing her body were so unknown her mind couldn't determine if her discomfort was from unmet need or shock at his technique.

Never had Mr. Bonner kissed her like this.

"Colleen?" he murmured against her lips.

"Yes, my lord?" She chased his mouth, but he tugged her head back.

"If I call you Colleen, you'd damn well better call me Max." He slid his hand from her back and down her thigh. The warmth from his palm penetrated her skirt and petticoat, but it was nothing like the scalding heat when he reached under her skirts and touched bare flesh. He skimmed back up her leg. Without anything between them.

Sweat beaded at her temple. Closing her eyes, she drowned in stimulation. Her breasts felt full, achy. And each stroke of his fingers on her inner thigh sent a longing pulsing through her core. She shifted closer, tried to open her legs wider.

"I'm waiting." He brushed his fingertips over the crease where thigh met her most intimate flesh. He drifted so tantalizing close, before pulling away.

Colleen blinked. "So am I." Sutton had already brought

her more pleasure in two minutes in his carriage than in her entire marriage. He couldn't stop now. "What is it you're waiting for?"

"To hear my name from your lips." He stared down at those lips, and without giving her a chance to comply, bridged the space and took them for another searing kiss. "Such sweet," he nipped at her bottom lip, "fuckable," his tongue sparred with hers, "lips."

Moisture pooled between her legs at his rough language. She'd never heard such a word coming from a toff. Something else that was highly improper and that she enjoyed more than she ought. Her lips curved, and she mumbled "Max" against his mouth.

Wrapping his hand in her hair, he feasted on her until Colleen grew dizzy. She tried to keep up, tried to match him thrust for thrust, but the slick slide of his tongue, the rough caress of his beard, all made it impossible to concentrate. Sunlight warmed her side, and she gave a passing thought to any witnesses that might see them. But it was a small window, and they were bumping awfully fast down the streets. Her body convinced her mind that it was worth the risk.

The hand on her thigh homed in on its target. She gasped, taking more of his tongue, and her knees snapped closed on instinct. Fortunately, instinct couldn't overcome the barrier of his hips. She was left open, exposed to his touch.

Max eased a thick finger between her swollen folds, and her muscles clutched him eagerly. He pushed deep inside, his digit sliding easily. Dropping her head back, she blinked at the carriage ceiling. She rocked against his hand and took what he gave her. How was it possible that Max with his one finger could make her feel more than relations with her husband ever had?

He dragged his finger from her body and slipped through her slick lower lips to the little bundle of nerves at the top of her sex. "So wet for me." He circled his finger around her nub, and she stopped breathing.

"Do that again." Her voice was barely more than a whisper.

"Hmmm." He palmed her outer lips, a nice feeling to be sure, but not what she needed. "For someone so prim and proper, you seem to have forgotten the niceties." Burying his face below her ear, he inhaled, and sucked her earlobe into his hot mouth. "How about a 'please Max'? In fact, I'd very much like to hear you say 'please Max, make me come.'"

If saying please would get her what she wanted, Colleen had no objections. "Please, Max, make me come." Any embarrassment she might feel at saying those words was well hidden by the flush that already engulfed her from head to toe.

He pressed his finger past her walls, sinking deep into her core. With his thumb, he circled her nub, the pressure a light tease. "Will you say my name, Colleen? When I bring you to crisis, will you scream your pleasure, let all of London know just who is in here satisfying you?"

Slapping her palms to the carriage ceiling, she pressed against the upholstered top, trying to push her body closer into his touch. "Oh God."

He smiled against her jaw. "I'll answer to that name, too, if you wish."

The carriage took a hard turn, and she swore the only thing keeping her on his lap was the finger pinned inside of her. He started a pattern, two hard thrusts followed by a leisurely circle of his thumb. Her muscles bunched tighter, her chest heaved. She was close, so deliciously close, she ... just ... needed ...

Max increased the pressure with his thumb, swirling at the same time with his thrusting finger.

Her spine arched, her nails dug into the cloth canopy. All her air was sucked from her and she grew dizzy. Her heart beat once, twice, and she flew apart, pulse after pulse of pleasure flooding through her body from her fingers to her toes. She rode the waves for as long as she could, Max's beguiling fingers never ceasing. A long moan tore from her throat.

Wrung out, she slumped forwards, her body molding around Max's torso like a wet rag over a rock. She drifted in a haze, feeling nothing but her lower body twitching periodically and the soft kisses Max pressed against her brow.

The sounds of London made themselves heard. Their carriage turned from a cacophony of noise into a quieter side street.

Max brushed his fingers against her thigh. "The sounds you make at your completion ... like a siren's call. I didn't think I could get any harder." One side of his falls dropped against her skirt, and he moved his hand to unbutton the other side.

The carriage slowed, and Colleen pushed herself up and looked out the window. They rolled past a neighboring building she recognized and came to a stop in front of The Black Rose.

The Black Rose. Her place of employment. A place where she'd managed to keep herself removed from the sin that went on inside those walls. Where she'd held firm to her morals.

Until today.

She couldn't say she regretted it. Her body was still too flushed with pleasure to acknowledge remorse. But she knew it would come.

The carriage shifted as the footman jumped off the back.

Colleen slapped at Max's hands. "Button yourself back up. We're here." Grabbing the daffodils by the stems, she pulled at the bundle. Half the blooms remained under Max's thigh where he'd sat on them. The rest of the bouquet was woefully crushed by her own knee. There was something symbolic in that, something she didn't want to contemplate.

At least the odor of the crushed flowers filled the

carriage interior, masking any other scents that might linger. She hoped.

Max pounded on the roof. "I'll tell them to go around the block."

"That isn't a good idea."

"Colleen." Frown lines marred Max's forehead, and he reached for her.

The door swung wide, and Colleen stumbled to the opening. She couldn't look at the footman, didn't want to see the knowledge of what she'd done, what he might have heard. She hurried down the steps and turned at the bottom.

Max filled the carriage doorway.

"I have to get back to work. The workers' luncheon won't serve itself." Patting her pocket to make sure her watch still lay inside, she spun on her heel and marched for the club's entrance.

She could feel the heat of his gaze between her shoulder blades. He had a right to be angry, but his ire didn't signify. Of all her sins, leaving a man wanting wasn't one of the top hundred.

In fact, turning the tables on a powerful man was a bit thrilling. Usually it was the man who had all the fun, with the woman left to fake a smile. She'd seen that well enough in her marriage and in The Black Rose. If the baron wasn't going to give her the money he owed, it seemed but the smallest of recompense to put her pleasure first.

She marched into The Black Rose, head held high. Revenge tasted sweeter than she'd ever imagined.

Chapter Seven

Max and Dunkeld sat in a carriage parked across from Garraway's coffee house. His friend rested his head back against the seat rest, his eyes closed. They'd barely said two words to each other since starting their surveillance. Pinkerton was meeting one of Zed's men at the coffee house, and they were hoping he'd have more information about his employer than the American did.

Dunkeld puffed out a small breath, the most sound out of the Scotsman Max had heard in twenty minutes. Not that Max was any better. Of their group of five friends, Dunkeld and Max had the most in common. Perhaps it was their size. It was easier for a large man to be taken seriously with his fists rather than his words.

Keeping his gaze fixed out the window, Max shifted. His left arse cheek was growing numb. He hated waiting.

"Something on your mind?" Dunkeld kept his eyes closed but he couldn't hide the tension in his body. The Scotsman was always ready for action.

Max merely grunted. There was nothing he needed to get off his mind; he just needed to get off. He still couldn't believe the little minx had left him there, cock weeping, with nary a thank you, or an invitation to follow her back to her rooms. He'd tried to corner her all through the frustrating luncheon, but she'd been slippery as an eel.

She'd enjoyed herself. Her sheath had gripped his finger so damn tight he'd almost gone off in his pants imagining her squeezing his cock in that wet heat. But for the most part, she was a proper little widow, and women like her didn't fornicate in the back of a carriage. She'd let her hair down once, and he could only pray she'd do so again.

Dunkeld peeled one eyelid open and examined him. Max ignored the scrutiny. When would Pinkerton show his face? The man had told them he had a meet set up at four in the afternoon, and it was nigh on that hour now. As Max saw it, if a person wasn't early, he was late.

"I should have chosen the position inside Garraway's," Max grumbled. "Their meat pies are damn good."

"And I wanted to follow Pinkerton on horseback instead of Rothchild." Dunkeld settled back against the cushions. "Looks like neither of us got what we wanted."

"With that massive beast you ride, you're too obvious." Leaning forward, Max eyed the hackney that rolled up. Someone other than Pinkerton climbed out, and he cursed under his breath. "You stick out like a vicar in a whorehouse." Rather like his Colleen in The Black Rose.

The Scotsman jutted his chin towards Max's crotch. "So do you."

Confound it, he'd been semi-hard all afternoon, thanks to his disappearing manager. He had hoped his friends wouldn't take note. Or would be polite enough not to discuss it. He glared at his friend. "Spend a lot of time looking at my Thomas, do you?"

"Only when the wee bit seems eager to greet me." Dunkeld yawned.

"It's not you it wants to greet."

Dunkeld opened that one damn eye again. "Do tell. Has one of the lady-birds at your new investment caught your fancy? That doesn't seem like you."

Max frowned but let that one slip past. "No lady-bird has drawn my interest."

His friend crossed his arms over his barrel chest. "The widow, then. That makes more sense."

"What the deuce are you talking about? What makes sense?"

Dunkeld tipped his head. He wore his hair

unfashionably long, gathered in a leather thong at the nape of his neck. The tail slipped over his shoulder. "You have higher standards than chasing a doxy. Not that you won't get your prick wet in a prostitute, but your mistress must be of a higher caliber."

"My prick doesn't discriminate." Max tightened his jaw. He was growing tired of the conversation.

"No, but your heart does." Dunkeld held up his hands as though expecting an attack. "You're always searching for the better life, one filled with perfect people doing perfect things. You're a dreamer. A suffering and noble widow you can save is right in your shire."

"I am not a dreamer." And why that word sounded like an insult, he didn't know. "I see life how it is. Every dirty, fucking bit of it."

"Yes." Was that pity in his friend's eyes? "And you always try to burn it clean."

Fingering the flint in his coat pocket, Max gritted his teeth. The problem with friends was that they knew him too bloody well. Understood his fascination with fire had deep roots. That he craved the fresh start that flames always brought.

It was his own fault. He'd set himself up as the torch in their group, using fire to smoke out the cutthroats the Crown sent them after. If he took a little more joy in the act than necessary, was that any of his friends' business?

The arrival of another hackney saved Max from finding a response. "Pinkerton's finally got his arse here. Let's go." He pushed out of the carriage and crossed the street, not needing to see if his friend followed. Dunkeld would. Max shot a look down the road but didn't see Rothchild. Unlike the Scotsman, the earl was prodigious at going unnoticed.

The door to the coffee house swung open before him, and two men stepped out. Max caught the door before it closed. Pushing into Garraway's, he made a mental picture of the room with one glance. Pinkerton sat alone at a small table in the corner, looking down and blushing furiously when he saw Max enter.

Montague and Summerset lounged at a table by the window, two servings of meat pies half-eaten before them. They didn't spare him a glance.

A serving girl bustled past. She jerked her head towards the center of the shop. "Get yourselves a free table. I'll be by in a jiff to take your order."

Max nodded, the brim of his hat slipping over his eyes, and he swept the bloody thing off in disgust. He could never find one big enough for his head; instead, the blasted things perched daintily on his curls rather than settling sturdily over his crown. Tapping the brim against his thigh, he weaved through the crowded coffee house, Dunkeld at his heels. He tossed the sodding hat onto an empty table and dropped into a wood chair.

Dunkeld settled himself more gently and rested his elbow on the table which tilted under his weight. He sat up, and the table rocked back into place. "Feck me, this won't do." He bent over, looking at the legs, trying to determine which one was uneven.

"Leave it be." Max lounged back in his chair. "We don't want to draw attention to ourselves."

"How can I leave it be? It will distract me the whole time." He waved over the serving girl. "Miss, do you have a paper?"

"Some coffee and a couple of those meat pies would be appreciated, too," Max said. His stomach rumbled agreement. That luncheon had been too liberal with the cakes and not enough with the meat dishes. But the workers at The Black Rose had seemed to appreciate it.

The serving girl pushed a lank strand of hair off her cheek with the back of her hand and nodded. She took off with admirable speed.

"Now, about this widow." Dunkeld propped an ankle on one knee. "What do we know about her?"

"*We* know how she became a widow. And whose fault her current matrimonial state is."

The door banged open and three boisterous young swells burst through. One had his friend in a headlock, laughing his arse off.

Pinkerton flinched at the noise. The American was nervous, and Max could only hope he was always nervous when he met with Zed's man. Otherwise, things could turn to shit very quickly.

"You forget who was with you," Dunkeld said quietly. "You had no way to know the wind would shift. You've set the same fire a hundred times, and it's never burned out of control. You can't keep putting yourself through the mill over it."

Max's eyes burned, but he looked at his friend evenly. "I started a fire that killed a man. That made my manager a widow. I hardly think a little self-condemnation is amiss."

And he still questioned that wind. It had been the only possible explanation for why the fire had spread to the building next door. To the clock shop. But he hadn't noticed any breeze that night. And he'd checked. He always did.

The Crown had considered that night a success. The evidence against a government official had been destroyed, and the man responsible for gathering it scared into submission. Liverpool had nary blinked an eye at the death of a Cit. Only Colleen had cared that her husband had died. Colleen, and Max.

The serving girl returned with two mugs of steaming coffee and a copy of *The Times* folded under her arm. She placed the coffees down, making the table rock, and handed Dunkeld the paper.

"Many thanks, lass." He folded the paper once more and shoved it under one of the legs. When he pressed on the tabletop again, it held steady. A small smile broke across his face, one that flattened when he turned back to Max.

"We've all made mistakes in our line of work." Dunkeld palmed his mug. "None of us have clean hands. You just have to think that the good you do makes up for the harm." His gaze turned steely. "We do more good than harm."

They told themselves that. It was the only way to sleep at night. But did Max believe it anymore? He didn't know. And he no longer wanted to wrestle with his conscience over everything he did. His retirement was the best idea he'd had in a long time. A simple life lay in front of him. One where fire was only used to bring warmth and pleasure, but never destruction.

Movement from the table next to their friends caught Max's eye. A man with more grey in his hair than brown lay down his paper and stood. He picked up his mug, sauntered across the room to Pinkerton's table, and took a seat.

The American gave the newcomer a shaky smile. Pinkerton must have made some jest that only he found amusing. He broke out into loud guffaws but the newcomer remained stone-faced.

"Your man isn't going to make it," Dunkeld said. "He doesn't have the stomach for the double deal."

He had stomach enough to threaten to cut a woman's throat. But, yes, looking at the man, Max doubted he would have had been able to carry through on the act. Max knew from past experience just how gruesome a slit throat could be. He swallowed. The world would be a better place if all men were as squeamish as Pinkerton.

"You don't suppose Montague or Summerset are close enough to hear their conversation?" Dunkeld asked.

"In this crowd?" Max shook his head. "I think Pinkerton is having a hard time hearing what the man is saying."

"I guess all we can hope for is that he will lead us to Zed. Or at least one step closer." Dunkeld sipped his brew and looked around for the serving girl. "Where are our pies? We could be here awhile."

"Or not." Bringing his leg down, Max sat on the edge of his seat. The older man had grabbed Pinkerton's forearm, shaking it around like a ragdoll. Something had made him unhappy. The man's gaze slid around the room, sharp as a blade. Max made himself busy with his coffee.

With a disgusted look at Pinkerton, the man drew to his feet and stormed from the coffee house.

Max threw some coin on the table. "Looks like we're up." With a nod to Montague and Summerset, he and Dunkeld headed for the front door while their friends made for the back. Dunkeld made a quick detour and hit the exit with two pies in his hand.

"What?" the Scotsman said at Max's eye roll. "Following someone isn't any easier on an empty stomach." Passing a meat pastry to Max, Dunkeld strode out onto the street towards their carriage.

Zed's man was climbing into a hackney.

Dunkeld said a few words to the driver of their carriage and nodded his head at the hackney Zed's man had entered. Their driver, a man they'd used before for such tasks, nodded and clutched the reins to the horses tightly.

Dunkeld climbed into the carriage. "I don't see Rothchild."

Max followed. "He's here. Somewhere." And with Rothchild, Montague, and Summerset on horseback, their chances of maintaining a line on their quarry were better than his and Dunkeld's.

They jolted into motion. Peering out the window, Max tracked the hackney. Their own driver maintained a respectable distance. The conveyance their quarry was in didn't have a rear window, and it would be difficult for the man to discover he was being followed.

The hackney coach turned down a side street, pausing by a cart weighed down with ale barrels, to let a street sweep cross before starting forward once more and rolling down the street.

Max almost missed it. The man was good, he'd give him that. If the nag harnessed to the cart hadn't done a little side-step, Max would never have looked anywhere but at the coach. He would have missed that the man had jumped out, using the cart to block himself from sight, and tucked himself behind the horse.

"We've been spotted. He's left the coach, and it looks like he knows someone is following." Max leaned forwards and clenched his hands. "Let's wait until we reach the corner and tell our driver to drop us off out of sight. If we double back, maybe we can still follow him without his knowledge."

"A wise plan." Dunkeld pursed his lips. "If only Summerset would have thought of it, too."

"What?" Max whipped his head around to look out the opposite window. Their friend galloped towards the ale cart, making it clear that he was aiming for their target. Zed's man peered over the horse's back, saw Summerset charging, and took off down a back alley. Max cursed. "Jesus. I swear, sometimes John has more jewels on his boots than he does brains in his head." Launching himself from the carriage while it yet rolled, Max hit the ground and stumbled. He straightened and took off after their fleeing quarry.

Summerset maneuvered his mount around the pedestrians on the sidewalk. He reached the entrance to the alley and kicked his heels into his mount's flanks. His horse took off, a spray of dirt flinging back from its hooves. Max's long legs closed the distance, and he turned into the alley right behind Summerset.

The man ahead got smart and began tossing barrels and empty crates in his path as he ran past the debris. Summerset urged his horse over and around, but lost time.

Max reached his friend and shoved past the rump of his mount. Summerset looked down, eyes wide and glowing.

Jumping over a barrel, Max yelled back over his shoulder, "This isn't supposed to be a good time, arsehole. We're here to catch the man." Actually, they were there to follow and gather information, but Summerset had blown that out of the water. Max didn't have time to give his friend snuff. Later. The yelling could come later.

"Can't we have both?" Summerset hollered from behind him.

Max pounded ahead, ignoring him. Turning at the next street, he was joined by Montague on his black stallion.

"He's turning the next corner," Montague said and kicked his heels in his horse's sides. Man and beast flew down the street. Max pounded after them, regretting not having a horse of his own for this task. Chasing down suspects was getting harder and harder.

Dunkeld rounded the corner ahead of Max, and Max was glad to see his friend's face was red and sweaty. "Why can't this bugger run in a straight line?" Dunkeld asked. "All these twists and turns are starting to make me lose my temper."

"Have you seen Rothchild?"

"He was circling around, trying to get in front of the bastard." Dunkeld jerked his head towards the next alley. "Onward?"

Max took a deep breath and forced his legs to move. It shouldn't be this hard to run down an aging man. But fear had the uncanny ability to make people stronger. Men could run faster and jump higher in moments of great distress. And being chased down by five angry men would distress anyone.

They converged as one. It would have been beautiful, if it hadn't been so deadly. Like a pack of wolves running down their prey. Their man darted down the wrong back alley, one without an exit, and Max and his four friends met at the alley's entrance. They watched as their target jumped at the far wall, his hands stretching for the top edge, but never able to grasp it.

Summerset, Montague, and Rothchild dismounted and tied their horses' ribbons together. Grimly, Max strode towards the panicked man, his friends flanking him.

The man jumped again, his fingers scrambling for purchase on the rough-hewn wood. When he slid to the ground, he left finger trails of blood streaking down the wall.

"Give it up." Max stopped ten feet away from him. "It's over."

The man's shoulders heaved. Slowly, he turned to face them. "What do you want?"

"You know what we want." Rothchild stepped beside Max. "Zed."

"You ask the impossible." The suspect shook his salt-and-pepper head. Pulling a knife from an inside pocket, he pointed the blade at their group. "You will never stop Zed. Zed is eternal."

Max darted a look at his friends, his stomach growing tense. "Zed is flesh and bone, just like all men." Stepping closer, he raised his hands, trying to look as unthreatening as possible.

"That's where you're wrong." He brandished the knife, his hand shaking. "Zed is indestructible."

"Put the weapon down and let's talk." Max took another step forward. "The game is over for you, but we can come to some arrangement. We'll make a deal."

"A deal! A deal with the devils who dare offend Zed." An unholy light gleamed in the man's eyes before his gaze went dreamy. "Zed seeks revenge. And what Zed seeks, Zed finds."

Max wasn't sure what the man saw, but he didn't think it was himself or his friends. A chill whispered down his spine. Something about the man's behavior struck a chord, reminding Max of something. The scents of sandalwood and saffron .... Hot and humid nights ...

"There is no deal for me. I will never betray Zed." The man pressed his back to the wall.

"He'll never know." Max inched even closer. If he leaned forwards, he would just be able to touch the man's hand. Or impale himself on the knife.

"Zed knows everything. Zed is everything. Betrayal is not an option."

Max's heart slowed to a sluggish pace. This man wasn't just loyal; he was a fanatic, mad in his devotion. He would be a hard man to turn against his master.

But he and his friends could be persuasive. Painfully so, if called upon. Max prayed it wouldn't come to that. He didn't think pressing a couple meridian points was going to cut it this time.

"Come now, man." Montague shifted to Max's left, creating a semi-circle around their foe. "It's over. Put down the knife and come quietly."

The man's eyes shifted, and a pit opened in Max's stomach. He tensed his legs. Something was about to happen. He could always see it in their eyes.

"Betrayal isn't an option." The man dropped his shoulders, his body relaxing, his face becoming as tranquil as the surface of a pond on a windless day. He looked up at the sky. "But I'm weak. I would break. I can't let that happen."

Before Max inhaled his next breath, the man raised his knife and cut a red line across his throat.

The blood was bright, stark against the man's pale flesh. The thin line grew, bursting wide, large spurts of blood turning his neckcloth red.

"Jesus!" Montague leapt forwards, grabbed him as he staggered. The dying man blinked, opened his mouth and collapsed into the duke's arms. By the time Montague lowered him to the ground, he was dead.

"What the sweet fucking arse was that?!" Summerset yelled.

Blood streamed from the gaping wound, soaking into the ground and wending in their direction. Summerset jumped back and raked a hand through his hair. "I mean, what the fucking hell?"

Montague pulled out a handkerchief and wiped blood from his hands. "The man was more terrified of Zed than he was of death."

"I think it's worse than that." Max eyed the body that

used to house a soul. A man with hopes and dreams and fears and faults. Soon it would be nothing more than rotting flesh. "I don't think he slit his throat because of fear. I think he did it for love."

"Love?" Dunkeld shrugged off his coat and covered the man's upper body. "You think he was a molly?"

"Not that kind of love." A drop of rain plopped on the dirt in front of Max. Then another. Perfect. Just fucking perfect. He'd never been a fan of the rain. "I've only seen the same mad fervor twice before, when I was in Hindustan. Both times I was facing a phanseegur. A thug who would do anything for his goddess, Kali."

Dropping into a squat, Max made quick work of checking the man's pockets. Found nothing. "He was willing to do absolutely anything for his master. For Zed. And that presents us with a huge problem."

Stomach rolling, he stood and faced his friends. Max clenched his chilled fingers into balls. "If Zed can convince people death is preferable to betrayal, we don't stand a shot in hell of ever turning his men."

Chapter Eight

Colleen was putting the final figure down on the next month's budget when she heard his footsteps on the stairs. She looked at her open office door, her heart pounding at the thought of seeing Max alone. It was a wonder that she even recognized his step when he usually walked so silently. He could move like smoke, his footsteps surprisingly light for such a large man. But something was different tonight. He trudged up the stairs like the weight of the world was yoked to his shoulders.

She half-stood, her body wanting to hurry to him, to ensure he was all right, before her better sense prevailed and she sat back down. He was a member of the nobility. Her employer. A man she had encouraged into indecent liberties. None of those factors were reason enough to justify such familiarity. Well, perhaps that last one. But she still couldn't quite sort out how she felt about their moments in the carriage, much less wonder at how the baron's feelings on their relationship might have changed.

Sliding her paperwork into a folder, she stacked it on the pile in the corner of her desk. When he appeared in the doorway, everything was neat and tidy, including her emotions.

She drank him in, relieved to see he appeared whole and hale if not a bit weary. His thick, dark hair was damp and his shoulders sagged, but nothing appeared amiss that a meal in front of a warm fire wouldn't fix. "Good evening, my lord. Is there something I can do for you?" Colleen sat up straight, pleased with how professional she sounded to the man who made her feel anything but.

One side of Max's lips curled up, a hint of a smile lighting his eyes, and Colleen ran those words through her head again. And flushed. Perhaps there had been something other than professional sounding about them, after all.

"For the club, I mean," she stammered. "Is there anything you need me to do for the club?"

Sinking into the chair across from her, Max stretched out his long legs and stared at the ceiling. "I already know, if there's something that needs to be done at The Black Rose, you'd have already thought of it." He sighed.

Colleen fiddled with her pencil. She shouldn't ask. She wanted to return to the business relationship they'd had before she'd botched everything up and that meant not asking personal questions. But he looked like he'd just lost a puppy. The words refused to stay put in her throat. "Are you all right, my lord? You look ... sad."

He lifted his head and rubbed the back of his neck. "I'm neither sad nor happy. Just had a tiring day."

"Oh." Touching a hand to the knot at the back of her head, she made sure her hair was still in place. "Are you here ..." She cleared her throat. "Would you like me to set up a room for you and one of our girls?" *Please say no.* "Several of the women are most eager to work with you again."

The corners of his eyes crinkled. "Work with me? Is that what you call it?" Stretching his arms to the ceiling, Max cracked his neck, linked his fingers together, and rested his hands on top of his head. "I assure you, Colleen, that playing with me is never a chore."

She swallowed. Why did he have to call her Colleen? Her given name was for stolen moments in a carriage. Not for two people of business in an office. "I didn't mean it that way."

"No." Uncoiling from his seat, he prowled around the desk and cocked a hip against it. His thigh brushed her forearm, and with regret, she drew back. "No, I don't suppose you did," he said. He rested a palm on the back of her chair and bent close. "I would love to play with fire tonight. If any day needed to be burned from memory, today is that day."

Her stomach knotted. He was going to touch another woman. Give her the pleasure he'd bestowed on Colleen only hours earlier. The back of her eyes burned, and she cursed herself. Why should she be upset? She'd made the decision to return to their professional relationship. She'd given herself one illicit moment that she could look back upon and treasure. One moment where she'd been impulsive and carefree. A woman in her position didn't deserve more than that.

He traced the curve of her cheekbone with his index finger. "But I don't want to play with just any woman. I want you."

Her jaw dropped. The pounding of her heart sounded unnaturally loud to her ears. Surely, he could hear it. "I don't know what to say."

"Say yes." He plucked the pins from her hair, one by one, laying each one on the desk in a neat row. Her hair fell in one thick coil down her back, and Max used both of his hands to shake it loose. Cradling her head in his palms, he drew her to a stand. "You don't need to be scared. I won't hurt you."

Her eyes slid half-shut, the feel of his strong fingers kneading her skull enough to put her in a trance. Each and every time Max had handled her had brought pleasure. Even when he'd dripped wax on her wrist. Especially then. That pinpoint of heat on her damp skin had been surprisingly delicious. A shiver rolled down her spine at the memory.

Another memory intruded, bringing with it the scent of burning wood. She'd been fascinated with that fire, too. The flames licking up the sides of her old home had been beautiful, entrancing in its destructive power when she'd thought all that burned was an empty building. The thought of harnessing fire for pleasure was a heady one. She understood Max's attraction to fire all too well. But it was also terrifying. Her stomach churned. Some forces couldn't be controlled.

"I don't"—she shook her head—"I'm not that kind of woman." How many times had she said that phrase before and meant something entirely different? When Lord Halliwell had asked her to play, and she'd sniffed in disdain, it was because she hadn't wanted to be one of *those* women. Loose morals. No self-respect.

Tonight, the phrase had changed, the words filled with regret. She wasn't the kind of woman who pushed her limits, stared down her fears. No matter how much she might wish she were.

"You can be any kind of woman you want." He pressed his forehead to hers, his breath flashing hot against her cheek. "Please, Colleen. I need this. Need you. There's no one else I want."

She bit her lip. His mouth was so close to hers, she only needed to tilt her head, move an inch, and she'd be there. A strand from his beard tickled her jaw, and she remembered how exciting it had been to burrow her fingers in deep and press her lips to his.

She bit back a whimper. She wanted this. Wanted him. But it couldn't be right. Anything that she wanted as badly as this had to be a sin. Gripping the lapels of his coat, she clenched her fists tight.

He grazed his lips over her cheek. Angling her head, Max licked around the rim of her ear, his wet tongue burning a fiery path. The heat settled low, melting her core, making her wet with need. When he sucked her lobe between his lips, she gave up the fight. Decided to trust her body to Max's care.

If this was a sin, it at least didn't hurt anyone but herself. She nodded, barely moving, but Max felt it.

He raised his head and stared down at her. Tiny gold

flecks in his eyes flashed in the lamplight, heating until his gaze looked like a forest on fire. "You're sure?"

"Not hardly, but I want to do it regardless." She shuffled closer, pressing her belly against the hard bulge fighting against his falls. She bit back a whimper. "We need to be careful, though. I can't get with child. Not in my position."

"I'll take care of it." Grabbing her under her bottom, he lifted, and she wrapped her legs around his hips. "I'll take care of you."

He strode around the desk and out the door. His thick length rubbed against her sex with each step he took, and Colleen rolled her hips, trying to increase the friction.

He growled, the reverberation thrumming from his chest, making her breasts ache. She expected him to take the back stairs down to one of the club's rooms, but he turned into her personal chambers. Bending over the bed, he gently lowered her down.

Colleen kept her arms and legs wrapped around him, tight as a python.

He kissed her, hard, pressing her head into the mattress. "I need supplies. The sooner I go, the sooner I'll be back."

She ran her hands over his hard shoulders. "Can't we just ..." She jerked her chin at the bed.

"We'll get there. Trust me."

Colleen arched and chased his lips. He tasted of brandy and tobacco and something sweet she couldn't identify. But it all mixed together to something unmistakably him.

He raised his head. "Let me loose."

With a heavy sigh, she let her hands slip from his shoulders and relaxed her thighs. Only to jerk them tight in surprise as Max pressed his palm to the vee of her legs.

One corner of his mouth edged up as he rubbed circles through her skirts. "I know you're needy, Colleen. Christ, I can feel how hot you are even through all these blasted clothes. I can't wait to sink into that heat." He pressed a kiss to her neck. "But let me do this my way. I need it tonight. I promise, you won't regret it."

He straightened and stepped back, his expression placid. If his hands weren't clenched into balls, and his length hadn't been jutting against his trousers, Colleen might have thought him indifferent.

"Take off your clothes," he told her. "I'll be back in a minute." He strode from her room.

Colleen let her head flop back on the bed. How did a man walk away at that moment? He had more self-control than a saint. And she was wasting time. She scooted off the bed and attacked the buttons on her waistcoat. She pulled her shirt up, her head popping free from the high collar. Her skirt and petticoat quickly followed leaving her in only a thin shift. After only a moment's hesitation, that, too, joined the pile of clothes on the floor.

She shifted on her boots, the cool air swirling around her bare skin. She'd never been ashamed of her body. It was functional, capable. But she'd never presented it as such to a man, either. Being fully unclothed felt a bit naughty.

Should she slip into her night rail? But then she wouldn't be as wanton, and that was a condition she wanted to revel in tonight. Perhaps a compromise.

Scooping her clothes up, she tossed them on her dressing table's chair. She lifted the coverlet of her bed, ready to jump under the sheets. The soft hiss of air behind her made her spin, the cover clutched to her chest.

Heat clawed up her face. Max stood in the doorway, several candles tucked under one arm. He held a bottle of liquor in his hand. His mouth was slightly parted, and his gaze raked her body.

"Don't cover up on my account." He stepped into the room and kicked the door closed with his heel. "I must admit that the view of you bending over the bed wearing nothing but kid boots stole my breath." He looked down again and smiled. "Nice boots, by the way. I see you've finally conceded and are wearing the new ones."

Crossing her legs at the ankles, Colleen leaned against

the bed. Then stood up straight and uncrossed her legs. "Um, just the one pair. I don't need anything else."

He laid his bits and pieces on her bureau. "We'll see." He tugged at the coverlet in her iron grip, and after a slight battle, maneuvered it from her hands. "You don't need a cover, Colleen. You're beautiful."

She didn't know about all that, but under his appreciative gaze, she did feel pretty. She threw her shoulders back. "I'm not without flaws." After seeing all the lovely young lady-birds traipsing around, bare as a babe, she'd come to see just how imperfect her body was in comparison. Not that such nonsense mattered.

Max strode to the banked fire and lit a thick ivory candle. He prowled towards her and held the candle up to her body, the small flame radiating only the faintest whisper of heat on her shoulder. Slowly, he moved the candle across her body, and inch by inch, that bead of heat bussed her skin. He drew his finger across her collarbone, following the path of the flickering light.

Circling around her, Max examined every inch of her bare flesh. "Where you see flaws, I see character." He dropped to his haunches behind her, and his breath skittered across her bottom. She shuddered.

"This here." He traced the inch-long pucker of pink skin on the back of her upper thigh. "How did you get this?"

"Fell on a saw."

He circled around, his face coming level with her most intimate parts. He brought the flame close to her ribs. "And this one?"

She rubbed the small crescent-moon shaped scar. "I was kicked by a horse before I was married." She remembered the pain of that one. The broken skin had been nothing compared to the broken rib.

"And these ...?" His eyes shot up from the silvery lines that decorated her belly. "You've had a child."

Those marks had hurt the worst of all. Reminders of all

she'd lost. "I had two. Neither survived their first year. One died of fever. The other croup."

He kissed the lines. "I'm sorry. There was nothing the doctors could do?"

Colleen huffed. "Those leeches? They didn't bother to come until after my babies were cold."

Max wrapped his arms around her waist, his beard tickling her lower abdomen. "And yet you endured your losses to become the incredible, resilient person you are. The take-no-prisoner's woman of business." He curved his lips against her belly. "Your scars show that you're a survivor. There's nothing more alluring than that."

Her chest grew tight. Max spoke of a better woman than she. If he knew what she'd done, the respect in his voice would disappear, and that knowledge lashed her heart.

Her mind became crowded with regret, when all she wanted to do was feel. She stretched out her hand, and he filled it with his own. "Come," she said, pulling him up. "Show me your fire."

Setting the candle on her bedside table, Max trailed his fingers up and down her back. He skimmed up her sides, along the swell of her breasts, and up her neck.

She shuddered. His touch was so soft. Delicate. Max treated her differently than anyone else in her life had, and it made her stomach twist and her heart pound. She bit her lower lip. He made her feel revered. The emotion didn't suit her. It was like her new boots. They were luxurious, but she didn't quite feel at home in them.

He coiled a lock of her hair around his finger. "I love your hair. It reminds me of a fire deep into the evening, as it's starting to cool. Years from now, when I'm sitting with a glass of whiskey and looking into the flames, I'll remember your hair and how soft it is between my fingers."

"I don't need pretty words," she whispered. But she couldn't deny that they did warm her heart. "I'm not one of your Quality ladies that needs to be wooed."

He just smiled. Leaning past her, he pulled a pillow

from the head of the bed, plumped it between his hands, and placed it in the center of the mattress. "Lay face down, with your hips over the pillow."

"My boots—"

"Can stay on." His smile started small and built slowly. "You look quite tempting in them and nothing else. Now quit delaying, woman."

A shiver of anticipation tickled her flesh. She climbed on the bed and crawled over the pillow, embarrassment and excitement dueling over the view she was presenting. Lowering onto the pillow, she rested her head on her forearms and crossed her ankles.

She heard bottles rattling and liquid sloshing. Craning her neck, she saw Max pouring the jug of water she kept on her bureau into her wash bowl and soaking a small towel. Using the flame from the white pillar, Max lit two more candles, one a dark blue, the other made of a deep crimson-colored wax.

He turned to the bed and tossed a thin leather string next to her hip. Running a palm up her calf and thigh, he said, "The sensations will be more intense if you close your eyes."

"When you're playing with fire?" she asked tartly. "I think not."

He smirked. "Suit yourself. For your first experience, that's probably wise. I'll pull my blindfold out later."

She narrowed her eyes at his jest then grew serious. "You will be careful?" she whispered.

He squeezed her shoulder. "There's absolutely nothing I want to protect more than you."

Colleen stilled. The sincerity in his voice hooked into her heart and tugged. She knew men said a lot of pretty things to women to get them in their beds, but Max actually believed it, if only for the night. He was a dear man, a better man than she deserved.

She released a long breath. She needed to relax. If she was going to lay aside her morals and her guilt for the night, she'd darn sure best enjoy herself while doing so. What was the point otherwise?

Max began undressing, and any second thoughts she had dissolved.

His coat he hung on the back of her dressing table chair. His top boots were neatly placed beneath. Silk rasped against linen as he drew his cravat from his crisp white shirt, the sound sending a ripple down her spine.

With one hand at the back of his shirt, Max pulled it over his head, and Colleen bit her lip. Good lord, but the man was impressive. As broad across the chest as a blacksmith. The muscles of his shoulders and arms were defined, and they twitched with every button he opened on his falls. He shoved the trousers an inch down his lean hips, exposing a thatch of dark curls.

Colleen's breath caught in her throat. She fixed her gaze on that crop of coarse hair, eager to see what lay below. She'd seen her husband's, of course. But she had a feeling that the differences between the two men would extend further than the color of their hair and the size of their chests.

She wasn't disappointed. Max pushed his trousers and smallclothes down his legs, his long length rising free. He bent over, obscuring her view, as he pulled off the remainder of his clothes. When he stood, every delicious inch of him was exposed.

She shifted her thighs together, moisture pooling between her lower lips. Every bit of the man before her spoke of power. From the determined set of his full lips, to the bulging muscles of his arms, to the ruddy head of his cock straining against his flat stomach. Maximillian Atwood, Baron of Sutton, was a formidable man.

He crawled on the bed beside her, the mattress dipping, and gathered her hair in a mass at the nape of her neck. She rested her head back on her forearms. Separating the locks into three sections, he braided it down her back, his thick fingers nimbler than she would have expected.

Picking up the leather string, he wound it around the tail of her braid. "Anytime you work around fire, certain safety precautions must be taken. I like to make sure no loose hairs have a chance to be exposed to heat."

Colleen's shoulders sank into the mattress. The feel of a man's fingers brushing through her hair was one of the more sensuous experiences she'd had.

"I also have a wet cloth nearby, so if anything is too hot for you, let me know, and I'll place the towel on the area." Tucking the braid up next to her head, he ran his fingers down her neck to her back, slowly rubbing away any tension.

"Isn't this supposed to burn?" Colleen asked. "How will I know if it's too hot?"

"Sting, yes. Some discomfort." He dug his thumbs into her shoulder blades, and she let out a breathy sigh. "And depending on your tolerance for pain, it can hurt, if you'd like. But we won't go that far tonight. If anything makes your eyes sting, let me know and I'll ease off."

Leaning over her body, Max picked up the midnight candle.

Colleen's stomach fluttered, and she swore she could feel the air he displaced brush across her sensitive skin. Screwing her eyes shut, she waited for the splash of wax. The shocking heat that she remembered from her wrist.

Max smoothed a palm up her spine, and she flinched, expecting something else. The bastard had the nerve to chuckle. She opened her eyes, ready to shoot a glare over her shoulder, when the first spatter of liquid heat struck her skin.

She sucked in a gasp. Her brain scrambled, trying to interpret the sensation, figure out if it was pain or merely shock she felt. By the time she made up her mind, that it had been only a low-grade sting, another dollop landed on her shoulder.

He ran his hand soothingly up and down her side. "Too much?"

She considered. Her skin was sensitive where the wax had landed, starting to tighten as the wax dried. Her pulse raced. Her fingers tingled with the urge to touch him. And she still thought she was mad to agree to this.

But she felt alive. Exciting. Nothing like a decorous woman of business.

She shook her head. "More."

The mattress shifted. Something velvety and warm dragged against her upraised bottom, and her core clenched, knowing just which part of Max it was.

The warmth of his cock was replaced by the heat of the wax. Gasping, she arched her back, the wax degrees more intense on the sensitive skin of her bum.

Max swirled the liquid heat around with his finger. "The blue wax looks striking against your fair skin. But this red wax ... I think this is my favorite."

Red, blue, white .... "Are you painting the Union Flag on my back?" From her perspective, the color of the wax didn't matter. Just the heat.

He chuckled. "Nothing that patriotic. Or organized. Only a pattern that pleases my eye." He trailed a line of wax over her bottom and down her upper thigh. She was starting to grow accustomed to the strange sensation. Her body welcomed the drizzled wax, instead of flinching away. She was content to let Max paint her any which way he wanted.

Becoming someone's canvas held its appeal. In that moment, she was wiped clean, a blank slate for Max to fashion as he wished.

Max crawled off the bed, quickly returning. He placed the bowl of water with the towel soaking in it by her shoulder. "That is there only as a safety precaution. I want you to relax, but tell me immediately if anything feels too intense."

Colleen licked her lips. "Um, what is it exactly you're going to be doing?" The wax had been an easy introduction. But the image of fire racing up her skin was something she couldn't fathom. Her heart pounded painfully behind her ribs. "I ... I don't want to burn."

"I'll only be touching your skin fleetingly with the flame." Max kneaded the base of her skull with one hand. "It will be like when you put out a candle with your fingers. You don't burn yourself when you do that, right?"

No, not when the contact was that quick. She was venturing into unknown waters. This went far past her comfort level. But she trusted the baron. Ever since the fire, he'd been there for her. A helping hand. She knew he felt responsible for her, and no other landlord would ever be so good to a tenant. Max didn't understand how little responsibility he bore for her situation. But he was a good man. And he would never hurt her.

Flame hissed to life behind her, and Colleen slid her eyes shut, trying to keep her breathing even. Every inch of her skin tingled in anticipation. And anxiety. This was the moment when she did the most impractical thing ever. Where she let herself become a different person, if only for a night. "You're certain I won't be burned?" Why was she allowing this again?

"Positive." He kissed her shoulder. "But I only want to do this if you want it. Tell me to stop and I will."

And never know what she might be missing? She gathered her courage. "No, I want this." She swallowed and nodded. "All right. I'm ready."

Max didn't waste time. Something soft and warm touched her spine, growing hot before flickering away. She eased out a breath. That wasn't so bad. Barely warmer than when she held her hands in front of the fire.

The next vertebrae down received the same treatment. A tingling kiss. Growing heat. Dancing away a moment before it became painful.

Her body grew restless. "What is that?" she asked.

"I've fashioned a small torch by wrapping one end of a taper with a brandy-soaked cloth which I then set alight." He ran his hand down her head and flicked the tail of her braid against her neck.

"And you're actually pressing the flame against my skin? And I'm not getting burned?" She licked her lips, a wave of dizziness swamping her mind. Things were moving so quickly, faster than she could sort out.

A man was laying flame to her body. And she was letting him. She was mad.

"Have you never played snapdragon?" He touched the flame of the torch to the crease of her bottom. The heat on her skin was transitory, but the heat that started further south built. "When you stick your hand in the flaming bowl to grab a raisin, you don't get burned then, do you?"

That snapped her back from the edge of fear. "Unlike some, I don't spend my time playing parlor games." She sniffed. "Some of us have to work." Cautiously, she wiggled her bum, inviting him to play with her more. She nervously waited for the next hiss of fire meeting skin. The faint odor of brandy teased her nose, and she swore she could hear the flames of the candles around her flicker.

"No need to get testy." He tapped her bottom with the fire in quick succession, each flash of heat ratcheting up her desire, like a tightening spring turned a gear. She rubbed her thighs together, squeezing her ankles tight. The tip of his torch found the crease at her upper thigh, lingered a moment, the sensation transforming from a prickle to an itch she couldn't scratch. She whimpered.

Placing a palm at the base of her spine, Max stilled her rocking hips. "The fire should tickle, perhaps turn into a sting, but not burn. Some people enjoy pain, but I don't want to leave a mark on your body aside from a fleeting red patch." He shifted the flame to her other upper thigh. "Does that burn?"

"Oh God." Warmth flooded her body, but nowhere near matching the heat on her thigh. The tips of her breasts scraped against the embroidery in the bed's coverlet as she writhed, driving her wild. She didn't know what it was she felt. There was a pinch of pain, yes. But it came and went so quickly, leaving in its place a lethargic ache. Her body missed the fire as soon as it was removed. "More. Please," she added, remembering that no matter what liberties she allowed with her body, the man was still her employer. And a baron. He expected the niceties.

She didn't want to insult him. Not if she wanted him to continue.

The gentleman he was, Max acceded to her demand. He set up a steady rhythm. Each tap of the torch was like a brush with a stinging nettle. And just when she thought she couldn't take anymore, she couldn't wait for him to start again. Anticipation warred with a sweet lethargy. How could something feel so intense and make her muscles sag into the mattress at the same time?

Max played her body like a drum, the rhythmic pattern making her mind drift. The stresses of the day, her worry over her flower shop, they all floated away. All that remained was the heat, a startling awareness of every inch of her body, and the man kneeling beside her, giving her pleasure.

"You said you needed this." Colleen cleared her throat then raised her voice above its drowsy murmur. "That you had a bad day. What happened?"

The drumbeat paused. "Nothing you need to hear about."

Well, Colleen couldn't have that. She looked over her shoulder, saw that the torch was well away from her body, and rolled. She positioned the pillow under her head and lay back, fixing him with a stern look. The wax on her back pulled at her skin and she shifted, restless. "I'm not some naïve green girl. I thought we'd already established that. I don't need you trying to protect my innocence. It's too late for that."

Max's gaze travelled from her face down her body. Cupping one heavy breast, he teased the nipple with the velvety pad of his thumb. Her skin puckered beneath his touch. "I know you've seen a lot," he said. "Too much. I don't want to add anymore filth to your head. And I don't want to think about it. I just want to burn it from my mind tonight."

Bending low, he licked her nipple with the flat of his tongue, his beard scratching her breast. Slowly, he lowered the torch, hovering it over her skin.

She stared at the flame, transfixed, her breath trapped in her throat. Her body wanted to arch into the heat, to bring the burn to herself, but she waited. Waited for Max to make his move.

He lowered the torch, bringing the flame to her damp skin with a whisper-light kiss. Colleen heard a faint sizzle, felt her nipple ache with pleasure, before he lifted the torch and sucked the tingling tip of her breast into his mouth. He pulled, hard, and she felt the tug all the way down to her sex.

His wet mouth did nothing to cool her fever. Digging her fingers into his beard, she held his head in place. Each suckle brought a whimper to her lips. He rolled his tongue and bit the soft underside of her breast.

Max was right. The time for conversation was over.

She looked down his body, saw he was as ready as she was. Tentatively, she trailed her hand down his stomach, grazed his length with just the tips of her fingers. Soft heat. Like the torch. Only Max pulsed beneath her touch.

She licked her bottom lip. "Have you burned away enough bad memories for the night? There are other ways I can help you forget." Running her middle finger down the path of one thick vein, she reached the base of his cock and changed direction, skimming his skin until she reached his crown.

His eyes burned hotter than the flames. "I've wanted to feel you come around my cock all damn day." He dunked the torch into the bowl of water, and it hissed out of life. He tossed the bowl on the nightstand, half the water sloshing out onto the floor.

Colleen didn't mind a spot of cleaning, not if it sped things along. But when Max lowered his large body to hers, she pressed a palm to his chest, stopping him. "Shouldn't we turn down the lamp?" It was nearly bright as day in her room. When Max was playing with fire on her body, making sure his vision was unimpeded only seemed prudent. But relations were meant to happen under the cover of darkness, as God intended. They'd already violated the unwritten rule of leaving as many clothes on between the bodies as possible. At least the lights had to be dimmed.

He drew his eyebrows together. "Why would we do that? I wouldn't be able to see you?"

"There's nothing important to see. It's the same body parts as every other woman." A little rounder than the girls of the club. Softer. Max didn't need to see that bouncing under him.

He smiled darkly and bracketed her hips with his knees, her head with his palms. He was like a large cat, pinning its prey, about to go in for the kill.

Her nipples tingled.

"Darling, before this night is over, I'm going to know every single inch of you. Taste every inch of you. And if I had the stamina, I would fuck every inch of you that I could." He lowered, his cock nestling into the vee of her thighs. Slowly, deliberately, he shifted his hips up and back, running his length lightly over the bundle of nerves at her apex. "But that might take two nights."

Gripping his forearms, she dented his skin with her nails. His smile widened. All right then. She'd already broken most of the rules of propriety. One more hardly mattered.

The touch at her clit was feather-light. Insubstantial. She tried to widen her legs, give him better access, but his knees blocked her. She whimpered in frustration.

"In fact ..." Lowering his head, Max scored her neck with his teeth, tugging at the soft flesh until she thought she would lose her senses. "In fact, I want you to see everything. Want you to see every hard inch of me sink into your sweet quim." Sliding one hand under her neck and one under her back, he rolled, pulling her body across his.

She planted her hands and knees around his body, finding her balance. Colleen blinked. The roles had reversed. She now had him pinned. Like a kitten might pin a bull mastiff. She knew he could throw her off with one finger, but the position of dominance still made her feel powerful.

With one palm on her bottom and the other wrapped around the thick base of his length, Max prodded her into position.

She swiveled her hips, felt him dip into her channel an inch, and backed off. Max dug his fingers into her skin and groaned. She smiled, pleased that she had the ability to torture him, too.

He looked up at her from heavy-lidded eyes. "I want you to watch as you slide onto me. Watch my cock tunnel into your body. Watch as our bodies become one." Anchoring a hand at her hip, he spread open her lower lips with his thumb, and flicked her nub. Her body jerked. She was so wet, she was surprised she wasn't dripping onto his length. She was more eager to *feel* every inch of him fill her, but if Max wanted her to watch, she could do that, too.

Guiding him to her opening, she widened her knees and eased him inside. She tried to go quickly, wanting him now, but after a couple of inches, her body pinched.

"Easy." He gripped both her hips, slowing her descent. He circled her clit with his thumb, and her head fell back. She stared at the chipped paint on the ceiling. She tried to sit down farther, but Max held her hips steady.

"I want you watching, remember?" His voice was hoarse. She looked down. His gaze was fixed on the point where they connected. His pupils were so wide, his eyes looked black.

She followed his gaze. His cock was purpling with blood, the tip disappearing into her body. She saw him twitch, felt the corresponding quiver in her sheath.

The hollow of her back grew damp with sweat. Resting her palms on his chest, she leaned forward and kept her eyes focused where he demanded as she slid down another inch. Both of their breaths caught.

She could understand his fascination. Watching her plump lips swallow him down was entrancing. The soft hair at her entrance glinted red in the light, glistening with her desire. With one hand, she slid two fingers between her lips and scissored them open, exposing her inner folds.

Max cursed, loudly and inventively. She smiled. She'd heard worse on her trips to the docks with her husband, but she liked knowing she brought out the uncivilized side in this man.

Max moved her fingers to her clit, then wrapped both his hands around her bottom. "Touch yourself," he commanded. "I want to watch you make yourself come."

Her cheeks heated. She didn't know if from embarrassment or lust. She didn't care. Not thinking it possible, Colleen grew slicker. With Max pulling her inexorably down, inch by inch she enveloped him. Whether from the position or because of Max, but she'd never felt so full. The pressure grew until she was sure she couldn't hold anymore. Max had reached her limit. With a grunt, he thrust his hips up and jerked her down, taking those last two inches and stealing the air from her lungs.

She dug half-moons into his shoulders. She'd been wrong. *Now* he'd reached her limit. She hoped. She was so filled, all her nerve endings sparking, that she knew there could be no more.

Until he rolled his hips. It was like a thousand tiny lightning bolts shooting through her cunny at once, followed by a thousand tongues easing the sting. Colleen couldn't stop the small moan that escaped from her lips. Then she knew. Max hadn't even come close to reaching her limit. This pleasure was only the beginning.

* * *

Max told his fingers to ease their grip, but they wouldn't listen. He knew he must be leaving bruises on her plump little arse, ten round marks that spoke of his need. Her body was already splashed with color from his wax. She didn't need any more. But his body didn't want to listen to reason.

Digging into her softness, he pulled her close again, matching the thrust of their hips, feeling the pleasure that slid over his cock flow through the rest of his body.

Colleen's sex was the slickest, softest bit of heaven that he could ever remember fucking.

She raised up an inch, and his hands slammed her back down where she belonged. A long, slow glide of her sheath over his entire length, from root to tip, would feel fucking amazing. But her wet heat surrounding him, squeezing him, was about as much as he could take. More than he deserved.

Colleen clenched her internal muscles and ground her pelvis into his, biting into her lush lower lip. Max just about lost his ever-loving mind.

Who knew buttoned-up women of business could fuck like this?

He needed to see just how far she'd let herself go. "Slide your hands up your stomach and cup those pretty breasts."

Eyes closed, Colleen sat back and followed his instruction. Her fingers glided over her ribs to her destination. She cradled her breasts, circling her thumbs over the nipples, and her sheath jerked around him.

Max rammed into her, wishing his cock was ten inches longer so he could pierce to the center of her. He needed more. Wanted all of her.

"Your nipples are so red and hard, like cherries just before they ripen. Pinch them for me."

She did, and the sound of her moan echoed around the room.

His body demanded release. It had never been this hard to wait on a lady's pleasure. Squeezing his fingers tight, he pulled her down. His nails dug into drops of wax, scraping them from her skin.

"You look so good, I need to taste you." He surged into her. "Will you offer up your sweet breasts for me, love?"

And like she'd been trained as a serving girl, Colleen plumped her breasts and leaned down, presenting her bounty.

Max ran his nose around the velvet pucker, inhaling the dusky scent of heat and woman. He circled the beaded nipple with the tip of his tongue. With one hand planted firmly on her bottom, he skimmed the other up her spine. His fingers rolled over smooth streaks of wax, broken up by the silky heat of her skin. He rested his palm between her shoulder blades, pressing her lower, and sucked her nipple between his questing lips.

Colleen jerked her hips, her body searching for relief, and Max was right there with her. He knew he should take the time, slow things down, suckle her until she begged for him to end it. He wanted to nibble at her lower lips, drink from her sex. Taste every inch of her skin, caress her, take deep, long strokes into her body. And he would.

But not now.

Right now, he needed release. Needed to find it with this woman who'd helped him erase the filthy memories with fire and wax. Let him forget for a couple of hours just how depraved human nature could be. The horror of the man's suicide was the faintest of memories. Max's need was all-consuming.

Hands on her hips, he brought them together. Rough. Hard. Every jolt set her breasts to bouncing. Every slap of skin on skin made him burn. A tingling heat built in his groin. He tried to ignore it, wanting this to last forever. Each time he bottomed out, the cutest little squeak passed her lips, but it wasn't enough.

He rolled, putting her to her back and staying between her thighs. Grabbing her hands, he pressed her palms flat against the headboard. "Hold on," he growled. As much as he liked Colleen's bouncing up and down on him, this was the position he liked best. A woman spread open below him. Taking what he gave her. Digging his knees into the mattress, he found his leverage and pounded home.

Her breasts still jiggled with each drive, and he filled his mouth with a soft globe. Her heartbeat pounded beneath his lips, her skin growing hotter. She wrapped her legs around his hips and arched into his touch. The heels of her boots dug into his arse.

So. Fucking. Good. Grabbing the top edge of the headboard, Max lifted his head, watching Colleen squirm beneath him.

"Oh, dear God," she whispered. "Please, oh please, oh please ..." Eyes wide, she implored him. "Faster," she whispered.

He didn't know if that was possible, but he would give it his all. Using the headboard as leverage, he slammed into her. His sweat dripped onto her left breast, and he licked it away. He tried to empty his mind of the picture of her, tried to stave off his impeding release. But even when he closed his eyes, Colleen swamped his senses. Her scent, her feel. He could see her as clearly behind his eyelids as he had with eyes wide open, so he gave in and looked his fill.

She thrashed her head from side to side, her sheath tightening around him like a velvet fist. If he could just hold on. One. Moment. More ...

His grunts matched the rattle of the headboard against the wall. "Come now, love. You have to come now." The need for completion bordered on pain.

Turning her face into the pillow, Colleen slid her finger between them. His next thrust bumped into the back of her hand, pressing it hard against her clit, and she went over with a cry.

Her muscles clamped down, sucking at his cock, triggering his release. With regret, he pulled out of her clutching heat and rocked against her belly. String after string of his sticky seed jetted from his cock, splashing across her softly-rounded stomach, and Max groaned at the exquisite relief.

He fell forwards, his nails clawing down the headboard as he collapsed onto the mattress. He turned slightly, keeping his weight off of Colleen, but keeping her body pressed close. He felt the slickness of her sweat, the stickiness of his release, smear across his stomach, and didn't care. He was content to lay where he was.

Colleen, however, was not. After her chest stopped heaving, she wiggled out from under him and scooted to the side of the bed. Pulling the half-full bowl of water onto her lap, she took the cloth out, and wiped her body down, spending quick attention to the vee between her legs.

Much of the wax had scraped off on the coverlet, but streaks still covered her back in a medley of red, blues, and whites. He smiled. It rather did look like a Union Jack. He scratched at the largest patch, and the blue wax peeled off in one large, satisfying piece. "Rubbing you down is my job. Give me a chance to catch my breath, and I'll lick you clean."

"I'm fine." Her voice was a harsh rasp.

Max pursed his lips. Rolling onto his hip, he wrapped an arm around her middle and pulled her around to face him. "What's wrong? Was I too rough?"

Her face turned pink. "No. That part was fine."

Max took the towel and bowl from her and set it next to the pillow. He might not be the world's best lover, but usually a woman liked to cuddle up to him after sexual relations. A sigh of contentment never went amiss. And a word or two of praise was always appreciated. But Colleen was a working-class woman. Who knew how they reacted?

"Talk to me," he said, his voice brusque. He cleared his throat and tried again. "If I did something wrong, I want to know."

Her blush deepened, and her adorable freckles looked almost purple. Pulling her legs up to her chin, she wrapped her arms around her shins. The toes of her leather boots dug into the sheets. "You aren't the one who did anything wrong."

Max's stomach clenched like a blow had landed. He took a deep breath. "You haven't done anything wrong, either."

"Haven't I? My husband's only been dead six months. I'm sorry, but this can't happen again." She rested her cheek on her knee. "I should still be in mourning, not traipsing around like a common Florence."

Max ground his jaw. "There was nothing common about what we did. And nothing wrong with it."

"Of course, you wouldn't think so." Rolling off the bed, Colleen hurried to her clothes and pulled her shift over her head. The threadbare cotton did little to hide her form.

Max planted his feet on the floor. "What the deuces do you mean by that?"

"You own and utilize a Venus club." She arched one auburn eyebrow. "A little bed-bouncing would be of no account to you." She crossed her arms, the hem of her shift riding the tops of her thighs. "I wasn't brought up that way."

Prowling towards her, Max grasped the tail of her braid. "And how were you brought up? To show the peerage little respect, act as though social classes have no distinctions, but then hide behind your working-class morality when it suits you? Is that what your mother taught you?"

"I have plenty of respect for my betters."

She damn well didn't and that was one of the things he liked about her. "So, it's just me that you feel free to debate, to question? Every other gentleman you'd bow and scrape before?"

She opened her mouth, but Max cut her off. "You curtsy to no one." Not sincerely leastways. He dropped to one knee. "And you're magnificent for it."

"Max, what are you doing?" She tugged at his shoulder.

Leaning forwards, he buried his face in her heat. Her regret spurred his anger, and he wanted to prove her wrong. Demonstrate that she was as weak when it came to matters

126

of the flesh as he. She couldn't just put him on the shelf when it suited her.

He pressed an open mouth kiss to her lower lips, tonguing the cotton, making it wet.

Colleen shifted. Her fingers gripped his shoulder so tightly she'd be leaving marks of her own. "We're supposed to be fighting."

Drawing back, he ran his finger over the seam between her legs. The wet cotton clung to her, molding around her cleft. "You feeling shame for what we did isn't a fight we're going to have."

"You can't control how I feel. Or what I'll argue about." Burrowing her fingers in his beard, she tugged his face up.

Max begged to disagree, and he played dirty. Ignoring the sting on his cheek, he lifted her shift, exposing her dewy curls. He ran his tongue between her folds, her musky sweetness exploding in his mouth.

"Max!"

"Is this something you want to give up?" He nibbled his way down one lip before swirling around her entrance. He lapped at her essence, not able to get enough of her flavor. "Will you let your notions of propriety take this away from you?"

"No," she breathed.

He fucking thought not. "I can make you feel so good, Colleen. Better than any man ever has." He sucked her clit into his mouth, swallowing thickly against the pain in the back of his throat. The only other man who would have tried would have been her husband. Max had taken Joseph Bonner's life, and now he'd taken his wife, as well.

There would be a special place in hell waiting for Max. But until that time, he planned on redressing that wrong as best he could. To take care of all of Colleen's needs. And kneeling before her in penitence seemed like a worthy start.

Wrapping one arm around her waist, he dragged her right leg up and over his shoulder.

She tugged again on his beard, this time holding him

close. "Lord of mercy." Her leg shook, and she wobbled in his arms.

Firming his grip, Max rose to his feet, Colleen half-sitting on his shoulders, and kept her pressed close to his mouth. She shrieked, her arms going around his head. Max couldn't keep the grin off his face as he tossed her onto the bed.

He crawled over her, and spread her legs wide, keeping his palms pressed to her inner thighs. "Now, where were we?"

Colleen flopped back on the bed and moaned. Any façade of respectability had crumbled away.

He buried his head between her thighs and let himself enjoy her decadence. Tomorrow he'd delve back into London's underworld, confront the worst of humanity. And remember the worst that existed within himself.

But tonight, he'd lose himself in bliss, fall into oblivion.

And drag Colleen over the edge right along with him.

Chapter Nine

Colleen pulled on a pair of cotton gloves, ignoring the hole at the tip of the index finger. A torn and tattered pair of gloves was a suitable accompaniment to how she felt. Worn out. Both physically and mentally.

The physical fatigue wasn't a problem. In fact, the soreness and lethargy had come as a pleasant surprise when she'd awoken that day.

And it had distracted her from her guilt.

Ever since her husband's death, she'd carried around a ten-pound sack of it. After last night, her load had doubled. It weighed heavily, dragging her steps, curving her shoulders. How could she let herself feel such pleasure when her husband wasn't alive to feel anything?

"Going somewhere?" Max pushed into her room, looking her up and down and frowning.

The fact that he hadn't knocked didn't pass unnoticed. "These are my private chambers. Please don't barge in. I might have been dressing."

His dark eyebrows shot up under his wild shock of hair. "Would it have mattered? Sorry, love, but there isn't an inch of you that I haven't already seen."

Colleen shrugged into her cousin's coat, making sure that her watch was secure in her waistcoat pocket. "No, I suppose not," she muttered. She cleared her throat. "Do you have plans for the afternoon? I was hoping to ask some questions in my neighborhood about this blackmail ring."

His muscles went rigid. "Were you now?" Pulling out a drawer in her bureau, Max removed a delicate pair of kid gloves and strode to her side. He tugged at the finger of one of her gloves, sliding it off her hand, before working on the other. He tossed them on her bed. "Anyone in particular you wanted to question, or merely an interrogation of the general populace?" Placing one of the new gloves between his teeth, he tried to work the other one onto her fingers.

She took the smooth leather from his fumbling hand and donned the glove herself. It was like she'd slipped inside a silken cloud. "I am nothing if not practical. I know that asking random people questions would lead to little result." Taking the other glove from his hand, she smoothed it on. This one pair of gloves, butter-soft and as supple as a second skin, likely cost more than she had ever spent on every piece of clothing she'd worn in her entire life.

Nausea ate at her insides. She was an ordinary woman from Wapping. That's where she was supposed to be, not playing dress-up with a nob.

And that's where she was going to return. She'd devised the idea of her own investigation that morning as her breakfast of toast and eggs threatened to come back up her throat when she thought about her actions of the past night. It was a compromise to herself, of sorts. She didn't know if she could give up Max's touch, no matter how big a sin their affair, not while she lived under his roof. He was too tempting. But she could make her time in residence as short as possible. Keep her folly to a short duration.

She set her shoulders. "If I want my flower shop, I can't wait around for you to find out who Zed is. I know some people, people who wouldn't turn up their noses on a bit of knavery, not if it paid the right amount of coin. If this crime ring was as big as you say it was, the sailors and dockworkers in my neighborhood would have heard of it."

He tugged the musty coat down her arms and tossed it by her waste bin. Opening the wardrobe, he eyed the contents, finally deciding on a hunter-green pelisse trimmed in velvet dyed a darker shade of green. "All right, if you know people to ask, we'll go talk to them."

Colleen blinked. She hadn't thought he would follow her counsel, much less invite her to join him in the investigation. She was so shocked, she let him put her arms into the sleeves of the pelisse and pull it onto her shoulders. "You think it's a good idea? That we'll get answers?"

"I don't know if we'll learn anything, but it doesn't hurt to try." Gently pressing her down onto her dressing table chair, he knelt and untied her old boots. "Lord knows I ran into a dead end. Literally."

She cupped his cheek. "That wasn't your fault." In the early morning, as they'd lain twisted in each other's limbs, Max had told her of the suspect they'd cornered. Of the horror the man had committed.

He turned his face into her touch. "Fault, no. But I can't understand how a man could do that. The look in his eyes was ... mad. He wasn't scared. He killed himself to protect someone he worshipped."

"Zed must pay his men an awful lot."

"That type of compulsion has little to do with money." He held up her ratty boots and frowned. "I thought you'd disposed of these."

Colleen pinned her arms against her stomach. "Those are the only pair of boots I own. I wouldn't get rid of them." Even though her feet had screamed in protest when she'd slid them inside that morning. It was amazing how quickly one became accustomed to borrowed comfort.

His eyes went hard. "All the footwear in this room is yours."

"You paid for them. I was merely borrowing them." Putting on her old boots had felt like a form of penance. A silly idea, perhaps, but her old boots also hadn't made her blush like a maiden when she'd looked at them. The beautiful kid boots would forever remind her of everything she'd done in bed with Max.

Shaking his head, he worked the new boots on her feet. She ignored the heat in her cheeks. "It is most admirable that you want to earn everything for yourself," he said. "But look on the clothes as part of your salary. I can't have a manager walking about with sores on her feet." He looked up at her and smiled. "It would decrease your efficiency."

Colleen pointed her toes, examining the boots. Wearing them again should be all right. She'd already broken them in, after all. They couldn't be returned. Spurning them because they reminded her of a wonderfully wicked night would be wasteful.

Standing, Max took her hands and pulled her to her feet. "Are you sure you wouldn't prefer one of your new dresses?"

"My own clothes do me well enough." She tugged at the hem of the pelisse. "I have no need for all that frippery."

"Of course." His lips twitched. "And you look enchanting in whatever you wear." Stretching out an arm, he guided her to the door. As they crossed the threshold, he lowered his head and whispered, "But you look best of all when you wear nothing."

The tips of her nipples tingled, but she pretended she hadn't heard him. She didn't know how to respond to such playful words, but they warmed her right through. But now wasn't time for such foolery, not when there was business to be done. She marched down the stairs and opened the door to the main room of the club. A couple of her girls were lounging on settees, chatting before The Black Rose opened. Colleen headed for Lucy.

"I'm going out for a couple of hours." Colleen ran a hand down her skirt. "Will you watch over things here?"

Lucy gave a pert salute. "Yes, ma'am. I'll make sure to batten down the hatches and keep everything running shipshape."

Colleen pressed her lips flat but couldn't help but find the vivacious girl charming.

Molly sat next to her, fiddling with her necklace, the large green gem glittering. She eyed Colleen and Max, a malicious gleam in her eyes. "And where might the two of you be off to? A little afternoon delight?"

This one, however, was the opposite of charm. Unless it came to a paying customer. Then she'd charm the trousers right off of him. "Where we're going is none of your concern. But if you have nothing to do but ask questions, I believe Mrs. Hudson could use some help cleaning the rooms down here."

Molly snorted. "You don't pay me nearly enough."

"Suit yourself." People were a queer lot. Colleen would have no qualms using a scrub brush to earn a living. But laying with men on demand ... that's what soured her stomach. Turning on her heel, she tossed over her shoulder, "Lucy, you have the helm."

Max followed her out and down the steps, pausing to give the footman instruction to bring the carriage around. He stood next to her on the sidewalk as they waited. "Was that a jest back there? Does Mrs. Bonner, strict, no-nonsense woman of business, have a sense of humor?"

She sniffed. "I don't know what you're talking about."

"Uh huh."

"Good managers strive to keep their workers happy." She stepped back as the carriage rolled to a stop before them. "A pleasant work environment encourages productivity."

Max opened the door, making the footman behind them grumble. "I don't think this is the kind of business that you can measure in increased productivity." He stroked his beard with one hand and extended the other to her. "I suppose we could measure the length of time the—"

"Yes, I was making a jest." Giving instructions to the driver, she took Max's hand and climbed into the carriage. She plopped on the seat and shook her head, exasperated. She didn't want to know what Max thought they could measure. She waited for him to close the door. "Now, I thought—"

The carriage swayed into motion at the same moment Max reached for her. Dragging her across his thighs, he sealed his mouth to hers, muffling her squeak of surprise. Her shoulder notched perfectly under his arm; her head finding its perfect perch on his biceps. She sank into his kiss, her body already accustomed to his touch, unconsciously yielding.

Until she felt sunlight warming her skirts and remembered the open carriage windows.

She pulled apart from him, breathing heavily. "Max! Stop."

"It's been hours." His beard scratched her throat before his soft lips glided across her flesh. "Hours since I've pushed inside your tight body. Since I've heard you moan. Why would you want to stop?"

His hands were all over her, caressing here, squeezing there. She couldn't find the strength to slide off her lap. Couldn't for the life of her remember why she should. Moisture gathered between her legs, and her breasts felt heavy and achy.

His fingers brushed against her pocket watch, pressing the round disk into her side, and she stiffened. Memories of her husband made it easy to find her propriety.

"It is daytime," she began, pushing herself off his lap, "and some things just aren't done in the daytime." She straightened her pelisse and touched the knot of hair at the nape of her neck. All in place.

"I see." Max pressed his lips flat but couldn't hide that they twitched.

"I don't see what is amusing about it. Just because I refuse to ... to ..."

"Dally in the daylight? Tup during the today?"

Colleen felt her cheeks heat, though from ire or embarrassment, she didn't know. "It is nothing to joke about. I may have relaxed some of my standards but that doesn't mean I'll flit about, willy-nilly, and lift my skirts where anybody can see me. It just isn't proper."

He didn't even try to hide his smile this time. "We could close the window drapes."

"No!" She tilted up her chin and sniffed. Insufferable man.

The carriage hit a hard bump, and her teeth jarred. Through the window, the masts of dozens of ships swayed with the river's current. The hollow knocking of hulls butting up against their berths beat a rhythm, the calls of the sailors and dockworkers a coarse melody. The music of the London Docks was as familiar to Colleen as Mozart was to Max. She looked down at her borrowed gloves, contrasting the fine stitchwork with that of her worn skirts. This was where she belonged.

"We're here." Colleen sat back, shaking off her melancholy. Time to focus on business. "There's an office in one of the back buildings where the dockmaster has a desk. I've met him before when my husband and I came to receive shipments of clocks from Amsterdam. If anyone would know what the men down here are up to, it's him."

They ground to a stop, and the carriage door was thrown open. Colleen blinked in the bright light before Max stood, blocking the glare with his torso. He climbed down and held a hand out for hers.

Gripping it, she stepped down, into the swirl of energy, the raucous laughter and shouts of London's East End. A man in wide trousers and a filthy shirt waggled his eyebrows at Colleen and gave a low whistle.

Max slowly swiveled his head to look at the sailor. He did nothing else, but the look on Max's face must have been enough. The sailor ducked his head and scuttled away.

"Speaking of proprieties, perhaps this isn't the best place for a woman to visit." Max turned back towards their conveyance. "If you'd like to wait in the carriage, I'll go ask some questions."

"The dockmaster doesn't know you." Tugging on his hand, she led the way to the office. "Besides, the men here are all talk. Nothing ever happened to me besides hearing some colorful language when I used to come here with my husband, and he was half your size. I don't think anyone will bother me now."

Max turned his hand, lacing his fingers through hers, his grip solid. Reassuring. "No, no one will bother you when I'm around."

Her heart fluttered at his words. She didn't *need* Max acting as her protector, but it did feel awfully nice.

Pushing the thin wood door on the ramshackle building open, he guided her in. When the door swung shut, it did little to block the noise of the docks from seeping in.

Several desks were pressed together with clerks poring over bills of lading and shipping contracts. "The man we want is back through here." Max followed her down a narrow hallway, and Colleen knocked on the door at the end. A triangle-shaped wedge of wood had broken from the bottom of the door, and Colleen could see a man's boots approach before the door swung wide.

"What do you want?" The man blinked and scratched at the whiskers on his neck. "Oh, Mrs. Bonner, isn't it? I haven't seen you hereabouts in a crow's age."

"Mr. Seagrumn." Colleen inclined her head. "I hope you've been well."

"Well enough." He stared at them and tilted his head to the side.

"I'd like to introduce you to Mr. Atwood," Colleen said, Max's surname sticking on her tongue. The men nodded at each other.

Colleen glanced back at Max. He raised his eyebrows at her use of the word 'mister' before his name but remained silent. Colleen knew the dockmaster's type. Men like him weren't impressed with titles. He'd be more forthcoming if he thought he was speaking with a regular chap. While Max's clothes were of the finest quality, the rest of his appearance didn't match that of a baron. She thought he could pass.

Colleen waited patiently for the invitation, a smile on her face. Mr. Seagrumn was a bit rough, but eventually he remembered the niceties.

"Oh. Uh, did you want to come in?" He stepped back, and Colleen hurried through.

She lifted the stack of papers on the one guest chair and settled them on her lap. The dockmaster circled around his desk and took his seat.

Seagrumn pointed at a squat barrel buried under a stack of documents. "You can sit on that, if you'd like," he told Max.

"I'll stand, thank you." Max rested his hands on the back of Colleen's chair, his fingers brushing her shoulders. "We appreciate you taking the time to see us."

"For the lovely Mrs. Bonner, of course." Grimacing, Seagrumn reached under his bottom and pulled out a rolled-up *Times*. "Though I don't think any of my ships are carrying clocks."

"I'm no longer in the clock business." Colleen pulled off her gloves, tugging on each leather finger. "What my associate and I have come here for today is information. I told Mr. Atwood that if anyone would know, it would be you." She gave the dockmaster a bright smile. "I remember how knowledgeable you were."

Seagrumn ran his thumbs under his braces, pulling the strips away from his round stomach and letting them snap back. "That's right nice of you to say, Mrs. Bonner. And coming from a sharp biscuit like you, I take it as a high compliment. If I can be of help, I will."

"That's what I like to hear." Max shifted behind her. "I'm looking for some men to help me with my new business enterprise. Mrs. Bonner said you're familiar with all the sailors and dockworkers who might take on odd jobs for some extra blunt."

Colleen frowned but held her tongue. This seemed an awfully roundabout way of getting the information they needed. Was Max going to hire each man down here and try to discover every other employer he had? The process would take months.

"Of course," Seagrumn said. "It's hard to raise a family on the salaries the lads make around here. Most are looking to make a bit on the side."

"Great." Max shifted behind her. "I only have one condition. The men I hire must be a bit ... flexible when it comes to their principles, if you understand what I'm saying. I can't have someone getting missish and run crying to a magistrate every time he has misgivings about the work. Nothing illegal, you understand. I just want it to be private."

Oh, Lord. Colleen glared over her shoulder at Max. What was he trying to do? Ruin her reputation so she could never do business in this neighborhood. True, sailors and dockworkers wouldn't be her main customer if she got her flower shop. But if word got out that she was running with some shady characters, the more respectable clientele wouldn't grace her doors, either.

"I see." Seagrumn scratched his jaw. "I don't—"

"We're looking for a blackmailer who goes by the name of Zed." Colleen leaned forward. "Any idea where we can find him?"

Max dug his fingers into her shoulders, and Colleen shrugged him away. "What? I don't want him thinking I'm in league with a devil." She turned back to Seagrumn and gave him a wide smile. "We only have the best of intentions in apprehending this criminal. Mr. Atwood doesn't really have a new business enterprise. He mistakenly thought that would be the easiest way to get information from you."

Max heaved a sigh, and she could almost feel the exasperation rolling off of him.

Seagrumn ballooned his cheeks out and released his breath in a hiss. "What in God's name have you gotten yourself into? You don't just go around asking questions like that." He peered at the closed door and out his grimy window. It was crusted over with dirt, letting in only the barest amount of light. The dockmaster needn't have worried about anyone spying on him from that direction.

"So, you have heard of him?" Max stepped around her

chair, closing in on Seagrumn.

Eyes wide, the man scooted his chair back to the wall, and Max halted. With a barely perceptible grumble, he stepped back and leaned against a bookcase, crossing his arms over his chest. No doubt his version of looking unthreatening. That look didn't really work on Max.

Colleen scooted to the edge of her chair. "We need to find this person. You must know someone who worked for his organization. I know the men around here are always looking for employment. An operation of this size would have drawn a lot of attention."

"Too bloody much attention." With a wary eye on Max, Seagrumn leaned forwards, propping his elbows on his desk. "A couple months ago, a government crowd came along, poking their noses in every pot and barrel down here. They took a heavy hand, throwing a lot of good lads in limbo, some that didn't deserve it."

"And yet, the Crown was still no closer to apprehending the head of the organization," Max said. He tugged at the corner of a loose document on Seagrumn's desk, perused its contents. "Were many men arrested from down here?"

"Lookee, I run a clean ship. None of my men were involved in anything like that." He shifted a stack of papers and plopped it on top of the document Max looked at, blocking his view.

"But there must be someone," Colleen said. "A sailor you know about, someone who needed a bit more blunt. We just want to talk to him. We're not here to get anyone in trouble." She peeked at Max from the corner of her eye. She hoped he wouldn't make a liar out of her.

Max dug into his pocket and came up with a leather pouch. He tossed it on the desk, and it landed with a solid clink. "We'd be most appreciative."

Seagrumn's fingers twitched, but he only touched the bag with his gaze. A hot, greedy gaze that almost matched the way Max had looked at her body last night.

"If I did know of someone, what guarantees do I have

that you won't tell him how you got his name?" Seagrumn dropped his face closer to the pouch. Colleen wouldn't have been surprised if the man could count each guinea simply by the bulge they made against the leather. "I can't have this coming back to me."

"I will have forgotten your name before I make it back to my carriage," Max assured him. "And, if your information leads somewhere, there will be more where that came from." He nodded at the pouch. "A lot more."

Seagrumn's pink tongue darted out, moistening his lips. He looked at the pouch, at Max, at Colleen, and back to the pouch. "Dancer."

"Pardon me?" Max looked as confused as Colleen felt.

"The sailor's name is Dancer. Harvey Dancer." Seagrumn scooped the pouch into a waiting hand. "And if you want any information from him, I'd suggest you don't joke about his name. He's right touchy about it."

"And this Mr. Dancer worked for Zed?" Colleen straightened. Perhaps Max could wrap up this investigation within the week. Pay her what she was due. That flower shop could be hers come Monday.

"I'm not certain, but the yahoo does a lot of odd jobs for a lot of unsavory people when he's not out at sea." Pushing to his feet, Seagrumn rounded his desk. "If anyone knows something about who you're looking for, it would be him."

Colleen stood. "And where do we find this Dancer?"

"Any time after five, you can find him at The Boar's Head. He drinks his earnings away just as soon as he makes them." Seagrumn opened the office door and waved them through. "And, that, my dear Mrs. Bonner, concludes our business, wouldn't you say?"

Never one to push her luck, Colleen thanked the man and strode from the office. Max padded softly behind her. One of the clerks glanced at them curiously before delving back into his work.

Outside the building, Colleen slid on her gloves. "Well, there you go." She strode for the carriage. "I can't understand why it's taken you and your friends so long to catch this Zed. Finding him seems like a fairly simple undertaking." She shouted instructions up to the driver.

"Let's wait to see what this Dancer has to tell us," Max said dryly, handing her up the steps. "It won't be so easy, I guarantee you."

She fluffed her skirts about her. "I don't know. I think I have a talent for this spy business."

Max stilled. "Spy business?"

"Oh, was that supposed to be a secret?" Colleen nibbled on her bottom lip. Men could be prickly about being outwitted by a woman. She blew out a breath and shrugged. She didn't have time for artifice. Max would have to come to terms with her knowledge. "A baron hunting a blackmailer only makes sense if you're personally being drained or if you're an agent for the government. You're not the type of man to do something that could be blackmailed over. Not something truly bad. That only leaves the latter option."

They sat in silence for a moment. "I don't deserve your praise," he said, voice low. "But I thank you for it."

He laid his hand on the seat between them, his finger brushing hers, and Colleen felt her heartbeat quicken. No matter how fast she tried to brick up the wall between her and Max, he found a way to knock it back down.

Clearing her throat, she brought the conversation back to business. "Like I said before, I think I'm good at this. When we talk with Dancer later, I'll bet you that I'll have him spilling everything he knows in five minutes."

Max snorted. "That is a theory we'll never know to be true or false. You're not going to The Boar's Head."

"I beg your pardon?"

Tugging his waistcoat down, Max kicked a boot up on the bench across from them. "For one who's such a stickler for proprieties, you seem most unwilling to follow the most basic tenets of decorum. Women don't go to taverns. It would be unseemly."

"Unseemly?" Colleen narrowed her eyes. "That's rich coming from a man who owns a Venus club and goes about as unshaven as a goat."

But damn him, he was right. A woman couldn't just walk into a tavern without attracting notice. Not unless she was disguised, somehow. As a serving girl? She tossed aside that idea. Acting wasn't one of her greater skills. She sighed. There was nothing for it but to let him go it alone.

Max ran his fingers through his whiskers, looking nonplussed. "You don't like my beard?"

"It's fine." She quite liked his facial hair and all the delightful places it could scratch. Not that she'd let him know it. "That's not the point." The carriage slowed, and Colleen peered outside. She pointed at Mr. Ridley's flower shop. "*That* is the point. However this gets done is all right with me, as long as I get my money to buy that shop." She chewed on her bottom lip, gaze fixated on the front window. Bouquets of bright yellow daffodils gave the store a cheery appearance. She wanted to go in but didn't want to have to tell Mr. Ridley she still didn't have his money. Couldn't bear to hear if he'd sold already to another buyer.

Max cupped her shoulder. "I'm sorry. I don't want to stand in the way of your dreams."

"But you did."

"Yes."

They were silent a moment, her staring at the flower shop, him burning a hole in the back of her head with the heat of his gaze.

"I do understand," she said finally. "Peoples lives are more important than one woman getting her flower shop. It still doesn't mean it doesn't hurt."

"I know," he said quietly.

She rapped on the ceiling of the carriage, and they lurched into motion. The driver turned down Duke Street. Their pace slowed, the street congested with carts and horses, and by the time they reached the shell of her old home, they were at a crawl.

She gasped and poked her head out the window. "It's gone!"

"I know." Max rubbed her back. "I had it demolished so a new building can go up. I should have done it months ago."

She stared at the square lot of dirt. The flat space bordered by two high buildings looked forlorn. Out of place. Colleen rubbed her hands down her skirt, twisting them in the stiff fabric.

"Are you upset?" Max asked. "I thought, not having to see it every time you went past, that it might be better for you."

She sank back into her seat. "No, it's fine. It's time it was rebuilt." She tried to figure out what she was feeling. Relief? The void of the lot matched the hollow feeling in her chest. That void had been filled with guilt and regret for the past six months, so the emptiness was a reprieve. The blank lot rolled to the edge of the window and out of her sight.

Max snuck his hand into hers, and she instinctively clutched it. Even through the thin layer of leather, she could feel his warmth.

"I want to show you something." Max edged closer, his thigh brushing hers. "Will you let me?"

Colleen stared out the window. She should go back to the club. Even though she'd decided to give him her body, she couldn't give him her soul, not if she wanted to live happily alone back in Wapping. Max was already coming to mean more to her than he should.

"Yes." She sighed. She was weak; she freely admitted this. But her need for a connection with Max overrode her disappointment in herself. Her husband had slept next to her, worked beside her, and never once asked her opinion. Never tried to determine what made her smile or laugh. She didn't fault Mr. Bonner. She had been little better as a wife. But now that she knew how it felt for a man to truly take an interest in her, she wanted to cling to that feeling a little while longer. "Yes, if you'd like to."

Leaning over her, Max shouted an address up to the driver. He settled back, keeping hold of her hand, pressing it to his thigh. They rode to his destination in silence. The only communication they had was the stroke of his thumb against the patch of bare skin between her glove and her sleeve.

They stopped before a large five-story townhouse in Mayfair. The sun slanted low in the sky, casting the bottom half of the honey-colored stone building in shadow.

Max handed her out and turned to the driver. "You can return to the club. I'll take Mrs. Bonner back."

"This is your house?" Colleen shouldn't be surprised a baron had such an elegant residence, but she'd thought Max's home would be a bit rougher around the edges, like the man himself.

"Yes." He guided her up the steps to the front door, and it swung open before them. A footman clicked his heels together and dipped his head.

"Good afternoon, Jackson. Have I received any correspondence?" Max handed his hat over to the young man.

"Not since you left this morning," Jackson said. "But I do believe the Marquess of Dunkeld is expected in a couple hours for dinner."

Max pursed his lips. "I'd forgotten." He glanced at Colleen. "I'll have taken Mrs. Bonner to her home and returned before then."

Jackson nodded. "I'll take your spencer and gloves, Mrs. Bonner, if you'd like."

Her fingers fumbled on the buttons. The footmen at the club held the doors for her, of course, but she was a working woman, of a servant's level. She'd never been a guest in such a grand house before, and it wasn't a comfortable feeling. Max helped her slide the garment from her shoulders.

Jackson's eyes flared when he took in her man's shirt and waistcoat, but he remained ever polite, taking her spencer with a small bow.

Max lead her through a grand foyer and down a wide hall. Her heels clicked softly against the marble floor. The swirling mosaic on the ceiling matched the tile pattern on the floor, and Colleen stumbled against Max's back, taking it all in.

He steadied her and threw open the double doors to a large sitting room. The back wall was made entirely of glass framed in diamond-shaped iron trusses and looked out onto a tropical jungle.

Colleen's step faltered. "What on earth ...?"

"Since you admire flowers so, I wanted to show you my conservatory." He cleared his throat. "This sitting room and the conservatory are my favorite rooms. I read in here most afternoons, enjoying the feeling of being among nature."

"I can see why." She drifted to the sheer wall and pressed her palm against the cool glass. She was facing another world, one of towering palm trees and wide ferns interspersed with explosions of colorful plants and bountiful citrus trees. Gravel paths wound through the lush garden, and the sun shone down through the clear ceiling, exposing the wildness and beauty of the space.

Max opened a glass door, removing the barrier between her and the flora. "Come. I'll show you around." He led her down narrow paths, identifying each plant and flower with its Latin and common names. The humid air hung heavy with fragrance, and she stopped frequently, smelling a bloom here, feeling the soft velvet of a petal there. The sky purpled above the glass enclosure. They were in a pocket of greenery surrounded by stone townhouses. It was beautiful.

"The conservatory in my country estate is, of course, much larger." Max pulled a knife from the top of his boot and cut a white rose from its stalk. The tips of the petals were splashed with pink. "But I spend so much time in London I had to build this. I find working with plants to be peaceful." He handed her the bloom, and she took it, careful to avoid the thorns.

Cleansing fire play at night and quiet gardening by day. The baron seemed to be a man in search of serenity. Not for the first time, she wondered about his work. Was seeing a man cut his own throat a matter of course when it came to spy work? Some men reveled in intrigue, but Max didn't seem to be one of them. Why did he do it?

She brought the bloom to her nose and inhaled. The scent was faint, delicate. "Perhaps when I buy my flower shop, you can be one of my suppliers. If I buy the shop," she added, her smile fading.

Max led her to a stone bench nestled between a blue *orchis* plant and a broad fern. Pulling her down next to him, he gripped her hand. "About your flower shop—"

"Let's not speak of it." Not when the sting of its loss had dulled into semi-acceptance. Cupping his jaw, she burrowed her fingers into his soft beard. "I'll leave it in God's hands. If he finds me worthy to have the shop, then Mr. Ridley will wait to sell it to me."

"Worthy? Why wouldn't you be worthy?"

She clenched her fingers in his beard. "People have to be held accountable for the choices they make. I haven't always made the right ones."

A wrinkle creased his forehead with his frown. "Are you speaking of last night? Of our affair? Because nothing about that choice felt wrong and everything about it felt damn good."

Colleen swallowed. She hadn't been thinking of that decision, but it was sure to be added to her list of mistakes. "Just because something feels good doesn't make it right."

"It doesn't make it wrong, either."

She shook her head. "I'm a widow. A Christian. I can't find it within me to regret what I've done with you, but that doesn't mean it was moral." She stared at his white cravat. "I try to act decently but around you, I fail."

He jerked his head away from her caress and stood. "Is it all that black and white to you? No room for mistakes? Or forgiveness."

Colleen blinked and slowly lowered her hand. "I would hope," she said, carefully choosing her words, "that when we all get judged that there is room for forgiveness. Especially if we regret our mistakes." She needed that to be true. The alternative was unthinkable.

Max paced to the end of the greenhouse, and she followed, unsure. His mood had changed so quickly.

Crossing his arms over his wide chest, he stared out into the gathering dark. "You want accountability. I don't know if I can give that to you. But at the least I can give you the truth."

She rested her hand on his arm. "What are you talking about?"

"Your husband."

"Joseph?" Now she was really confused. What on earth did her husband have to do with Max? Unless, he knew. Colleen felt the blood drain from her face. Did Max know her secret?

"The night your husband died, I was tasked with a job." Max caught her gaze in the reflection of the glass. His eyes looked darker than usual, black orbs that sucked in all the light. "A man had given his brother letters to keep safe. Letters from a young, unmarried daughter of a well-respected banker."

"What—"

"Let me finish. Please."

Colleen nodded.

"The man was a footman in the young lady's home and had started a flirtation with her. From the girl's account, the letters she wrote to him were fairly innocuous. But after the bastard had assaulted her, stolen her innocence, they could be looked upon in a different light. That's why he kept them. As protection against retribution. He told the father that if he were prosecuted, he'd publish the letters, show that the daughter had encouraged him."

Colleen's stomach churned. The world could be a horrible place. But she still didn't understand why Max was telling her this.

"The girl's father didn't want disgrace to fall on his daughter. Willing or not, her reputation would be ruined. She was no longer a maid. So, he didn't turn to the authorities. Rather, he turned to a friend in a high place." Max's shoulders bunched, hard as boulders. "Word came down that messages should be sent. I was to deliver the message to the brother. That familial bonds don't extend to concealing illicit letters or aiding brothers who had angered the wrong man. Someone else delivered a different and harsher lesson to the footman."

She shook her head. "I don't understand. Why are you telling me this?"

He continued like she hadn't spoken. "Since it's known that I have a talent for setting fires, I was called into service. On a night when I knew the brother would be away from home, I broke into his house and set up hot spots. Small fires fueled by hastening agents I knew would burn out quickly. The brother's home, those letters, and the chandlery below, would burn. But nothing else."

"A chandlery?" She fell back a step. Her heart pounded painfully, and she pressed a hand to her chest.

Max turned, piercing her with his gaze, not letting her hide. "I set the fires and escaped across the street to watch. You see, I like to watch." He advanced a step, and she retreated, not wanting to hear this. But he wouldn't let her escape. "I watched as the flames cast flickering shadows through the windows. Then as the small fires met and grew into a larger conflagration."

Colleen's hip smacked into a raised flower bed, the corner of the wood box sending an arc of pain down her leg. She kept stumbling back. "You set the fire?"

"So many things went wrong that night." He shook his head. "The fuel didn't burn out as quickly as it should have. The winds shifted, blowing embers next door."

Her shoulders hit a glass wall. "You set the fire," she breathed out.

The tips of his top boots nudged her toes. He loomed above her, his expression harsh. "Yes. It was no accident, as had been reported. No candle that burned too close to a curtain. I was supposed to destroy the man's livelihood. Burn the girl's letters." Flexing his hands, Max raised them to her shoulders, hesitated, then dropped them to his sides. "I'm responsible for your husband's death. You're a widow because of me."

She couldn't breathe. Couldn't move. The light streaming from the sitting room focused into small pinpricks in Max's eyes, everything else going dark.

The Baron of Sutton hadn't randomly appeared in her life. He wasn't a kindly landlord trying to help her recover. He was an arsonist, and a liar, and was as guilt-ridden as she.

Her chest caved in on itself, and she sucked down gulps of air.

And he still didn't know the truth.

That he wasn't the one responsible.

That it was Colleen who had killed her husband.

Chapter Ten

"Will you move your arse?" Max growled at his friend. "But do it slowly, or you'll tip over the damn phaeton."

Dunkeld shifted, dropping the flannel-wrapped bricks he'd been arranging on the floor. Sinking back into his seat, he raised one burnished eyebrow. "Well, someone's got their smallclothes in a twist. And I'm not the one who chose this dainty little contraption over our usual carriage. Why did you put two hulks like us in a phaeton?" Dunkeld peered over the side. "The springs will never be the same."

"Who gives a flying fuck about the springs of a rented phaeton?" Max cracked his neck. A breeze drifted under his beard, cooling his throat. He tried to remember how the air felt against bare jaw, before he'd grown his beard as a way to distinguish himself from the rest of the sots of the ton. Colleen thought the beard made him look like a goat. He swallowed. That was most likely the kindest thing she would think of him from now on.

"We should have stayed for a round at The Boar's Head after learning that your Dancer was at sea. Your demeanor would be much more pleasant with a drink or three in you."

"There's nothing wrong with my demeanor," he bit out. "And the man's not *my* bloody Dancer." Absurd name.

"What's the matter?" Dunkeld asked. "The lovely widow turn you down?"

Max clenched his jaw and refused to take the bait. If a friend couldn't take a little unreasonable carping, then what good was he?

Dunkeld's gaze sharpened on their target. Pinkerton emerged from a bakehouse, a long baguette wrapped in paper tucked under his arm. Twitching the reins, Max set a slow pace to follow the American.

"I ran into Lady Fletcher on St. James street the other day," Dunkeld said. He leaned back in his seat and propped one boot up on the front bar. "She asked after you. If you need to rid yourself of excess energy, I think she would be more than willing to accommodate you."

"Not interested."

His friend swiveled his head to look at him. "That woman has the ripest breasts in London and she's generous enough to share them. And you're not interested?"

They were spectacular breasts. And Lady Fletcher was as adventurous as she was well-endowed. But his cock didn't even twitch at the prospect. Besides, "They aren't the ripest in London." Those belonged to the woman who was probably even now plotting her revenge. His mouth watered, remembering the velvety softness of her nipple on his tongue. The succulent pink of her areolas. The way the delicate skin had puckered under the heat of the flame.

Shifting in his seat, Max could feel his friend's incredulous stare. Fuck it, he didn't owe Dunkeld any explanations. And he wasn't going to share any stories about Colleen. His friends already knew too much about his bed sport. He wouldn't subject Colleen to their scrutiny.

"And who, pray tell, does that honor fall upon?" Dunkeld shifted onto one hip. "Not your bonnie new manager, by any chance? Are you ranking her breasts higher?"

"Don't talk about her that way," Max growled. Pinkerton stopped at a haberdashery, and Max pulled the phaeton to the side of the road. The American looked up and down the street, nodding at Max and Dunkeld before slipping into the store. Max pressed his lips together. The man made a terrible spy.

"So, it's that way, is it." Shaking his head, Dunkeld

heaved a sigh deep enough to rattle their chaise. "My bachelor friends are dropping like flies."

"No. It's not like that." Max glared. "She's a good woman and doesn't deserve our ribaldry. Now, can we focus on the task at hand and stop talking about my sexual pastimes?"

"Or your lack thereof?" Dunkeld smiled blandly at him. "Of course, but we need something to pass the time. Zed is being most uncooperative by not trying to kill our fellow." He shifted his weight, and the springs squeaked in alarm. "We've been following Pinkerton for two hours hoping someone would attack him. My arse is sore. I think the least you could do is entertain me with your sad love life to take my mind off of it."

It had been a mind-numbing two hours. They'd told Pinkerton to go about his daily business, but to make sure to keep them in sight. With the way Zed handled betrayal and failure, Max figured eliminating the American would be his next step. When Pinkerton's handler didn't report back, Zed must have suspected something was awry. And the crime ring's leader was crazy enough to kill first and ask questions later. He'd want to shut Pinkerton up permanently. But after trailing the man to the barber, the tailor, and the public library, even Max was tempted to take Pinkerton down. Anything to ease the boredom.

"Your manager seems a wee bit puritanical." Pulling a small flask from an inside pocket, Dunkeld took a swig and handed it over to Max. "I don't think she'd be the type to play. Perhaps you should look for a more hospitable lass."

Max grabbed the flask and resisted the urge to chuck it at his friend's head. "I'm cutting you off. Your civilized accent is slipping."

Dunkeld made a rude gesture, and Max bit back a smile. He knew the Scotsman meant well. He and his friends wanted more from a lover than just a willing lay. Why choose a woman who couldn't fulfill all one's needs? It was only setting oneself up for disappointment.

But Colleen had responded to his play. Had arched her body into the flame. Max tipped the flask to his lips, felt the whiskey burn a path down his throat. And he'd killed her husband.

Why the fuck had he told her? If he was only to have a brief affair with her, there was no reason to confess. But she was so forthright and honest. She deserved to know who she was giving her body to.

Not like that would be an issue anymore. He and his big mouth had guaranteed the end of playtime with Colleen.

"I told her what I did."

Dunkeld was silent for a weighted moment. "You told who, exactly what?"

Max tore his gaze off the storefront. "I told Colleen. Mrs. Bonner. And you know what."

Dunkeld cursed, loudly and for a long time. His brogue became thick the more heated he became until Max could only understand one word in two. The horse in the phaeton's harness skittered uneasily.

"Are you a bloody, feckin' eejit?" Dunkeld thumped Max in the chest. "Do ya know the trouble she could cause?"

Rubbing his breastbone, Max scowled. "She isn't like that." He paused. That wasn't quite true. Colleen was loyal and steadfast, yes. But she also believed in consequences for one's actions. And her loyalty had been to her husband. Why wouldn't she go to the authorities? He'd confessed to killing her husband. It was her logical next step.

Max's shoulders rounded. Even though the sun shone brightly, the afternoon air was chilled, and he tucked his hands up under his armpits. "Even if she did speak, it wouldn't matter," he said woodenly. "I'm a member of the House of Lords and she runs a Venus club. Who do you think the courts would believe?"

His friend grumbled but settled back into his seat. "There is that. Liverpool wouldn't like hearing the name of one of his men bandied about in the streets, but there wouldn't be any legal consequences."

Pinkerton emerged from the haberdasher's. A crisp new top hat sat at a jaunty angle on his head. The American looked at his reflection in the mirror, fingered the brim, and turned up the street.

"We shouldn't have given him any coin until after we catch Zed." Flicking his wrist, Max turned the phaeton into the street at a slow plod. "He shops like a woman." Not like Colleen, though, who turned up her nose at the idea of buying new clothes. She was far too practical for such rubbish. Max hadn't missed the lustful gaze when she'd examined her new boots, however, or the way her fingers had returned again and again to the velvet trim of the spencer he'd put her in. When he returned to the club, would he find the new wardrobe nothing but a pile of ashes? He couldn't imagine she'd want to see anything from Max again.

He snorted. Of everything he'd ruined by confessing his guilt, the fact that Colleen wouldn't wear the clothes he'd bought her was the stupidest loss of all to mourn. He truly was an eejit.

Dunkeld elbowed him. "There," he said, his voice quiet and deadly. He nodded across the street at a man dressed in rags. The other pedestrians veered away to avoid the man stumbling like a drunkard. For a moment, Max wondered what had caught his friend's attention. But then he saw it. For an ape-drunk, the man was able to catch himself neatly before actually falling, and for all the zigs and zags, was walking an amazingly straight path. Right towards Pinkerton.

"Ha!" Max sent the horse galloping into motion. The phaeton zipped around a hackney and darted ahead of a carriage. "Now you see why I rented a phaeton?" The miscreant was ten feet from Pinkerton, and nobody knew better than Max how quickly a knife could be thrust between a man's ribs, puncturing his heart. In two seconds, the assassin could have finished his job and be back on his way. The speed and maneuverability of a phaeton became important factors when a man's life hung in the balance.

Pinkerton paused on the sidewalk, shifting one of his purchases to the other arm, oblivious to the danger bearing down on him.

Lining the chaise next to the fake drunkard, Max tossed the reins to his friend and leapt. He hit the man's back and took him down five feet from the American. The man bounced on the dirt, his squawk of surprise cut off in a hiss of air when Max landed on his back.

A grim smile tugged at Max's lips. Finally, something he could pound. Prey to take down. Ever since Colleen had fled his house last night, an itch had settled under his skin. An itch he couldn't scratch. He dug his fingers into the back of the man's neck, just until the point where he could feel the fine bones of the spine start to shift.

"Who the fuck," he ground out, "is Zed?" Max was sure three of his friends would roll their eyes at the inelegance of his interrogation technique. Luckily, those three weren't here. Dunkeld liked to bust heads as much as Max did. And Max was getting tired of this fuckwit Zed. The criminal mastermind was leading them on a merry chase, and it was time that came to an end.

"I think it usually works better if you give a man space to draw breath." Dunkeld's boots came into Max's view, and his friend rocked onto his heels. "The man's face is purple. I don't think he could answer you if he wanted."

Max grunted. But what his friend said was true, so he sat back, careful to keep his knee in the small of the assassin's back and the man's hands in sight.

Pinkerton stepped forward, his face pale. "That man was going to kill me?"

Max hadn't forgotten that the American had threatened to do the same to Colleen, so felt little sympathy.

The man beneath Max shook his head, his face scaping across the dirt. He squeaked, cleared his throat, and tried again.

Nudging the man with the toe of his boot, Dunkeld

sniffed. "I think he's trying to deny that accusation." A crowd began to form around them, and the burly Scotsman clenched his fists and glared. The lookie-loos dispersed.

"I'm not trying to kill anyone!" The man tried pushing to his hands and knees, and Max put more weight onto his back. The miscreant flopped to the ground. "I swear. I would never hurt anyone."

"You were following this man." Max jutted his chin at Pinkerton. "And you're pretending to be in your cups. That leads me to believe you were up to no good."

"Let me roll over, and I can prove it." The man clasped his thin hands together on the dirt above his head, as though praying. "Just let me show you."

Max glanced up. His friend reached into an inside pocket, letting his hand rest on the butt of the gun Max knew he kept there. Dunkeld nodded.

Rolling to a crouch, Max released the pressure on the man's back.

Slowly, like a rat struggling through mud, the man rolled to his side and sat up. Keeping his eyes on Max, he flicked open one side of his coat. Row after row of handmade pockets had been sewn into the lining, most of them bulging with watches, coin, and jewelry.

Max sat back on his heels and cursed. The man was a bloody thief.

"I saw this chap spending freely and didn't think he'd mind if I relieved him of some of his blunt." The thief opened the other side of his coat, showing even more pockets. "But I don't hurt people. They don't even know I've lifted anything until they get home."

Perfect. They'd been trying to chum the waters for a shark and instead they'd attracted a guppy. Just to be certain, Max patted the man down, finding a diamond-studded cravat pin and a fine lady's bracelet but no weapon of any kind.

He stood and stretched his back. "I think today is a bust."

Bending, Dunkeld grabbed the thief by his collar and heaved him to his feet. He pointed down the street, and the man took off without a question.

"Wait." The baguette slipped under Pinkerton's arm, and he hefted it higher. "You're just going to let him go? He was going to try to rob me."

"And we're not bloody Bow Street." Max turned to his friend. "If anyone else was following him, they're not now. Let's call it a day."

Dunkeld nodded agreement. He jerked his head at Pinkerton. "What about him?"

"It's not my day to watch him. That's a fight between you and Summerset."

"Fine," the Scotsman grumbled. Lifting a hand, he hailed a hackney. "I'll take him to my place. Try again tomorrow?"

Max nodded and climbed into the phaeton. He watched his friend grab Pinkerton's baguette and rip off the end before tossing the loaf back to the American. Pinkerton juggled the bread and his satchels before dropping everything. Dunkeld hollered for Pinkerton to get his arse in the hackney, and Max smiled. The first genuine one of the day.

Turning the chaise around, Max headed back to The Black Rose. He'd let one of his footman return the contraption. Max wanted to see Colleen. Wanted to see if she looked at him with disgust or hate or .... No. Those could be the only two options.

Without Dunkeld weighing them down, Max and the horse made it to the club in good time. Max tossed the reins to the footman and gave the beast a good shoulder rub. "Find a treat for the animal and then return it and the phaeton to Haworts on Mayweather."

The footman nodded, and Max climbed the steps and entered his club. He went to give the man at the door his hat and realized it no longer perched on his head. He must have lost it during the scuffle. Finger-combing his wild hair as best he could, he looked for his manager.

And didn't find her. "Lucy." He waved the girl over. "Do you know where Mrs. Bonner is?"

The blonde gathered her silk robe tightly about her. "She had an errand to run. Didn't you get the note she sent to your home?"

"I haven't been home." Max narrowed his eyes. "What errand?"

She sucked her plump bottom lip into her mouth and let it out with a pop. "She got a letter and left. How am I to know where she went. She's my employer; I don't question her."

"Technically speaking, I am your employer." Something about the way the girl wouldn't look him in the eye set Max on edge. She knew more than she let on. "And if you would like to keep your employment here, I'd suggest that you tell me what you know."

Lucy examined her cuticles. "I only saw the letter because Mrs. Bonner has been asking me to help her out more and more. You know, like an assistant."

Sweat gathered at the small of his back, and his fingers itched to shake the words out of the chit's mouth at a faster pace. But he knew when to show restraint. Besides, Colleen had probably gone to visit her cousin, or the flower shop. No reason to be concerned.

"Yes, she's mentioned how helpful you've been." Max kept his voice friendly. "What was in the letter?"

"A request that she meet someone at St. Katherine's church." The girl chewed on her bottom lip. "It wasn't a friendly request, at that."

"And she went?" Max's eyebrows hit the ceiling. "Alone? The damn fool woman didn't take a footman with her at least?"

Lucy furrowed her brow. "Well, she first asked for Bob, but he hadn't come in yet. Rufus said he had to wait for the wine delivery. Sam has been feeling poorly and is still out back in the—"

"When did she leave?" he interrupted her.

"About thirty minutes ago. She should be getting there about now. But—"

Max didn't wait to hear Lucy's next words. He ran for the door, bursting through before the doorman could open it. The footman was halfway down the block in the rented phaeton. Max pounded after them, a shout choked in his throat. That little idiot. Even with Bob, Rufus, and Sam down, there were still plenty of other servants she could have taken with her. Or better yet, she could have missed the meeting and given Max the letter, letting him handle the situation. He was going to throttle her when he found her.

The footman had set the horse at a slow clop, and Max soon caught up. Without a word, he hauled the footman down from his seat, ignoring his yelp. He put a foot on the step then changed his mind.

"Help me unharness the animal," he shouted at the servant. In under a minute, the horse was free. Grabbing its mane, Max swung up onto its bare back and kicked his heels into the horse's flanks. He shot forward, leaving an open-mouthed footman and listing phaeton behind.

Without hesitation, he guided the horse to his target. Thankfully, he was familiar with St. Katherine's location. It was across from Simon's, and he knew the way there almost as well as he knew his way home.

The horse pounded down the streets, rattling his bones. He hadn't ridden bareback since he'd been a child and his seat wasn't comfortable. After he throttled Colleen, he'd ask her to kiss it and make it better. If she forgave him for the fire.

If he found her alive.

Digging his heels into the heaving flanks of the horse, Max flew towards St. Katherine's. And prayed.

He reached the creamy white cathedral and raced the horse up the broad steps. Before the front doors, he slid from his mount's back, stumbled, and pounded into the narthex. Colleen would have been with the man for ten minutes. Ten minutes where she was unprotected. Vulnerable. A person could be beaten to death in moments. Choked to death in under sixty seconds. If the attacker had a knife or a gun ...

He burst into the nave, chest heaving. The door slammed behind him, the hollow echo ringing through the empty church. Candles flickered along the walls, and a gray light filtered through the high windows.

Pacing the center aisle, Max looked down every row, expecting to see a crumpled body lying on a pew. He reached the altar and turned, resting his hands on his hips. Where was she? A shadow flickered to his right, the toe of a boot sliding behind a large pillar.

Max took a step towards the hidden figure, and the main door swung open.

A woman's silhouette stood outlined in the rectangle of light. "Max?" Colleen called out. "What on earth are you doing here?"

His leg muscles gave way, and Max had to lock his knees to stay upright. "Colleen." His voice was more whisper than rasp. She was alive. And whole.

Footsteps skittered to his right, running away from him. Max caught sight of the swirl of a black cloak and a squat hat. A side door clanged shut. He looked from Colleen, to the outlaw's escape route, and back to Colleen. Shoulders tight, Max prowled towards the obstinate woman, not willing to take the chance that the man who'd fled had been the only cutthroat Zed had sent.

He grasped her elbow and hustled her from the church.

"Shouldn't we go after him?"

"No," he bit out. The horse was gone, and Max hoped the animal was smart enough to find its way back home. A hackney rested at the curb, the driver lounging against it, twirling his hat in his hands. He opened his mouth when he saw Colleen, but Max ignored him and pulled her around the conveyance. Max headed across the street, practically dragging Colleen behind him.

She twisted, looking back at St. Katherine's. "I don't understand. We've been afforded the opportunity to speak to another member of the blackmail ring. Why are we letting him get away?"

"Speak? Do you think all that man wanted was a conversation?" They climbed the steps of the stately building that faced the church.

A footman swung open the door at his approach and sketched a bow. "Lord Sutton."

Max pressed Colleen into the foyer, his shoulders finally unclenching when she was safe within those four walls.

"Where are we?" Colleen tugged at the hem of her spencer, one of her new ones, Max noted, and peered around the lushly-decorated foyer. "What is this place?"

"My club."

Her auburn brows disappeared beneath her sweep of hair.

"My other club. Simon's. I'm a member here, as well."

The head butler hurried towards them, deep creases marring the man's forehead. "Lord Sutton. So nice to see you this evening." Spreading his arms, he tried to herd them back towards the front door. "But I can't allow your guest to enter. The members haven't voted to allow women tonight."

Nor almost any other night. Rothchild's wife was the last woman to grace these halls. Max ground his back teeth together. The rules were starting to irritate him. "It's not entry I need, but the use of a carriage. I assume my guest is allowed in one of those, even if it does belong to the club?"

"Of course." The butler nodded at the footman, and the younger man stole from the room. "Can I bring you and your guest something to drink while you wait? A cup of tea, perhaps?" the man asked, giving Colleen an indulgent smile.

"I don't know about you, but I could use a shot of Irish whiskey." Colleen adjusted the brim of her hat. "It's been a hell of a couple of days."

Max snorted, a portion of his anger easing. The butler looked shocked at her language, and truth be told, so was Max. But she was right. It had been a hell of a couple of days.

"We're fine," Max told the man. "We'll just wait here until the carriage comes around."

"Of course." Pressing his lips into a white slash, the butler gave one last disapproving look at Colleen and oozed down the hall.

She fingered the chain of her pocket watch. "I hope I didn't just get you blacklisted. But I don't like hearing I'm not welcome merely because of the accident of my birth."

"I'll survive."

"Then do you want to tell me why you were at St. Katherine's?" She cocked her head. "You received my note in time?"

Max's anger roared back at full force. "No, I didn't get your damn note. I went to the club and learned you were actually fool enough to go meet a stranger alone, I raced here as fast as I could."

"I didn't plan to come here unattended, but none of the servants were available to come with me."

"There was still the footman at the front door, the stable boy—"

She sighed. "I had to leave *some* people at the club so it would function." She nodded to the front door. "I did ask the hackney driver to wait for me so if Zed, or whoever it was he sent, tried anything outside the church, I would have a measure of protection."

"And if he tried something inside St. Katherine's?"

Colleen opened her mouth. Closed it. "No one would harm a woman inside a house of God. It's a sanctuary," she said in a hushed voice.

Max inhaled sharply. "You'd risk your life on the assumption that everyone is as pious as you?"

She lowered her gaze to the floor and toed the carpet. "By my estimations, it was worth the risk. I took precautions, and besides, Zed is a businessman." She raised her chin and stared up at him. "I know businessmen. If he could obtain my cooperation, the information I would provide to him would potentially be worth in the tens of thousands of pounds. He wouldn't hurt the golden goose."

"Don't assume everyone will act as rationally as you would." He crossed his arms over his chest. "It's a good thing your driver was slow and I was able to arrive before you." His hands tremored at the thought of what could have happened to her if she'd arrived on time, and he dug his fingers into his opposite biceps to hide it.

"The horse pulling my hackney threw a shoe." She flicked a piece of lint off her sleeve. "I was delayed."

He shook his head. "That horse saved your life."

"You don't know that." Colleen stepped into him, and the scent of her soap tickled his nose.

The front door opened, and a footman stepped through, cutting off Max's sharp retort. "Your carriage is here." The boy pointed to the front steps. One of the club's landau's, a study in black and gold with the initial 'S' painted onto the door, waited for them.

Taking Colleen's elbow, Max herded her out the door and down the steps, keeping an eagle-eye for anyone approaching. He tossed her into the carriage, one hand on her hip the other on her lower back. The feel of her warm body, alive and bristling with irritation, soothed the worry that had dug its claws into him ever since he'd fled The Black Rose.

Colleen slapped at his hands. "I'm in already." Flopping onto the plush bench seat, she scowled at him. "We could have just taken my hackney." She peered through the window. "Oh. He left. I owed him another bob."

He climbed in behind her and slammed the door shut. "You thought you would purchase sufficient protection for a bob?"

She scooted to the end of the bench, as far from him as possible. "I don't see how you can act as though you're the injured party. We agreed last night that it would be for the best if our relationship was once again a purely business one. My employer doesn't have the right to reprimand me unless it comes to the administration of The Black Rose."

Max huffed. Agreed? After he'd confessed his crime, Colleen had gone white as a snowdrop flower and told him she could no longer continue with their affair. That she needed time alone to think. He hadn't *agreed* to anything.

Max slid next to her, letting his thigh rest against hers. Needing the contact. "You have every right to hate me. And you have every right to keep me from your bed. But I will keep you safe, even if it goes against your will." Pinching her chin between his thumb and forefinger, he turned her head to look in her eyes. "Is that understood?"

"Would it change anything if I disagreed?"

"It would not."

She jerked her chin from his grasp. "Then it is pointless to say I don't understand."

"Perfectly pointless." On one thing, at least, they could agree. He pounded on the ceiling, and the landau jerked forwards.

They rolled through London, Colleen staring out the half-lowered window. When she finally spoke, Max started.

"I don't hate you." Her voice was barely more than a whisper.

Max swallowed. He wanted to believe her. Needed her forgiveness. "How could you not? I took so much from you."

She twisted, tucking one knee up on the bench to face him. Grabbing his hands, she held them close to her chest. "We all deserve forgiveness for our sins. Don't we? There can't be some mistakes that are irredeemable?" She dug her teeth into her bottom lip. "Can there?"

Max cocked his head. Was she letting him off the hook or asking for forgiveness herself? But then, there was nothing Colleen could have done that would warrant absolution. The greatest sin in her mind was having an affair as an unmarried woman. He didn't want to dismiss her worries but needed to convince her that what they'd done had hurt no one. There was nothing to seek forgiveness for.

"I hope," he said slowly, "that if the harm we caused wasn't intentional, that if we try to do the right thing, that we can atone for anything. And if we haven't hurt anyone by our actions, then I don't think there is anything to ask pardon for."

For men like him, much needed to be forgiven. The line between doing what was right and doing the right thing was blurred and bent. Did the good he and his friends secured override the less desirable methods they employed to achieve it? But on one score he was certain. "For someone like you, someone who leads a decent, solid life, mercy is always available. There is nothing you could do that would be very bad."

She gave him a small smile. "Let's hope you're right." Resting her shoulder against the bench, she sighed. She lowered their joined hands to her lap, and his fingers twitched.

So close to her heat. It was a crazy reaction. But the fear that had pounded through him had to go somewhere. And it turned into lust. He brushed his thumb along her skirt, along a small bump in the fabric that covered the crease where her hip met her thigh. A caress so small she couldn't have felt it.

She shifted her legs. Her head, already so close to his resting on the bench back, dropped to his shoulder. "I don't want to keep you from my bed, any more than you want to leave it." The words were honey-coated whiskey. So sweet, and they started a low burn deep within Max.

More boldly, he palmed her thigh and slid his hand up and down her leg. The landau took that moment to grind to a stop. The footman from The Black Rose opened the door, his forehead clearing when he saw Max and Colleen inside.

"Welcome back, my Lord." The boy reached up to

hand Colleen down, but Max brushed him aside.

Bustling her into the club, he guided her directly to the stairs up to her private rooms. Lucy shouted a question across the room, and he slammed the door at the base of the stairwell in answer. All questions could wait. Colleen had forgiven him. He'd gone to bed the night before believing he'd never taste this woman again, and he'd been given a second chance.

A man didn't waste a second chance.

Colleen pushed his hands off her bum. "I'm moving as fast as I can."

"Not fast enough." He turned her around on the step above him and slung her over his shoulder, enjoying her shriek. Taking the remaining stairs two at a time, he made for her bedroom.

The bottle of brandy and the candles still sat on her bureau. He couldn't wait to tease her body. But first, he needed release. The fire could wait until he was in a clearer state of mind. Impatience and flame were never a good combination.

He tossed her on the bed and grabbed her ankles, dragging her hips to the edge. Her shrieks turned to laughter. Her skirt rode up to her hips, exposing creamy thighs and knee-high stockings. Shucking her boots, he stroked his hand down her calf, danced over the back of her knee, and drew down her stocking. The other bit of silk received the same treatment. When his hands traveled up her bare legs, they didn't stop at her knee.

She jerked when his fingers grazed her sex then let her thighs fall wide. Finding her clit, he rubbed circles around it, loving the way her face flushed and her mouth fell open.

She popped open the buttons of her spencer and flapped the loose ends against her body. "That feels so good."

Pressing his index finger into her channel, he glided along her slick walls. "I can see that. But trust me, it's going to feel better." He knelt and lowered his mouth. Colleen rested her feet on his shoulders, curling her toes into his coat at the first lash of his tongue.

Spreading her lips, Max licked the slick skin inside, lapped at the juices spilling from her opening. With his teeth, he nibbled on her outer lips, tugging at them before returning to her core. He plunged his tongue inside, wishing it were longer, wanting all of her.

"Oh God." Her calves clenched against his ears and released. "Your beard is scratching me."

He lifted his head, brows drawn. "Do you want me to stop?" This damn beard was becoming more cumbersome by the minute.

"No!" Threading her fingers into his hair, she drew him back down. "No, don't stop."

"Hmm." She shivered, and Max vibrated his lips against her sensitive flesh again. Plunging two fingers inside her, he found her clit with his lips and pulled.

Her hips jumped from the bed, her feet digging into his shoulders. Pulling her closer to his mouth, he pinned her in his embrace. Her quim fluttered around his fingers, and his cock throbbed in response, wanting in.

But his fear from that day wasn't forgotten. When Colleen started thrusting her pelvis, when her moans reached a fevered pitch, he pulled his head away.

She flopped to the mattress. "Don't stop!"

"For ten minutes today, I was near out of my mind with panic," he said. "Ten minutes where I imagined the worst. Ten minutes that I couldn't get to St. Katherine's fast enough. I think you owe me for those ten minutes."

She pushed up to her elbows and glared down at him. "What are you jabbering on about?"

"For each of those ten minutes, I'm going to bring you to the edge." A smile stretched across his face. "But not over. Never over. Not until we reach the tenth peak." He lowered his head and paused. "Oh, and by that tenth peak, I'd better have heard an apology for making me worry and a promise you'll never do anything so stupid again."

"Apologize! I will no—oooh." She bounced back on the bed, her whole body going limp as he applied himself back at her opening.

She was utterly delicious. Like smoked honey. He could spend all day feasting between her thighs. Which was a good thing, because he was going to be here awhile. Her legs quivered, her nails dug into his head, and Max pulled back, resting his chin on the edge of the bed.

Colleen cursed with feeling.

"Where did such a proper woman learn such filthy words?" he asked, nuzzling her thigh with his cheek.

"I told you I spent many an afternoon down on the docks accepting our shipments." She rocked her hips into his face. "You pick up things."

Max chuckled. He started in on her again. Each whimper, every curse, made him throb painfully behind his smallclothes. He had to give her credit. By the sixth time he'd brought her to the peak, he thought she would have cracked. It wasn't until her seventh climb, when she was reaching down to bring herself her own relief and he had to trap her hands, that she finally broke.

"I'm sorry! So, so sorry." She writhed and pounded her heels into his shoulders. She landed some solid blows. But not hard enough to make him stop.

"And?" Curling his tongue, he arrowed it in and out of her tight sheath.

"And I won't do it again!"

Planting an open-mouthed kiss on her nub, he smiled, satisfied. "Good girl. Now, only two more climbs, and you'll get your reward."

She wailed, thumping her fists against the mattress. Max remained unmoved. He'd promised her ten, and he was a man who kept his word.

By the time they reached her tenth climb, Colleen was in tears. He took pity, shifting from leisurely swipes to a good, rigorous tongue-fucking. She needed to come, fast and hard. Slipping two fingers into her scalding heat, he curled them, finding that cushion of flesh that drove women mad. He locked his lips around her clit and sucked, and she came with a sob.

Her channel clamped down around his digits, the pressure so strong it crossed his eyes. Unable to wait a minute longer, Max pushed to his feet. He flipped Colleen to her stomach, her legs dangling off the bed, and shoved his trousers and smallclothes down his hips. Lining his straining cock at her opening, he pushed home, into her throbbing heat.

He fisted his hands into the coverlet and dropped his head. He wanted to stay in this woman forever.

Colleen's knot of hair was half undone from all her thrashing, and he pulled out the remaining pins. Combing her hair out along the bed, he bent and pressed a kiss behind her ear. "You doing all right?"

A small sigh escaped her lips. "I'm lovely. Do what you will. I'll just lie here."

Pushing her skirt up to her lower back, he gave her arse a playful pinch. "Are you giving me permission to use your body as I see fit?" He rocked his hips back and thrust deep. "Thank you, love. I think I will."

It didn't take him long to get close. Her core was liquid heat, a velvet glove. Every thrust raised the hair on his arms and sent sensation shooting to the base of his spine. He forced his body to slow. Easing his cock back, he felt every tight clutch of her muscles. Only the tip of him remained in Colleen's body, his shaft shiny with her juices. Digging his fingers into her hips, slowly, so goddamn slowly, he pressed back in, every inch she swallowed him tightening the screws on his control until he was ready to snap.

"What do you say, love?" He covered her back with his chest and bit down on her earlobe. "One more time?" He slid his hand up between her leg and the bed, his fingers questing for her bundle of nerves.

She groaned. "No more. I can't take anymore. Just find your pleasure and be done. This was supposed to be for you."

Max stilled. "What does that mean?"

"Nothing." Wriggling her arse, Colleen glanced back over her shoulder. "It just means I want you to find release. Want to show you that I don't hold any grudges."

He reared up. "Is this some sort of pity fuck, Colleen?"

She tried to push up, but Max kept one hand bunched in her skirts at the small of her back. The other stayed pressed against her clit. "Honestly, do you care right now why I invited you back to my bed? And it's not like I didn't get anything from it. I just wanted you to know, about the fire—"

"A forgiveness fuck then." His chest burned, and bile rose in his throat. He didn't understand his reaction. A fuck was a fuck, no matter what was going on in his manager's head.

He glowered down at her, trying to figure out just what he was feeling. His pulse pounded in his temples and his cock, a strange twin beat. He needed to be guided by his head more, his prick less. This uptight woman of business was getting under his skin, and no good could come from that.

But it was the throbbing in his cock that won out. Swiveling his hips, he slammed back home. Her sheath felt like a hundred greedy tongues licking him all at once. How was a man to resist that?

Pummeling into her, he took her every moan as an affirmation. She thought she could just lie there like some twisted good Samaritan, gifting her body for his release? Like she was too good to find pleasure from his cock, that this was only for him? To hell with that.

Rage. That was what he was feeling. Not usually an emotion he brought to bed. But balls deep, he wasn't going to waste the energy. He'd probably saved her life today; given her a job three months ago when she needed one; even paid off that old flower shop owner so he wouldn't sell before Colleen could pay him. And she was still too bloody good for him? If she thought she could spread her legs, give him a benediction, and be done, she could think again.

His fingers began a soft seduction. Swirling a slow circle around her clit with each thrust of his hips before pinching down on the nub. With his other hand, he pushed her skirt high up her back. Her arse joggled each time he slapped into her, her normally fair skin flushing pink. With his boot, he knocked her legs wider, drove deeper.

Lighting raced along his cock. Gritting his teeth, he dug deep. No fucking way he was going without her. She thought she was wrung out from her edges? She didn't know what being so damn drained from coming and coming until her entire body quivered like one giant exposed nerve felt like. But she would.

Sliding his thumb between the cheeks of her arse, he circled her other opening, rimming the tight muscle there.

Colleen dug her nails into the coverlet, fisting the embroidered fabric. Her small white teeth speared into her bottom lip and her sheath went so tight she nearly forced him out.

"You like that?" he asked. He pummeled into her, his balls drawing tight. Colleen might be better than him. More decent. Have a heart big enough to forgive the unthinkable, and God knew he didn't deserve her forgiveness. Pain stabbed his heart, and his fingers faltered for just a second. Jesus, he didn't deserve her forgiveness and yet she'd given it so freely. But he couldn't think of that now. The enormity of what he'd done, what he'd taken, would swallow him whole.

So, he focused on what made them equal. When his cock was fucking her body. His tongue, his teeth, his fingers. She might rise so far above him in her conduct and integrity and honesty that he couldn't even reach her feet to kiss. But her body came just as hard as his when they screwed. Her surrender was just as true.

His balls slapped her arse. Hooking the tip of his thumb into her tight, rear channel, he let his body go. The bed shook and inched across the floor. Colleen kicked a foot up, her heel hitting his thigh. She tried to claw her way across the bed, but her core clutched at his length, pulling their bodies together.

She arched up, her hair falling down her back, as beautiful as a fiery sunset. He clamped down on her arse, her skin whitening around his fingertips. The soft sucking noise of her body grasping at his echoed in his ears. He grew thicker, harder. Colleen screamed, her channel fisting him hard. And he was done.

Thousands of pinpricks of fire raced up his cock. A pleasure so acute it hurt gathered at his spine and shot through his length. At the last moment, he pulled out, not wanting to leave her milking heat, but with just enough sense left to know he must.

His release spurted across her arse, marking her pink skin. Pulling his thumb from her, Max spread her wide, and speared his cock through her cheeks, drawing out each shuddering jet.

Colleen pressed her face into the mattress and groaned.

Staggering back, he stared at her, arse up, still clothed except for her skirt flung up to her waist. His seed glistened in streaks across her reddened skin. The room was silent except for their breathing.

Buttoning up his falls, Max withdrew a handkerchief from his pocket. With regret, he wiped her clean. Removed his taint. He smoothed down her skirts, shame mixing with his anger. Stepping back, he waited for her censure.

Max was good at reading people. His friends, his enemies. The most minute facial expressions didn't go unnoticed. But when Colleen rolled over and sat up, her emotions were a complete mystery.

She scooted to the edge of the mattress and slid off, her skirt falling into place. Except for her hair falling loose and her feet being bare, she could have been on her way to work. Walking to one of her wardrobes, her stride a bit wobbly, she shrugged out of her spencer and hung it within.

Still without speaking, she made her way to the far side of the bed. The thing had scooted out of place, sitting diagonally to the wall. Leaning her hip into the mattress, she pushed, trying to get it back into position.

Max grabbed the bottom post and pulled it straight.

"Thank you," she said, her voice clipped, as proper as a fucking queen.

Max crossed his arms. "Are we going to talk about this?"

She sat on the bed, her shoulders drooping. "I don't know what I'm doing, Max. I was right before when I said we should remain business associates. We're not right for each other, for so many reasons." She pulled out her pocket watch and gripped it in her hand. "And yet, when we're together, I don't want to think on those reasons. Or worry about the immorality of my actions. I feel like we're going round and round but not getting anywhere."

He sank down beside her. "Where would you like to go?" he asked quietly. Was she asking about his intentions? He wiped his palm on his trousers. Was he ready for a commitment?

Her lips twisted. "Don't look so worried. I'm not expecting you to ask for my hand."

Max frowned at the tone in her voice, like it was the most absurd thing in the world to think of a permanent attachment between them.

"In fact," she added, "it might be just the opposite."

His frown deepened. "What does that mean?"

She rubbed her thumb across the face of the watch before tucking it back in its pocket. "I married when I was quite young. I've only been with my husband, and now you. You've opened my eyes to new experiences and maybe ..." She sucked in a large breath, her chest heaving. She closed her eyes. "Maybe I need to explore more to figure out what I want."

Max clenched his fists. "Are you saying you want to fuck other men?" No bloody way.

Her face blanched. But she didn't deny it.

"From little Miss Morality to an adventuress? That hardly sounds like the Colleen I know."

She knotted her fingers together and pressed them into her lap. "You don't know the real me," she whispered.

"Apparently." He stood, his stomach knotting, turning to stone. "Isn't it fortunate you run a whore-house? Plenty of men available to you. Go find one to fuck and tell me how your explorations fare. See just how well your body responds when it's another man's hands touching you." The second the words were out of his mouth, he regretted them. The last thing he wanted to do was encourage her to find another lover. Have another man trail his fingers down her spine. Squeeze his prick into her tight—

Max's vision blurred. He blinked away the tiny red spots that had formed.

"Perhaps I will." She jumped to her feet and planted her fists on her generous hips.

"Good," he bit out.

"Fine."

One benefit to not undressing to tup, Max didn't need to waste time looking for his clothes before getting the hell out of there. With a curt nod, he stormed from the room and pounded down the stairs. He flung the door open, and it bounced against the wall.

The three-piece band he'd hired was practicing in their raised alcove above the main room. Only a couple girls were out, chatting with the footmen before the customers arrived. A servant walked about with a candle in his hand, lighting the lamps along the wall. The man turned down the hallway to the back rooms, the corridor becoming brighter with each wick he set ablaze.

Molly sidled up to Max, a drink in her hand. She trailed a finger along his sleeve and cocked her head coquettishly. "Greetings, stranger. You're looking awfully tense. Anything I can help you with?"

"Yes." He took her glass and threw back a swallow of port. His tongue twisted at the cloying sweetness. He handed the glass back to her. "Thanks."

"Not quite what I had in mind." Playing with a heavy red stone dangling between her breasts, she raised a plucked brow. "You look like a man with a lot on his mind. Too many worries aren't beneficial to a person's health." She smoothed her palm down his cravat. "I can make you forget. At least for a while."

Rolling onto her toes, she whispered in his ear. "I can take the heat. Anywhere you want to burn me, you can. Anywhere."

Unwillingly, his cock thickened at that invitation. Molly was a beautiful woman, but he'd never played with her before. She was too practiced. Malicious, even. To truly enjoy working with fire, a bond of trust needed to exist between the play partners. Something in Molly's eyes warned she could never be trusted.

"Not tonight. But thank you for offering."

She laughed, a musical tinkle. "So polite. Enough to make a lady wonder."

Max looked back at the stairwell. Would Colleen be coming down tonight? Would she make good on her threat? "Wonder what?"

"If perhaps you might have a longing to try something different. At least for one night." She stroked her hand lower, over his waistcoat. "Haven't you ever wanted to lose yourself, Sutton? Let go of the reins, just for a little bit?" She stepped close, pressing her breasts into his arm. "Let me take control for the night. Relieve you of your burdens. You won't have to think about anything except how hard I make you come."

He grabbed her hand before it dropped lower. Blood pulsed through his length, and he was torn between pressing her palm into his groin and tossing it off of him. He knew what his cock wanted. Finding release in a woman who wanted nothing more than to make him happy. And he couldn't deny that the novelty of taking orders from a domineering woman as skilled as Molly didn't hold its appeal.

But this time, his big head won out. "Afraid not. That doesn't interest me." At least not with a woman he couldn't trust. If Colleen ever wanted to play the strict nursemaid with him, perhaps crack a ruler along his palm, that could be another story.

His stomach sank to his toes. Colleen wouldn't be doing anything with him anymore. His shoulders slumped, and Max desired nothing more than to be alone in his sitting room, with a book in his hand, and a gallon of whiskey by his side. There was another way to forget aside from a back room at The Black Rose, and Max intended to drown himself in it.

Molly shrugged, the wide strap of her gown slipping off her shoulder. Max was sure it had been intentional. "Your loss," she said. "If you ever change your mind, I'll be waiting." She turned. "It's the least I could do for my new employer," she tossed over her shoulder and sauntered away.

Her employer. Max strode from the club. Ignoring the footman, he hurried down the block and hailed his own hackney. Clambering inside, he blew out a breath. At least that was one worry he didn't have about Colleen. She would never have slept with him just because he employed her. Or to try to seduce money and gifts out of him. No, she was so damn honest she informed a wealthy baron, a man who could give her anything she desired, that she wanted to sleep with other men.

He slumped in his seat. He couldn't fault her. Just because his emotions had become involved in their affair didn't mean hers had to. And she was right. She'd only been with two men. How could she know from such a small sampling where her passions truly lie? He'd hoped—

He ground his fist into his thigh. It didn't matter what he hoped.

The carriage rattled towards his home. Large and empty except for his plants and his servants. Colleen deserved better than him. She'd been remarkable enough to forgive his greatest transgression. She was a goddamn saint.

And he was a lonely bastard, still trying to figure out right from wrong. He needed his work with the Crown to end. He'd waded through the swamps of England long enough; he needed to get out before he sank. Once he was home, at his country estate, working with his plants, everything would make sense again. It would be easy to not cross certain lines. Easy to not have to hurt someone for the greater good.

Life would be undemanding. Trouble-free. Simple.

And he would be alone.

Solitude, something he'd always loved, no longer seemed easy.

He'd taken from Colleen, taken something precious.

But she'd taken from him, too. His comfort with seclusion. And he didn't think it was something he'd ever get back.

Chapter Eleven

"Another sodding wasted day." Dunkeld picked up a horseshoe and tossed it at the upright handle of a sledge hammer. It hit the wood and bounced off. "Why won't anyone try to kill this bounder?"

Max and his friends had been following Pinkerton around for hours, waiting for an attack that never came. Montague and Summerset had shadowed the American to his bank and to the docks. Pinkerton had asked about the cost for tickets back to America. Rothchild trailed their man to the butcher and again to the bakehouse. How many baguettes could one man eat? Hoping to draw out an attack, they'd instructed Pinkerton to stroll to the outskirts of town. See if the isolation would inspire an assault.

It hadn't.

The six of them lounged in a blacksmith's hut, its owner called in to tea by his wife. They hadn't been invited. Looking at their dusty, motley group, Max couldn't blame the woman.

Montague took off his hat and wiped his cuff across his forehead. "Pick this up again tomorrow?"

"I'm going to need new shoes if you want me to walk ten miles again tomorrow." Pinkerton sat on a crate, his legs stretched in front of him. He broke off a wedge of bread and chewed.

Dunkeld swiped the baguette from the American. He took a large bite off the end. "You'll walk barefoot if we want you to."

Perched on a sawhorse, Summerset wiped a spot of dirt

from the heel of his white, leather boot with his silk pocket square. "We might be in the country, but must you act like an animal?" He glared at Dunkeld. "Keep your mouth closed when you eat."

Dunkeld opened his mouth wide, showing Summerset the half-chewed bit of bread.

Montague sighed. "Gentlemen, can we focus? Our current plan of attack is leading us nowhere. Any new ideas?"

"Aside from Pinkerton's and Zed's threats against Mrs. Bonner, we don't know what Zed is up to." Max had left men posted around The Black Rose to watch for anyone unknown entering the club. And to follow Colleen if she was daft enough to leave on her own again. "The *Teresa May* should be pulling into port in a day or too. We can try finding Dancer again at The Boar's Head."

Rothchild picked up a stone and flung it against the wall. "I'm tired of being lead around by our noses. My wife still has nightmares because of this arsehole. It's time to put him in the ground."

Montague squeezed Rothchild's shoulder. "It will happen. Be patient."

Dunkeld picked up a large haybale and tossed it over his shoulder like it was nothing. "We're all a bit on edge. Let's say we take a breather." Kicking the gate open, he strode from the hut and flung the bale against the side of the wall. Everyone else drifted out as he stacked two more bales on top. Pulling Pinkerton over by his collar, the Scotsman told him to hold some boards against the stack. Dunkeld wrapped rope around the hay, fixing the wood to the bales.

He wiped his hands. "There. A target."

A smile danced around Montague's lips, and the duke bent down and slid an eight-inch blade from the inside of his Hessians. "Shall we make this interesting? Closest to that knot in the center board wins fifty pounds from the losers?"

"Agreed," Rothchild said. Everyone else nodded.

"Why don't we make it even more interesting?" Dunkeld disappeared into the hut and emerged with a red apple that the smithy had kept in a basket for his shoeing clients to nibble on. "Pinkerton, sit before the boards and we'll put this on your head."

Scowling, the American grabbed the apple and marched back into the hut, slamming the gate shut behind him.

"Humorless fellow, that one." Dunkeld took off his coat and unwound his cravat. "I don't know why we're bothering to keep him alive."

Montague stepped forwards, took aim, and threw his knife. It spun in a tight spiral and sliced into the board, three inches from the knot. "Pinkerton is a victim, too. We can't lose sight of that." He strode forwards and yanked the knife from the wood.

Max took his own knife, a five-inch blade, and threw. The point slid into the wood an inch closer than Montague's. He smiled. Max gestured for Rothchild to step up.

Rothchild shrugged. "I'm not carrying."

Dunkeld pulled out his knife, flipped it over so he held the blade, and presented the handle to Rothchild. "What's mine is yours."

Circling his throwing arm, Rothchild took his place in front of the target. "For the record, Pinkerton has been less than useful." He loosed the knife, and it hit the outside edge of the wood. He grimaced. "Zed must know we're trying to trap him. I think we should send the American on his way."

"I agree. I'm tired of feeding and housing that man," Summerset said, bending to adjust the lace that trimmed his boot. Quick as a whip, he flicked his wrist. His small blade flashed in the sunlight and buried itself on the other side of the knot from Max's mark. "I'm closer."

"Like hell." Max tramped forwards and peered at the boards. "I'm clearly closer." Probably. Shit. Summerset always made it easy to forget. With his ruffled shirts and obscenely bright clothes, it was hard to remember that of all his friends, Summerset was the deadliest. As elegant as a Bengal tiger, and as vicious when provoked.

"No need to bring out the ruler." Yanking an axe from a tree stump, Dunkeld stomped next to Summerset. In one graceful swing, he brought the axe around his shoulder to his back, gripped the handle with two fists, and heaved.

Max dove out of the way, the sound of wood exploding behind him. He rolled onto one knee, panting. "Son of a bitch!" The blade of the axe had severed two boards in half, digging into the hay behind it. The handle quivered with latent energy. The target knot was nowhere in sight.

A wide grin lit up the Scotsman face. "I win."

It was hard to argue with that, although Summerset tried. Max found Summerset's knife and plucked it up. He handed it to his friend. "Concede defeat. I'd say obliterating the knot counts as getting closest." He turned to Dunkeld. "I'll send over a bank draft when I get home."

Summerset grumbled but nodded. With two fingers, he plucked his lime-green handkerchief from his pocket and waved it at Max. "There's a trough of water for the horses over there. You might want to clean yourself up a bit so you don't resemble one."

Rothchild snorted. "I always thought he more resembled a bear. Now one that's rolled around in the muck."

A rumble built in Max's chest, but he smothered it. With a glare at the arseholes who were supposed to be his friends, he brushed out his beard, dirt sprinkling down. Taking his blade, he angled it, trying to catch his reflection. "The beard isn't that bad. Is it?"

Montague coughed discreetly into his fist. "It's a unique look. Makes you stand out in the House of Lords."

"So, you think I should shave?"

"Absolutely," Summerset said.

"I didn't want to say anything," Rothchild demurred.

"About damn time." Dunkeld picked up his axe. He tossed it into the air, let it revolve once, and grabbed the handle. "Your face is as unfashionable as a bit of Haymarket ware at Buckingham Palace."

"You're one to bloody talk!" Fisting his hands, Max glared at the Scot. "No one has had hair that long since Louis Fourteen."

"We'll worry about Dun next," Summerset said.

Damn and blast. First Colleen, now his friends. He tunneled his fingers into the bush and rubbed his jaw. He liked it when Colleen tugged on his beard, drawing his head down for a kiss. But perhaps a clean cheek would be best. He pursed his lips. Since Colleen didn't seem to want to see his face right now, perhaps a new one would soften her.

Decision made. "I'm shaving it off."

"Excellent." Summerset tucked his handkerchief away and clapped his hands together. "Now, my man will not only give you a clean shave but can do something with the rest of your hair, as well."

Max eyed the earl's perfect coif, with two locks artfully coiled at his brow. As pretty as a woman's. "No, thank you."

Dunkeld slapped the flat end of the axe-blade into his palm. "Don't need a valet. I'd be more than happy to take care of it for you myself."

Not liking the glint in the Scotsman eye, Max took a wary step back. "Thanks, Dun. But I've got it covered."

"Nonsense," Montague said. All four men advanced on him. "You can always count on your closest friends to get the job done right."

Bloody hell. Max stepped back, stumbling over a broken wheel discarded in the weeds. His friends saw their advantage and made their move. Max spun on his heel and ran as if his life depended upon it.

Like dogs chasing after a fox, the sots efficiently hunted him down. Their laughter drowned out his fruitless curses.

* * *

"It was a clear question." Colleen rocked back in her chair and laced her fingers across her stomach. She pinned

Molly with a stern stare. "Did you lock Suzy in the necessary and take her standing appointment with Mr. Harper?"

Of all the problems with being the manager for a Venus club, suffering from boredom wasn't one of them. In the last three hours Colleen had fired her wine dealer, freed a couple from the ropes they'd tangled themselves in, and stopped Suzy from tearing out Molly's hair.

She'd been busy putting out fires. Fingering the chain to her pocket watch, Colleen's shoulders sagged. But not busy enough to help her forget the words between her and Max. The anger in his eyes.

"There isn't a lock on the outside of the door to the necessary." Turning in the chair, Molly draped one leg over the chair's armrest, swinging her foot.

"No, but the mop stick through the door's handle did the trick."

Molly looked unperturbed. Stretching her arms up, the girl arched her back. Colleen dropped her gaze from the high, pert breasts pressing through the thin layers of white silk net. She eyed her own breasts. Sturdy. Drooping a bit. Average. And, for a short time, functional. Max hadn't seemed to mind her more used version, but with all the fetching options around here, he was sure to turn elsewhere.

As she wanted him to, Colleen reminded herself. Pushing him away last night by feigning interest in other men had seemed easiest. Easier than admitting to her guilt and seeing the disgust in his eyes. Easier than letting herself indulge in fantasies of a future life between them that could never be. No, it was better to end this now before they grew even closer.

His feelings for her had deepened. He'd revealed that as he'd thundered at her for going to St. Katherine's without him; shown it through the fear in his eyes, the desperate press of his fingers into her skin. And her feelings ... She sighed. Well, their relationship would have to come to an end, and the more intimate they became, the harder it would be. Max deserved better than her.

The bastard hadn't needed to agree with her quite so quickly, however. Even encouraging her to lay with other men.

"The customer didn't complain, did he?" Molly asked, drawing Colleen's attention back to the conversation.

Tossing her quill on the desk, Colleen leaned back. "No. He seemed quite satisfied with the change. But"—she ignored the Cheshire-cat grin spreading across the girl's face—"I won't tolerate that behavior. Do it again and you're out."

Molly shot to her feet and leaned across the desk. "Don't threaten me," she hissed. "If I go, there are many men who would follow me. Many. You'd be wise to remember that."

Colleen's scalp prickled, and she slid her quill off the desk. Molly looked ready to claw her face, and Colleen didn't want anything pointy that could be used as a weapon within reach. Years of living outside the bounds of civilized society had obviously affected this woman. But even though they were in a vulgar business, that didn't mean their behavior had to match it. Colleen wouldn't allow it.

She pushed to her feet, tugging down the hem of her waistcoat. "I do know you're one of the favorites, and you would be missed. But that doesn't mean you're irreplaceable. Now, pull yourself together, watch your tone, and let's try this again, shall we? Interfering with the other girls' customers will not be allowed. I will protect their right to make a living, just as I would yours. Try to behave in a manner that you would like to be treated and we will have no problems. Agreed?"

Molly's pretty mouth twisted in a scowl, but she was smart. She knew when to back down. In a fashion. "Of course, my liege." She flounced to the door. "I guess the rumors weren't true. Anyone who was taking that strapping man's cock couldn't be so unbearably miserable."

"What?" Heat clawed up Colleen's neck. "What rumors?"

The brunette looked back over her shoulder. "The girls thought you and our new owner were having relations, as you might say. They thought your prim-and-proper act was just that; an act. But now that I think on it, I should have known it wasn't true."

Colleen licked her lips. "Shouldn't you have?"

"No." Molly leaned against the doorjamb and crossed her arms under her chest. "Aside from the fact you're much too tedious to let loose, Sutton's behavior would have proved the rumor false. Just last night when we were"—she flashed her teeth—"together, I could tell how tense and unhappy he was. He isn't the picture of a man who is sexually satisfied." She laughed. "I'd hate to think you were a mediocre screw, not when you're surrounded by so many good examples of how to please a man." She winked. "In any event, I'll let the girls know they were wrong about you and the baron, shall I?"

"Please," Colleen said faintly.

With a waggle of her fingers, Molly was gone. Colleen slumped into her chair and buried her face in her hands. She didn't know which was worse. The gossip about her debauchery or the knowledge that Max had jumped in someone else's bed so soon after hers.

No, she knew which was worse. Even though she'd wanted Max to move on, his actions still lanced her like a betrayal.

Molly could be lying, of course, spiteful little thing that she was. But even if Max hadn't lain with her last night, it would soon happen. If not with Molly, with someone else. Colleen rubbed her temples, but the low throb didn't dissipate. Couldn't he have at least waited until this business with Zed was over and she'd moved out of The Black Rose? So she didn't have to see him with another woman?

She took deep, calming breaths. She had a business to run, and no time to concern herself over such frivolities like the piercing ache behind her breastbone. Her feelings were of little consequence. Colleen rose and exited her office. When she pushed out into the club's main room, her shoulders were square and her chin held high. The burn prickling at her eyes she could do little about.

Lord Halliwell was across the room, a girl sitting on his lap. He looked up and down Colleen's standard uniform, and his eyes lit up.

At least someone found her superior to the other women. Colleen gave him a polite nod and turned away. She found Lucy in the entrance hall, chatting with a footman.

"Can I speak with you a moment?" Colleen asked.

"Of course." Lucy followed her to the cramped office off the kitchens. "Did I do anything wrong?"

"No." Colleen gave the girl a warm smile. Lucy was the one club worker who didn't give her trouble. "I've been giving you some added tasks around here lately, and I'm wondering how you find them. Do you enjoy the additional responsibility?"

Lucy blinked. "Yes. I think I do." She sat back on the broken table they used as a desk. "Although, additional tasks should come with additional pay, don't you think?"

Colleen kept her smile to herself. A woman of business after her own heart. "That is something we can discuss. If you were to formally take the position of assistant manager, a new salary can be negotiated."

The girl's jaw dropped, her eyes growing wide. "Assistant manager?! Are you in earnest?"

"Yes. I won't be manager here forever, and when I leave, I think you might make a good replacement." Colleen's heart pinched. When she left, she'd never see Max again. "It will give you a hiring advantage if you have experience as the assistant. It will be a lot of work—"

Her words were wrung out of her on a gasp as Lucy threw her arms around Colleen and squeezed tight.

"Thank you, thank you, thank you!"

Colleen laughed and patted the girl on the back. "I take it you'd be interested in the position?"

Lucy pulled back, her eyes damp. "You have no idea how much. I never thought I could be anything more than ... well, you know." She dropped her head.

Colleen paused and examined the girl. All the women had seemed so content in their positions. This was the first glimpse she'd seen that even though they lived more comfortably than most Cits, and pocketed more in a night from their wages and gifts than Colleen had seen in a month at her and her husband's clock shop, that the women might want for more.

"Are you unhappy here?" she asked gently.

"No." Lucy smoothed down her skirts. "This situation is much better than what I grew up in, and I'm very grateful. But I'd like a husband. A family. And I don't know any man who'd be happy with his girl doing this. At least, no man I'd want."

"Well"—Colleen pulled a ledger from a shelf over the desk—"if you'd rather spend tonight tallying our kitchen's inventory and figuring out what we need to order for next week, the job is yours. But we won't be reordering from our wine supplier." She frowned. "I need to find a new one."

Opening the ledger, Lucy ran her index finger down the column of numbers. "Why? Mr. Landry has sold to us for years."

"Well, he's either been cheating you for years or decided to try his tricks with a new manager, thinking I wouldn't get wise to his deception." Colleen's conversation with the man still left her unsettled. He'd been patronizing and ingratiating in equal measure and completely shocked when she'd shown him the door. Irritating man. "I discovered the wine he'd delivered had been watered down."

"Huh." Lucy bit the inside of her cheek and stared into space.

"What?"

She shook herself. "Nothing. I'm sure it's nothing."

"But ...?" Colleen shut the door, needing to suck in her stomach as she squeezed it past her body and a cabinet. "My assistant manager needs to keep me apprised on what happens in the club, even if it is only suspicions."

"I saw Molly leading Mr. Landry to one of the back rooms a couple of weeks ago." Lucy shrugged. "I would have thought that with the money we pay him, plus the added incentive of Molly's company, that he would have taken extra care to treat The Black Rose well. I'm surprised is all." Sniffing, she perched on the upside-down amphora they used as a stool and moved a candle closer to the ledger on the desk. "I shouldn't be surprised, however. Greed knows no limits."

Colleen's stomach churned. "Very true." Certainly, her greed hadn't. Her greed hadn't been for more money or a better life than the common Cit. But she'd been greedy, nonetheless. She'd been tired of the sterility of the clock shop, of her marriage, and desperate for change. She'd prayed for change. Begged God for it.

And he'd punished her for her dissatisfaction by giving her what she'd asked for.

She'd stared at her home as it was being devoured by fire, and she'd thought that her husband would now have to change his mind. That he would want to run the flower shop with her. Escape from the gears and springs, from the endless ticking of a hundred clocks. She'd stared at her life as it burned, and she'd been happy.

She'd been happy until it had been hours and her husband still hadn't returned home. Until the next day when she'd been told his body had been found in their bed. When she'd realized that her carelessness hadn't been a gift from Heaven but retribution.

And when Max had pressed her into service at The Black Rose, she'd thought it naught but further punishment. That it was her lot to be surrounded by depravity and immorality.

Lucy scratched her head with the tip of a bit of lead as she examined the ledger, her face alight. Colleen watched her, her throat tight. She'd judged Lucy unfairly for her profession. But the girls here were supporting themselves in honest work. A simple business transaction where no one was hurt. If her cousin hadn't taken her in after the fire, if Max hadn't given her this job, what depths would she have sunk to survive? Colleen wasn't fit to judge anyone.

"Lucy ..." She hesitated. "How did you get involved in this? You're smart, sensible. Surely there were other options."

Lucy looked up and blinked. "Other options? Maybe. But at fifteen I couldn't think of any. It was either this or starve. And I didn't want to starve."

Grasping her hands together behind her, Colleen leaned back against the door. "Of course not. But ... you seem so happy. Isn't it difficult, what you do? I mean, with how society views the profession, isn't it hard to, I don't know, to face yourself in the mirror each day?" She was fumbling for the right words, but it seemed important that she know. At some point these women had taken an irrevocable step across a line society drew, yet they all managed to laugh and find joy in their lives. Colleen had done worse. It had been an accident, but worse just the same. If these women could find peace with their actions, mayhap Colleen could move past her guilt, too.

Lucy carefully closed the ledger and put her elbows on the table. "My first time, I worked at another house, nowhere near as grand as this. There, you were lucky to have clean sheets on the bed each night. I cried after every man for three days." She clenched her fists, her knuckles going white. "But at some point, you grow up. You can't live life second-guessing your every move. Berating yourself over every mistake. And at the end of the day, you realize, it isn't that big a deal. Just one body part slipping into another. If a man wants to pay for that, I'm happy to oblige him. And once you realize letting a man rut between your legs isn't the be all end all that we're raised to believe, it all becomes easier. Each man becomes easier. We all do what we have to survive. It's not something I'm proud of or ashamed of. It just is."

Colleen nodded slowly. Lucy had always seemed young. All the girls did. But they weren't girls. They were women, probably just a year or two shy of Colleen's age. And Lucy had experiences and wisdom Colleen couldn't match. Perhaps instead of giving the orders all the time, Colleen should listen a little more. She might learn something.

"Thank you for your candor." Colleen fingered the chain of her pocket watch. Her last link to her past. "I'll tell the other women to arrange the schedule without you tonight. Let me know if you have any questions." She slid out the door, closing it softly behind her.

Her mind a muddle, she plodded to the main room. One of the candles in the large chandelier was out, but she didn't think anyone else would notice. Everyone else's attention was on seeking joy. Pleasure. She'd had a brief glimpse into that world, reached unbearable heights, but once again she was a spectator looking in. It didn't matter that it had been of her own choosing in order to save Max and herself from certain heartache. Colleen had never felt more alone.

A glass of champagne was lifted to her face. Colleen blinked, and the face of Lord Halliwell came into focus behind the glass. He pressed it into her hand. "You look like you need this, my dear. Are the books not balancing tonight?"

She sniffed at her glass, and tiny bubbles tickled her nose. What the hell? She tossed it back. "Not everything is about numbers for me, my lord." Rolling her head, she tried to loosen the knot that had taken up residence where neck met back. "I hope you are having a pleasant evening?"

"It could be better." He snagged another flute from a passing serving girl and handed it to Colleen. "The number one attraction to this club has so far been out of my reach."

She frowned down at her glass. Men. Hoping to use alcohol to do the persuading for them. She wasn't the sort to drown her troubles. Drinking to excess only led to more problems. If she was going to make a mistake, she would do it sober.

But another tiny sip wouldn't hurt.

"The Black Rose has many attractions more alluring than me." She looked up at the earl. "I think you persist in your pursuit only for the challenge I present."

"Perhaps." Swirling an amber liquid around in his snifter, Halliwell shrugged. "But I must confess that your natural authority appeals to me much more than a performance put on by a doxy. Is that so wrong?" He stared at the floor, the tips of his ears turning red. "Do you find my interests so repellent?"

Scuffing the toe of his boot through the thick pile carpet, the earl looked very much like the wayward little boy he wanted to pretend to be. But he was sincere. And more endearing than she'd ever noticed.

Resting her palm on his sleeve, she squeezed. "You don't repel me. And there is nothing wrong with wishing to cede control to someone else for a bit." After all, that was what he truly wanted. An authority figure to tell him what to do, to tell him right from wrong. Give someone else power over his actions.

She understood how freeing that could be. Allowing Max to play with her had shown her that. A pulse pounded in her throat. That was over with now. She'd kicked him from her bed, and he was moving on to other partners. The back of her throat ached. If she were smart, she'd do the same.

"Mrs. Bonner, I don't want to assume." Halliwell shifted closer. "But it sounds as though your feelings have changed. Would you consider spending some time with me in one of the rooms? We'd go only so far as you're comfortable with. You'd make the decisions."

She jerked her head back. "My lord, you must know

how out of place I feel with all"—she flapped her hand at the room—"this. I may not think it as wrong as I used to, but I couldn't ... I wouldn't know how ..."

He stared into his snifter. "Of course. I didn't mean to presume."

If she were smart, she'd do the same.

Her feelings for Max had deepened as their intimacies had progressed. Was that a result of their physical relationship or solely due to the man Max was? He'd moved on, treating his affairs as though they were nothing more consequential than sharing a dance with a woman. If she ... joined with another man, could that be the means of lessening her attachment to Max? The thought of lying with Lord Halliwell turned her stomach, and she pressed her hand into her abdomen.

Each man becomes easier. Lucy had no issue separating out her emotions from the act of sexual congress. It was just one body part going into another, as the girl had said. Repetition seemed to be the key for diminishing the significance of the act for Lucy. She developed no tender feelings for her customers. She remained untouched by heartache when a client turned to another woman.

It seemed only sensible that Colleen should at least attempt to exorcise Max from her heart. She couldn't spend the rest of her life aching for a man she could never have. She chewed on her lip. Perhaps, if she told Max the truth—

She cut that thought off before it flowered. There would be no forgiveness from Max. No understanding. She wouldn't expect it for her crime. And she couldn't pursue a relationship with him without telling him the truth. Keeping something like that from the man she loved would eat at her every day. So, her choices were either live alone for the rest of her life while pining for the baron or do something to restore her peace. She gave a small nod. It was only practical.

She stepped closer to Halliwell and a wave of dizziness swamped her. She swayed on her feet. What was she doing? She was an unmarried woman, She'd only sinned with Max because, well, it was Max, and she loved him. It hadn't felt wrong to be in his arms. And what would Max think if he ever found out?

Plenty of men available to you. Go find one to fuck and tell me how your explorations fare.

She rolled her shoulders back and straightened her spine. She loved Max, God help her. And he'd told her to fuck another man. He'd been angry and hurt at the time, but he'd said the words just the same. And he hadn't taken them back, even though hours had passed and emotions had cooled. He'd taken his own advice, found another partner, and it only remained for her to do the same.

Colleen swallowed. Halliwell wasn't bad looking. His chin was a little weak, his hair a bit thin across the crown of his head. But his eyes were kind. Rather sad, like a hound dog's. If she were to let anyone touch her, to try to rid herself of the memory of Max, she could do no better than a gentle man like the earl.

She slugged back her second glass. The rush of alcohol didn't change her decision. But the slight spin in her head made the words easier to speak. "Yes. If you still wish it, meet me in the Emerald Room in ten minutes." Her mouth was as dry as a desert, and she eyed Halliwell's whiskey enviously. "I can't promise you'll get what you want from me. I have no practice in this sort of thing. But I'm willing to try."

His eyes lit up. Grabbing her hand, he pressed it to his lips. The man's obvious delight made her more resolved in her decision. She didn't know if this would help her get over Max, but at least it would bring one person happiness. There was something satisfying in being the instrument that brought joy.

"Mrs. Bonner, I am all that is grateful." He rubbed his hands together and rocked onto his toes. "I can follow you to the room now."

"Ten minutes." It would take that long to gather her

nerve. "I assume you have a watch and know how to tell the time?"

Halliwell nodded, an excited pup.

Colleen pursed her lips. Telling a man what to do shouldn't be too difficult. Not if he was as eager to please as the earl. "No earlier. No later. I'll be waiting."

Spinning on her heel, she forced her feet to keep an even pace. No need to flee. She would be in charge. She spoke with the other girls, informing them that Lucy was out for the night and that the Emerald Room was booked. Colleen got more than one raised eyebrow, but it made no matter. The rumor mill would have fresh grain to chew upon, of that Colleen had no illusions.

Her footsteps were muffled as she trod the hallway to the back room. Blood pounded in her temples and her heart raced. Placing a palm on the wall, she closed her eyes and took a deep breath. The paper-hanging felt rough beneath her skin. She could go to her office and run a price analysis of what it would cost to cover the walls in a nice silk damask. Or even a sumptuous leather. Solid work that didn't involve disrobing in front of a near stranger. What on earth was she doing? Proving something to herself? Or to Max?

Pushing in the door to the Emerald Room, she shuffled through and pressed it closed. She rested her shoulder blades against the wood and let her head thud back. She could do this. Just one body part going into another. And once she understood there was nothing sacred to the act, it was nothing but physical sensation, her attachment to that infuriating man would disappear.

Pushing off the wall, she crossed to a low bureau made of a Brazilian teak. She'd chosen this room because of its normalcy. It looked like the bedroom in a grand house. The walls were covered in a cream paper hand-painted with delicate strands of ivy. The bed was a four-poster mahogany, large and sturdy. The coverlet was a hunter green, matching the thick carpet. The large mirrors on the wall across from the foot of the bed, and on the ceiling above it, were disconcerting. But at least there were no cupboards full of whips or paddles. No hooks along the ceiling or walls. She could pretend she was a normal woman, inviting a lover into her home.

She slid open the bottom drawer and examined the negligees that lay folded within. None of the frothy concoctions appealed, but she'd have to come out of her clothing eventually, and she didn't want Halliwell disrobing her. She chose a white silk robe with large red poppies printed across it and quickly changed. Folding her own clothes neatly, she stacked them on an armchair, tucking her boots beneath.

She curled her toes into the plush carpet. She still had a couple of minutes but didn't know what to do with them. She drummed her fingers along the top of the bureau. This wasn't significant. She was among a group of women who slept with a different man every night with no ill consequences. And she was now a widow. Such liberties were more accepted for widows.

Bile rose in her throat. Was she mad? She didn't have to lay with another man to move past Max. Her love would lessen in its own time. She'd move out of The Black Rose, hopefully into the apartments above the flower shop, and she'd never see the man again. Her attachment would gradually fade and she'd have her flowers, bursting with colors and fragrances, to gladden her spirit.

Colleen pressed her palms into her eye sockets, fighting against the tears. The flower shop had started as a beautiful dream. It now seemed sad and hollow.

When the door swung silently open it was almost a relief. The tumble of thoughts rolled to a stop, and all she was left with was the slippery feeling of dread.

Halliwell stepped through, two more glasses of champagne in his hands. He kicked the door closed. "In case we get thirsty." Holding the flutes up, he strode forwards then jolted to a stop, champagne sloshing over the rims. "You changed."

She fingered the collar of the robe. "Yes. Something easier to slip out of."

"I liked the waistcoat and"—he motioned to his neck—"the high collar." His eyebrows drew together. "This looks all wrong."

Of course. Colleen bunched the silk robe in her fists. He liked the idea of a stern disciplinarian, and she came to him like a mistress. This is why her girls were paid well. Playing a role was harder than it looked.

She set her shoulders. "My attitude doesn't change with my clothes. If you want the discipline of your nursemaid, I assure you I can do that just as well in a robe. Just pretend I've caught you out of bed after we'd gone to sleep."

A smile lit up his face, and it was in that moment Colleen knew she couldn't go through with it. She gripped the sides of her robe, pulling them more tightly across her body. Halliwell looked so happy, and she was more miserable than the day of her husband's funeral. There was only one man she wanted touching her. And it would be better to go a lifetime without Max than to try to replace him with a poor substitute.

Now she only needed to figure out how to get out of this situation without angering one of the club's most high-spending members. "Lord Halliwell—"

"Gussie."

"Er, yes, Gussie." She cleared her throat. "I was thinking perhaps to find another girl to join us. Someone a bit more experienced." And someone who could take over as Colleen quietly slipped from the room.

He narrowed his eyes. "I want you. You're not changing your mind now, are you?"

"Of course not." She tried for a light laugh. It came out sounding like the honk from an untuned organ. She wiped her palms on her hips. Think. She'd see Molly take charge of men several times. It couldn't be that difficult. Sometimes ... sometimes she never even touched them.

The edges of Colleen's lips curved up. That was it. Make Halliwell happy by bossing him around a bit and keep herself happy by never letting him touch her. Her customer would be satisfied and wouldn't quit the club in anger, and she, well, she'd rather be up in her rooms with a cup of tea, but this alternative was acceptable.

She blew out a breath. She could do this. "Now," she said, searching her mind, "you've been quite naughty. You need to promise that when I say it is bedtime that you will stay abed." She cringed. Never had she sounded such a fool.

Halliwell lowered his head. "Yes, Nanny."

The bile rose in her throat again. That sounded all kinds of wrong. This wasn't going to work if she had to hear him calling her nanny. "I think it best you don't talk to me." She needed to end this quickly. Berate him a bit, tell him to find his own pleasure because a nanny would definitely *not* be a party to that act, and escape. As easy as balancing the ledger.

Shuffling to the bed, she gripped a post and stared over Halliwell's head. "Take off your clothes." What would a toff's nanny do? Have him say his prayers? Tell him a bedtime story when he was tucked up under the covers?

"Don't you want to help me disrobe?" She heard him set the glasses of champagne down. "My nanny used to always help me undress and give me a sponge bath."

She kept her eyes fixed on the far wall. "Yes, well, I'm a different sort of nanny. I think the less we look upon each other, the better."

"Why don't you just wear a blindfold and be done with it?" he asked petulantly.

She arched an eyebrow and considered. Not having to see him as he took care of himself would be a definite bonus. Plugging her ears when the time came also wouldn't go amiss. "That's an excellent idea. I'll do that." She hurried past him to her folded clothes and removed her handkerchief. She folded it in half as she scuttled back to the bed. "When you've undressed, stand in the corner and, uh, think about all the naughty things you've done today." She wrapped the kerchief around her eyes and tied it behind her head. Darkness enveloped her, and she took her first full breath. She could handle this without seeing him.

She sat on the bed and scooched back until her knees hit the mattress and her feet swung free. "Are your clothes off yet? If there's water in that pitcher on the bureau, give yourself a quick rubdown. Oh! And say fifty Hail Mary's. While crossing yourself. You've been extra bad today."

"Fine," he muttered.

She bobbed her feet. This wasn't so bad. Even a bit diverting, if she did say so herself. She might have a real talent at this sort of thing. The Hail Mary's were most likely the wrong religion for the earl, but he could have had a French nanny.

Should she try to fake an accent?

Her lips silently formed the words 'Mon Dieu' and 'oui oui'. Did she know any other French words? Lucy could probably teach her some good ones. A cool draft brushed her back and she shivered. Fabric rustled, and she wondered if she should yell at him for disrobing so slowly. There was a thump, another, and she figured his boots had hit the floor.

"Are you putting your things away?" Hmm. That accent came out sounding more Germanic than French. She tried again. "Good boys need to be tidy?" She stretched out her legs, pointing her toes. Much better.

A strong fist gripped her ankle and pulled her bum to the edge of the mattress. She fell onto her back with a shriek, the mattress bouncing beneath her.

He slid his palms up her calves and pulled her legs apart.

"Lord Halliwell!" She pushed up onto one hand and shoved his hard chest. Frowning, she poked him a couple more times. His chest was suspiciously firm. And so were his shoulders, and his biceps ...

She sucked in a breath. She knew these muscles. And those hands on her legs ... She knew the calluses on those palms.

Hope sparked in her heart. The contact was so familiar. It couldn't be from the milksop earl. Her thoughts jumbled and tears welled behind her eyelids. Somehow, Max had removed the earl from the room. It must have been those two thumps she'd heard.

She should push him away. Stay true to her resolve that their separation now would be for the best. But she couldn't. Not when he touched her.

She trailed her hand up his neck, eager to cup his cheek and bring him in for a kiss. And froze. She rubbed her thumb back and forth over his jaw.

His smooth, clean-shaven jaw.

She kicked her legs, hitting something solid, and leapt across the bed to escape Halliwell's touch. Dragging off the blindfold, she blinked at the brightness. "I'm sorry, but I can't—"

"Can't what?" The man standing next to the bed was shockingly new. A face she'd never seen before, had only imagined. "Tell me, you little fool, what is it exactly that you can't do?"

Chapter Twelve

Colleen could only gape. It was most definitely her baron glaring down at her. He was without a coat or cravat, his white shirt draping loosely around his frame. His broad shoulders heaved with pent-up emotion. His pine-green eyes glittered with anger. But his face ...

"What happened to your beard?"

He rubbed a palm across his bare jaw. "I shaved. Didn't want to look like a goat." A muscle twitched in his cheek. "But I guess I needn't have bothered. Not if you're going to spread your legs for any man that strikes your fancy."

Her relief was short-lived. Colleen sucked in a breath. "You told me to look for other men!"

"I didn't think you were stupid enough to actually do it!" He shook his head. "Halliwell? Truly? I must say that disappointed me."

"Lord Halliwell at least is a kind man." She climbed onto the bed on her knees and shuffled forwards, jabbing at the air with her index finger. "Not like that shrew, Molly, that you tupped. You don't get to judge me."

He crawled onto the bed and prowled towards her on his hands and knees, as sinuous as a leopard. "I've never bedded, or played, with that woman."

"Oh." That brought Colleen up short. That shrew *had* lied.

Quick as a snake, he grabbed her behind her knees and flipped her to her back. His body covered hers, pinning her down. "Can I judge you now?"

The front of her robe gaped open, and the starch of his

linen shirt tickled her skin. Unbidden, she arched into him, her body demanding the contact even as her head yelled at her to stick to her resolve. She'd had good reasons for ending their relationship. Reasons that protected both Max and—

He took her mouth, stealing her will. All her arguments scattered before his onslaught. Max was kissing her. She knew it was wrong, that it would be better if she moved on from him, but couldn't find it within herself to care.

Wrapping her arms around his back, she returned his kiss. Opening her mouth, she tangled her tongue with his. Each slide sent a delicious chill rippling down her back. He nipped at the tip of her tongue, then suckled, and she melted into the mattress. Max lay heavy on her, his weight comforting, delicious. She needed to feel more of him and she slapped at his shoulder until he gave her the space to pull an arm free from her robe. He tore the garment from her body then pressed her back into the bed. Grabbing her wrists, he locked them into the coverlet by her head. He took hold of her bottom lip between his teeth and pulled his head back, abrading the swollen flesh, until her lip released with a pop.

"You're a fool." Max pinned her with a glare.

"Yes." She was a fool. She was willing to ignore the knowledge that their future could only end in heartbreak in order to stay in his arms in the present.

"I don't own your body." He nipped at her collarbone. "I can't forbid you from offering yourself to other men." His clenched jaw showed just how unhappy he was by that fact. "But I'm damn sure going to make it so you'll never want to again."

"I didn't want to then," she admitted. Burying her nose in the hollow where his neck met his shoulder, she breathed Max in. "I'd changed my mind and decided not to go through with it. I was only going to boss him around a bit and then leave." She cupped his cheek and stared into his eyes. "I couldn't let him touch me. I only want you."

His eyes glittered and his body went still. Only his chest heaved. "Truly?"

"Truly," she whispered.

Dropping his head, he pressed his lips to her collarbone and breathed out a shuddering breath. Then his lips spread in a wide smile against her skin.

He raised up, bracketing her hips with his knees. "Now that we've got that sorted"—he gazed hotly down her body—"whatever shall we do?"

Her nipples puckered under his examination, and she restlessly rubbed her thighs together. "Well, for what I have in mind, you are wearing altogether too many clothes."

"That is something I can remedy." He brushed his mouth against hers before rolling off the bed. He shucked his shirt, the light from the gas lamps flickering off the bronze skin of his back. His boots and pants quickly followed.

Colleen bit her bottom lip. The man was perfection. Every inch of him hard and chiseled. Shadow and light played along the planes of his corded thighs, the rise of his tight behind. She reached out a hand, needing to feel him, but he stepped away, leaving her hand outstretched and empty.

Striding to the bureau, Max pulled a taper from a three-pronged candelabra. He lifted the glass cover off an oil lamp on the wall and lit the candle from the flame. He turned, and Colleen's breath caught in her throat.

Every time she saw him she never failed to have a reaction. His length jutted from the soft nest of dark hairs, semi-hard, but long and thick. Unabashed, he stalked towards her, his cock bobbing. When he reached the bed, she stretched her hand out again and gently cupped him.

Max let her explore. Wrapping her fingers around him, she fisted him down to his base. Achingly slowly, she slid her hand up and rubbed her palm over his crown. Her hand came away sticky.

"On your back," he ordered.

Colleen rolled and scooted to the middle of the bed. Her fingers tingled with excitement, and her gaze tracked every flicker of the candle's flame.

"I don't have a torch available to bounce the flame off of you, but there is a bottle of brandy on the side table." Max traced a pattern on her stomach with his index finger, her skin fluttering wherever he touched. "I would love to paint a pattern on your skin with the alcohol. Then see it come to life with flames."

She froze. "You want to actually set me alight? Not just touch me with the flame?"

Max sat next to her, shifting close. "Yes. Brandy burns at a low temperature. It will ignite, the flames streaking across your body along the path I create, warming your skin just until you start to squirm before I smother the flames." His voice was low and dusky. With the back of his fingers, he caressed the swell of her breast. "It is the purest expression of trust between a man and a woman that I know."

If he had plunged a dagger in her heart it couldn't have hurt more. She closed her eyes and fought against the tears. He trusted her. Enough to want to share this most intimate act.

And she was lying to him.

She understood what he meant. There was no way she could keep her walls, stop him from seeing straight into her heart, if she opened herself up to Max and his fire. She would be completely exposed.

It was something she desperately wanted. And something she couldn't allow. The look in Max's eyes as he gazed upon her was too precious. She couldn't lose it. Not yet.

"No." She shook her head. "I'm sorry, but no. I'm not ready for that." Would never be ready.

His Adam's apple bobbed up and down. Without his beard, Colleen could read him so much more easily. At that moment, she wished she couldn't. She hated to see his disappointment.

"No need to apologize," he said. "I understand. You need to completely trust the person holding the candle."

Her lungs squeezed tight. "I do trust you. Just ..."

"Not enough for this."

Jackknifing up, Colleen rolled to her knees and cupped his smooth cheek. "I trust you more than anyone. But I don't think I can let someone actually set me on fire. For me, that's a step too far. Please understand."

He turned his face, pressing a kiss into her palm. "I do. And I would love nothing more than to paint your body with wax from this candle. If that still appeals to you, lay back. If it doesn't, I'm happy to blow out every damn flame and take you in the dark. I'll take you any way I can get you."

Colleen's throat grew thick. Pressing her lips to his neck, she felt the strong beat of his blood pulsing through his body. No man had ever said anything so dear to her, and she would treasure the words forever.

"Keep the candle." She rolled back and stretched her hands to the headboard. "Make me squirm."

Max crawled over her. "My favorite job." Keeping the candle held aloft, Max worshipped her body with his mouth. His lips tickled the hollow of her throat. His teeth scraped along her ribs. Everywhere he touched was a tease, a nip, a lave. By the time he was done, her skin was so sensitive, it felt as though only the thinnest threads held her together.

She reached for him. "Come here."

He shook a finger and pushed her hands back. "Open up," he said, nudging her jaw.

Brows lowered, she opened her mouth, and he stuck the taper into it. She squawked around it.

"Just one second." Laughter filled his voice as he took the belt of her robe and tied her wrists together. He knotted the end of the sash around the truss of the headboard.

She glared at him around the candle, feeling as absurd as she must have looked.

He plucked the taper from her mouth. "Thanks."

"That was disgusting." She licked the pillow next to her, trying to scrape off the taste of wax.

"But it accomplished what I wanted." Straddling her body, he sat down, the hair on the back of his thighs tickling her hips. "Now, be a good girl and thrash around a bit." One side of his mouth curled devilishly up, and he tipped the candle. A drizzle of white wax rained down on her left breast.

The heat shocked her, and she jerked. Making his smile deepen. "Fiendish bastard."

"Guilty as charged." Her other breast received the same treatment, and Max bent low to blow a soothing stream of air across the abused flesh. He kissed the underside of her breast then licked a path around the crease. "Have I told you how much I adore your breasts? They are quite extraordinary."

Rubbing her thighs together, Colleen let out a shuddering breath. "No different than other women's. Maybe a little bigger." And riding lower than other women's, like Molly's. But Colleen couldn't ever remember Max looking on Molly with any sort of appreciation. Never the way he looked at Colleen. So perhaps there was truth to his words; that he did esteem Colleen's body more highly. Dear, foolish man.

"Plump and soft and mine." He twirled a nipple between his thumb and forefinger, gradually increasing the pressure. "It's that 'mine' part that I like best of all."

She gasped. The bite of pain sent a corresponding tug deep in her core. Releasing her nipple, he sucked it into his wet mouth, soothing the sting away. Only to drizzle searing wax over the reddened nub.

Colleen's mind fractured. Her body tried to twist from the sting even as her sex grew slick with wanting. Colleen pulled at the silk band. "Oh, God. Max, please."

He smiled and slid lower on her body. He circled her belly button with his tongue and plunged that naughty muscle into her navel.

She arched her back, not understanding how every flick of his tongue in that most innocuous of places could make her core twinge. It was though there were a string attached from her belly button to her center. Every flick of his tongue made the string vibrate, sending small shock waves to her most intimate flesh.

She'd never loved her belly button more.

Raising his head, Max tipped the candle, and a splash of wax filled the hollow of her navel. It burned hot, almost painfully, before banking into a comforting warmth.

Colleen closed her eyes and sagged into the bed. She was done struggling against the sensations. Her body had tensed before each drip of wax, and after each assault tried to sort through the sensations, organize them into pain or pleasure. It was exhausting.

Her mind drifted, a lovely haze settling in her brain. Peace descended. No more anticipation. No more fight. Max blazed a trail of wax from her navel to the top of her cleft, and her skin welcomed the burn. Accepted whatever he meted out.

The mattress dipped, and Max spread one of her legs wide, then the other. He settled in between. "I missed you last night." The soft pad of his tongue licked between her folds.

Colleen let her thighs fall wider. "I know what you missed."

He nipped at her outer lip. "When I tell you I missed you, take me at my word." Circling his tongue around her opening, he eased the tip into her sheath. He fucked her with his mouth, slow and thoroughly.

"Yes, Max." She would believe anything he had to say at the moment.

"Hmmm." The vibrations of that sound thrummed across her aching skin, and she moaned softly. He lapped at her essence. "I like it when you're compliant."

Bending her knees, she dug her toes into his sides. "Yes,

Max."

She needed more. The baron was the type of man to enjoy a stroll on a country lane. Colleen just wanted to cut across the fields and get to her destination. His unhurried manner was one of his more annoying characteristics.

He spread her folds with his fingers, and his breath ghosted across her moist flesh. As delicate as a cat, he licked her clit.

Colleen bit her lip. His tongue was like velvet: luxurious and soothing one moment and irritating the next when brushed against the grain. It drove her mad and had her begging for more.

She had no warning. One moment his tongue was coiling around her clit like she was his favorite lemon ice, and the next the hiss of wax hitting wet skin sizzled through the air, followed quickly by searing heat. Directly on her tender bundle of nerves.

She arched off the bed. She would have hit the mirrored ceiling if her hands hadn't been bound to the headboard. Her clit throbbed, pulsing angrily. The beat pounded in time with her heart, filled her ears, until the pain softened to a pleasing ache that spread throughout her body. "Max!" She didn't know if her exclamation was a reprimand, a plea, or plain shock. Most likely a combination of all three. Her eyes flew open to see the taper hovering dangerously close above her core.

One side of his mouth tipped upwards. "As you are being so accommodating, my love, how about an apology for the apoplexy you nearly gave me when I heard you were occupying this room with Halliwell. All the girls were chittering on about it." With his thumb, he slowly circled her clit. "That was three minutes of my life I'd never wish to repeat."

"What?" Her body felt heavy, lethargic. Except for the growing need to be filled. She wiggled her hips, trying to find relief. "You demand an apology now? Another one?" What was it with him seeking out her atonement at the most inappropriate of times? And really, he was nearly as responsible for her actions this time as she was by encouraging her to seek out another man the night before. It hardly seemed just that she be the only one to grovel. "I already explained that I had changed my mind."

"Yes, but there were still those three minutes when I thought the worst and found you closed in a room with a naked Halliwell." He blew a steady stream of cool air across her tortured nub.

She groaned. "This is hardly fair." Insufferable man thought he could get the upper hand on her. Bend her to his will. "You have me in a position of advantage."

He chuckled. "I know." He kissed the inside of her thigh, his jaw skating across her damp skin. Where his beard used to abrade, inflaming her skin as it scraped across, the caress of his smooth cheek sent delicate shivers racing through her body. Both sensations were equally enjoyable.

She ran numbers from her ledger in her mind, trying to distract her body. She would not break so easily. If she bought candles from that new shop by the docks, she could save an average of—

Max lowered his head and plunged his rolled tongue inside her channel.

Colleen fisted the silk belt, her wrists grinding together, and rocked her hips into his face. "I am most sorry. So very, very sorry."

"There, that wasn't so difficult, was it?" His eyes crinkled mischievously. "And as you were so sincere, here is your reward." He tipped the candle, and the air hissed, her clit burned.

She couldn't keep the scream in her throat. She throbbed. It felt like all the blood in her body had pooled in that one spot, like every nerve was threaded through her nub. Nothing else existed except her pounding need.

He bent and lashed her with his tongue. He swiped from her clit to her opening, lapping up her juices, plunging deep inside.

Colleen stared at the ceiling, her breath clogging her throat, watching their reflection. His head was buried between her thighs, her skin flushed pink, the white wax splashed starkly across her torso. The muscles in Max's shoulders bunched and released as he moved his head. It was the most stimulating sight she could imagine.

Her need built, her body tensing. Digging her heels into his thighs, she thrust her hips up to meet his mouth. He brought her to the crest, held her there, and just as she peaked, he tipped the candle, scalding heat swamping her senses and blending with her ecstasy.

She screamed her throat raw, her body convulsing violently.

Max thrust two fingers into her channel and rode her orgasm out as long as possible. He blew out the candle and tossed it aside.

Colleen's lungs burned from breathing so hard. Her reflection blinked down at her, a dazed look upon her face. Not giving her time to recover, Max swung her left leg around his head, held both of her ankles to his right shoulder, and prodded his cock at her entrance.

He slid inside, stretching her walls, firing up her over-sensitized nerve endings. He pressed in until the front of his thighs met the backs of hers.

"Sweet Jesus, you feel good." Max kissed her ankle, wrapping one strong arm below her knees. He rocked his hips back then thrust forwards with a grunt. "Such a sweet little cunny."

Her channel twitched, still recovering from her last crisis, but Max tunneled past the tightening muscles. Colleen whimpered, her inflamed inner walls feeling every ridge and vein on Max's cock as he dragged through her flesh. She clawed at the headboard, trying to find purchase. Pressing her palms flat against the smooth wood, she pushed into his strokes, leveraging every ounce of pleasure.

Max dug his fingers into her skin, denting the flesh of

her legs. His bollocks slapped against her bum, a rhythmic counter tempo to his grunts. The headboard rocked into the wall, the entire room shaking with the sounds of his pounding. Colleen couldn't have cared less if the entire club heard them.

Every slide of his length made her nerves tingle. Each time he bottomed out, something pinched deep inside of her, something no man had ever reached. Her body climbed once more.

Max dropped his head back, eyes wide open on the mirror. "Fuck, I love the way your breasts bounce when I drive into you. Perfect breasts. My breasts," he growled. His hips rocked faster, pounded harder. The tendons on his neck flexed and strained, and a bead of sweat slipped from under his newly-shorn hairline, rolling down his cheek.

He lowered his head, his eyes boring into hers. Reaching one hand down, he slipped his thumb between her thighs and scraped a layer of wax off of her clit.

Colleen's entire body jerked, and the fabric of her robe's belt broke from the headboard. She wanted her whole body coated in wax just so she could feel Max peel it from her skin, piece by piece. He'd already scraped away the walls to her heart. Her body deserved no less of a treatment.

Max sucked the tip of his thumb into his mouth. He lowered his hand, bringing it back between her legs. He rubbed the slick digit around her nub. His fingers dug into her stomach, the motion of his hips growing jerky. "Are you close? Please tell me you're close."

Colleen could only nod. He was so big inside her, his length growing harder and larger so that she couldn't feel where he ended and she began. Max increased the pressure of his thumb, bringing her to the edge. He pummeled into her once, twice, fire chasing down her walls, and she exploded.

Fisting the coverlet, her whole body clamped down and shook with her tremors. "Max," she moaned. Black dots swum before her eyes, and she let go, letting the bliss envelop her.

Max hugged her legs tight, gave a roar, and thrust into her one last time. Heat flooded her core, and his length twitched inside her channel. Closing his eyes, he bit her calf, holding on until the pulses tapered off. He shuddered one last time inside her body and rested his head against her ankles. "Oh, fuck, that was good."

Colleen blinked and tried to find her voice. Good didn't even come close to describing what they'd just done. "Mmm hmm."

His body stiffened. "Oh fuck!"

Raising her arms above her head, she stretched her back languidly and tugged her hands free from the belt. She settled on her side. "You're starting to repeat yourself. I think we already covered how good it was."

"No." He slid out and rolled off the bed. Digging through his coat pocket, he pulled out a handkerchief. "Dammit, I forgot to pull out. I put you at risk." Striding back to the bed, he cleaned her up, the pressure too heavy on her tender skin to be comfortable.

She tucked her legs to her chin. "Well, that's not going to help." She rolled to her back, feet planted on the mattress, knees to the ceiling. She stared at her reflection in the mirror. This wasn't good. A commoner getting pregnant by a member of the ton never ended well for the woman. Or the bastard child. "I wouldn't worry overmuch. The chances of my getting with child are low." She placed her palm on her stomach. "But if it happens, I'm keeping the babe."

Grabbing her wrist, Max pulled her up to sitting. "And who's arguing that you wouldn't?" he demanded. "Do you think I'd order you to give it up?"

"No." She laid her hand on his chest, burying her fingers in his soft pelt. He would take care of any child. He or she at least wouldn't starve in the streets. "In eight years of marriage I was only in the family way twice. Let's not worry until we need to."

"All right." He cupped the nape of her neck. "But you'll let me know?"

Wrapping her arms around his waist, she rested her cheek on his chest. "I will." They breathed together. "I'm sorry about the fire. I wanted to do it for you, but I couldn't."

"I know." He kissed the top of her head.

"When did you start playing with fire? It's such an unusual predilection." Bringing something so dangerous to her bed never would have occurred to her.

His hands stilled on her back. "I've always been interested in fire. It seemed natural to incorporate it in all aspects of my life."

"But there must have been something that sparked your interest?" She smiled. "So to speak."

He was quiet, rubbing his hands in circles on her back. She didn't think he would answer. Finally, he said, "Fire has always been beautiful to me." Sighing, he released her and sat on the edge of the bed. He tugged on her hand, drawing her down beside him.

"There's much I don't remember about my early years, but I do remember the poverty," he said.

"But, you're a—"

"Baron, I know." He pulled out the few pins left in her hair and combed the thick mass down her back. "My father was a second son and a bit of a scoundrel. He was supposed to go into the church, but he wasn't very good at it. It was hard for him to wake up in time for the service, let alone write a sermon. After repeated complaints from parishioners of his drunkenness and licentiousness, my grandfather, the third baron of Sutton, cut him off. After that, let's just say my father, my mother, and I didn't live well."

"I can imagine," Colleen said faintly. She knew the type of man his father was. She'd seen many in her old neighborhood. Too drunk to put in a day's labor, relying on the meagre wages of their women to keep them in their cups. "And your mother? What did she do to provide for you?"

"She wanted to help." Max's shoulder tensed against hers. "She would have become a charwoman to help put food in our bellies, but father wouldn't hear of it. The wife of the son of a baron, even a second son, didn't find employment."

Colleen took his hand, threading her fingers with his. "What happened?"

He shrugged. "My uncle died. He was returning from the Continent, and the ship he was on sank in a storm. Grandfather wrote for us to join him at Meadowlark, the seat of the barony, since my father was then in line for succession."

"And the fire?" She chewed on the inside of her cheek. There was so much more to the story than he revealed. The fear of a boy going to bed with his belly aching for food. The uncertainty of not having a parent he could trust to see them through. It was a story all too common in London, but one she didn't expect from the Baron of Sutton.

"The day my grandfather's carriage came to collect us, my mother gathered all our clothes, everything except for what was on our backs. She piled them in the yard." Max stared at the wall, as if seeing that long-ago scene. "She set everything on fire and she held my hand as we stood there and watched it all burn. There was a lot I didn't understand, but I knew the fire represented a new beginning. A clean start. My mother was crying she was so happy. That fire was the most beautiful thing I'd ever seen."

They sat in silence, holding hands. Colleen rested her head against his shoulder. Her throat was thick, but it didn't matter. There was nothing she needed to say. She was content to merely sit next to this man. Her future was uncertain. Her plans in a disarray. But she wouldn't regret a minute of her time with the baron. He truly was the finest man she knew. And she would treasure every moment they had together.

He cleared his throat. "Regardless, that feeling never left me. Growing up, whenever something bad happened, I would start a small fire, usually on the manor grounds, and the flames would settle me." He turned and looked down at her, his mouth twisting. "My grandfather and parents were not amused, as you can imagine. But they couldn't stop my fascination."

"Thank you for telling me." There wouldn't have been many people he'd told. Colleen sat up tall. "I'm honored."

Max opened his mouth, looking like he wanted to say more, then snapped it shut. He scratched his cheek. "Damn, it feels strange without my beard. It will take me a while to become accustomed to."

Scooting off the bed, Colleen gathered her clothes and began to don them. "You don't have to get used to it. You could always let it grow back." She missed his bushy, bear-like appearance. Though she must admit, the face under all that hair was startlingly attractive. The beard had hit chiseled cheekbones and a tiny dent in the center of his chin.

"Summerset would never forgive me if I did that." Max grimaced. "He almost wept in joy when the hair came off."

"Interesting friends you have." She pulled her shirt over her head and turned for the waistcoat. She plucked it off the bureau, and something thudded to the floor.

"You lost something," Max said, tugging up his trousers.

Colleen clutched the garment to her stomach, staring at the gold watch nestled in the green carpet. Half of a chain swung loose from the buttonhole of the waistcoat.

"Colleen?" Max moved towards her.

"It's nothing." She cleared her throat. "The chain to my watch broke."

"I'm sorry." He shifted behind her then stepped around and picked up the watch. "It was important to you. I'll get you a new chain."

A new chain to her past. She shrugged into the waistcoat, took the watch, and slipped it into her pocket. "No, thank you." No more chains. "It isn't worth replacing." Smoothing down her skirts, she smiled up at Max. "Now, tell me how large an apology I owe Lord Halliwell. Was he merely annoyed at being displaced or was he harmed in the process, as well?"

The tips of Max's ears flushed red. "He received no less treatment than he had coming to him."

"Ah. So free membership for half a year, along with prostrating myself with contrition."

She stepped past Max, and he grabbed her elbow. "No prostrating yourself with him in any form."

"That was only a figure of speech." She patted his hand. "Now, are you hungry?" Her own stomach grumbled. "I know the cook has some lovely pheasant down in the kitchens. Tonight is Lord Manderley's weekly appointment. You know how he likes his bacchanalian feast, and there is always plenty left over." She caught his expression. "Everything that goes into the red room is disposed of. I'm speaking of food that is never sent up."

He blew out a breath. "In that case, do you think there's enough leftovers for seven?"

Pausing at the door, she frowned back over her shoulder. "How hungry are you?"

"With you, I feel like I'm always starving." He patted her bottom. "But tonight isn't just about my appetites. Darling, we have company."

Chapter Thirteen

Max leaned back in his chair and rubbed his full stomach. The cook at The Black Rose was quite remarkable. He'd never tasted a juicier bird. The hollowed-out carcass on the table attested to the fact that everyone agreed.

He and his friends sat around the long, rough table in the kitchen of the club, drinking watered down wine and feasting on what hadn't made it to the table for one of their strangest members. There were times when Max thought that Manderley truly believed he was a Greek god.

Max glanced at Colleen, seated to his right. After seeing one of Manderley's scenes, Max had to admit the idea of Colleen hand-feeding him grapes and other succulent tidbits with one hand whilst stroking his cock with the other, wasn't a bad one. Maybe Manderley was onto something.

The club was quiet, now closed, and workers and customers alike had gone home.

"What now?" Summerset tossed a wing, picked clean, down on his plate and wiped his fingers on a towel. He jerked a thumb at Pinkerton. "We've placed this man in every window of every club, coffee house, and tavern, and no one has taken a shot at him. Zed obviously doesn't think he's worth the time to try to kill"—Summerset ignored the American's objection—"and we're left feeding and housing the annoying sot. I think we need a new plan."

Everyone but Pinkerton and Colleen muttered an agreement. It felt as though they were giving Zed more time to retrench while they passively dropped a line in the water.

Max had always preferred a more active hunt. If he saw a fish he wanted, he would dart his arm in the pond and grab for it. It was time they stopped letting Zed dictate their actions.

"Any ideas?" Max asked and looked around. Montague tapped the flat end of his knife's blade against his mouth, looking thoughtful. Rothchild stared at the ceiling. And Summerset looked more interested in cleaning the grease from his fingers.

Only Dunkeld spoke. "I think we've been dangling the wrong bait. Zed has shown an interest in one person, and it's time we used her to flush out our prey."

Everyone swiveled their heads toward Colleen. She had a bit of bread raised to her lips, and her eyes darted to the surrounding faces.

"No." Max threw his own towel on the table. "We will not parade her about waiting for someone to put a bullet in her head. Absolutely not."

"But that was fine for me?" Pinkerton asked, outraged.

He was ignored.

"Maximillian, we wouldn't let that happen," Montague said gently. The duke rested his elbows on the table. "We'd have to stay close to her, of course."

"Too close." Summerset kicked a jewel-encrusted boot up onto the corner of the table, and Dunkeld knocked it down. Summerset grunted. "If we did this, Sutton couldn't come along. He'd be in her petticoats the entire time, and Zed would never try to strike."

Heat flushed through Max's body. He clenched his fists. "Go to hell. You're not using my woman as bait. And if you try to do so without me there, I swear I'll—"

Rothchild pushed him back into his seat and patted Max's shoulder. "Everyone, calm down. No one wants to take down Zed more than I do, but we won't put Mrs. Bonner in danger if Max is against it."

"Interesting that no one's asked my opinion," Colleen said, a brittle smile curving her lips.

"It's. Not. Happening.' Max's glare encompassed everyone, including Colleen. She was just the sort of woman who'd put herself in danger to help others. Noble. Determined. Daft. Max needed to make his decision abundantly clear to everyone involved. "We find another way."

Dunkeld shrugged one shoulder. "I understand," he said in a quiet voice. "But sometimes danger can't be escaped. She's already a target."

"Well, we're not going to make her a more appealing one. And that's final." Colleen opened her mouth, but Max cut her a look. "Final," he repeated.

Rising to her feet, Colleen took her plate to the sink. "Since it appears I need permission for my own actions"— she dipped into a low, insolent curtsy—"may I adjourn to the cellars for another bottle of wine, my lord? I promise to hold tight to the rail going down the steps and tread carefully. No injury to my person shall occur."

His friends raised their eyebrows and looked to see how Max would respond. A smile ghosted across Montague's lips, and Max frowned. He knew how the duke's mind worked, knew how he would handle such impertinence from a lover. Max didn't want Montague's mind anywhere near Colleen's bottom. Standing, he tossed his plate at the duke, who caught it to his chest, startled.

"You go ahead," Max told Colleen. "We'll clean up here in the while."

"Bring two bottles," Dunkeld hollered at her retreating back. "We need to drink twice as much of that swill to feel anything."

She waved her fingers over her shoulder and disappeared down the narrow hall.

Summerset wrinkled his nose. "We're going to clean up?"

"Put your plate in the sink." Max planted his fists on his hips. "It won't kill you to help out."

All the men cleared their places at the table.

"What are you going to do with me?" Pinkerton asked. "My wife and son will starve if I go to prison."

"That isn't our problem," Dunkeld said. But Max and his friends eyed each other uneasily. Twisting a towel between two meaty hands, Dunkeld grumbled, the sound trapped deep in his throat. "But you've tried to help us. And the prisons here are full enough with our own criminals. We don't need Americans taking up all the spots. I can give you some blunt to start over."

Pinkerton widened his eyes, looking hopeful.

A shadow moved, and Max peered out the window to the small yard behind the club. Something glinted in the moonlight.

"Down!" Max kicked out at Pinkerton's thigh, knocking the man sideways just as the window above the sink exploded in a hundred shards of glass. The men dove to the ground. Pinkerton clutched his arm to his side and groaned. A starburst of torn fabric erupted from the shoulder of his coat, a darkening stain spreading from the hole.

Rothchild flipped the large table, bowls and bird remains flying. Max dragged Pinkerton behind the barrier, joining Rothchild and Summerset. Montague holed up in a nook beside the pantry and Dunkeld pressed his back flat against the cupboard underneath the sink. All men save Pinkerton had pulled out their pistols. They hadn't trusted the American with a weapon.

The pane of glass in the door that led outside shattered, and they all ducked. They were easy pickings in the well-lit kitchen, yet Max could see nothing outside in the pitch of night. Narrowing his eyes, he took aim at the oil lamp on the wall and shot it out. The spilled oil ignited on the floor, and a slow blaze crept across the wood planks towards Summerset.

His friend whipped off his coat and smothered the flame. "Careful what you're doing! I think I'd rather be shot than burn to death."

Max let his eyes adjust to the dark, ignoring Summerset. That small amount of oil would have burned itself out before putting anyone in danger. The moonlight limned the edges of the windows, casting a faint glow.

Dunkeld edged up from his squat and peered through the bottom of the window. "I see two men." The pane next to his head took a shot and splintered in two. He ducked back down. "At least three men."

Perfect. While they'd been eating like gluttons, Zed had chosen that moment to spring an attack. Max could have kicked himself for letting his guard down, even for a moment. He glanced to the hallway entrance and prayed Colleen didn't step through it, into the line of fire.

A tall figure melted from the shadows behind Summerset.

"John!" Max shouted. He swung his gun towards the attacker, his movements seeming too sluggish.

Summerset rolled, his hand slicing out. The form screamed, hopping on one foot before toppling over. Summerset was waiting, knife in hand, and slit his throat with the same ruthless efficiency as he had the man's Achilles tendon.

Max released a deep breath. That had been too close. The attackers had infiltrated the club. His hand froze. There was an entrance to the cellars from the yard. It was kept locked from the inside, but Max didn't want to give the bastards any time to break it open. Not with Colleen down there.

Summerset wiped the blade of his small dagger on his sleeve and shifted back behind the table. "One down."

"Fucking hell," Pinkerton whispered.

"What?" Summerset shrugged. "I didn't want to waste a bullet."

Montague pointed at Dunkeld and made a swirling motion with his hand. The Scotsman nodded. "Give us some cover," Montague said, and without waiting to see if they complied, he and Dunkeld slithered to the doors and disappeared outside.

Max, Summerset, and Rothchild each took a turn leveling a shot out the broken windows, hoping it was enough of a distraction.

"You have a two-shot?" Rothchild asked Summerset.

John held up a pearl-handled pocket pistol. "Three barrels. I have two shots remaining."

"I have to reload," Rothchild said. "Watch my back."

Rolling to his feet, Max crouched behind the table. "I'm going to check the rest of the building. Watch—"

A scream tore through the night air. Coming from the basement.

Max popped to his feet and ran like the devil himself was on his heels. He pounded through the doorway to the hall, jerking his head as a chip of wood frame exploded from a bullet strike, scratching his cheek. The door to the cellar was five feet away and stood open. Max plunged inside and took the stairs three at a time, stumbling at the bottom and hitting his knee to the stone floor.

A candlestick rested on a large barrel, the small flame of its taper bouncing in the draft. He heard a grunt, a low curse, before Colleen's sturdy frame hurtled around a row of casks.

He took in every detail in a second. The small tear in the shoulder of her shirt. The way she clutched her skirt high in front as she ran. The look of panic in her eyes that melted to relief when she caught sight of him.

The fucking bastard who was three steps behind her, knife clutched in his hand.

Max took two running steps forwards, pushed Colleen behind him, and planted his fist in the attacker's face. His nose broke with a satisfying crunch.

The man staggered back, his legs as wobbly as a newborn fawn's. His eyes rolled back in his head, and he collapsed in a heap.

Grabbing the back of Max's coat, Colleen tugged him towards the staircase. "Let's get out of here."

"No. There's more upstairs." Max picked up the candle and strode to the base of the short flight of steps that led to the yard. The cellar door was closed and the bolt remained in place. The arsewipe must have come down the club's stairs. "You're safer here. I'll take the man upstairs, and you barricade the door until I tell you it's all right for you to come out. Understood?"

Tiptoeing to the crumpled body, Colleen tentatively stretched out a hand and snatched the knife that lay inches from his trouser. "How do you suggest I barricade myself inside? Carry wine barrels up the stairs on my back to lodge against the door?"

That was a good point. The door from the club didn't lock on the inside. Still, he could have done without the impudence. Not while their lives were in danger. "Fine. I'll leave the body here and take you up with me instead. But you will stay behind me and do as I say. We don't know how many men are up there, but I'm certain each of them is eager to kill you." Bile rose in his throat with the words.

She raised her hands in a placating gesture, almost cutting her ear with the blade. "I'm not the spy. I'll do as you say."

Pulling the knife away from her face, Max sighed. "Just don't stab me in the back, please." Taking her free hand, he tucked it to his side and started up the steps. When they reached the top, he blew out the candle and waited for his eyes to adjust.

The door swung open, and Max pounced. He grabbed the man by the throat and throttled him against the wall.

"Max!" Summerset wheezed. He clawed at Max's hands. "It's me."

The hiss of a flame meeting an oil-soaked wick sizzled in the air. Montague lit one of the wall lamps, illuminating the hallway, and replaced the glass cover. "I wanted to make sure we could all see this," he said mildly. "It's always amusing seeing Summerset get his daylights darkened."

Max dropped his hand. He brushed Summerset's

shoulders. "Apologies. How many did we capture?"

Rothchild strode down the hallway. "None," he said, his lip curling with disgust. "All either dead or escaped."

"Blast." Max grabbed Colleen around the waist and swung her out of the doorway, enjoying her little yelp. He bounded down the stairs. It should have been black as pitch in the cellar. But the cellar doors were flung open, letting the blue of the quarter moon illuminate the space. No body lay on the floor.

"Sodding hell!" He plodded back up the stairs. "My man got away, too."

Dunkeld tramped into the hallway, Pinkerton a step behind with a red-soaked towel pressed to his shoulder. The Scotsman crossed his arms over his chest. "It's like these men are smoke. Deadly, but we can't seem to grab ahold of them."

Colleen leaned against the wall and closed her eyes. Her chest heaved up and down, and her fists were buried in the folds of her skirt.

Max ground his teeth. She'd had more frights than anyone deserved. And she'd faced them all, as resilient as a soldier. He'd been looking forward to pounding information out of someone, and now there was no one to loose his aggressions upon. He eyed Summerset. No, it wouldn't be nearly as satisfying pounding on a friend.

Only one other way that he knew of to pour out his frustrations.

He took Colleen's hand. "I'm taking her home with me. The club is no longer safe."

"What about me?" Pinkerton's nasal accent sounded like the whine of a child.

"I think it's time our friend rejoined his family." Montague tucked his thumbs in the pockets of his waistcoat. "Perhaps we can send him on his way somewhere safe, like back to America."

"Good idea," Summerset said. A gleeful smile stretched across his face. "After all he's done for us, Pinkerton is going to need protection back to Scotland to rejoin his family. Seeing as he's injured. Don't you think?" he asked Dunkeld, as innocent as a babe.

The marquess crossed his arms over his chest. "No. He can find his own way there. We owe him nothing."

Rothchild snorted but managed to smother his laughter. "Summerset is right. And you are the obvious choice."

"You're going to freeze your bollocks off!" Summerset didn't bother trying to restrain his mirth. "Scotland at this time of year. You and Pinkerton will have to snuggle together in the inns on your travels. I hope—"

Dunkeld planted his elbow in the earl's gut, cutting off his sentence to gasp for air. "'Effing slags, all of you." Turning to Colleen, he bowed his head. "Pardon my language, ma'am." He cracked his neck and took a deep breath. "Come, Pinkerton. Let's get you to a doctor and deliver you to your wife."

The Scotsman strode away. Pinkerton took a couple steps, then turned back. "I just wanted to thank all of you. It is really most—"

"Just go." To Max's mind, the American was getting more than he deserved. He turned to Montague. "Can you contact Liverpool? Ask him to have this cleaned up by the time the club opens tomorrow?"

The duke nodded. "He won't be happy we've come away without any witnesses again. But a little tidying up is the least he owes us."

The men separated. Max pulled Colleen up to her rooms and found an empty valise. "Pack what you think you'll need for the next couple of weeks."

Silently, she moved among her wardrobes, placing a couple of pairs of new boots in the bottom of the kit.

Max frowned. "What? No argument?"

Colleen pressed her lips together. "As has just been proven, this building is easily accessible to men who want to cut my throat and ..." She balled up a gown and tossed it in the valise.

Grasping her shoulders, he turned her to face him. "And what?"

She shrugged. "The man made it quite clear he wanted something more before he killed me. I think my fear excited him." She patted Max's chest. "I am quite happy to go stay in your house until this is resolved."

Folding his arms around her, he pulled her close. He buried his nose in her hair and just enjoyed being surrounded by her. Her arms, her scent, her strength.

Somewhere during that embrace, he knew. Having her in his home for the next couple of weeks wouldn't be enough. He would need her forever.

Chapter Fourteen

Colleen turned a corner and stepped around the man posted at the end of the hallway. She snapped the gardening book that she'd found in Max's library shut and made an about-face, hoping to find some solitude.

She bumped into the man trailing behind her.

"Gentlemen." She huffed. "I know the baron has engaged you to watch over me, but this is a little much. Wouldn't your time be better spent securing the entrances to his house rather than following me about?"

The man standing in the hallway stared forwards. "Apologies, madam. The baron was explicit in his orders. We're not to let you out of our sight."

Yes, she'd been made aware of that when one of his men had followed her into the necessary. To the man's credit, his face had flamed red when he'd realized his mistake, and he'd darted back. Colleen had still slammed the door on his blush.

After making love to every inch of her body the night before, Max had disappeared, leaving her under the watchful eyes of his servants and the men he'd hired to guard her. She appreciated that he wanted to keep her safe. The reality, however, of having strangers peering after her like she was a monkey in a menagerie, was less than enjoyable.

"All I want is to read in the sitting room. Alone." She wasn't the fastest reader, and the book she'd chosen was chock-full of long Latin names. Numbers were more her strength. She didn't need some hired ruffian peering over her shoulder, watching her fumble her way through the tome. "Can that be arranged?"

The men looked at each other and shifted their weight.

Colleen drew her shoulder blades towards her spine. "I see. Then please call a carriage for me. I will be going to the club. That is still allowed, isn't it?"

The one man dipped his head. "Yes, madam. As long as we accompany you."

After what had happened in The Black Rose the night before, the supervision there was welcome. In Max's home she felt safe. She'd lost that feeling in the club. But work didn't stop because she was beset with dread.

Without a word to her shadows, she returned to the room Max had given her – one with a door connecting to his own chamber. She collected her spencer and a reticule. The book wouldn't fit inside her bag, so she tucked it under her arm. She hoped to read in her office, free from scrutiny.

Her guard stood by the bureau, silent, his gaze darting to the connecting door to the master bedroom. Colleen refused to feel embarrassed. A month ago she would have been mortified by an affair of hers becoming public knowledge. But she was an independent woman, and Max wasn't a man a woman should be ashamed of.

Chin high, she strode from the room and down the central staircase to the foyer. A footman opened the front door, and another guard melted from the wall. With a man five steps in front of her and one five steps behind, Colleen paraded to the carriage and climbed inside. One man followed her in, the other joining the driver up top.

She had to admit she was becoming accustomed to the service granted to the guest of a baron. It would be disappointing to return to opening her own doors.

Her heart twisted and flipped behind her breastbone. Losing those minor services would be nothing compared to losing Max. The feel of his mouth, the beat of his heart beneath her cheek as she fell asleep, his warm laugh buoying her spirits. Those were the things she would miss. That was what would be hard to live without.

The carriage pulled to a stop and the door opened. The slanting afternoon sun caught the second-story windows of the club, the glare causing her to blink. Cheery petunias lined planter boxes below the first-floor windows, and Colleen smiled as she always did when she saw them. Who would guess what went on within the building when such an innocent flower graced its walls?

Climbing the steps with her entourage, she entered The Black Rose. The muscles in her back clenched tighter the deeper she went into what had become her home. A home that had been teeming with men trying to kill her and Max's friends.

Wanting to see the worst and get it out of the way, she headed for the kitchen. She jolted to a stop in the doorway.

"Something a'matter, ma'am?" one of her guards asked.

"No." She drifted to the sink and placed her palm on the cool glass of the unbroken window. She looked around. The table had been righted, all the broken dishes cleaned up. The kitchen smelled of fresh paint. Colleen looked for holes in the walls and couldn't find any.

Max's friends could make a fortune if they opened a cleaning business. Colleen pursed her lips, impressed. The cook of The Black Rose stumbled in, a burlap bag full of fruits and vegetables hugged tight to his round stomach.

He nodded to Colleen and hefted his load onto the counter. "Mrs. Bonner. I wanted to thank you for the new equipment. The copper pans conduct heat much better than the old ones we had."

Colleen had no idea what he was talking about. "You're welcome. I say only the best for the best."

The cook's pink cheeks plumped with his grin. He looked at the two men flanking the doorway and tilted his head. "Giving a tour to new members?"

One of the men coughed into his hand.

"Er, no." Picking an apple from the bag, Colleen rubbed

it on her sleeve. "There's been a threat against one of our members. Nothing to worry about, I'm sure. But we're taking extra precautions."

With a reassuring smile, she headed towards her office. Lucy was on a settee in the main room, sewing a bit of lace onto a gown and chatting with some other girls. Colleen changed direction and approached the group. "Good afternoon, ladies. Lucy, can you join me in my office?"

Lucy nodded, eyeing the guards. She put down her gown and followed Colleen across the room to the entrance to Colleen's private rooms. They climbed the stairs, one of the guards remaining at the base of the staircase, the other following them up. He took up position next to the door inside Colleen's office.

She frowned. "As you can see, there is no one in the office but us. And no windows or doors besides that one to enter from. Please wait outside."

"Madam, I'm supposed—"

"I know what you were told, but you have a head of your own. Use it." She tapped a toe. "You'd do better making sure no one unwanted comes through that door."

He nodded, took one last look around the room, and ducked outside.

Colleen shut the door with a decided click.

"Have a seat," she told Lucy and circled behind her desk to do the same. "As assistant manager, I wanted to apprise you of a situation."

"All right." Lucy perched on the edge of the chair. Instead of her usual negligee or gossamer-thin gowns, she wore a basic morning dress. Cut a bit lower in the chest than Colleen's liking, but much more business-like than before.

Colleen folded her hands together. "You should know there has been a threat against the club. I will be telling other workers that one of our members requires increased security, hence the presence of guards. But it is the Baron of Sutton and me the threat seems to be against. I don't want to alarm anyone, but if you could tell people to keep an eye out for anything untoward, I would appreciate it."

"Those men out there," Lucy said, pointing a finger over her shoulder, "they're here to protect you?"

Colleen shifted in her seat. She was as uneasy with the idea of men watching her every move as she was with the idea that someone wanted to harm her. Her anger simmered. What had she ever done to this Zed creature? She'd ignored his letters? Refused to give him the information he wanted? That hardly seemed cause enough for all this fuss.

"Yes." Placing her palms flat against the cool wood of the desk, Colleen nodded. "And to watch over the rest of the club." She would make sure of that. It was more than just her life at risk. "Although by having such a show of force, I'm certain that the blackguard wouldn't dare attack us now."

"All right. I'll let the girls know to be extra careful."

"Good."

Lucy leaned forwards. "Can we discuss business now? I came up with a list of purchases we'll need for the next month, and I think I found us a new wine supplier." The woman spoke rapidly. Taking a folded piece of paper from the inside of her sleeve, she pushed it across the desk.

Colleen picked it up and ran her finger down the proposed list with its tidy scrawl of projected costs running down the side. "This all looks in order. Good job."

Lucy flushed. "I was talking with Bob, our footman. He also works at White's, and he's friendly with the manager there, and he says his wine guy is the one to use." She pulled another piece of paper, this time a small scrap, from her other sleeve, and gave it to Colleen.

Colleen eyed the woman's sleeves, wondering what else lay hidden within. She took the name and address of the other supplier. "Thank you. I will contact him today and have M— Sutton run a history. This is most helpful."

"And you'll tell the baron that I found him? If I'm to

become the manager, I need our employer to know I helped."

Colleen's reply, that of course she would give credit where due, was interrupted by a shout in the hallway. She shot to her feet and ran for the door, flinging it open. The guard posted down below came pounding up the stairs and took his position in front of Colleen.

She frowned and sidled around him. The other guard had one meaty hand wrapped around Molly's elbow and was dragging her from Colleen's bed chambers.

"What on earth is going on out here?" Colleen asked.

"I caught her peeping around your room." The man shook Molly's arm. "She says she works at the club."

"She does." Colleen pressed her back against the doorjamb and pointed into her office. "Let's bring her in here." She turned to Lucy. "Thank you. I think we're done."

With a curious look at Molly, Lucy scooted past the group and inched down the stairs, casting glances back over her shoulder every other step.

Molly jerked her arm from her captor's grip and sauntered into the office, head high. One of the guards made a move to follow, but Colleen held up a hand. "You won't be needed for this." She closed the door and faced the scourge of The Black Rose. Perhaps scourge was a tad dramatic, but Molly had turned into a severe annoyance.

"Was there a particular reason you were in my chambers?" Colleen circled behind her desk and plopped in her chair. "Something you were looking for?"

"A shawl." Crossing her arms over her small frame, Molly gave a delicate shiver. "I left my wrap at home and was hoping to borrow one."

That was a good line, Colleen had to give her that. Molly was quick-witted. She was also a consummate liar. "Well, I'll be happy to provide you with a covering for your return trip home. Your services are no longer needed here."

Molly's jaw dropped open, genuine shock blanking her

face. "You can't dismiss me. I'm the best incognita The Black Rose has."

"That may be true, but your skill is surpassed by your deceit. I won't have workers I can't trust. Not anymore." Picking up a piece of lead, Colleen rolled it between her palms. Trust was a precious commodity. One she should be willing to give if she expected it returned.

She shook off thoughts of Max. This was business. "You can collect any belongings you have stored here, and I'll direct a carriage to take you home." Standing, she stretched for the ledger on the shelf behind her. "I'll tally up your past wages and settle with you before you go."

Molly jumped forwards and slapped the journal from her hand. It fell onto the desk, cover open, the pages inside bending against the wood. "You can keep your pin money. I don't need it."

Colleen didn't know anyone who didn't need money. Not enough to ignore a week's worth of wages. She cocked her head and righted the journal, smoothing the pages. "Do you have someone taking care of you? Perhaps the gentleman who showers you with expensive jewels?" A new stone rested above the girl's low neckline. Deep blue and as large as a lump of coal.

Molly stepped around the desk, making Colleen stumble back. "Do you think there is only one man who knows my worth? That I won't have fifty such idiots lining up to beg me to be their mistress?" She poked a sharp nail into Colleen's shoulder. "I could buy this club ten times over." She blinked and pressed her lips together in a slight grimace. "Yes, I think I'll order one of my patrons to buy this club out from under you and toss you to the street. Because that's where you belong. You're nothing more than trash, and no amount of fancy gowns the baron buys for you will change that."

Molly had backed Colleen around the desk and across the room. The solid weight of the door hit Colleen's bottom, and her shoulders sagged. Only three inches away were the two men hired to protect her. She hadn't thought she'd need their assistance ridding the club of a lightskirt, but the spite in Molly's eyes told a different story.

"I'm glad that the termination of your employment won't cause you any setbacks." Colleen made her voice brisk and businesslike. No need to antagonize or show concern. "And, of course, if you require references, I would write of your great popularity and skill." Her character would receive a less complimentary mention, however. "Now, as we've nothing more to discuss, I bid you good eve'n." She fumbled behind her back for the latch, not wanting to take her gaze off of Molly. She jerked the door open, scooting to the side.

One of the guards stepped forward, looking irritated. "Any problems?"

"None." Colleen wiped her damp palms on her skirt. "Molly is going to collect her things. Will you arrange for a carriage and driver to take her where she wishes and escort her out?"

He nodded, his gaze tracking Molly's every breath. Colleen would have to commend Max on his choice of guard. Annoying as they were being underfoot all the time, she appreciated that they weren't deceived by a pretty face and a tight bodice. The man recognized Molly for the trouble she was.

The girl's face shuttered. She strode through the door without acknowledging Colleen or the men. It was as though none of them existed to Molly anymore.

Colleen waited for the door at the base of the stairs to snick shut before returning to her office. She sat behind her desk, and the tension in her body seeped away. The club's profits would take a blow, but releasing the woman was the right choice for the long-term. Her attitude poisoned the other workers.

Molly's boastful words rang in her ears. She did seem to have an arsenal of suitors at her disposal, which left Colleen with one question: why had Molly remained at The Black

Rose?

Perhaps the lady-bird's suitors weren't as ardent as they appeared. A trinket here and there hardly meant they were willing to set her up in the luxury she so obviously thought she deserved. The clients might appreciate her varied talents, but that didn't lead to a sustained interest. At his core, could a man love and support a woman he didn't trust?

The small muscles in her neck knotted. Were she and Molly so different? Molly put on an act with her men, deceiving them each night into believing she was a different sort of woman. The woman they most desired.

Colleen was lying to Max. Letting him carry the weight of her guilt. Letting him believe she was a better woman than she was.

If she told him the truth, he might fire her. Perhaps not deliver on her premium. But it was the knowledge that he would never look at her again with worship in his eyes that made her own eyes burn.

That was the loss that would cut the deepest.

* * *

"I can't drink another sip of this horse piss The Boar's Head passes off as ale." Summerset wiped his mouth with the back of his sleeve.

Max raised an eyebrow. His friend must truly be disgusted to forego using his pocket square. Or perhaps the horse piss was stronger than he thought.

He glanced across the crowded tavern. Montague and Rothchild were nursing their drinks, seemingly underwhelmed with the brew, as well. All four men wore clothes borrowed from their footmen and valets in order to conduct their surveillance of the public house Dancer was known to frequent. The man's ship, the *Teresa May*, had docked that day, and the first stop of any sailor worthy of his name was his local tavern.

"Dunkeld's journey up to Scotland isn't looking so bad

now, is it?" Max lifted the mug to his lips and pretended to take a sip. Aside from the rancid flavor, he needed to keep his wits about him. Dancer was starting to feel like their last chance to find Zed. Max was growing tired of going around in circles.

"I did have a lovely new winter coat made that would have been perfect for Scotland." Summerset fingered the rough collar of his shirt. "Braving a bit of cold would have been preferable to wearing ... *this*."

Max snorted at the horror in his friend's voice. "You didn't have to come tonight. Montague, Rothchild, and I would have managed fine without you."

"So you think. Without me, you might not have noticed that a man of five feet and a couple of inches with deep-set eyes and cadaverous cheeks and sporting disgusting tufts of hair out of his ears has just seated himself at the bar."

Max kicked a boot up on the table and glanced over his shoulder. "How did you know the man's description?"

Summerset stared at his nails and buffed them against his coat. "After you gave us his name, I had my men run my own check on him. It came with a description of his personal appearance."

"A colorful one at that."

Summerset shrugged. "What now? Do we wait for him to get deep into his cups? Perhaps speed the process along?" He patted the breast of his coat. Summerset was a bit of a chemist, and Max didn't want to even guess what drug lay bottled within. "Or do we follow him and hope he leads us to Zed?"

Max pushed to his feet and cracked his neck. "None of the above. I'm tired of chasing after our prey like a pussy cat. I say we take a more active approach."

"All right," Summerset drawled. "What, exactly, does that ... hey, wait up!"

Max felt the earl fall into step behind him, saw Montague and Rothchild rise from their seats. Knowing his friends would stand beside him, Max didn't hesitate. He walked up behind Dancer, grabbed the back of his neck, and dragged him from his stool. "Last order. Let's go."

Swatting at Max's hand, the man stumbled to one knee. Max dragged him until Dancer regained his footing.

Two burly sailors stood, and Montague and Rothchild blocked their access to Max and Dancer, staring them down. Summerset followed Max to the rear exit, walking backwards, assessing any potential threat.

None came.

Kicking open the back door to the alley, Max pushed the sailor outside and into a rubbish heap. Empty bottles rolled along the dirt, dislodged from his sprawl.

Dancer rubbed his back. "What the bloody hell are ye fuckwits on about? I just came in from a month's paddle. If you won money off someone, it weren't me."

The door squeaked open, and Montague and Rothchild slipped through.

Max rubbed his forehead. "I'm tired, I'm hacked off, and I've run out of patience. To save time, I'm going to tell you what we know." Dropping to a squat, he brought his face level with the sailor's. "Your name is Harvey Dancer and you live off Brook Street. You have a lady friend who lives in Lambeth and whose children call you Uncle Harry. You've worked for Bellweather Shipping for eight years, and until three months ago, also took on the odd job with a crime organization run by the self-named Zed." Max had his own men, and they could run background checks with the best of them. They had failed to mention the ear hair, however.

Dancer started to protest, his chin drawing back into his neck.

Max slapped his face. "Focus. You could spend from here to eternity denying your connection to Zed, and we wouldn't believe you."

Rothchild stepped forwards. "Perhaps answers would be more forthcoming if I applied a little pressure."

Perhaps. But they'd already encountered one man who

preferred death to talking. Max didn't have the time to test the pain limits of another fanatic. Besides, it wasn't information he was after.

"Let's save that as an option, shall we? If Dancer refuses my simple request." After riffling through Dancer's pockets and removing his only weapon, one small blade, Max stood. He planted his fists on his hips. "You are going to deliver a message for me. Tell Zed I want to meet. Just him and me, at a location of his choice. Tell him my only objective is to rid England of his presence, and I'm willing to pay handsomely to set him up in a residence abroad."

Rothchild inhaled sharply through his nose. Max knew his friends wouldn't approve. They each wanted their pound of flesh. Max just wanted it over. He wasn't so foolish to think that Zed would take him up on his offer. But they'd tried roundabout ways to find the crime lord without success. It was time for the direct route. He was going to offer himself as bait.

The eight men he'd set to follow Dancer back home made a solid secondary plan.

Max tossed a small bag of coin at the man's feet. "Every delivery man deserves payment. Tell Zed that the Baron of Sutton has issued an invitation. Deliver this message, and you're out." Toeing his boot under the bag, he tossed it, and it hit Dancer's chest with a thump. "Fail to deliver it, and the consequences will be severe."

Clutching the sack to his stomach, the sailor looked between it and Max. Slowly, he nodded and heaved to his feet. "I hope you know what you're about. You don't just invite the devil to a party and expect him to drink the punch."

Summerset rolled his eyes. "Everyone's a damn poet these days. I blame Wordsworth."

Dancer shrugged. "It's your funeral if you meet with Zed. But I warn ye, that one don't have both oars in the water." Tugging up his collar, the man sidled past Montague and Rothchild and scuttled down the alley.

Montague slapped dust from his thigh. "Interesting technique. I thought for sure you'd be the one I had to stop from inflicting too much damage."

Summerset huffed. "Ever since he's given his manager carte blanche, he's gone soft."

"Soft?" Rothchild raised his eyebrows. "With those tight, little waistcoats the woman wears, I would have thought it would be the opposite."

"Enough." Slashing his hand through the air, Max glared at his friends. "You wouldn't tolerate me making lewd comments regarding your wives, would you? Show Colleen the same respect."

"We respect all women," Montague said mildly. "But there is a difference between jesting about a man's wife and his mistress. Rothchild's joke was no more than we've all said to each other before."

"Unless Mrs. Bonner is more than a mistress?" Rothchild gave him a sympathetic smile. "I apologize for my remark. It won't happen again."

Max nodded his thanks. He turned and made his way out of the alley.

Summerset trotted by his side. "No," he said, shaking his head. "I won't allow it."

"What are you on about?" Max asked.

"Another friend becoming imprisoned in a life tenancy." Summerset waved his arms in the air. "We've already lost two men. I won't allow another."

"What?" said Rothchild as Montague huffed "I object!"

"We haven't lost anyone." Hitting the street, Max looked for their driver. The man was down the block but put leather to horse when he saw Max wave. Max strode down the sidewalk, meeting the carriage half way.

"Really?" Summerset clambered into the carriage behind him and scooted over to make room for the others. He jabbed a finger at Montague. "Where are you heading now that our work is done for the night?"

"Home. To Liz."

"Uh, huh. And you?" He knocked Rothchild with his knee.

"To Montague's to collect Amanda." He shrugged. "The sisters wanted to spend their evening together."

"So, instead of going to King Street or The Black Rose as we used to, the two of you are going home. To your *wives*." Derision dripped from his words like water from an icicle. "You've been domesticated."

"Don't include me in that group. I've spoken no vows." Max tugged the hem of his waistcoat.

"So, after we drop off this lot, do you want to go to a hell? Find a little trouble?" Summerset asked, skeptical. "I know a couple of women who would be more than happy to entertain us."

"Can't."

"Because you're going to your Mrs. Bonner?" Summerset shook his head sadly. "Domesticated and you don't even realize it yet. Pathetic."

Max shoved his friend, and the carriage rocked with the ensuing scuffle. Max had to admit his heart wasn't in it. Going home to a woman he cared about each night might be tame, but it did sound pleasant. Montague and Rothchild were lucky bastards.

He thought of Colleen's forgiveness and hoped that he might be allowed into the ranks of lucky bastard, as well. He took Summerset's elbow to the ear with equanimity and settled back into his seat. His life was changing, and even though his friend might not be pleased with the outcome, Max was. His jobs for Liverpool would soon be a distant memory, and he could spend his days relaxing with Colleen, puttering around the conservatory, helping her run her shop.

No, things were looking up. Even under the heavy cloud Zed cast over their lives, the bad times wouldn't last. With a remarkable woman like Colleen at his side, his future was bright.

At Montague's townhouse, Max practically kicked his

friends from the carriage.

"Hey!" Summerset stumbled to the sidewalk and ran a hand through his hair. "This isn't my stop."

"I'm certain Montague can lend you a horse. I'm going in the opposite direction." And didn't want to waste a minute before returning home. To Colleen.

Crossing his arms, Summerset shook his head. "At least I still have Dunkeld. That lout will never leg shackle himself."

Max ignored that. "I'll notify you if I hear back from Zed."

"His response might be a bullet to the head." Rothchild closed the carriage door and rested an arm in the open window. "Have you thought of that?"

"I have." Max shouted directions up to the driver. "We'd be in no worse position if Zed rejects the idea of a meet than if I'd never issued the invitation."

"Except you could be dead." Rothchild shook his head. "Don't underestimate the threat."

"I don't." Sitting back, he pounded on the ceiling, and the carriage started to roll.

Rothchild slapped the side, a wordless farewell.

Max knew his friends were concerned about him. They all put themselves at risk, but with Zed focusing on the club and Colleen, Max couldn't deny he stood closer to the line of fire.

He wasn't overly worried. Zed was a threat, but Max was prepared. His life was finally falling into place, and he wouldn't let anything stand in his way.

Not when, for the first time, he felt like he had everything to live for.

☐

Chapter Fifteen

Max peered through the row of plants, searching the shadows. The guard positioned at the door between the sitting room and the conservatory swore Colleen was within, but so far Max had seen no evidence of it.

"Colleen?" His voice seemed to melt into the glass walls. A rustle came from his left, and the woman he was looking for materialized next to the trunk of a palm tree.

Rolling to her feet, she brushed dirt off her bottom and came to meet him. "You're home earlier than I expected. You weren't able to find Dancer?"

"We found him." Wrapping his arms around her waist, he drew her close, resting his chin on the top of her head. The smell of her soap was faint beneath the citrus scents of the nearby lemon trees, but it was there. And it settled him like no nightcap ever had. "Let's go to bed."

She pulled back. "Well, what happened? You can't just tell me you found him and leave it at that."

"Can't I? You shouldn't have to worry about men like Zed."

She leveled him with a look, crossing her arms over her chest.

Max sighed. She shouldn't have to worry, but she would. And much as he hated it, Colleen was involved. Placing a hand at the curve of her back, he guided her towards the sitting room. "I asked the man to deliver a message to Zed. Nothing more. I hope Zed will reply with a time and place for the two of us to meet."

"That's a silly idea." She nodded at the guard and led

the way down the hall to the stairs. "And it will be the three of us meeting."

That was an argument he didn't want to have. Not when his bedroom was mere feet away. But there was no way in hell Colleen was going to accompany him to meet with the devil.

"I think the financial incentive I offered Zed to leave England, coupled with his desire for revenge, will make the meet happen," Max said. "He'll be curious. And we'll use that to trap him."

Colleen stopped in front of her chamber's door, but Max herded her on to his. Pushing it open, he dragged her inside, kicking the door closed behind them. "Now," he began, shrugging out of the coarse coat, "no more talk of criminals tonight. Nor the club. I want you all to myself, your mind focused on what I'm going to do to your body."

She licked her bottom lip, sending a shaft of desire straight to his groin. Her mouth was so utterly fuckable, and the need to feel her lips wrapped around his cock pounded under his skin.

Tucking his fingers into the top of her waistcoat, he yanked her forwards, enjoying the sweet way she sucked in her breath. He unbuttoned her vest and tossed it on top of his coat. Her skirts and shirt soon joined the pile. Swinging her into his arms, he strode to the armchair in front of the low table before the fireplace. Warmth from the flames heated his back as he lowered her into the chair. He sat on the table and placed one of her feet on his thighs.

"Max?" she asked as he slid off her boot and stocking. She took a deep breath. "There's something I've been meaning to speak to you about."

"Oh?" He lifted her foot and bit down on the fleshy pad of the ball. "I did say no work or Zed talk."

"Yes, but ..." She raised her bent arms, grabbing the top of the chair behind her head. The motion gave her back a delightful arch, lifting her nipples to point straight at him.

He placed her bare foot on the bulge behind his

trousers and picked up her other foot. She rubbed her toes around his hardening length, distracting him from his task.

"Whatever it is can wait." Fumbling, he scraped her stocking off and chucked it behind him. "Right now, I'd rather you use your mouth for a different purpose."

With a shy smile so unlike his Colleen, she scooted to the end of the chair and leaned her face forward. "I like kissing you, too."

Toeing off his boots, Max stood and stripped off his clothes. She looked up at him, a tiny crease etching her forehead. Placing a hand on her shoulder, he stopped her from rising.

"If you have no objection, I'll take my kiss a bit lower than my mouth."

Colleen followed his gaze down, her cheeks turning pink when she caught his meaning. She licked that damn bottom lip again. Her hand was no longer tentative when she reached for his cock, and she stroked him from base to tip, her grip firm. But uncertainty filled her eyes as she inched forward and brought him to her mouth.

Her moist lips grazed his tip, the lightest of touches. When she exhaled through her nose, the delicate stream of air fluttered around his crown, like he was being kissed by a fluttering butterfly.

It was a singularly erotic sensation.

He forced his hands to remain loose on her shoulders though they ached to ball into fists. The contact was a tease. A promise. One that he needed her to deliver on.

Closing her eyes, she eased her head from side to side, dragging the soft cocoon of her lips over his head. He wanted to let her explore. To take her time to discover just how to pleasure him.

He wasn't that patient of a man.

"Open your mouth, love." He nudged her lips with his cock. "Everything you're doing feels good, but I need a little more." Cupping the back of her head, he pushed inside a couple inches. "Fuck. Just like that."

Her hot little mouth closed around him, the velvety rub of her tongue on the underside of his length an overwhelming contrast to the wet slide against the roof of her mouth.

She pulled back and wiped saliva from her lip. "Am I doing it right?"

She was unpracticed, inexperienced. And none of that mattered. More than just the fact that a woman's mouth on his cock would always feel good, regardless of expertise. It was Colleen's mouth. Colleen's eyes staring up into his.

Perhaps it was wrong of him, but the fact she hadn't pleasured her husband in this way sent a bolt of satisfaction spearing through his gut. He was her first.

Plucking the pins from her tight knot, he shook out her thick hair. He rolled a burnished lock between his fingers. "Anything you do down there will be right. Except, take care with your teeth, please." He chucked her chin and smiled.

Gripping his base, Colleen nodded. Eying his cock like a column of numbers in her ledgers, something she needed to figure out, she stretched her mouth wide and guided him inside.

Pleasure skittered along his length, gathered inside his bollocks, and arrowed up his spine. Her mouth was fucking heaven. After his retirement from service to the Crown, this would be his primary occupation. He could spend hours with Colleen's mouth wrapped around him. Or her cunny. Any part of her. She was perfect. Sweet, honest, determined. And so willing to give pleasure.

Rocking his hips, he tried to sink a little deeper, watching her face for discomfort. She opened wider, her eyes watering a bit, but accepting his entreaty.

"Fuck yes, suck me deep." He cupped her cheek and felt his length inside her mouth. Her cheeks hollowed, the soft suction pulling at his skin with each drag.

She gargled, coughed, and Max pulled back, letting her catch her breath. Tenderly, he used his thumb to wipe the corners of her mouth. "Is this all right?"

Her breasts heaved. "It's different. But you taste good."

"I hope you continue thinking that." He couldn't wait to come down her throat. Empty himself while buried inside of her. He'd done that in error once, but nothing had ever felt better.

She ran her palm up and down his length, her saliva easing the glide. Inhaling deeply, she brought him back into her wet heat. Her lips stretched around his shaft. Reaching around, she gripped his arse and pulled him closer. Every inch he disappeared into her mouth ratcheted up his need. The sight was mesmerizing, and he couldn't take his eyes off of it.

She sucked and slowly bobbed her head. Blood pulsed through his veins, making him throb in her mouth. He buried his fingers in her hair.

"Look at me," he said, his voice as rough as gravel. "Give me your eyes."

She looked up, her gaze pinned to his face as she took him ever deeper.

Max was done. Ruined for any other woman. The look in her eyes slayed him. The trust. The sincerity. So fucking pure, so far removed from his life for the government.

His hips jerked forward. His body needed to fuck, to take whatever the woman kneeling before him was offering. And she was offering a lot.

Cradling the back of her head, he held her steady and took her mouth. Slow, steady strokes that tested his patience. Need crawled down his back, and he pulled her even tighter.

She moaned, the vibrations shuddering down his cock.

Widening his stance, he took it deeper, his crown nudging the back of her throat. His bollocks tingled, drew up tight. He held himself still, his nerve endings screaming, tipping over the point of no return.

He groaned. "I'm coming, love. Suck me hard. Swallow every drop of me down."

She closed her eyes, cheeks hollowing, her eyebrows drawing close in concentration. At her first deep drag, he exploded. Pulse after pulse of ecstasy raced through him, weakening his limbs, making him dizzy. Bending over her head, he grasped the arm of her chair with one hand and poured himself out.

Into the woman he loved.

She broke away, panting hard. Hugging him around his legs, she rested her cheek on his thigh and tried to catch her breath.

Max could only stand, legs locked and quivering, and hope that feeling would return to his feet before he collapsed onto Colleen.

"Goddamn," he said when his voice returned.

Colleen looked up at him and scratched a nail down his stomach. "You liked that, I see."

Max snorted. An answer wasn't necessary.

"Then you're going to like this even more." Placing a hand on the seat cushion, Colleen pushed to her feet. Max grabbed her waist to help her up. Resting her hands on his shoulders, she took a deep breath. "I want to be with you tonight, the way you want. I want you to show me how you play with fire."

Max's heart stuttered, came to a complete stop, before bursting into motion. He'd wanted this from the first moment he'd seen her. But she had to be certain. There was no room for indecision when it came to fire. "I need you to think carefully about this. It's all right if you're not ready. I'll—"

She laid a finger across his lips. "I'm certain."

His cock was still out of commission, but every other inch of skin buzzed. Excitement raced through his veins, but he forced calm. Calm would keep Colleen safe. Safe and satisfied. "All right. Go get on the bed. I'll get the supplies."

Striding to the side of the room, he rang the bell for a servant. Colleen yelped and ducked under the covers when someone scratched at the door. Pulling the door open just wide enough to speak through it, Max made his request and closed it. He gathered his washing bowl, a pitcher of water, and a towel. Opening the chest at the foot of his bed, he pulled out a decanter of brandy and a small torch. He set them on the table next to his bed. Picking up a candelabra near the door, he lit the candles and set it next to the bed.

Colleen held the covers up to her nose. "What did you ask the servant for?"

"You'll find out." He found a thin leather strip and crooked his finger. "Now, sit up."

With an eye on the door, she swung her legs around, and Max crawled behind her. He gathered her fiery hair into one hand and combed it out with his fingers. He separated her hair into three sections and braided it down her back, fixing it with the leather band.

Another scratch sounded at the door, and Max kissed her shoulder. "Don't worry. I won't let him see you." Hopping off the bed, he took the cloth-covered bowl from his footman and shut the door with his foot. The servant couldn't miss that Max was naked. And Max was under no illusions that installing Colleen in the room next door to his wouldn't lead to gossip amongst his servants. But Colleen was a widow; such things were more accepted.

But he shouldn't wait too long before making the situation right.

"What's in the bowl?"

Max pulled it out of her reach, the bowl chilling his hands, and set it on the far side of the bureau next to his bed. "Later. First, I want to prepare your body. Lie back."

She did so, staring at him steadily, her eyes fathomless pools of trust.

Her dusky nipples pointed to the ceiling, and Max started there, his mouth and hands tasting and teasing every inch of flesh. Fire dancing along the body created a surge of pleasure. But dancing over already aching and sensitized skin increased the pleasure three-fold.

He nibbled along the soft flesh on the underside of her breasts. Kneaded and chafed the skin over her ribs. He worked his way down her body, down each leg, not forgetting even the littlest toe.

Her thighs fell open, an invitation. The hair along her lower lips was damp with her desire, and Max's mouth watered. But he didn't want her sated. Not yet. "Roll over." He tapped her thigh, nudging her along.

She grumbled, shooting him a pointed look, but turned to her belly. He worked his way up this time. His fingers skimmed up her inner thighs, slipping close to where she needed him, but never quite making contact.

"Max!" Part angry taskmaster. Part entreaty. All delightful.

Blood pooled in Max's groin, and he bent down and bit her round arse. Her neediness, her wet and inviting sex, none of it would distract him. Not when he'd finally received an invitation to really play.

He chafed and rubbed every inch of her back and bottom until they turned pink. He dug his fingers under her shoulder blades and scraped down her back. The pressure left fleeting streaks of white skin before pinking back up.

Rocking her pelvis into the mattress, Colleen closed her eyes, breathing heavily. Max licked a trail up her spine, and she arched into his caress. Leaning over, he picked up the decanter and drizzled brandy along the path his tongue had taken. A small pool of liquid gathered in the hollow of her back.

He lapped at the brandy. "When I set the liquor aflame, you should feel heat. Your skin should tingle, some even say it tickles. And just when the sensation starts to deepen, just before it becomes too intense, I'll put it out."

Colleen clenched the pillow beneath her head. "All right." She glanced over her shoulder and smiled. "I won't lie and say I'm not apprehensive, but I'm ready. I trust you." She sank into the pillow, her eyelids fluttering shut.

Gripping his cock, Max eyed the woman laid out

beneath him and stroked. The absolute faith. The vulnerability his partner had to lay bare in order to allow him this privilege. Those were the things that made his blood burn. That made him throb with want.

There were no barriers between him and Colleen. No secrets.

Laying the towel in the water, he placed the bowl next to Colleen. He pressed a soft kiss to her shoulder and made sure her braid was out of the way.

Drawing out the moment would only increase Colleen's fear, and he just wanted her to experience pleasure. Max doused his torch in the brandy and held it over the candle's flame, watching it burst to life. Without hesitation, he set the torch to the brandy on her skin.

* * *

The small hairs on the back of her neck rose, her muscles tensing in shock. A lightning bolt speeded up her spine. She sucked in a breath as the heat grew, and grew, until she was just about to call out. Max smoothed a cool, damp cloth up her back, extinguishing the heat before it turned into a burn.

She released a shaky breath.

Max squeezed her hip. "How was that?"

Colleen took a second to consider. The skin over her backbone felt tender, and tingly, but there was no pain. "Was I truly on fire?"

He chuckled. "You truly were." He bent over her, and his cock nestled against her bottom. "It was beautiful. The fire raced up your spine, following the path of the brandy before I snuffed it out," he whispered, his breath hot on her ear. Sucking the lobe into his mouth, he gently bit down.

Lust dug a hook into her center and tugged. "More," she breathed out.

The mattress dipped. "All right. But I don't want you to overheat. Open up." He tapped her lips with something hard and frozen.

Her eyes flew open. "Ice? That's what the servant brought?"

"Yes."

She opened her mouth for another question, and he popped the shard inside. She wanted to complain about his highhandedness, but the ice felt refreshing in her mouth, and she settled for a decided sniff. She let the ice melt, sucking on the cold water it released.

Max laid another frozen piece at the nape of her neck. Shivers flooded her body as he traced the length of her spine with the ice. Her body shuddered under a different kind of burn. Following the damp trail with his mouth, he placed hot, open-mouthed kisses along each vertebra, warming up what he'd just chilled.

Colleen bit her bottom lip and dug her fingers into the pillow. Hot, cold, hot. Her senses couldn't keep up.

Gripping her leg, he tugged her knee up until it was bent beside her hip. "Open up," he repeated.

Colleen nibbled on her ice, uncertain what he was asking. When he slid another slick piece inside her core, she just about choked. "What?! Cold!" she yelled around her mouthful.

"Don't you want me to warm you up again?" He drizzled liquid across her bum and drew patterns through the brandy with his finger. Colleen wiggled, her body trying to escape the frigid intrusion, when the skin on her bottom flared awake. Streaks of heat raced across her arse. The warmth battled with the ice spreading through her core until her toes curled and a whimper was torn from her throat. Max swiped the wet towel over her skin, the cloth abrading the sensitized flesh.

Colleen drooped, every muscle as limp as an underwatered flower. She was as wrung out as though she'd walked the entire length of London.

Max set more and more lines of brandy alight, the burn on her skin receding less and less between each treatment, making her squirm. All her ice had melted, and she almost wished he'd insert another piece. She wanted to crawl out of her skin. Wanted him to touch every inch of her body with his torch. Anything to ease her ache. "Max!"

"Need something, love?"

Did she need something? Colleen needed for Max to stop sounding so smug. So controlled. She was clawing at the sheets, and he was as collected as a duchess taking tea. His mastery, over the fire, over her, burned away her barriers. She was exposed, laid completely bare. She needed Max to breach the space between them. Make them one.

Reaching back, she took hold of the stiff length. He felt as hot under her palm as the torch. She tried to guide him to her channel, but he pulled back.

He zig-zagged a chunk of ice across her back. "Are you sure you're ready? I haven't put flame to anyplace very wicked. And you haven't begged nearly enough."

She chucked her pillow over her shoulder at him.

He swatted it away with a growl. "All right then." He tossed the bowl onto the side table, water sloshing over the rim, and doused the torch in the bowl. Grabbing her hips, he jerked her bum up and entered her with one long stroke.

Colleen moaned, the relief exquisite. She didn't need anything else but Max deep inside of her. Filling her up. Making them one. She breathed deep and enjoyed the moment.

The respite didn't last long. Max pulled out until just his crown remained notched in her body and slammed back home. He set up a punishing rhythm and the heat crept back, even hotter than when he played with fire.

Crawling over her, Max threaded his fingers through hers and pressed her chest down into the mattress. He continued thrusting, the angle changed, different nerve endings sparking. "I can't get enough of you, Colleen." He bit her shoulder.

He covered her like a blanket, enveloping her in his strength. He held her down, controlled the pace.

Controlled her responses. And she was happy to let him, here in this bed. She'd lost control of her life, of her heart, and nothing had ever felt so right.

She tried to remember each delicious slide. Every exquisite tremor Max created in her body. And prayed they wouldn't be her last memories of him. Because she could no longer keep her treachery a secret. He deserved to know.

He thrust faster, his breaths coming in short heaves. His frenzy, his need for her, drove her own passion higher. That a man like Max could want her was something she'd always cherish. Her body coiled tight, all of her muscles clamping down. Max's pace faltered before redoubling with effort and pounding back home.

Burying her face in the sheets, Colleen let out a strangled gasp and went over the edge. Pleasure rippled outward from her core, shaking her body.

Max cursed. He pulled out and ground into her lower back, groaning. Liquid heat splashed across her skin, reminiscent of the fire that had seared her flesh.

He rolled to his side, pulling Colleen with him, holding her close. Their skin cooled and their breathing slowed.

Max kissed her neck. "That never gets old, does it?"

She laced her fingers with his, palm to palm, and held his hand over her heart. She brushed her lips over his knuckles. "No." And it never would. Colleen swallowed, the back of her throat burning. "I need to tell you something. Something I should have told you earlier. But I've been scared."

Brushing a lock of hair back from her cheek, Max held her tighter. "You have nothing to be scared of. I won't let anything hurt you."

"It's not that type of scary." She closed her eyes and took a deep breath. Her heart pounded painfully behind her breast, and she almost changed her mind. But it wasn't fair to Max. He needed to know the truth.

"You didn't kill my husband, Max," she whispered. "I

did."

She waited, motionless as a rock, her pulse racing. He didn't respond. Colleen bit her lip. He must not have heard. She opened her mouth to repeat it, but Max moved first. Jumping to his hands and knees, he flipped her to her back.

He stared down at her, his face expressionless. "Say that again."

"Whatever you're thinking, it wasn't like that." Clutching his wrist, she held on tight. The words tumbled from her mouth. "My husband was supposed to be gone that night, spending the evening with some friends. I was in our office when I smelled the smoke. The chandlery and our clock shop shared a backyard. I went outside and saw the fire."

Max sat back on his haunches, a horrible resignation creeping over his face.

She dug her fingers into his skin. "I heard calls for the bucket brigade. Knew they'd be there shortly to put out the flames. And for a moment, I wished it was our shop that was burning. That it was all those clocks going up in flames. So, when I ran back inside and my hip knocked an oil lamp from the desk, I didn't react at first. I just stared as the flames spread across the floor. Then the curtains caught, and the fire seemed to be everywhere. I escaped outside. My husband wasn't supposed to be home," she repeated. "I didn't call up to warn him. I didn't mean to hurt anyone."

"But you did." Jerking from her grip, Max rubbed his wrist. As if trying to remove her mark.

"It happened so fast." She swallowed as blood pounded behind her temples. "You don't know how stifling my life was. I felt like I was being buried alive, buried under the weight of all those clocks. I hated that shop. But I didn't mean for it to happen. I just thought that, finally, God was answering my prayers."

Max rolled off the bed and gathered his clothes. He tugged on his trousers, his movements jerky. "I wondered how the fire could have spread. I thought there must have been a gust of wind I didn't account for. Something I'd missed. This makes more sense."

Colleen crawled to the edge of the mattress. "My husband came home early. His friend later told me he had been complaining of a headache. I never knew." Every night she thought how things would have been different if she'd only yelled, woken him from his slumber. If she hadn't waited those long seconds watching the fire eat across her office, if she'd tried to smother the flames.

"I reckon that makes it all right then."

She twisted the sheets in her fingers. "I never said it was all right."

The muscles in Max's back bunched as he pulled on his shirt.

"Look at me," Colleen begged. There was no way the kind man who'd rubbed the sting from her sore feet, who'd made sure she had employment, and a roof over her head, there was no way *he* could turn from her now. Not when they'd come to mean so much to each other.

But when Max looked up at her, it was the face of a man Colleen didn't recognize who met her gaze.

"I'll have one of my men return you to the club. You've performed in an exemplary manner as manager of The Black Rose." Striding to the wall, Max rang for a servant. "You're welcome to remain in that capacity as long as you wish."

Pain stabbed into her stomach and she bent double, her forehead hitting her knees. "I thought—" She broke off and gasped for air. "I thought you'd understand."

"I do understand."

She looked up, a seed of hope taking root. Max smiled politely and handed Colleen her clothes.

Everything in her withered and died.

"I understand that when I confessed to you, you remained silent," Max said. "I understand you are more adept at subterfuge than I'd thought. Even though killing your husband was an accident, you still might have faced criminal prosecution. You couldn't risk that. Your safety is more important than honesty, after all."

Mechanically, Colleen slid into her shift and skirt. She shook out her crumpled shirt and slipped her arms through the sleeves. "Believe it or not but being punished wasn't at the top of my concerns."

Someone scratched at the door.

Colleen held his gaze. "I didn't want you to think poorly of me. But I couldn't keep silent any longer. I didn't want you to bear the burden of a guilt you didn't earn. I didn't want there to be anything between us. Not even a secret."

"I'm most appreciative." Max turned for the door and pointed to the floor by the fire. "Your boots are there. When you return to the club, please remember to stay by your guards. They are there for your protection."

Noble to the end. He treated her as a stranger, but Max treated strangers well. It was one of the things she loved about him. He treated everyone with respect until they showed themselves undeserving of it.

She should be grateful. She'd shown him her worst. Instead of scorn, he gave her a pleasant smile and a polite goodbye.

It hurt worse than if he'd struck her. But it was nothing more than she deserved. Jamming her feet into her boots, she looked around for her waistcoat and put it on. Pulling the gold watch from its pocket, she squeezed it in her palm. She wouldn't cry in front of him. Her tears would only make him uncomfortable.

She paused by the door he held open. One of her guards stood across the hall, looking at the floor. Colleen ignored him. "I'm sorry," she told Max. "You'll never know how much."

He stared over her head and nodded.

Without a backwards glance, Colleen marched for the stairs. She was a survivor. She'd made it through worse.

Somehow, she'd make it through Max.

☐

Chapter Sixteen

Max slid a second knife into his boot. He smoothed down his trouser leg, making sure the handle of the blade wasn't visible.

"I can't believe Zed agreed to this meet." Summerset flipped his own knife from handle to blade, a mesmerizing blur of silver in the candlelight. They were all gathered at Montague's townhouse preparing for the night. Zed's response had arrived swiftly. Dancer had shown up on Max's doorstep, missive in hand and a large, purpling bruise around his eye.

Max wondered how long Zed would let the man live. The crime lord seemed to have limited tolerance for those that could lead the Crown to him. Dancer had slipped past Max's men to contact Zed but he couldn't evade a tail forever.

Why would Dancer, or any man, continue to work for someone after his abuse. Was the money that good or was the sailor as devoted as so many of the others to their mysterious leader? The man didn't seem like a fanatic. Fear must hold him in place.

Checking the powder in his double-barreled flintlock, Max pushed the lackey from his mind. He needed to push all extraneous thoughts from his head if tonight was going to be a success. If they caught Zed, Max wouldn't have to worry about protecting Dancer's worthless life.

He took aim at his reflection in the large gilt mirror across the sitting room. Colleen's lovely blue eyes stared accusingly back at him. Max swallowed and shook her image from his mind.

Rothchild lounged on a settee and took a pull from his cheroot. "Zed may have agreed to meet, but that's no guarantee he'll show. We need to handle this carefully. I'm certain he'll have just as many men surrounding St. Katherine's as we do."

"But he said he'd come alone," Summerset said, eyes wide, tone mocking. Gripping his knife by the blade, he executed a neat spin and hurled it at the wall above the fireplace. The blade buried deep into an oil portrait of a homely older woman dressed in a stiff-bodiced mantua. The handle of the knife stuck out right between her beady eyes.

"Confound it!" Montague entered the room and slammed the tray he was carrying down onto a low table. Marching to the wall, he yanked the knife out and ran his finger along the puckered slash of the canvas. "This was my great-grandmother, you lackwit. What in the blazes were you thinking?"

Montague's wife, Elizabeth, put down her own tray and moved to her husband to rub his back. "I'm sure it can be repaired. Until then, I'll have a footman put her in storage. Besides, this gives us a space now to put up that new Vermeer you bought for me." *Thank you*, she mouthed to Summerset behind Montague's back.

The earl winked back at her. "I need all the target practice I can get to prepare for the night ahead," he said innocently.

Montague growled and ripped the painting off the wall.

Rothchild leaned forward and picked up a small sandwich. "I don't believe I've ever been served by a duke before. Have you taken a cue from your lovely wife and decided to playact as a servant?"

The smile Elizabeth shot Rothchild wasn't nearly as warm as the one Summerset had received. "My husband thought it best that our servants weren't made aware of your preparations for the night. He's given them the evening off.

And if you require anything else, you will have to fend for yourself. I'm off to your house to spend the evening with my sister." Bending down, she pecked a kiss on his cheek. "And it wouldn't hurt you, brother, to experience a little of how the other half lives."

Rothchild took Liz's hand. "Tell my wife not to worry."

"How can we not?" She looked to Montague and laid a hand on her abdomen, a look passing between them.

Max's heart twisted like a wrung-out rag. He recognized the look. Love. Adoration. It was the same one that Colleen had given him yesterday. Before she'd revealed her perfidy. Before he'd told her to leave. He rubbed his jaw, a scratchy bristle. He hadn't bothered to shave that morning. There was no one to impress.

"Both Amanda and I have tried to think of ways to help you in this endeavor." Liz straightened and smoothed her skirts. "But all our thinking has come to naught. The best we can do for you this time is to stay out of your way and trust that you will take care."

"Come." Montague smoothed a strand of hair from his wife's cheek. "I'll show you to the carriage." Taking her hand, he led her from the room. He whispered something in her ear that made her gasp and smile, and they disappeared down the hall.

Summerset snorted. "The duchess must have—"

"Take care what you say of my sister-in-law," Rothchild said mildly. "I'd hate to have to kill you defending her honor."

"—must have a spine of steel to train Montague so well." Summerset glared at his friend. "I'm quite fond of the duchess and wouldn't insult her, as you damn well know."

Max rubbed his forehead and dropped into a chair. He wanted nothing more than to climb into bed and forget the past twenty-four hours. "Gentlemen, can you please shut your traps? I'd prefer to focus on the task ahead and not have to listen to your incessant bickering." Moderating the level of his voice, he continued. "Let's go over the plan one more time."

"What's to plan?" Summerset dropped onto the chair next to Max, draping a leg over the armrest. "You go meet with Zed. We try to take out his men before they take you out. Simple." He nudged Max's thigh with the toe of his boot. "I'd be much more interested in discussing what's put your smallclothes in a bunch."

Montague came back into the room and paused midstride. "I fear I've come into this conversation at an inopportune moment."

Rothchild waved a scone at Max. "Sutton is acting like a grumpy bear. Seems to be trying to outdo Dunkeld in the man's absence." He took a bite and jabbed the half-eaten pastry at Summerset. "That one is using his extraordinary gift with words to try to learn why Max is upset."

"Ah." Montague poured himself a cup of tea. "I can't imagine it's easy knowing you will be walking into a trap in a couple of hours. That could account for Sutton's mood."

Max sat up straight. "Are you saying I'm afraid?"

"He is getting up there in years," Rothchild said. "I hear a man starts to feel it in his bones. That could be the problem."

"I'm a year younger than you!" Max threw himself back in his seat. Truly, his friends were all arseholes.

"You're both wrong." Lacing his fingers together, Summerset rested his hands on his stomach, twirling his thumbs. "It's because of a woman, or a lack thereof. I can tell when someone isn't satisfied. An excess of vigor that hasn't been spent can lead a man to snap at his bosomfriends over the smallest of jests."

Max remained silent. Fuckwits. Each and every one of them.

Three faces swiveled in his direction. Too late, he realized his mistake.

"So that's it then. Your manager." Montague raised a golden eyebrow. "Has a rift developed between the two of you?"

A rift. More like a goddamned canyon. "Nothing has developed between us."

Summerset snorted. "It took you long enough to realize that your Mrs. Bonner didn't have what is needed to keep you happy. How could a clock-maker's wife feed your unique appetite? After we apprehend Zed, I'll take you out, let our little arsonist play—"

"Enough!" Max dug his fingers into the upholstered fabric of the armrest, anything to keep them from throttling his friend of a decade. "She fed me fine." Perfectly.

"What happened?" Montague asked. He poured a glass of something stronger than tea and handed it to Max.

He downed the whiskey, enjoying the burn along his throat. It distracted him from the pain squeezing his chest. Leaning his head back, he stared at the ceiling. "What I say here goes no further." He didn't need to see his friends nod to know they would agree. "You all know I was working for Liverpool when I set fire to the shop next to Colleen's."

"Guilt seems like a poor reason to start a relationship with a woman," Rothchild said.

Max snapped his gaze down but saw no judgment in Rothchild's eyes. "Perhaps it was. But that point is moot. For it isn't my guilt that is the issue. It's hers. She confessed to me that when she saw her neighbor's shop burning, she accidentally knocked over a lamp, setting fire to her own. She's responsible for her husband's death."

He stared into his empty glass. How the guilt must have wracked her. Kept her up at night as it had him. He didn't know how he'd missed it. All the signs were there. Her reluctance to wear the clothes he bought for her. How she always fingered that damn watch, her link to her husband. For a man who prided himself on reading people, the lapse was unforgivable.

Summerset pursed his lips. "If it was an accident, what is she guilty of?"

"Of keeping the truth from me." Of not being the woman he'd thought she was.

"What are you going to do?" Montague asked.

"Nothing."

"You will continue your affair?" Rothchild nodded. "Good for you."

Max frowned. "Of course, I won't continue the affair. It's over."

"Why?"

Max couldn't believe Rothchild even had to ask. "She lied to me. She listened to my confession and kept her own close to her chest. A good woman would have come forward the day after the fire and told the magistrate what had happened, not waited to acknowledge her own guilt until—" *Until he'd fallen arse over teakettle in love with her.* He bit off his words, not wanting to admit his own folly to his friends.

Scraping his fingers along his jaw, he slouched in his chair. He didn't blame Colleen. Not really. No one wanted to expose their guilt. But everything he'd thought he knew about her, her character, her honesty, had been a lie. Perhaps if he'd—

A jewel-encrusted boot sparkled in the corner of his vision, lashing out and striking his armrest. His chair rocked up onto two legs. Max wind-milled his arms, trying to regain his balance, but his body slid to the side of the chair and his weight tipped it over. He crashed to his side, his temple bouncing off the Aubusson carpet.

Max blinked in surprise.

"Bloody fucking hell!" Montague yelled. "First my great-grandmother's portrait. Now my Chippendale chair. Stop destroying my property, you gormless git!"

Pushing up onto one hip, Max glared at Summerset. The man had the audacity to look unrepentant, still aimlessly bobbing his boot through the air.

"Sutton has a tendency to be a self-righteous prick." Summerset shrugged. "He needed to be tossed on his head."

Montague righted the chair and wiggled the broken

armrest. "You could have done that without breaking my chair.

"Or my head." Max pushed to his feet.

Rothchild poured himself a cup of tea, stirring in some sugar. "I wouldn't call him self-righteous, per se." He took a delicate sip. "I don't think Sutton thinks he's a better person than everyone else. But now that Mrs. Bonner has fallen from the pedestal he'd placed her on, she's no longer worth his time."

Heat flushed through Max's body. "What the hell do you know about it?"

Montague laid a hand on his shoulder, and Max shrugged him off.

"Come now," Montague said quietly. "You can't deny that you have a rosy ideal of how you think life should be. And that includes romanticizing the women you're with." Montague poured him another glass of whiskey, only half full. "Inevitably, you're disappointed when circumstances and people don't live up to your expectations."

"Mrs. Bonner is made of flesh and blood." Rothchild leaned forward in his chair. "She'll make mistakes. But I've never seen you so torn up about a woman. You've certainly never shaved for one before." He shook his head, his mouth twisting wryly. "Are you certain you want to give her up for one mistake?"

Summerset cleaned his nails with his blade. "To be fair, it was a large mistake. She killed her husband. How could Sutton lie next to her at night easy in mind? She might set fire to the bedsheets."

"Don't be ridiculous." Max raised his glass to his mouth, paused. "A child's pour?" He frowned. "You think I'm acting like an infant so give me only an infant's portion of whiskey?"

Montague sat on the armrest of the settee. "You'll need all your senses about you tonight. Only being prudent."

Max grunted and knocked the swallow back. He fixed Summerset with a glare. "Colleen doesn't make a habit of tipping over lamps."

"Your money must have been a great inducement to the woman." Summerset started flipping his knife again. He must have known he would need to have a weapon at the ready by continuing to speak of Colleen such. "A baron in her bed. Quite the step up from a clockmaker."

"He didn't make the clocks," Max gritted out. "Only sold and repaired them." He didn't need to defend Colleen's honor. Such an accusation was absurd. Colleen had never asked him for anything except the money she had earned.

Summerset tapped the blade against his lips. "I suppose it could have been the bed sport that attracted her. A widow knows what she's missing and must look for comfort somewhere. It's convenient she manages a Venus club. Now that you're done with her, she'll have easy access to a replacement."

Blood pounded in Max's ears. Summerset surely had a death wish. Friend or not, if he laid one more insult at Colleen's door ...

"I hear that Lord Halliwell—"

With a roar, Max hurled his glass at the fireplace. It shattered against the brick the same moment Max's hands encircled Summerset's neck. "Shut your filthy mouth." He yanked John to his feet. "I swear to God, if you say one more word against her, I will knock out all your teeth and shove them down your throat to choke on."

Montague and Rothchild each took an arm and pulled him off Summerset. The earl bent at the waist, heaving for air. Swiping his blade off the carpet, he straightened. The look he shot Max was much too smug for a man who'd nearly been strangled.

Montague shoved Max onto the settee. "Settle down. Summerset can be annoying, but he's useful in a fight. We'll need him tonight."

"Yes, he's so shiny and pretty he makes excellent cannon fodder," Rothchild added. "Everyone's aim is drawn in his direction. At least let his death be useful."

"All of you can sod off." Planting his boot on his chair, Summerset slid his knife under the tight cuff of his pantaloons. "I cut to the truth of the matter much sooner than you all did. We don't have time to play around tonight."

"What truth is that?" Max's chest tightened, his breath drawing short.

Summerset stared at him, his blue eyes losing their superciliousness. They reminded him of Colleen's, and Max shrugged away that uncomfortable thought. "You've never cared about a woman's next partner before," Summerset said. "Once done, you wish a woman merry and go about your day. But not with this one. What's changed?"

His friends waited for his response, all bearing silent witness.

Max opened his mouth. Shut it. He shook his head. "So, I care about her. What does that matter? She ..." She hadn't led a blameless life? She hadn't conformed to his perfect ideal of a woman? In defending her from Summerset's attacks, Max was reminded of how grand a woman his Colleen was. One error in judgment didn't change the rest of her character.

Digging his fingers into his scalp, Max groaned. "Christ, I'm an idiot."

"We already knew that," Summerset said. "We want to know if you actually"—he wrinkled his nose—"love that woman?"

Max flopped onto the settee and dropped his head onto the backrest. He stared at the trompe l'oeil of the sky painted on the ceiling. An emotion as lauded as love shouldn't feel like this. Like his heart had been ripped from his chest, shredded to small pieces, and shoved back inside the cavity to rot. Like each day of his life would be a misery if it didn't start with Colleen lying beside him.

"Jesus fucking Christ," Summerset swore. "I've lost

another one."

Ignoring him, Max looked to his two friends who knew something. "What do I do? I sent her away."

Montague tilted his head. "To your club? Hardly the far side of the world."

"But what I said ..." He'd been so cold to her. Had locked down his emotions. Didn't let the hurt in her eyes sway him from his course. Guilt gnawed at him.

"We all know you're not perfect, either." Rothchild knocked Max on his shoulder. "She'll have to do some forgiving of her own."

Max nodded, his resolution firming. He was a determined man, used to getting his way. Colleen was a proud woman, however. He swallowed, his throat going thick. Earning her forgiveness wouldn't be easy.

But he'd do whatever it took. Colleen might not be perfect, but she was perfect for him. He'd been a fool to ever think otherwise. Catching Zed was the second most important thing he had to do that night.

Sliding to the edge of his seat, Max rested his elbows on his knees. "Let's go through the plan again. Mark out all our positions. I want this done quickly and cleanly."

"What's the rush all of a sudden?" Summerset asked.

"I have new plans for the evening and I can't waste time playing around with a blackmailer."

* * *

Colleen shut the lid on her borrowed valise. All of her belongings fit easily inside; she would take nothing that Max had added to her wardrobe. Sitting on the lid, she dropped her forehead to her knees. The finality of the act struck her and a shudder tore through her body.

Her time with Max was over. She needed to face that. She'd told him the truth, shown him who she truly was, and he didn't want her.

She took one breath. Two. Each inhalation sending pain clawing through her chest. She pushed past it. She'd endured the loss of her husband and the accompanying guilt. She would endure the loss of Max.

A footman knocked on the door. Colleen rose and took the note from his hand. "Thank you." It only took one glance to confirm its contents. "Can you take my case down?" she asked the man, pointing to where it sat on the floor. With a nod, he hefted it to his shoulder and disappeared from the room.

Colleen sat on her bed and read the note more closely. Her cousin, although terribly inconvenienced by her sudden request, would honor his duty and allow her a spot in his daughters' bed. So long as she remembered that poor Jonny had grown another inch and required new clothes. That Julia was feeling most indisposed and would appreciate help around the house.

So long as Colleen remembered her place.

Well, there was nothing for it. Beggars couldn't be choosers. And living under the yoke of her cousin was infinitely preferable to spending one more night under the roof of the man who'd broken her heart.

Grabbing her old coat, Colleen marched down the hall. She thought about stopping in her office, writing Max a note. But what was left to say? He would know where she was. The guards that still trailed her every step would see to that. And she couldn't imagine Max would be anything other than relieved by her absence. She was doing them both a favor by removing herself from his presence. A favor to Max and a mercy to herself.

A guard at the bottom of the stairwell held the door open. "Where are we going, madam?"

"To Wapping. I have family there." She swallowed down the bile in her throat. "Just give me a moment to speak with Lucy, and I'll be ready to leave."

She found the woman working in one of the back rooms. She was one of three girls with two male customers writhing together on the absurdly large bed of the Amethyst Room. A large crowd had gathered around the scene, and the hands of those watching were disappearing into as many unheard-of places as those of the participants on the bed. Just another night at The Black Rose.

The moans and shudders seemed to be reaching a peak so Colleen stepped back out of the room and waited, leaning against the opposite wall.

Lucy hurried out a few minutes later, securing a billowing silk robe about her. "Did you want something?"

Colleen raised one side of her mouth. "Even with your attention diverted amongst so many people, you still noticed my entrance. I'm impressed."

She shrugged one slim shoulder. "In my work, you have to keep one eye on the door at all times." She took in Colleen's coat. "You going somewhere?"

"Yes." Clasping her hands together, Colleen gave the girl a tight smile. "My employment at The Black Rose has come to an end. I will be leaving its management in your hands. Now is the time to impress Lord Sutton. Prove to him that he doesn't need to hire anyone else to run the place."

"But ..." Lucy opened and closed her mouth. "It's too soon. I haven't learned enough."

"You found us another wine supplier, didn't you?" The door to the Amethyst Room opened, and Colleen guided Lucy down the hall to the main room. The band was playing a lively tune, and several people were dancing a rather drunken jig. "And you think you've found a replacement for Molly."

The woman nodded, worrying her bottom lip.

"That is management," Colleen assured her. "Keeping supplies well-stocked, heading off disasters. I know you keep tidy ledgers. And you know how to manage all the personalities here. Everything else you can learn as you go. And if you have questions, I will be staying with my cousin. You can contact me there."

"What will you do?"

Colleen hadn't thought that far ahead. Pulling a pair of

threadbare gloves from her coat pocket, she tugged them on. "I will find something." Hopefully, if Max apprehended Zed tonight, he would make good on his long-ago promise of a premium. If Mr. Ridley's flower shop was no longer for sale, well, there would be others. She would find a way to achieve her dreams.

Something pinched behind her breastbone, and she rubbed her chest. Dreams were funny things. They had a way of changing without a person even being aware of the transformation. Her flower shop, full of energy and life, didn't seem so sparkling as it used to. Just another place where she would spend her days alone.

Shaking the melancholy from her mind, she clasped Lucy's hand. "I have every faith in your abilities. Remember, there is no shame in asking for assistance when needed." She pressed a brass key into the woman's palm. "My office is now yours."

"Thank you." Lucy flipped up the collar of her robe. "I guess I should change. The manager of The Black Rose shouldn't wander about in a negligee."

"Go to the wardrobes upstairs." Colleen checked her reticule, making sure she had all she needed. "The baron fitted them out with all the uniforms you could ever need."

With one more well-wish, Colleen was on her way. She strode outside to the carriage waiting at the sidewalk. The guard held the door open, giving her a hand up.

Facing front, Colleen settled in, clutching her reticule tightly on her lap. Her guard sat next to her, and the carriage rolled forwards in silence.

Every fiber of her being longed to push back the window's curtain and watch as her home for the past several months faded from view. As though prolonging her sight of the building would prolong her connection to Max. She might have done so had she been alone.

The carriage stopped, the streets around them silent.

She rapped on the ceiling. "Is there a problem?"

No answer.

Frowning, her guard lowered his window and stuck his head out. "I don't see anything blocking us. Why aren't we moving?"

Colleen glanced outside. The man was right. The street lay dark and empty before them. The Black Rose was situated on a narrow side street in a business district that bedded down at night. Perfect for men to keep their club membership private.

She bit her lip. The emptiness was unnerving. The club lay only thirty feet behind them. "Perhaps we should turn around?" Get out and run was more to point, but showing her fear never helped anyone.

Leaning forwards, the guard wedged his shoulders through the window until he was halfway out. "I don't see our driver. Nor the other guards who're supposed to be following." Flicking back his jacket, he reached for a pocket pistol. "Hell. Stay—"

Something thudded. The guard's body jerked, then fell slack, hanging half out the window.

The door on her side of the carriage was flung open, and Colleen shrieked. Slapping at the hands that reached for her, she lurched to the other side of the carriage. The guard had been reaching for a weapon, and if she could only get her hands on it ...

She felt for his pocket, kicking out at the body trying to clamber inside with her all the while. Her thumb just brushed cold metal when the guard's body swung out of her reach as the door on that side opened. The poor man slid from the window, crumpling in a heap at another dark form's feet. The shadow reached for her just as a hand encircled one ankle.

Colleen renewed her struggle, knowing it was hopeless. The odds were stacked against her. She wouldn't win. Whatever these ruffians wished to inflict upon her, they could.

But that didn't mean she wouldn't spend her last breath fighting.

Chapter Seventeen

Rain tapped against the stained-glass windows, the sound a low tattoo throughout the marble chambers of St. Katherine's cathedral. Max leaned against a column at the far end of the nave, looking deceptively casual, but every muscle in his body was coiled tight.

Zed was late. Max popped open his watch. Two minutes and forty seconds late to be precise. Tucking the timepiece away, he looked at the crucifix hanging behind the altar. Jesus looked as impatient as Max felt. Catching Zed had fallen in his list of priorities. Right now, Colleen was laying her head down on her pillow, thinking he didn't care. That problem seemed more important to rectify.

That's what his heart said. His mind knew better.

He checked the doors and hallways that led into the nave, wondering where the trap would be laid. Just like Max, Zed would not be arriving alone.

A door squeaked open by the front entrance. Max's body hummed, his restlessness spiking when he saw the slight, cloaked figure walk down the side aisle. A woman would prove a good distraction.

Her slippers made no sound on the stone floor. She stopped by the first pew and dropped to one knee before sliding onto the bench. She stared at the altar, the hood of her cloak covering half her face.

Easing around his column, Max searched the rest of the church. All remained still. He cocked a shoulder against the column and crossed his arms over his chest. He slid a hand into an inside pocket and gripped the butt of the pistol hidden within.

He was tired of waiting. "Are you here for me?" he called, his voice startling loud in the church.

The figure didn't flinch. "Of course." The voice was low, melodic, as soothing as a fire on a cold winter's night.

It sent a shiver of dread straight down Max's spine.

He took a step closer. "Do I know you?"

She laughed. "I would like to say intimately so, but, sadly, I've never had the pleasure."

"Show yourself."

"As you wish." Gracefully, she lifted the hood, pushing it off her head, exposing a twist of glossy brown hair. Molly winked at him. "I'm not usually the one taking orders, but I'm open to new experiences."

It couldn't be. Max searched the corners of the church again, expecting Zed to appear at any moment.

He and Molly were alone.

"You are Zed?"

She inclined her head.

"How?"

Draping an arm along the back of the pew, Molly raised an eyebrow. "Don't you really mean 'why'?"

"I know why." Making a quarter-turn, Max pinned his gaze on the shadows dancing beneath the lip of the front doors. His men or Zed's—Molly's—he didn't know. "Greed, of course. The motive was always obvious. People are such grasping, common little creatures. It's not surprising you'd be the same."

"Hah! I've been leading you and your friends around by your noses for the past year. I'm hardly common."

Max gripped the end of the pew. "You're smarter than most, I'll grant you that. But someone of true intelligence would understand that honor is worth more than money."

"Now you're just speaking nonsense." She traced a pattern in the grain of the wood. "You don't truly think your friends outside are going to help you, do you? My men have already identified each and every one of them and are disabling your force as we speak."

They would try, Max had no doubt. But he trusted in the abilities of his friends. "How do you get men to kill, and die, so easily for you? Money and threats only go so far. Some of your followers, it's as though they are in a trance."

She shrugged, her cloak slipping off to expose a pale shoulder covered by a slender red strap. "If that's what you want to talk about, all right. I discovered early on in life how easily men could be swayed. At first, just by spreading my thighs." She wagged a finger at Max. "Your sex truly has no self-control when it comes to the snake between your legs. The secrets I learned were delicious."

Max didn't doubt it. Many a campaign had been defeated by a seductress. "Men can speak too freely, especially if prevailed upon by some pretty young chit. But I saw someone cut his own throat rather than betray you." He raised an eyebrow. "I don't care how sweet in bed you are, no doxy is worth that."

She laughed, a light, tinkling sound. "Do you think that's all I am to my men?" Leaning forwards, her eyes caught the flickering lights of the candles on the altar. "I am the alpha and the omega. The reason my men get out of bed in the morning. Earning my approval is their sole purpose in life."

"You used your skills from the club, your authority as a dominating woman, to affect these men's minds." Max could see it. When a person submitted him- or herself, they made themselves vulnerable, physically and mentally. A mad-woman, talented in her craft, could use that susceptibility, bend it, until the people she dominated depended upon her for the very air they breathed. "Is that why you stayed on at The Black Rose? Lord knows you didn't need the money. Why keep working there?"

"It isn't work when you enjoy it. Besides," she said, adjusting the strap of her gown, "one can never have enough money. The secrets I learned at the club, the men I brought into line under me, definitely made it worth my while."

There was a scuffle, a groan, beyond the front doors. Max's friends were close. Fascinating as Molly's mental defect was, it was time to wrap up this chapter in Max's life. "We have the church surrounded. You have to know the Crown won't let you escape." He cocked his head. "Why did you engage with us? Why not take your ill-gotten gains and buy a villa in Tuscany?"

She jumped to her feet, shaking with fury. "What gains? Six months ago, you and your friends laid waste to my network, froze half my net-worth."

Yes, and if their calculations were correct, the remaining half was still more than most earls could hope to see in their lifetime.

She advanced a step. "I always return a favor. A cut for a cut. I owe you for the trouble you caused and it's time that I delivered."

She was mad. Max could see that in her eyes. He wondered if Liverpool would account for her illness when he decided her punishment. "My friends are waiting at the front door," he said gently. "Come with us quietly, and let's avoid further bloodshed."

"Isn't that sweet?" Running her palm down the ermine trim of her cloak, she smiled. "You think it's your friends at the door." She flicked her fingers in a shooing motion. "Well, go check. Let's get that last bit of hope of yours out of the way."

Max stepped back, uneasy, and glanced at the double doors. Of course, it was his friends beyond it, waiting in the narthex. Molly might have a lot of men under her control, but Max and his friends had all the resources of the Crown behind them. Liverpool wanted Zed caught; he hadn't been stingy in the amount of men he'd sent.

"Go on." She bit her lip, looking coy and girlish, and nothing like a criminal mastermind.

Keeping an eye on her, ready to pounce at the first sign of her flight, Max made his way to the doors. It was time to end this charade. Maybe once Molly saw she was surrounded she'd give up her delusions.

He flung open the left door, ready to ask his friends what had taken them so long. An unfamiliar male face stared back at him. Max frowned. Liverpool had many men. It could be someone Max hadn't met.

It wasn't until Max had convinced himself of that fact that he saw the arm the man had a grip on. The body attached to that limb was hidden behind the second door. With a tobacco-stained smile, the man tugged on the arm and Colleen stumbled into the doorway. Her face was pale except for the purpling between her left eye and temple. Her hair had long ago escaped its pins and flew about her head in a crimson tangle.

Instinctively, Max reached for her. The man holding her took a step back and pressed the edge of the blade he held with his other hand beneath her breast.

Max's feet rooted to the ground. He swallowed, his mouth dry as the desert, and let his arms drop to his sides.

Understanding crashed on him likes waves, swamping his brain, making him dizzy. His friends wouldn't be coming. If they'd been able, they would have rescued Colleen already. He was all that stood between the woman he loved and the vengeance of a lunatic.

"I must admit I don't understand what it is you find appealing in her," Molly said from behind him. "But I'm so glad that you do care. It makes it that much more satisfying killing a person when someone who loves them is there to watch."

Chapter Eighteen

The man holding the knife to Colleen jerked his head, indicating Max should step back, and he obeyed. Max's gaze was transfixed on the knife, that three-inch length of steel that could destroy his future.

"It's going to be all right," Max said. Trying to reassure Colleen or himself, he didn't know.

She nodded and lifted her chin. If Max didn't know her better, he would think she wasn't afraid. As though having a man hold a knife to her was an everyday occurrence. But he did know her better. Saw the slight quiver of her lips before she set them into a firm line. Saw her hands clench into fists beneath the cuffs of her cousin's old coat.

The group of them marched to the altar. Molly, Max, Colleen and her captor. "This church, hell, this entire city block, is surrounded by government men," Max said. "You're only rational choice is to give yourself up."

"All those men are currently battling my own." Molly stepped up on the altar and lifted a taper from a three-pronged candelabra. "I practically have my own army. But thanks for your concern. Besides, I love this church. It's so peaceful." She took a deep breath and sighed. "Even after your men blocked off all the underground tunnels that I used months ago, I still came here for the quiet."

"You worked at the club." Colleen tugged at the arm her captor still held, but the man jerked her back into his chest. She frowned. "Why write to me asking for information on the members? You most likely knew more about them than I did."

"Why not?" Raising the candle high, Molly stepped close, the flame throwing flickering shadows on Colleen's face. "You annoyed me, so it seemed fitting to involve you. Also, if the manager of The Black Rose was giving me information, no one would wonder how I came to know the secrets that went on behind those walls."

Max nodded. "Putting Madame Sable, and then Colleen, on your payroll deflected attention away from you. Smart."

Molly dropped a low curtsy. "Why, thank you, my lord."

"Trying to kill her when you invited her to this very same church would have ruined that deception, however." Glancing at the front doors, Max prayed for a miracle to burst through. They remained shut. "That wasn't so smart."

Molly snorted. "When I sent her that note?"

Max nodded and inched closer to Colleen. The man holding her adjusted his grip on the knife, and the blade twisted against her waistcoat. Max's lungs froze.

"I wasn't going to do her in then." Molly ran her fingers through the candles' flames, her gaze transfixed on the flickering fire. "My man was just going to offer her more money for information."

Colleen dipped her chin and raised an eyebrow, giving Max a look.

He pressed his lips together. Yes, she'd been right about Zed's motives, but this was hardly the time to tell him 'I told you so.'

"When I had the club attacked, I definitely wanted her gutted then, however. Her and that backstabbing American." Molly cracked her neck and stared at Colleen, her eyes as flat as a dead fish's. "You shouldn't have threatened to dismiss me. You shouldn't have insulted me so."

Colleen's jaw dropped. "I didn't insult you. I rebuked you, and it was well-deserved. You can't kill someone over a well-deserved rebuke."

Max shifted closer to the man holding Colleen, closer to

the knife. "Don't bother arguing with a madwoman. You'll never win."

"I'm rich, beautiful, and powerful." Molly shrugged gracefully. "I believe I would be called eccentric rather than mad. Now," she said, raising an eyebrow, "I know how much you enjoy fire. Don't you think Mrs. Bonner would look lovely all aglow?"

Before Max could stop her, Molly stooped over and touched the flame to Colleen's skirts.

"No!" Max roared, jerking forwards.

Colleen kicked out, her boot knocking the candle from Molly's hand and catching the lunatic on her shoulder.

Molly fell to the ground, her rear end hitting the floor hard. She narrowed her eyes. "Cut her throat!"

The world slowed. Max saw the blade inch towards Colleen's neck, but he was too far away to stop it, too sluggish. A side door banged open, and Max didn't care if it were friend or foe coming through. He stared into Colleen's deep blue eyes, drowning in their depths.

She blinked, and the world snapped into motion. Colleen twisted, grabbing the man's wrist, using her body weight to pull his arm down.

Max kicked Molly aside. Seeing the knife arc back towards Colleen's neck, he grabbed the blade, putting a barrier between it and her skin. Ignoring the sting to his palm and fingers, he wrenched the assailant's arm up and pulled Colleen away.

There was a shout, a pistol fired, but Max focused on pounding the man beneath him unconscious. When the man went limp, Max tossed him aside and whirled to face his next challenge. St. Katherine's had filled, men pouring in from every entrance, a battle royal between Molly's men and the Crown's. Energy flooded his body and his limbs screamed for action. Max's gaze found Colleen, huddled in a pew next to an unconscious body, safe from the fray.

A man he didn't recognize rushed past, and Max grabbed the back of his collar and throttled him to the ground. One stomp to the jaw later, and he turned for the next target.

Summerset rolled past him down the aisle.

Max gave him a hand up. "You took your bloody time getting here."

"Zed has a fucking army out there." Summerset brushed dirt off his sleeve. "The man had us pinned down from every direction."

"Woman." Max shoulder-checked Summerset as a foot soldier took aim at his friend from the altar. Max leveled his own pistol and took the man down. "Zed is Molly from The Black Rose."

Summerset stumbled. "What? You must be joking."

Sweeping the leg of a man battling with Montague, Max shook his head. "I wish I were. But our criminal mastermind is none other than the chit who likes to whip men till they beg." Max spun, looking for his next opponent. "We were all just too blind to see it."

"I did say it could be a woman." Summerset looked over Max's shoulder, his eyes going wide, and threw his blade. A body thumped to the floor behind Max.

"But you didn't actually believe it."

Summerset shrugged, and they both turned and engaged more opponents.

The fight wound down. Liverpool's men began dragging out those still living of Zed's army. Shaking the sting from his cut hand, Max zeroed in on the mastermind herself, standing behind a table on the altar.

"Now do you believe it's over?" Max asked. He and his friends stepped forwards, forming a wall. "Put down your weapon, woman, and give yourself up. There's no other option."

She circled the table. Her hand was steady as she swung a pistol in a line between Max and his friends. "There are several options available, you just don't see them. I do."

"Only one of them ends with you walking out of here alive." Max took a step forwards, hand outstretched. "Give me the gun."

"Careful," Rothchild said. He raised his own weapon, joining Montague and Summerset in leveling on Molly. But Max could read the hesitation in their eyes. They'd faced much bloodshed in battle, but never had they shot a woman. Hurting one went against their nature, even if she was a crime lord.

Max took another step. "Molly, you're an intelligent woman. Think in the long term. Surrendering now is your best option."

She tilted her head. "Oh, I have thought of all my options. In the second it took you to come that one step closer, every possibility has flown across my mind. There is only one choice I'll be happy with." She smiled and threw her shoulders back, tipping her chin up high. "Inflicting as much damage as possible before I go down."

Max steeled himself. He saw it in her eyes. She was going to shoot him, and there was nothing he could do. His friends wouldn't pull their triggers in time. After she shot him, one of them would take her down, but not before.

He looked up at the stained-glass window high above the altar, not wanting Molly's face to be the last thing he saw. His last thought before the gun went off was that at least Colleen would be safe.

The reverberation of the shot echoed around the stone chamber, and Max frowned. There should be pain. He blinked, looked down, and saw Molly's slight form crumpled on the altar, a circle of blood staining the stomach of her silk gown.

Shoulders unclenching, Max turned, wondering which of his friends had taken the shot. The three men had their pistols pointed at the ground and were staring down the aisle at Colleen.

She lowered her arm, smoke drifting from the barrel of her gun. Tossing the used weapon on the body of an unconscious man, she shuddered. "This belongs to him."

Chapter Nineteen

Colleen tapped her fingers along the rim of her glass, the brandy within untouched. She'd sat with the same glass of liquor for the past two hours, ensconced in a chair in Max's sitting room, as government men came and went. Each of Max's three friends had given statements of the events, all glancing her way when they came to the end of their tales.

She'd killed someone. And this time, it hadn't been an accident. She'd found a weapon in the man's pocket, pulled it free, and aimed at Molly's head. When it had become apparent that she was going to shoot Max, Colleen had pulled the trigger. Without hesitation. Without remorse.

What kind of person was she?

Max had placed her in the chair when he'd brought her to his house. Had given her a drink 'to settle her.' And had left her alone since. Probably too disgusted to even look upon her face.

The Earl of Summerset took a seat across from her and crossed one leg over the other. He fingered one of the artfully coiled locks of hair that curled across his brow. "That was a nice shot. Have much practice with weapons?"

Colleen pursed her lips. "I was aiming for her head. I think I hit quite a bit lower."

"Still." Picking up a decanter from the low table that lay between them, the earl poured himself a glass. "How are you faring?"

What an odd question. "I am unharmed. Molly's the one who's dead."

"It's never easy." He leaned forwards. "I only wish I had

taken the shot, saving you from it."

The backs of her eyes burned. This conversation didn't make sense. Why should she be saved from anything?

Summerset raised his glass. "To the living." He lifted it to his lips and paused. "I made a toast, now you take a sip."

Colleen followed suit, ignoring the fact she detested the taste of brandy. The liquid burned a path down her throat and cleared some of the fog from her mind.

Tossing his drink back, Summerset slammed his glass on the table. "You might not think it now, but everything will look better in the morning."

The Duke of Montague and the Earl of Rothchild joined them. "Trying to get the poor girl half-sprung?" Montague asked. "I think she's had it rough enough without you pursing her. Sutton won't appreciate it."

Summerset smoothed the tail of his cravat down his chest. "Sutton isn't here, and she is." He gave a pointed look to the duke. "Alone."

Tracing the rim of her glass with her thumb, Colleen sighed. "You don't need to keep me company. I'm all right."

"Of course, you are," Rothchild said. "But that doesn't mean that after an evening like tonight, you wouldn't want some companionship. I think we all need another drink after tonight." He fixed the duke and himself glasses and topped up Colleen's and Summerset's. "To the end of Zed." He held his glass up.

"To friends having one's back." Montague raised his glass.

Summerset crossed one leg over the other. "To adventures that come out right in the end."

They looked at her expectantly. She was supposed to come up with a toast now, too? She had a hard enough time just sitting there quietly, not turning into a puddle of sniffles and tears. Now they expected poetry?

She lifted her own glass, her hand trembling. "To lucky shots." To saving Max. Even if that confirmed in his mind just the type of woman she was. She threw back the liquor and bent over coughing.

A warm hand rubbed her back. Max's hand. She jumped out of her chair in surprise.

"Sorry." He lifted his palms, his left one wrapped in a thick bandage. "I didn't mean to startle you."

She coughed a couple more times into her sleeve. Clearing her throat, she said, "I didn't hear you come in."

"I've never been far." Max poured a glass of water and gave it to her. "Just dealing with business in another room."

She swallowed the cool draught, but it did nothing to alleviate her sudden thirst. Why was he looking at her like that? Gone was the indifferent stare of the night before when he'd told her to leave. She'd expected disgust. Perhaps gratitude at saving his life. Not ... admiration?

"Well, I think it's time we all went home." Montague clapped his hands together. "I know my wife and Rothchild's will be worrying."

Summerset settled back in his chair. "There's no one to worry over me. I think I'll have another drink."

The duke grabbed Summerset under the elbow and yanked him to his feet. "Don't make me hurt you."

"Well, I should at least see if Mrs. Bonner needs an escort home." Summerset turned to her and dipped his head. "My carriage awaits, madam."

Max growled. "What the devil—"

"Thank you. I was on my way to my cousin's house in Wapping when I was taken." Colleen put her glass down. "It's long past time he expected me." Fatigue tugged at her eyelids. She desperately needed a good night's sleep. Maybe then she could understand what Max was about.

"You're going back to your cousin's?" Max planted himself in front of her. "You detested that man's house."

"I never said that."

"You didn't have to." Planting his hands on his lean hips, Max bent over her. "I could just tell."

"And now his home seems like the better alternative."

Swaying slightly, Colleen tried to gather her strength. Every muscle in her body drooped, aching for rest. Even the two-foot space on her nieces' bed seemed appealing. She'd sleep so deeply she wouldn't even feel Mary's nightly kicks. Head down, she stepped around Max and gave Summerset a weak smile. "I'm ready when you are."

Max glowered. "I need everyone to get out of my house, right now." He gripped her elbow. "Except you."

Staring at the carpet, Colleen waited until the men filed out. The door to the sitting room clicked shut behind them. "I've asked Lucy to run the club until you find a new manager. Although I'd recommend you give her a try. She's impressed me with her competence."

"I couldn't care less about The Black Rose at the moment." He circled around her, his very nearness making the fine hairs on the back of her neck stand on end.

"No, I don't suppose your club is at the top of your concerns. Not after a night like tonight." She could scarcely meet his gaze, glancing everywhere but at him directly. "Even in your line of work it can't be every day you witness a woman murder another."

He stopped behind her, his chest brushing her shoulders. "You hold a strange definition of murder. Molly was about to shoot me."

"And instead I shot her." An act she couldn't regret. Not like the fire that had killed her husband. But now she was responsible for the loss of two lives. Max hadn't been able to forgive the one. "I'm sure you're grateful, but I don't need any thanks. I don't want to prolong our farewell any longer than it needs to be." She turned and looked up at him. He hadn't shaved that day and a thick stubble darkened his cheeks and jaw. A hint of the man she'd first met. Her fingers tingled with the urge to reach up and stroke his face. Instead, she raised her hand chest high. "Let's shake goodbye and part as friends."

Max looked at her hand, eyes narrowing. "Friends?"

Oh, God, he didn't even want that. A giant fist grabbed

her around the middle and squeezed, wringing the air from her body, crushing her until it felt as though her heart would burst.

He despised her.

Trembling, she lowered her hand.

Max grabbed it before she could turn tail and run. Encircling her wrist, he whipped it behind her back and pulled her body snug against his. "Are you so daft as to think that we could only ever be *friends*? That I'd let you walk out that door and out of my life?"

The vise around her chest loosened, and a sob burst from her lips before she could control it. Blood pounded behind her temples. "But you wanted me to leave. Last night, you said—"

"Don't repeat it." One hand held her in place against his body, the other skimmed up her spine. "And if we're to have a successful future together, you'll have to learn to ignore half of what I say. I can be a bit of a numbskull. Ask any of my friends."

"Are you saying you forgive me?"

"When I thought about it, I realized there wasn't much to forgive. Your husband's death was an accident. It was a mistake not to tell the magistrate, but you must have been scared."

She bit her lip. "I should have told you. Not let you believe you were responsible."

"Yes, but when?" He swallowed, his Adam's apple bobbing. "You wouldn't tell me something like that until you trusted me completely. I should have taken your admission as the honor it was. I'll regret till the day I die how I reacted."

Hope reared its head and stole her breath. But she'd been here before. Laid her heart bare. His touch was clouding her mind when she needed to think clearly. Stepping away, she turned to the glass wall separating the conservatory from the sitting room. She walked forwards until she felt the cool glass against her palms.

"Do you want me to continue managing The Black Rose?" She couldn't imagine a relationship as his mistress, installed in an apartment, waiting for him to come to her. She needed honest occupation. If her flower shop was no longer available, perhaps staying on at the club wouldn't be so bad. The place had grown on her.

"If you want. You are a superior manager." His reflection closed in on her. He stood directly behind her, raising his hands to hover over her shoulders, but never touching. "I know my wishes. But I want you to find your happiness. What is it that you want?"

Colleen stared into the conservatory. The moonlight threw strange shadows of blues and greys amongst the plants. What did she want? She'd thought she'd known. But her desires had taken a new direction since meeting Max.

Stepping to the side, Max pulled the door to the greenhouse open. "Come. Let's take a stroll." He held out his uninjured hand, his gaze rock steady.

Her stomach fluttered. She stared at his hand, big, rough, capable. Inviting. Sucking in a deep breath, she slid her palm into his and followed him into the humid heat of the conservatory.

"Have I told you about the amaryllis at my greenhouse at Meadowlark?" He tugged her close. "This time of year they're nothing more than shoots poking from the dirt, but in a couple months the plants will explode with color. It's one of the most beautiful sights in the world." He stopped under the shadow of a palm tree. "I hope to show it to you."

A bead of sweat slid down Colleen's spine. "How would I go to Meadowlark? As a business acquaintance? A mistress? A ...?" She couldn't voice it. It was too absurd.

Max had no such qualms. "My wife, should I be so fortunate. I wish to marry you."

Colleen heard every thud of her heart. The scent of the nearby jessamine overwhelmed her senses. The idea was fantastic. Absurd. "The baron and the woman of business?

It sounds like a bad novel."

"The story of Max and Colleen. It sounds wonderful to me. But"—he reached into an inside pocket and pulled out a folded piece of paper—"before you answer, I want you to read this. You should know all your options. I want you to pick me because you want me; not because you feel like you have no other choices."

She snatched the parchment from his hand, rolling her eyes but knowing he couldn't see it in the dark. He was offering her a life with the man she loved. What option was better than that? "The moonlight isn't strong enough for me to read this. And I don't need to. Of course—"

Flint sparked against steel. Kneeling on the path, Max blew a small flame to life on a dried palm leaf. He held the light up to the paper. "This won't last long, so read quickly."

Shaking her head, she snapped the paper open. Beautiful, stupid man. How he thought she'd—

"What is this? A bill of sale?"

"For your flower shop." Max cursed and dropped the leaf, stamping out any lingering flame. "When I reneged on our deal for your premium, I knew I couldn't let my decision steal your dream. So, I struck a deal with Mr. Ridley." He tucked a strand of her hair behind her ear and cupped her neck. "It was your money I used. The money you'd earned. The deed is in your name. No one can take it away from you."

Even though she could no longer read the words, she stared at the paper. Her flower shop. Her dream.

She looked up. Moonlight limned the firm jawline of the man who'd made it happen. "You think I'd choose this shop over you? Maybe we shouldn't marry. I don't want to be joined forever with a blockhead. But—"

His whoop cut her off. Grabbing her about the waist, he swung her in a circle. "I heard yes." He covered her lips with his own, and their tongues tangled. He tasted of whiskey and heat, the spirit sweeter coming from Max's lips.

Breathless, she pulled back. Tried to regain her previous

thought. "Besides, I don't have to choose. I can have both. You are a man of business. I see no reason your wife should be any different. If a baron having a Cit for a wife doesn't destroy your reputation, I don't see why having a wife who also runs a flower shop should do you any worse."

He nuzzled her neck. "Trust me. Of my friends who've married, you are by far the most respectable bride. Like Montague and Rothchild, I care not how society regards me."

She dropped her head back, exposing more skin. Loving the way he took advantage. "Of course, if we marry, I'll no longer own the flower shop. Everything becomes yours. Blasted, idiotic law," she muttered.

Max growled against her throat, and she patted his arm. "I didn't say that would change my mind. But it wouldn't go amiss for you to bring up the issue with your fellow lawmakers in the House of Lords."

"Duly noted." He raised his head. "But you do know that what's mine is yours, too. Everything I am, everything I have."

She melted. Threading her fingers in his hair, she nipped at his throat. "And I will manage everything of yours with economy and efficiency."

"I have no doubt." He cupped her neck then slid his hand down lower.

Her breast tingled under his caress. "But with all the time we'll be spending at Meadowlark, I'll have to find a local manager for the shop. With so many delightful ways to occupy our time, I wouldn't want to waste every day working."

Dipping his head, he sucked her earlobe into his hot mouth. "Leisure time is one of the many benefits of marrying into the peerage," he agreed. Softly, he cupped her cheeks between his hands and stared down at her. He brushed his thumb over her lower lip. "You're an amazing woman, Colleen Bonner. Just as you are. Do you understand me?"

She understood. She saw the self-recrimination in his eyes. The regret for their fight.

The love.

He loved her. Not because she maintained the ledgers for his business. Or in the hopes she'd bear his children. This would be a marriage so unlike her first.

The back of her throat ached. "Even now you know I'm not perfect? Are you sure you still want me?"

He rested his forehead against hers. "Perfection is overrated. You're smart, and determined, and have completely captured my heart. Who needs perfection when I have all that?"

Well, when he put it that way. "You know that leisure time you spoke of?" She smoothed a hand down his cravat, over his flat stomach, and lower. "How about we go enjoy some of that?"

A growl reverberated up from his chest. "Your wish is my command."

She danced back, dodging his exploring hands. "I'll meet you in your room. Give me ten minutes." She'd need at least that to make herself somewhat presentable. Not that Max ever seemed to mind how she looked.

He stalked after her, matching her step for step. "I always considered myself a patient man. Until I met you. Ten minutes is too long."

"I'll make it worth your while." She paused at the glass door, enjoying the sight of Max in his conservatory. Taking in her new world. A world of life and love. Fire and heat. "Oh, and Max?"

He raised an eyebrow, his stubble making him look rough and dangerous. "Yes, my love?"

"It's a bit chilly tonight. I hope you can think of some way to warm me up." With one last look at her man, Colleen sauntered from the room, knowing he was but a step behind.

She smiled. Burning the midnight oil had taken on a new meaning for her. And every delicious, red-hot second of it was going to be amazing.

* * * *

About the Author

Like almost one-third of all romance writers, Alyson Chase is a former attorney (okay, maybe a slight exaggeration, but not by much). She happily ditched those suits and now works in her pajamas writing about men's briefs instead of legal briefs. When she's not writing, she's probably engaged in one of her favorite hobbies: napping, eating, or martial arts (That last one almost makes up for the first two, right?) She also writes humorous, small-town, contemporary romance novels under the name Allyson Charles.

Connect with Alyson at:

www.alysonchase.com
www.facebook.com/AlysonChaseAuthor
Twitter: @1alysonchase
Email: alysonchaseauthor@gmail.com

Made in the USA
Middletown, DE
28 August 2018